KALISUN SERIES

The Kalisun Initiative

Kalisun Initiative:
The Price of Progress

And coming soon . . .
Kalisun Initiative:
Age of Saturn

Library of Congress Cataloging-in-Publication
data is available.

For information about permission to reproduce
selections from this book, write to
Watermount Projects
1000 West Chase Street,
Greenville, Michigan 48838.

http://www.watermountprojects.com/

Visit this book's website at
https://www.facebook.com/KalisunInitiative

ISBN: 978-0-9914448-2-3

Cover art by Andon Monk
Interior art by Jared Claybrooks
Interior and Jacket design by Melissa M. deJesus

THE KALISUN INITIATIVE: THE PRICE OF PROGRESS

BY

NICK WYCKOFF

The Watermount Projects

Boston   Greenville   Huntsville

ACKNOWLEDGEMENTS

This book was originally the second half of the first book in the series. When I decided to cut the book in half I knew there would be challenges being consistent across both books, particularly with the level of technical detail present. Additionally, I wanted to incorporate feedback from readers regarding the format and story arcs. None of this would have been possible without my editor Sarah Widdup who helped me both clean up the story telling and keep the story arcs linked up. I want to extend a thank you to her and to all of the readers who took the time to provide feedback to make this a more engaging story.

Phoebe, Saturn Orbit

Key Staff

Director: John Hatfield

    Aide: Ed Styles

    Aide: Jim Dover

    Enforcer: Joe

Congressional Liaison : Molly Caan

Deputy Director: Brenner Minuit

Eden Cave Lead: Sasha Reynolds

Hangar Chief: William Stokes

Armorer: Chief Warrant Officer Bobby Graves

Lead Sensor Officer: Higgins

Operations Chief: Sloan Goldsmith

Chief Weapon Scientist: Doctor Erik Bilks

Lead Planetary Scientist: Doctor Dave Rogers

Special Projects Lead: Doctor Walter Kapple

Particle accelerator Lead: Doctor Christie Elliot

Radiation Studies: Doctor Kyle Winters

Materials Research Lead: Doctor Surjit (Sam) Malhotra

Contract Researchers

Doctor Meckler

Doctor Von Tremel (Incarcerated for attacking Kalisun Marines)

Moon Base Training Center, Earth Orbit

Key Staff

Kalisun CEO: Ed Stokes

MBTC Director: William Forsythe

Kalisun CEO: Ed Stokes

MBTC Director: William Forsythe

Congressional Representative: Sanders

    Chief of Staff:Matt Kline

Phoebe, Saturn Orbit

Military Staff

Marine Commander: Major Eric Stringer

   One company of Marines

   One squadron of SARines

   Master Sergeant: Eugene (Gene) Marin

   Senior Drill Instructor: Leblanc

Wing Commander: Major Ava Sirano (G-Loc)

   Three squadrons of Mongoose with supporting Angels

   One hundred Angels in mixed configurations

   Captain Jamal Martin

   Captain Jasper Wilcox

   Lieutenant Lori Sinclair

   Lieutenant Kimmie Sinclair

   Lieutenant Terns

   Lieutenant Hopper

Tug *Atlas* Captain: Jacobs

Moon Base Training Center, Earth Orbit

Military Staff

Wing Commander: Joseph Prieter

   Five squadrons of Mongoose Fighters with supporting Angels

   One hundred Angels in various configurations

   Commander Badger Squadron: Jamie Wilks

Ground Forces Commander: Colonel Davies

   Intelligence Lead: Julio Menendez

   Five total companies of Marines

   Three SARine Squadrons

   Lead SARine: Darnel Morris

   1st Company: Captain Jill Belle

   2nd Company: Captain Williams

   3rd Company: Captain Spears

PROLOGUE

After a series of proxy wars flared into a major war between the United States, China and their allies, a mandatory peace treaty was dictated by the United Nations. The treaty stipulated that all warring parties must substantially reduce their military strength and refrain from open hostilities. The world could not tolerate another nuclear exchange, it could not tolerate the tide of human suffering that engulfed nation after nation as the two sides struggled for dominance.

Both sides ignored the treaty, building up bases on the moon in an attempt to hold the high ground. China built sprawling complexes advertised as science bases to rebuild their national pride, while the United States gave money under the table to an international company, the Kalisun Initiative, to establish a sophisticated army in secret on a base orbiting Saturn.

KSI had plans of their own however. While they spent a sizable portion of the money on creating weapons and a combat force for the moon, they also built an experimental interstellar ship. When the ship returned from its first test, an unexpected ball of intense radiation preceded it, wrecking havoc across the solar system and plunging Earth into chaos.

Now, just weeks after the event, the war on Earth's moon has erupted into a major confrontation between the Chinese and KSI forces while much of the population of Earth is without food, water and electricity. As KSI tries to fend off the Chinese onslaught they are forced to confront the damage they caused; but the fallout from the flight test has one final surprise in store for the men and women of the Kalisun Initiative . . .

THE KALISUN INITIATIVE

VOLUME TWO

THE PRICE OF PROGRESS

CHAPTER 1

John Hatfield, Brenner Minuit, Sloan Goldsmith, and Molly Caan clutched the safety bars on the rover as Ed Styles shot down the tunnel back to the main base. The chemo-luminescence from the surrounding rock made surreal shadows flash by as they bounced down the rough tunnel that pierced deep into Phoebe, one of the moons of Saturn.

Hatfield, Brenner and Sloan each sat in silence, watching as data from the base's external sensors streamed across their helmet heads up displays. Debris-tracking maps sparkled across an overview of the Saturn system, with a single colored streak flashing through the debris. With each sensor update, the error volume of the unknown object's sensor track continued to shrink from possibly passing the moon, to possibly impacting the moon, to impacting the hidden shipyard on the far side of the base.

Molly sat squished between Sloan and Brenner in the back bench seat, a last minute addition to the rover. She did not have the benefit of wearing one of the command suits. Her suit was more protective than functional, focused on short-term survivability rather than being a mobile command suite. Her position within this company of men and women was even more limited. She was neither corporate leadership nor engineering expert; instead she was an involuntary guest, part indentured servant, part hostage.

As the rover jostled back and forth, the bulk of the two command suits and their pervasive mottled charcoal color schemes gave Molly a sense of claustrophobia. The nauseating, shifting colors of the camouflage system had activated when they had started using the command battlenet. A glance to the left showed Sloan's helmeted head tilted downward in thought. Molly's suit couldn't access the command net, excluding her from the conversation while the leadership of the KaliSun Corporation's Saturn Base sifted through what the base sensors could tell them.

A particularly nasty bump jarred her teeth together and made her eyes tear up. She looked to her right at Brenner, who was quickly typing something into his wrist interface. His armor was shifting in front of her eyes like a grey and charcoal lava lamp. With a start she realized the emblem on his shoulder of a naked red-haired woman swinging a sword also had its own camouflage pattern now, the pale flesh tone of the caricature shifting into deep mottled greens and browns as though she had been body painted with jungle colors. Only Hatfield's armor seemed mostly unchanged. Just a subtle dulling of the maroon and yellow coloration as it shifted to blood red and lusterless gold. She glanced down at her own suit, neon-blue and lightly armored. No weapons, no symbols, no mission patches or designations, and gave a sigh.

With a shuddering, skidding stop, the rover came to a halt near a large airlock at the end of the tunnel. The group piled out and stood under a small static electricity shower that sent waves of charged particles over their suits. The sharp, electrostatically charged dust particles floated free from their suits and drifted toward the positively charged dustbin under the shower. Molly watched as Sloan flexed the various joints in her suit, causing dust to squirt from its crevices and folds, before stepping into the shower after her.

They passed through the airlock and into the corridor beyond, the artificial gravity suddenly clutching at their suits. Two Marines guarded the airlock, and they saluted Director Hatfield as he passed by. He sketched a quick salute, followed by Brenner and Sloan, and half trotted toward the Command Information Center.

Throughout the military side of the base Marines and their more highly trained search and recovery brethren, the SA-Rines, moved aside as the Director passed through. There were more guards on duty than normal due to the recent terrorist plot by one of the researchers on the base, making the passageways congested and active. Pilots wandered in and out of the briefing rooms as they attended their training classes and operational reviews, their lighter armor dwarfed by the heavier SARine and Marine armor. These combatants were all veterans of the Earth wars, their armor decorated with insignia representing their former ranks and awards. They had been hired by the KaliSun Corporation to form the backbone of a new space military to contest the Chinese in the quest for dominance of the Earth's Moon.

Molly felt a scowl cross her face as she looked at the Marines guarding the entrance to the command deck. The KaliSun Corporation had been hired to train these fighters, given money to design their armor, weapons and equipment. They had been allowed to hire away some very competent members of the US military for this operation, under the belief that when the army was ready, they would turn it over to the Government. It was all done under the table, a violation of the international treaties that the US had been forced to sign as part the Armistice between themselves and China. But instead of turning the military assets over, they had kept them for themselves, sparking a new war with the Chinese—a war that thankfully had been contained to the Earth's Moon so far, but that could easily spiral out of control into further nuclear exchanges on Earth.

One of the pilots passing them in the hallway looked her in the eyes, a startled expression on his face. Molly realized she must be glaring angrily out of her faceplate and hastily composed her features. Her situation with Director Hatfield was very delicate, it would not be wise for him to see that she was still upset at the recent turn of events. Things had been so promising just a year ago; she was the Chief of Staff of powerful US Senator, organizing a trip to Saturn Base to inspect their investment with the KaliSun Corporation.

There had been promises that upon her return she would get a promotion within the Democratic National Party structure; a leadership role had been strongly hinted at. But then, her fortunes turned.

First Senator Hernandez's lover and assigned intelligence operative got caught snooping where he shouldn't have been. Hatfield blew him out an airlock and pretended it was an accident. The death was bad enough, but the Senator compounded the problem by spiraling into a revenge fantasy against Hatfield. She teamed up with a resident researcher who was an undercover asset from the CIA. His time on the moon hadn't been kind to him, bringing on paranoia and his own set of revenge and depression issues directed at Hatfield.

The two of them had acted out against the Director as the Senator was scheduled to fly home, severely injuring several Marines and a SARine in the process, as well as taking Molly herself hostage. She involuntarily gulped at the memory, reaching up as though to rub her throat through the suit. The Senator had threatened to cut her head clean off, holding a scalpel against her throat right up until Deputy Director Brenner and a squad of SARines intervened and disabled her. The cut Juanita had left on her throat had healed, leaving a slightly raised ridge of scar tissue near her jugular vein, a vivid reminder of how close she had come to being killed.

Her situation had not improved much from there. The Senator's actions had prevented her from catching the freighter back to Earth. As a result, she was stuck on Phoebe, a dimly lit rocky moon in one of Saturn's most distant orbits, with no way home and far too much knowledge of what the KaliSun Corporation was up too. Hatfield had given her two choices—assist the Corporation in their goals at Saturn Base, acting as a staffer and liaison back to Earth if one was needed, or walk out an airlock. He certainly knew how to motivate people.

They were passing through the wardrooms that served the internal Command and Control spaces now, taking every shortcut available as updates flowed to the three Corporation officers walking in front of her.

She briefly considered whether it would have been better to choose the airlock option over serving these people, before rolling her eyes upward to ask for guidance. The problem was they were very likable people when dealt with individually. At times she felt a bizarre friendship with some of them; intellectually she realized it was probably a form of Stockholm Syndrome. Her mind was searching for friendship with those who were the least immoral. Perhaps an unconscious desire to avoid being completely cut off from human relationships while she was trapped out here.

But the fact remained, they had manipulated currency markets, the Federal Reserve and Congress in order to obtain the funding required for their own personal drive towards interstellar space. In the process they had crippled the world financial markets, defrauded the government and created shadow monopolies across the globe.

All of that had happened before their first test flight of the interstellar space drive went awry, launching a giant ball of glowing plasma and emitting waves of high-intensity radiation throughout the solar system. The Southern Hemispheres of Earth were plunged into darkness, technology across the Northern Hemispheres suffered sporadic failures, satellites died, cults dedicated to the 'mini-sun' sprang up world-wide, limited nuclear exchanges between several countries, air travel was grounded and basic human services essentially stopped.

During the first week, things had held together. But as the power stayed off and food grew short, riots and looting had begun in some areas. The US had deployed its entire National Guard and the majority of its armed forces in an effort to prevent the situation from getting out of hand, but recent budgetary and treaty cuts had left them a hallow force.

Whole swaths of the US had devolved toward local security solutions; vigilantes and militia.

Molly felt a lump in her throat as she thought of the chaos these people had inflicted on the world, chaos caused by ego and hubris. She shook her head slowly inside her suit. The worst of it was that the relatively young cold war between the United States and China and gone white hot on Earth's Moon, with Chinese forces launching surprise attacks on the KaliSun Moon Base Training Center and its research facilities. The Corporation had managed to fend off those attacks and launch an attack of their own, significantly damaging a sprawling Chinese base and killing hundreds of people. In the days that followed almost daily skirmishes were reported on the Moon, as well as several Chinese saboteur attacks on the base at Saturn. The whole situation was deeply unsettling for a person who was, at their heart, uncomfortable with war.

They entered the CIC and Molly was immediately struck by how tense the atmosphere was. Hatfield, Brenner and Sloan removed their helmets and attached them to their suits, straddling the special saddle benches designed to handle the bulk of a command suit. Molly shucked her helmet too, and sat in one of the oversized observation chairs in the back.

Hatfield waved at the Sensor Officer. "Higgins, we've reviewed most of your projections but I need you to take me through how we got where we are."

The Sensor Officer stood up and looked back at their chairs. Her blonde hair was tucked in a neat ponytail that trailed down into her jumpsuit. She was an attractive woman, with light blue eyes and pale skin. "Sir, we were conducting the ephemeris study you requested in the aftermath of the *KALISUN* returning, and detected several anomalies we could not explain. Right now we are using trilateration techniques to try to narrow down the variables and determine what it is we're seeing."

"What's ephemeris?" Molly asked, not intending to say it out loud and looking abashed when the majority of the people in the CIC gave her an odd look.

Higgins looked at the Director questioningly. When he gave her a nod to continue she turned toward Molly. "Ephemeris is a database we maintain that tracks all of the objects in our near vicinity. We also use ephemeris data to track the positions of major sources of gravity in the solar system as a whole, and to provide safe paths for ships to travel in. We currently have eleven surplus X-band radars from Earth stationed around the rim of the base crater and in various other locations that are constantly scanning the Saturn area for objects. Frequently an object's orbit changes as it encounters other bodies in the local vicinity. We have to redo the database completely every few months for that reason, Saturn is a much busier place than Earth."

"Surplus radars eh," Molly said meaningfully toward Hatfield, who glanced over at her and waved dismissively.

"Another time Ms. Caan. Ok Higgins, so you told me you are using trilateration, but that really only works if you have objects to compare. Everything I saw on the way over here indicates there is no object."

"Ah yes, sorry sir. As we were conducting the study it became apparent that some objects we have long tracked were missing. Then we noticed some of the larger ones had been moved from their typical orbits. As we went looking for the missing ones we actively observed several items disappearing from our displays. Most of the objects were small, but we detected several large ones that vanished as well, especially in the Phoebe ring. We directed IR detectors from the *Heritage* and our own telescopes at the area and discovered that there is a volume of space that is regularly annihilating material. It appears to be moving more or less directly at the shipyard."

"And you can see the debris getting destroyed but not what's destroying it?"

"We can see energy discharges consistent with objects being vaporized on the IR sensors, and actual visible flashes on the telescopes," Higgins said, motioning to one of her techs to pull a time-lapse video feed up on the display.

Hatfield pondered it for several moments in silence before he spoke up. "So, we have an object approaching us that is destroying material in its path. It appears to be heading toward the ship we just recently flew that might produce a very damaging ball of radiation, and we can't see the object at all?"

"Correct sir. There is no visible structure there, but we're certain something is coming."

"Did you interrogate it with the LADAR?" Brenner asked as he studied the IR footage.

"We attempted to, the return we get back indicates we're firing into an infinite space. No reflection at all beyond dust and small rocks."

"Could it be drive residual from the KaliSun? I mean we've never used it before, maybe it created some kind of funky space time tear and we're just seeing it approach us now," Sloan interjected.

"Highly doubtful I think," Brenner said. "It's more likely something with very good optical camouflage. How big do you think it is, Higgins?"

"Between fifty and six hundred meters long, and perhaps thirty to sixty meters wide. We think it's roughly ovoid in shape," she said with an apologetic frown.

"That's the best you can do?" Hatfield said, a mild tone of rebuke in his voice.

"We're extrapolating on the absence of data rather than actual hard data, I think that's the best we can do without flying out there and seeing if we can run into it," Higgins replied stiffly.

"Flying out there might not be a bad idea," Brenner said.

"What, so one of those pilots can run into an invisible wall? Not sure you should ask for volunteers for that mission, might not get anyone," Sloan said sarcastically.

"They wouldn't have to hit it, just fly near it and shoot at it. If they shoot short bursts, we should be able to determine what the thing is, based on the speed it destroys incoming rounds," Brenner said defensively. "Maybe it would even drop its camouflage so we can see it."

"Who is it?" Molly asked. "Chinese? We certainly don't have anything that can fly stealthily like that. We put most of our eggs in your basket with regard to space flight systems," she added bitterly.

"I don't think it's a US system, probably not the Chinese either. Neither of them could build something six hundred meters long and not be seen by somebody," Hatfield said softly.

"Who then?" Molly prodded.

"Might not be a who. It could be a rock, or something we've never seen before. Maybe a chunk of dark matter from the depths of interstellar space? Who knows?" Sloan said.

"Just the same, I think we should go to General Quarters," Hatfield said pensively. "Recall all pilots and Marines. Start sealing this place up, non-essential personnel to Shelter in Place locations immediately."

The communication tech to Hatfield's right nodded once and immediately began keying information into his control board. A deep bell rang throughout the entire station; normal broadcast radio, music channels and digital programming halted as alerts flashed through the system. Quickly, the tech cut down the volume for the CIC and communicated orders to the civilian and military hangar units to begin closing the non-essential hangars and prepare for combat. The walls and floor reverberated with the sound of boots pounding down the passageways, and a new display popped up showing the current order of battle for the station, with a health and status bumper next to each unit. Units that were already geared up and ready to go quickly reported in, and the board started to turn green.

"Brenner, get Major Sirano on the radio, inform her of the situation. Higgins, I want you to interface with Chief Graves down on the military hangar side, get him up to speed on what you think is coming. Work out a mechanism to utilize the estimated flight path of the object as an overlay for the Angel's engage-on-remote track system. That should enable the Angels to provide the fighters with a HUD icon to shoot at."

Both Higgins and Brenner acknowledged Hatfield's order, but Higgins paused before executing it. "Just one other thing sir. About forty minutes before we started investigating this object, we noticed a strange, uh thing, in the clouds of Saturn. We've already forwarded it to Dr. Rogers for immediate analysis."

"What kind of thing?" Hatfield asked curiously, his eyes squinting at her intently.

Higgins wordlessly displayed the video image on the main screen. The clip was only eight seconds long, with some supporting still photos displayed in monitors to either side of the main screen, but it left the room silent. A long, thick object appeared to be swimming through the clouds.

"It looks sort of like an eel, but those little frilly things running down the side look like a cuttlefish. Or maybe I'm just making that up," Sloan said as she squinted at the footage.

"Have we ever seen anything like this before?" Brenner demanded.

"No, in fact we thought at first it might be something on the telescope optic. I sent somebody to check, it's clear. Ah sir, we don't have any way to judge the scale of it. But the cameras found it pretty quickly while watching that nearby cloud formation for one of the science teams. In order for that system to automatically detect something in a cloud bank it would have to be ... " Higgins trailed off as Brenner caught on.

"Fucking huge," Brenner said softly.

"Yeah, pretty much," Higgins said before going silent again.

"Any idea at all how big it is?" Hatfield asked.

"Not really, that big cloud formation near it might be a good reference point. That's why we sent it to Dr. Rogers. Honestly, before we dug into it too much, we noticed the invisible thing coming at us."

"Uh oh," Sloan said, her faced screwed up in dismay.

"What?" Brenner and Hatfield replied in unison.

"Uh well, you know we've never gotten too deep into Saturn's atmosphere during any of our exploration missions. What if the radiation ball was bright enough to spook this thing up from the depths. Maybe there is life down there. I mean it looks like a fish, maybe we made it sick or something and now it's floating on the surface thrashing and dying. Maybe its big brother is swimming toward us right now ... invisibly," she said softly.

"Let's not make this worse than it has to be," Hatfield said firmly. "We will investigate the invisible thing and then you will know. Until that time, keep the knowledge of that video clip on a very, very short leash. The last thing we need is people panicking because they think we pissed off some aliens."

"What happened to it after the end of the video clip?" Brenner asked, looking apologetically at Hatfield.

"It drifted back down into the cloud deck. Chief Goldsmith is correct in some respects. Our initial analysis suggested it was similar to an Earth sea snake that swims by undulating its body through the water. It's just that, well, it's so big," Higgins responded.

"So it surfaced, thrashed around, then shortly afterward we saw the invisible object?" Brenner pressed her as Hatfield started to grow impatient.

"Yes, but I really don't think they're connected. The object plowing through the dust is too far away from the planet right now to be related, at its present speed it would have had to have launched a week ago or so to get where it is now from Saturn proper," Higgins replied, casting a nervous glance at Hatfield.

"I doubt they are connected," Hatfield said firmly.

Sloan looked him, assessing his mood, before she asked, "Why is that?"

"Because if that snake was like our unidentified object, we would never have seen it down there. It is immaterial, the *Heritage* can use her secondary sensors to scan that area looking for it again, but the object heading at us covertly needs to be dealt with. Right now," Hatfield said, looking around the room. "So focus on the ten-meter target people, before it kicks our teeth in."

The CIC stirred back into a hive of activity as the base shifted to combat status. The command sections of the military side of the base partitioned themselves automatically, blast doors dropping at strategic points, checkpoints and heavy weaponry sliding out of recessed sections in the walls to repel boarders.

The watch officer studied his screens before turning back to Hatfield. "Director, mil side of the base is at Condition One. All pilots have been issued a recall, Marines are in armor and on station. SARines are prepping. Far side civilian areas are preparing for combat. Security details have been deployed. We have a group of pilots en route from the Morale Improvement Center to hangar eight via the tram. As soon as they're clear, we'll lock the tram down.

The Director looked up at the Order of Battle screen, scanning through the red health and status units that gradually flipped to green. He turned to Brenner with a determined look on his face. "Brenner, organize the welcoming committee for our guests."

Brenner nodded once firmly, rapidly issuing orders via his keyboard and using his sub-vocal radio to communicate directly with Hangar Chief Bobby Graves.

CHAPTER 2

Dr. Christie Elliot slid slowly down the wall to sit on the bench next to Dr. Surjit 'Sam' Malhotra, tugging at the neck of her pressure suit as she did. He silently handed her data and power plugs to connect her suit to the wall, and looked around the room.

"This is getting to be an undesired trend. I'm not a fan of the shelter-in-place amenities," Christie said dejectedly.

"Oh, it's not so bad. At least the company is pleasant," Sam said encouragingly.

Christie gave a furtive glance at the other corner of the room, where the contract researchers were gathered in what sounded like a raging bitch session about the situation. "Well, some of it is. How long do you suppose they'll take before they get up the nerve to come bother us?"

"Oh, ten or fifteen minutes at least I'd imagine," Dr. Kyle Winters said with a smile. "Although I'm sure Sam knows better than I, given he used to be one of the contractors instead of one of the family."

Sam gave a barely audible grunt, stealing a glance at the visiting researchers who had rented space at the facility for their work. "If things haven't changed, right now the academics and senior corporate researchers are arguing about who should be in charge of the pissing contest. It really does bring the worst of democracy and autocracy together when you mix those two species of scientist."

"We really need to get assigned to another SIP. Or break them up into different ones if we're going to keep getting locked in here with them," Dr. Walter Kapple said with an undertone of disgust in his voice.

"I brought it up to the Director a week ago . . . " Kyle said.

"Yeah and what did he say?" Walt asked.

"'Duly noted. But remember your presence has a calming

influence on our colleagues when times are tough,'" Kyle said in a reasonable impersonation of Director Hatfield's voice.

"Or maybe a source of agitation for them, somebody to vent at," Christie said.

As they watched, three of the contractors got up and started their way, walking with firm, purposeful strides, all older males. The rest of the contractors were overtly watching from the corner.

Christie looked up as they approached. "Ah Dr. Meckler, nice of you to pay us a visit. Is there anything we can do to assist you?" she said pleasantly.

Meckler ignored Christie, instead choosing to address Dr. Winters. "So Kyle, what is the meaning of today's interruption? More *radiation* problems?" he said snidely.

Dr. Winters looked up at the three of them patiently. "Clearly we're going to have to review our alarms and alerts with incoming scientists. That was a battle stations alarm, not a general alarm or a radiation alarm."

"A what?" asked the spindly scientist to Dr. Meckler's left.

"Battle stations. As in prepare for combat operations. We secure the base so any depressurization event that might occur won't cause a massive loss of atmosphere," Christie said in the same tone of voice Dr. Winters had used.

"Combat operations against what? We're at the ass end of the solar system, there is nothing out here to fight!"

"I have no idea. We weren't told anything at all. So far all that's coming out over the data nets is a recall for all military personnel and a command to shelter-in-place for all non-essential staff," Dr. Winters said.

"This is the third time we've been trapped in these tiny boxes in the last six weeks. This is unacceptable! We have a very small window to accomplish our research out here, these continued interruptions make it virtually impossible to get any work done!" Dr. Meckler thundered down at them, his hands on his hips, his face turning darker and darker shades of red.

"As you may recall, the last time we were sent to the SIPs, there was a major radiation storm that swept over the base, killing a number of our employees and sickening others. This is for your safety and the safety of your teams Dr. Meckler."

"And just what caused that radiation storm? A storm we have never seen the likes of in all of recorded history just happened to pop up right after you told us to hide in the radiation hardened shelters. It beggars belief that you had nothing to do with it!" Dr. Meckler said as he gestured overhead toward the surface angrily.

"Well, I certainly had nothing to do with it. I was as unaware of the situation as you were if you recall. What caused it has been the source of much discussion of late, but I can assure you the radiation hazard was real. I . . . I can confirm it was very dangerous," Dr. Winters said, his voice breaking as he remembered the sickening sight when they took the protective armor off one of the SARines who'd been directly exposed to nearly seventy Gy of radiation, effectively cooking him within his armor. In all the years he had done radiation exposure research, he had never even heard of that level of exposure.

"Oh I don't doubt it was real. I'm sure it was real, look what it did to Earth. I am also sure your company was responsible for it. I think this bullshit about stuffing us back in the SIPs again is just so they can cover up whatever caused that thing. You're all a bunch of crooks, but one day you'll get caught. Caught and punished!" Dr. Meckler spat at them.

"Like I said, I have no idea. I perform research out here to better understand radiation and cancer. I am rarely invited over to the other side of the base. Nobody in this room spends much time over there. I think you are missing the bigger point however; when the base does military exercises, they use their own internal communication system. Do you remember a single recall order going out over the public PA before? We've been in here nearly thirty minutes; even test blasts for the alert system are preceded with "For the Exercise" prior to being used. Did you hear that? No."

"So what, you are saying this is a real combat alarm? Please. Other than that idiot Von Tremel and a few people you've accused of being spies, there is nobody out here looking to cause trouble."

"It could be the Chinese. We are at war with them now. It could be something else, we don't know right now," Christie said.

Dr. Meckler waved his hand dismissively down at Dr. Elliot as she spoke, and continued to berate Dr. Winters. "I'm going to demand a refund of our fee to be out here." He paused dramatically, pointing around the room. "For all of us!"

With that, the trio of contract researchers stomped off toward their corner, with Dr. Meckler receiving a lukewarm reaction to his outburst.

"Bit of a prick isn't he," Christie said as he walked away.

"He's a titan in his own mind," Walt said disgustedly. "I wonder what he'll do when he finds out that really wasn't a drill? The Marines I saw heading for the tram section looked pretty keyed up for an exercise."

A ping from her wrist interface got Christie's attention. There was a single message from Sloan pulsing red in the display. Sam leaned over and looked at her wrist, then back at her expectantly.

"I know you guys are friends . . . maybe she's telling you what's going down?"

Christie smiled awkwardly and shielded the display from Sam while she opened the message. She stared at it. She reread it again, the color draining from her face. Concerned, Sam reached over and moved her hand away from the screen so he could see. When he read the message he stiffened suddenly and looked over at Dr. Winters with concern clouding his face.

Across the room, in the corner, one of the research technicians had been watching Christie from a distance and saw the look on her face. He reached back and tapped his buddy, nodding in her direction. They watched with intent as they saw Sam's expression, followed by Dr. Kapple's.

Christie held her wrist display up for Kyle to read. He licked his lips and looked at it. The message from Sloan was simple.

Keep your suit at the ready. Possible Alien contact.

Hangar Chief Bobby Graves boosted off the floor in a long, graceful leap, landing next to the squadrons of Mongoose being prepped for launch. Mongoose were fearsome looking craft, a three-pronged, spear-shaped spaceship, with a cone at the back end instead of a shaft. With the engines embedded in the slope of the cone and the tines loaded with countermeasures, thrusters, missiles and a single gun each, the ship just looked predatory.

Chief Graves watched as each Mongoose was pulled into a weapons jig by tugs operated by his techs. The jig looked like a short tube with robotic arms tucked away into recesses within the walls. As the Mongoose slid into place, its skids locking with a sharp metallic clack, the arms reached down to open access ports around the rear of the ship. Once the access ports were opened, the arms began to load the Mongoose with mechanical precision. Fuel powder ported into the fuel tank, fuel catalyst grids extracted and inspected before being replaced or reinserted into the ship. Ammunition feeders lowered themselves down to interface with the magazines for each of the three guns, feeding caseless ammunition into system at high speed. Alternating colors swiftly passed into the Mongoose as high explosive, fragmentation and kinetic rounds were fed into the magazines. A small arm lowered down directly in front of the cockpit, spraying a fine mist on the artificial sapphire glass cockpit before carefully scraping it clean as a final prep for launch.

Once the jig released the Mongoose, the tech pulled the ship free before dismounting and opening the cockpit up so the pilot could climb in. Chief Graves watched as the Mongoose were towed toward the launch tubes. With growing concern he glanced at his command suit's HUD clock. This was taking a long time, he thought to himself.

An alert flashed along the bottom of the HUD indicating Brenner was contacting him. He braced himself and accepted it.

"Where are we at Chief?" Brenner asked patiently.

"We have seven birds almost in the launch tubes. The other five of the squadron and G-LOC's ship should be ready in twenty minutes or so."

"Twenty minutes?"

"Yeah, we weren't exactly organized for a section scramble. We still had a lot of the equipment in protective storage due to that radhaz event."

"Ok, so when can you get me two squadrons in ready to fly?"

"Another hour, maybe ninety minutes if we cut some corners. When do you need them by? Drop dead time."

"Right now the incoming unknown will intercept us in about four hours. It seems to be slowing down a bit, but we want to make first contact with it outside the engagement envelope for the base guns, so we have time to react. So call it two hours until we go with whatever you can get into space."

"WILCO. Be advised, the two combat space patrol birds are already outside and doing their racetrack, but they will need to refuel at two hours and thirty minutes. So you might want to bring them in early."

"Yes, agreed."

"Ok Brenner, I need to get cracking on this. I'll update you in thirty."

"Bobby wait," Brenner said suddenly, forestalling the Chief from cutting the connection. "We need to consider the possibility that we can't kill whatever this is with normal weapons. I want a couple of our experimental missiles on

Angels in a standby orbit well away from the conflict. If it goes poorly, we'll send them in."

"I have a few Erik worked up that will fit on the Mongoose as well. Do you want me to load the CSP birds with those when they come down for fuel?"

There was a pause as Brenner considered his suggestion before he finally asked, "Are they safe to use?"

"I think Erik fixed most of the targeting bugs. Even so, I'd try to fire them at close range so they don't have time to get into any mischief."

"Who are the CSP pilots?"

"Crawford and Simmons."

"Are they with Sinclair's squadron? She did the testing on the new weapons platforms, right?"

"Yes, she's already in the launch tube waiting on your go. They're the two tail-end birds, eleven and twelve. Decent experience."

Seconds melted away as Brenner went silent. "Put the missiles on G-LOC's bird and the two CSP guys. They can form a section to deal with second contact. That way we have G-LOC out of range of defensive fire until we see what the response is. Also, shift two of the trainers into spots eleven and twelve in Martin's squadron, that should fill them out."

"Ava's going to want to be up front with that squadron for first contact."

"I know, but they already have a squadron commander and I want to make sure she survives long enough for us react to whatever pops out of the dark at us."

"Ok, but can you be the one to tell her? I have to focus on getting us ready."

"You know, for a guy as big as you are, you sure want to avoid confrontation with her." Brenner chuckled over the radio, stress evident as it rasped in Bobby's ears.

"Gotta learn to pick smart battles Brenner. Aggravating Ava Sirano is never particularly smart."

"So I've learned. Brenner out." The Deputy Director of

Saturn base abruptly signed off as something else drew his attention away.

Chief Graves gave a sigh into his suit microphone before calling to one of his assistants. The man spun around, looking for the Chief's command suit as he answered immediately.

"Karl, I need you to pull some of the specials out and load them on Major Sirano's bird. Keep a few out to load on the two CSP birds that will land soon."

"Got it chief, what about the Angel's loadouts?"

Graves looked over at the Angels as they prepped for battle. Several of them were almost ready, but the missile birds were all still unloaded, with crews struggling to get them into the rarely used weapons jigs. "Go ahead and load up three of them with a mix of tactical space attack missiles and anti-space missiles. I have no idea how big this thing is, so we'll just have to be ready to fight a range of things. I'll be there in a minute to try to get the Angel crews motivated."

"Solid copy sir." Karl spun back to the task he had been working on, finishing it quickly before bounding off toward the munitions elevator that led down into the weapon storage area.

Graves counted the birds that were loaded up in the launch tubes, flashed instructions to the guys handling Sirano's Mongoose, and used his boosters to make a long leap across the low gravity of hangar eight to land amongst the Angels.

The Angels were the all-purpose utility spacecraft of the KaliSun Corporation. They could be modularly modified to be troop transports, electronic warfare platforms, science vessels or missile boats, all based on a single common framework. They were called Angels because the patterned electronic warfare emitters on the top and the bottom of the wings, and the shape of wings themselves, looked like an Angel's wings from a distance. He approached the first of the Angel flight, one of the quick reaction force Angels, set up for troop transport.

A nearby tech was lugging two tubs of ammo for the top turret into the back, to be loaded by hand into the turret magazine. The tech was joking with the men working to fuel the Angel and prep it for flight. The entire group seemed nonchalant about the affair, competently but slowly going through the pre-flight checklists.

Graves keyed his suit radio to their frequency and cut loose. "Why are none of these birds ready for flight? General Quarters sounded almost twenty minutes ago and you have nothing ready yet? What the fuck is going on?"

The lead tech spun around, just now realizing that Graves was there, and stammered his reply. "We're just going through the pre-flights chief, we have a lot of Angels to get up and half the team is on down time right now." His voice trailed off as he saw Chief Graves stomping closer to the group.

"Did you hear 'for the exercise' on the announcement for General Quarters?" Graves asked aggressively.

The tech looked at his team, confused, before eventually answering. "Uh no sir."

"That's because this isn't a fucking drill. We have a real threat of unknown origin inbound and we stand a very real possibility of having all our space assets destroyed in the hangar. Now get your ass in gear or I am going to kick it so hard you get a free vacation on Titan."

The crew immediately scrambled back to their jobs, working at a much faster pace, as Graves stomped over to the next bird. The crew chief there had evidently been listening in as his team was working like the Devil was stalking their souls.

Graves stopped, looking around the hangar. The first Angel, one of the sensor control birds, was riding its taxiing skid toward the takeoff grid, pulsing the engines in a pre-flight warm-up as it went. At least they might get something into space before it was too late, he thought grimly to himself.

CHAPTER 3

B renner, report," Hatfield ordered, as he stared up at the mission clock as it tirelessly ticked upwards.

"We are one hour from initial detection. Two squadrons of Mongoose will be prepped and in the launch tubes within the next thirty minutes. We have a quick reaction force of twenty marines and six SARines prepped in four Angels, supported by four missile boats, some EW/ECCM and a pair of command and control Angels that have been flash programmed to use the training simulation software to paint a target for the Mongoose to shoot at."

"The ground radars here will do the heavy lift on detection and track and send it to the C2 Angels. The Mongoose are going to fire at the training image with just their guns until they find the object. If we get a solid detection on the object, G-LOC will make a determination at the time as to whether to engage with Mongoose dumbfires or to let the Angels fire at it with ASMs or TSAMs."

"Brenner, how good is the track image going to be going through all those layers?" Hatfield asked intently.

"Well, it's a guess being filtered by software that doesn't have a high level of accuracy to begin with. So we may miss a lot."

"Make sure they use short bursts. I don't want to find it then have nothing left to shoot at it with. What about lunar side security?"

"The mil side is Condition One with all checkpoints reporting green, weapon systems reporting green and non-essential sections have been placed into lockdown. Non-essential personnel have been sent to the shelter-in-place that is deepest into the base. Far side research section and the Morale Improvement Center are reaching full readiness inside the next ten minutes. We had some difficulty getting all the researchers to SIP in a timely manner. The Promenade and

MIC are in lockdown at this stage, with all radiation and meteor shields in place. In ten minutes the pilots who were on leave in the MIC should be back to hangar nine, unfortunately four of them are incapacitated at present."

"Incapacitated how?" Hatfield asked absentmindedly as he studied the data that Brenner was feeding to his HUD.

"Been up too many hours and some alcohol. They are within regulations, just not suitable for flight."

"Have them suit up and observe from the ready room, we might still need them. What about the hangars?"

"All research hangars and transient hangars are in full lockdown, meteor armor extended and damage control crews awaiting action in their SIP. Hangar eight and nine on the mil side are in full combat launch status, with two squadrons loaded in the launch tubes. Hangar seven is the dedicated emergency recovery hangar for damaged birds. We have Marine security details in each hangar in case of any unexpected guests. The anti-meteor defensive batteries are all showing green right now, with full ammo in the hoppers and the gunnery crews on station. We're in about the best position we can get to right now."

"Notify the tugs and make sure they're ready for flight. We may need them to run for cover if this turns ugly. Are they fully fueled?"

"I know Jacobs keeps *Atlas* fully fueled, we'll check with the others just to make sure."

Hatfield drummed his console, deep in thought, while Brenner waited patiently. One of the hatches behind Molly opened up and Erik Bilks struggled through it, trying to wiggle into his command armor as he stumbled into the CIC. Brenner gave him a bemused stare before returning his attention to Hatfield.

Erik stopped next to Molly long enough to finish closing up his suit, putting his helmet between his knees as he scanned the displays intently. He leaned over and whispered to her.

"What's going on? I was uh, occupied in the MIC when the recall went out."

Molly favored him with a look of mild reprove. "Occupied doing what?"

Erik leered juvenilely at her. "I was at Phoebe's. Getting in some stress relief with a lovely girl named Melanie."

She rolled her eyes at him, still not fully comfortable with the fact that some of the taxpayer money that had been given to the KaliSun Corporation had gone to building whore-houses and casinos in the MIC for morale purposes, but given the situation she decided to drop it for the time being.

"The sensors woman over there said they used the surplus radars you guys acquired from us to detect some kind of in-visible object heading our way."

"Good deal on those radars, got them at fire sale prices," Erik said distractedly as he punched in the codes to fully activate his encryption suite in the command armor, gaining access to Hatfield's data.

Molly's lips pressed into a thin line as she ground out her response. "So I heard. You practically stole them."

Erik's response died on his lips as he saw her expression, his eyebrows furrowed for a moment before his face cleared. "Oh, right. Sorry about that. We were uh, just doing our patriotic duty to help defer the cost of downsizing your military." He flashed his dimples as he gave her a feral grin, fully aware that she considered the Corporation's actions criminal.

Molly scowled at him and turned back to face the displays in the center of the room.

"So just to clarify. Something went bump in the night, we can't see it, the Director brought us to General Quarters and we are about to go see what it is," Erik said quietly.

"Sure," Molly said with a snarl before she sighed and looked back at him. "Sorry. Yes that's what I understand." She paused, frowning. "Oh and I think they saw an alien swimming through a cloud on Saturn."

Erik, caught in the middle of taking a pull off his suit's water system, snorted it back out through his nose, tears welling up in his eyes. "What was that?" he said between wheezes.

"I don't know, some big snake or cuttlefish they saw in the clouds of Saturn."

Sloan glanced up from her display with a patient look at Erik. "Put your helmet on, I'll show you. I've been staring at it for fifteen minutes, I still can't tell what it is. It's almost translucent in parts and seems to be very large."

Sloan waited while Erik watched the video several times on his helmet HUD before he took it off and put it on the deck next to him. "Well, that should be interesting. The far side nerds are going to have kittens when they find out."

"They aren't finding out any time soon," Hatfield said, looking up from his display to give Erik a baleful stare. "Not until we know what it was and what is coming at us. I need you on the radio to Chief Graves. He wants to brief the pilots on your new specialty missile."

"We're using that? Uh boss, that's really not a good idea. We don't have any good full-scale test data. We don't even know what it will do to a ship if it's too close."

"Consider this the start of operational testing. If we don't stop that thing, it's going to hit Phoebe. Hard. Now get on the radio to Graves and make sure those pilots understand the blast radius on the damn thing."

"It's not really a blast radius . . . "

"Erik." Hatfield gave him a stern look.

"Ok, I'm on it." Erik pulled his helmet back on and turned his face shield opaque while he called Bobby Graves.

CHAPTER 4

What is this garbage about me being in the rear formation?" Major Ava Sirano barked into her helmet radio as she stormed across the hangar toward Chief Graves.

"It's not my call Ava. The DD wants you back from the point of contact in case whatever it is shoots back or blows up unexpectedly," Chief Graves said apologetically, trying to minimize the schematics that Dr. Erik Bilks was feeding him so he could see her clearly through his faceplate.

"Bullshit. This is the first combat we've had since the war and I have to sit in the back like a damn school teacher."

"Well not exactly, he also wants to give you a new weapons package. Something with a lot more punch than the other pilots are going to get. But it's only partially through testing, so he doesn't trust the first year pilots with it yet. Not enough experience shooting normal missiles, never mind this thing," he said as he waved over toward her blood red Mongoose as it was manually loaded with several hot pink colored missiles.

"Why the hell is that pink?" she said with disgust in her voice.

"He wanted to make sure nobody grabbed one by accident. It's the same reason our nukes are neon green, you have to be pretty stupid to accidentally load one," Graves said as he watched the last missile being attached to a hardpoint just to the right of her cockpit.

"And just what new deathtrap has Erik made for us today? The last three of his creations have been nothing but trouble."

Silently Graves added her to the conference call he was on with Dr. Bilks. "He was just about to tell me as you came stomping up here."

"Morning Major," Erik said cheerfully into the call.

"Don't give me that shit Erik, we're in a hurry. I want the quick and dirty on these weapons. So don't play around,"

Major Sirano said, using the same voice she used to get the attention of the new pilots she trained at the base.

Erik audibly gulped over the radio before pulling the other pilots who were supposed to be using the missiles into the conference call. Across the hangar, several pilots who had been doing pre-flight inspections of their spacecraft paused and began watching the conference call on their helmet HUDs. It was unnerving to watch them freeze in place as their attention was diverted, but the maintenance crews had seen it happen before, so they ignored it, taking over the pre-flight checks.

"Ok, basic premise for the pink weapons on your ships. This is a new semi-guided missile, the kind we normally refer to as dumbfires for the Mongoose. They have a substantially upgraded warhead but use more or less the same guidance systems. So line them up with your target, press the designator button, wait until it beeps green, then pull the trigger."

"The warhead will take an image of the last thing you were aimed at and tell navigation to go seek it out. Just like in your training. The one big difference here is that the warhead is not an explosion device. It's basically a paste of special material with some very special sub-atomic particles suspended within it. Think of it like protons and electrons, but smaller, and they don't play well with others. When the missile is detonated, an explosive compression occurs, vaporizing the holding material and jamming these little sub-atomic particles into each other at high speed. The particles will annihilate each other resulting in a wave emitted omni-directionally. The wave does lots of damage. Don't be within one hundred meters of the target or else it's very likely it will kill you, through your ship's defenses. Any questions?"

Jed Simmons answered with a thick north Texan accent. "What kind of wave does it emit?"

"It's complicated and we really don't have much time for that math."

"Just tell us, we might not get it now, but you never know," Simmons persisted.

"Uh it's kind of a quantum gravity wave. The grade school version is that when these particles are in proximity to each other, they create a gravitational field. That's what we use to make artificial gravity on the base, strips of these particles buried in the floor to make gravity fields. The closer they get, the stronger the field is. So when we make artificial gravity we are basically just moving two blocks of different particles closer or farther apart. When they actually make contact, they annihilate each other, and emit a large amount of energy. Very large in fact, disproportionate to what they should be able to due to well, it's complicated, but basically due to quantum potential energy. So the release of energy follows behind the last gravity wave that's emitted. That gravity wave is very strong due to the close proximity of those particles before they touch. The gravity interacts with the target object, distorting it, overcoming the weak nuclear and electromagnetic forces within the molecules. This results in the structure of the object being weakened and then impacted by the expanding energy emission from the contact between the two different types of particles. In theory, it should destroy the target. Make sense?"

"Sure," Simmons drawled back at him.

"Really?" Erik asked, surprised.

"Sure," Simmons repeated with a laugh.

"The explanation for the gravity system is in our training material Dr. Bilks," Ed Crawford said helpfully. "Major Sirano made it clear we needed to memorize that material."

In the background they could hear Erik try to change channels and ask somebody why the gravity manipulators were being taught to the pilots. Major Sirano gave a sigh and interrupted him. "Erik, you are still on our channel. As for who authorized the data release, it was me. They need to understand how those work or else they may try to fiddle with the generators in a survival situation and get killed. Now is there anything else?"

After a mumbled comment Erik came back through clearly. "Yes, don't shoot it near your friends and don't shoot at point blank range. We're still not exactly clear on what happens when you hit objects with high potential energies, like fuel sources or, uh, other things. Maybe don't shoot it at a nuclear reactor."

"Maybe?" Major Sirano asked impatiently.

"Yeah, we have no test data. But one simulation seemed to indicate that you could experience very bad results if it hits a fusion or fission pile. The gravity wave might compress it, detonating it, or worse."

"What's worse than a nuclear reactor going critical?"

"I have no idea. But there's always a worse in weapons testing."

One of the Angel pilots muttered over the channel. "If he doesn't know how these things work, maybe we shouldn't shoot them."

"I told the Director not to use them!" Erik whined.

Before anyone could comment further, the Director broke in. "Erik, stop complaining. Major Sirano, these are to be used at your discretion and very carefully. This is a non-ideal situation against a ship that may be far more technologically advanced than we are. I need a trump card in my pocket—you're it. I'm holding you in reserve because I trust your judgment. Now I need you all to live up to that expectation and make sure you don't get killed during first contact. Hatfield out."

The Angel pilot again said something under his breath. "I thought this was a private channel ... "

"There is no such thing as a private channel where the Director is concerned. Now get to your ships, complete preflights and lock into the tubes," Major Sirano said, gesturing Chief Graves over towards the back of her Mongoose.

She quickly disconnected from the conference call and initiated her point-to-point laser link communication system with the Chief. "Bobby, I don't trust Erik's toys. He's pasted too many of my pilots so far. I want you to have some extra SAR birds loaded and ready. If we pop this thing off, there's no telling how big the exact explosion will be. I suspect it's tied to the material it interacts with, and we have no idea what that will be. So keep your head on straight and be ready to ride to the rescue."

Chief Graves looked at her, flexing his prosthetic hand as he remembered back to their last assignment on Earth. She'd pulled him out of the hangar deck of the ship after shrapnel from a Chinese ballistic missile had sliced through his arm like a scalpel. Now she was asking him to be ready to save her. There was no doubt in his mind—he reached out and gripped her upper arm armor and gave it a squeeze.

"You have nothing to fear on that account Ava," he said as the memory clouded his eyes.

Dr. Christie Elliot looked up quickly as one of the contractor researchers exclaimed in excitement and gestured at the monitor he'd been playing with. She reached over and nudged Sam awake before unplugging herself from the charge ports for her suit and standing up. She ambled over to the group gathering around the monitor. Some of them were trying to tell the researcher what to do, others were pointing at things on the screen and asking him questions.

"What did you find?" she asked evenly.

The group protectively tightened up. Nobody responded to Dr. Elliot's request. She looked from person to person expectantly before sighing softly to herself.

"That was not a request. What have you found?" she said, keeping her voice level.

"Don't worry about it *Doctor* Elliot," Meckler said sarcastically.

Kyle Winters walked over, placing himself between Meckler and the slow burning fuse that was his coworker. "I'm worried about it, as well as your attitude. Remember you are a guest at the KaliSun Corporation's research facility. Now answer the question."

"I paid rent to be here, I am no guest," Meckler said defiantly.

"Yes, and the terms of the occupancy agreement clearly stipulate that you are a guest; it actually says, "While you are on KaliSun properties you are to be considered a guest, subject to all of the rules and regulations that other guests must abide by." One of those rules involves inappropriate use of IT equipment. So the lot of you, back away from that station and explain what you are doing. Right now."

"Or what? You'll call those thugs outside to come in here and beat us?" Meckler said.

Dr. Kapple walked up to stand by Winters. "Kyle, consider his mental state before we proceed."

Dr. Winters eyes narrowed in thought. "Yes, excellent point Dr. Kapple. But we still need to know what they've done to the emergency equipment in the SIP." He turned back toward the researcher who was standing at the monitor terminal as Dr. Meckler sputtered in front of him. "Please, route your monitor to the big screen so we can all see it."

The researcher hesitated, looking to Meckler for guidance, but when he realized that Meckler was not going to say anything helpful he frowned and pushed the display to the large screen on the far wall. For a moment, the screen dropped to a black, then flickered to life showing a partial view of the crater the base resided in. The camera angle had been zoomed in on the far military hangars. Dr. Winters looked at it for a few moments then looked back to the researcher.

"Maybe I'm just old. But I struggle to see why you're so excited. There is nothing going on out there."

Meckler regained his composure and stepped close to Winters, nearly chest bumping him like a coach arguing in baseball. "Exactly! Nothing is happening! No military fight, no reason to jam us in these little shelter rooms. It's all bullshit, all of it!"

Christie looked at the researcher running the terminal. "Where is that camera feed from?"

"One of Dr. Rogers' ephemeris optical tracking cameras. I reprogrammed it, so we could tilt it down into the crater," he said defiantly.

Christie and Kyle exchanged glances before Kyle spoke. "Change that and shift it back to the control of the central hub. Now."

"No," Dr. Meckler breathed in Kyle's face.

"Did you order him to hack the camera? Did you let Dr. Rogers know before you did it?"

"Yes of course I ordered him to do it. I lead these people and we won't tolerate being kept in the dark anymore!" he said, making an expansive gesture toward the clustered researchers. Christie rolled her eyes toward the overhead lights and mumbled under her breath. "Great, another crazy like Von Tremel."

Dr. Kapple reached out and grasped Winters' arm. "Kyle, we should really call the base doctor in here to see to him. You know as well as I do, that if this mental state is left untreated it could lead to serious harm."

"Mental state? You think I'm crazy? I'm not the one who lies to people so they can kidnap them—you did that. I am not the one who keeps making up excuses to shove us into this tiny room while you go through all of our data . . . "

"Almost exactly like Von Tremel." Christie gave a resigned grunt.

"He may not have been very friendly, but I've come to believe he was right not to trust you. He was right that you were stealing our data. What other reason could you have to keep us out of our research labs? You have people in there right now, going through our stuff," Meckler said with a patronizing tone.

"I seriously doubt that," Kyle said, with the resigned tone of a man whose patience was being worn out.

"Oh really? Show them," he ordered the researcher at the terminal. On the main screen a small window popped up, showing several Marines with a SARine in the lead entering one of the research wings, weapons at the ready as they cleared the room and moved on to the next room, searching for something. Dr. Meckler stepped closer to Winters, glaring at him from just inches away.

"As you may remember Dr. Meckler, I was involved in the Indian Military for several years during the latest Kashmiri conflict. Those men are not stealing data. That formation and their actions indicate they are searching for somebody. You don't need a submachine gun to go through computer files," Sam said as carefully as he could.

Several of the contract researchers looked back at the monitor, troubled expressions on their faces. It had not been that long ago that a double murder had occurred in the researcher barracks. No explanation for who had committed those murders was ever given, although during the radhaz event afterward, a number of the researchers had been arrested and detained. Nobody had heard from them either. A short girl who worked for one of the medical research companies suddenly gave a startled exclamation and started pointing at the big screen excitedly. "Look, look! What are those?"

All eyes in the room turned toward the big screen, several of the researchers pushing past Meckler and Winters to get a closer look.

"I count, ten, twelve. Wait, they keep on coming. It looks like two dozen of the small black ones taking off from the holes in the cliff face!"

"Hey look, some of the Angels are taking off too!" another researcher shouted, jabbing his finger in the direction of several of the ships taking off from one of the hangars in formation.

"What are those little ships? Hey look, another three just left the cliff. Uh that one is painted blood red! What is going on?" the researcher asked, worry creeping into his voice.

Christie shot an alarmed look at Sam and mouthed. *"Sirano just launched?"* Sam gave a silent nod and began sending a message on his wrist interface.

Meckler grabbed Winters' arm and pulled him closer, their faces nearly touching. "What is going on?" he demanded.

Winters shook him off and gave him a shove as he stepped away himself. "I honestly have no idea. They sounded General Quarters, secured the base and now are launching fighters en masse. I'd guess we're under attack you ingrate."

The female researcher standing under the display turned and looked at him. "You have spacefighters? Combat ships? But those are banned under treaty . . . "

Winters shrugged at her. "That's not my department. We do science, not war."

Further conversation was curtailed as the main hatch leading from the SIP room burst open and a squad of Marines with two SARines exploded into the room. The lead SARine did not hesitate, striding right up to Dr. Winters and speaking rapidly through his external speaker.

"Somebody has hacked into grid twenty's sensors, shutting down several of our defensive radars, shunting video feeds from some of the optical sensors to the researcher center before they are readdressed to come to this SIP. Who did it?" the SARine demanded quietly, his massive command armor adding menace to his words such that he no longer needed volume.

Instantly several of the contract researchers pointed to Dr. Meckler; a smaller number pointed to the man at the terminal who had paled to an almost translucent shade of white. Without hesitation, two of the Marines knocked Dr. Meckler to the ground, binding first his hands and feet, then tying the two bindings together behind his back. A SARine standing outside the door stepped forward as the leader motioned it was safe to enter. He strode angrily over toward Dr. Meckler.

"My name is Joe. You are going to answer me honestly or you are going out the airlock with me, without a helmet."

"Fuck you," Dr. Meckler snarled at him.

Joe reached down and plucked him off the floor, slamming his suited figure awkwardly into the nearby bulkhead twice, before tossing him back on the floor. "First question. Are you currently involved in a plot to destroy this base?"

Meckler spat a stream of bloody spittle in his direction, missing by a significant margin. Joe reached down and lifted him up with one arm, his armor augmenting his strength significantly. With casual ease he threw him back down on the floor with a tremendous crash.

"Next question, are you currently in communication with the hostile force approaching the base?"

Meckler sat up woozily and looked around the room, begging for assistance. But there was none to be had. The man who had been manning the terminal was pinned to the ground with a Marine's knee to his back and a weapon tucked snugly against the base of his skull. The KaliSun employees were looking at him with disgust, and the rest of his colleagues were either paralyzed with fear at the sudden violence, or staring at the big screen, their eyes wide with fear at the mention of an attacking force. Meckler's head lolled to the side in his suit as he faked passing out, hoping Joe would leave him be.

Joe wasn't fooled. He pulled a small vial out of his suit and squirted something foul up Meckler's nose, causing him to roll over, hacking and cursing as the smell overwhelmed him. "Answer the question Dr. Meckler."

"I didn't know we were being attacked. I thought you making up the attack so you could go through our research. We saw you on the camera going through our areas."

Joe shot a look at Winters, who confirmed that Meckler

had said just that earlier. "We were going through your re-search lab because it showed up as the source of the hack on our defense systems. Now, tell me what you did. We need to turn the grid back on immediately."

"I don't know, he did it, not me!" Dr. Meckler said as he gestured with his head over toward the other captive, wheezing through a bloody nose and mouth.

Joe motioned toward Dr. Meckler. "Strip his gear, bag and tag him. We'll finish up with this later." Two Marines stepped forward, stripping away his space suit then putting him in a durable plastic bag for transport to the holding cells. Joe walked over to the other researcher.

"What's your name?"

"Richard."

"Your full name dumbass."

"Richard Barkley."

Joe paused as his suit took the name in and began scanning through the employee database. He read in silence, his faceplate transparent so that everyone could see his face. Finally he nudged the captive with his boot. "Alright Dick, tell me exactly what you did to the system." Joe motioned to one of the other SARines who walked over to the terminal and jacked his suit in, typing in overrides and clearance codes so that he could access the entire system.

"Dr. Meckler told me to hack into the system so we could prove that you were going through our files and that there wasn't any real..."

"Yes, I gathered that. You did something to the defense network. I don't care who told you to do it. What did you actually do?"

"Uh, well, uh, I claim the right to an attorney."

Joe reached down and turned the researcher's chin up toward him. "Listen to me asshole. You turned off one of the tools we were using to track a very dangerous enemy that is approaching the base. There won't be a trial for this. I'm going to take you apart until you tell me exactly what you did."

"If you kill me you will never find out."

Joe looked at him, a grim look on his face. Finally he spoke, low and quietly but in such a way that everyone in the room could hear. "Your file indicates that you have two sisters, as well as several nieces and nephews. I have just transmitted your name to our contacts on Earth. If you don't cooperate, we will hunt them down and kill them. If the base falls to this attack, we will hunt them down and kill them. Are we clear?"

Barkley gulped, his eyes darting from face to face in the room, searching for somebody to challenge the hulking SARine. All he saw was fear and the eyes of several of the younger researchers pleading him to cooperate. He gave a resigned sigh.

"I used a general root password to access the power grid for the science experiments and shut it down. Once it was down, I selectively turned power back on for several cameras but not for the security equipment that supported them. So I was able to access the camera feeds but the normal security features didn't work. I routed it all through my computer in the Research Center."

"We have blocked all general root passwords from working on the system. Where did you get one that worked?"

Richard looked away from Joe. "What does it matter, just type in the code on the screen of my tablet. That'll let you turn the rest of the system back on."

Joe looked at the SARine working on the terminal. He held up the tablet, showing the locked screen. Joe prodded the captive with his foot and indicated over at the tablet.

"BigTits4A!!, is the password," he said dejectedly as a few nervous outbreaks of laugher briefly swept the room. The SARine at the terminal entered the password into the tablet, nodding over at Joe when it worked. He looked at the password on the tablet screen and punched it into the terminal. As it worked on accepting his access into the system, he reached down and plugged a small flash memory system into the tablet, copying all of the data onto his personal data key as he worked. Within seconds, an interface window popped up on the main display. He began keying in commands, his armored fingers surprisingly nimble as they raced across the keyboard.

On the screen a list of power distribution panels appeared. As the crowd watched intently the SARine reactivated each of the power hubs, a small depiction of the power grid in the lower right hand part of the screen flashing as each component went back online to green. As he worked, the lead SARine stared blankly at the wall, discussing the situation intently with the Command Information Center.

"CIC says power is green across the board now, estimated ETRO for the sensors is twenty-three minutes," the lead said to Joe, who gave a satisfied nod.

He aimed a light kick at the man on the floor. "Who gave you the code?"

"Why does it matter? Maybe I came up with it on my own."

"It matters because you can either answer when I ask politely, or you can answer while I'm ripping your knee caps off slowly, by hand. It's a matter of pain and suffering on your part," Joe said evenly, his eyes staring balefully out from his command armor.

Barkley swallowed hard before answering. "Von Tremel gave it to me, couple of months ago. He said I should be prepared in case something ever happened."

Joe exchanged a glance with the lead SARine. "What else did he give you?"

"Not much, just some stuff to hold on to for him."

"Where did you put it?" Joe said impatiently.

"It's in the frame of my bed. Inside it," Richard said miserably.

Joe looked over at the SARine working the terminal. "Are we stable or is this thing going to flake out on us the moment we leave?"

"It's stable I guess. I can't cut the camera feeds he routed to this room without doing a system restart though. That'll add about twenty-five minutes until the sensors come online. The radars need to reboot, but won't need the full system to restart."

The lead SARine assessed that information before looking over to Dr. Winters. "I'm leaving you in charge with two Marines stationed in here. You are to restrict access to any computing devices in the room unless it's you. If you have problems, the Marines can handle it, or you can have them contact me. Try to stop anyone from doing anything stupid." He looked over at Joe, who was standing over Barkley, looking down at him impassively. "Joe, can you take these two assholes down and dump them in the holding cell? I'll report our status to Major Stringer and Master Sergeant Marin."

With that, the SARine lead swept out of the room, trailing his Marines and the SARine who had fixed the power grid. Joe gathered up his charges, glaring at the two Marines who were staying behind. "Keep it under control in here and watch your backs."

Christie looked up at Joe as he walked past, dragging his two captives. "Did you actually send a kill order to Earth on his family?" she asked him quietly.

"No, of course not. But he didn't know that." With that, the SARine walked out the door leaving the KaliSun employees with the terrified contract researchers.

CHAPTER 5

Lieutenant Kimmie Sinclair nosed her Mongoose into formation as she cleared the launch tubes. She watched as the last of the launch indicators faded from her HUD, scanning her weapon systems to make sure nothing had been jostled loose during the rapid acceleration down the tube. She'd been sitting in the launch tube for nearly an hour by the time they were cleared hot to take off, and the waiting had taken a toll on her mental sharpness. She shook her head angrily to try and get back in the game.

Over the radio she heard the Squadron XO check down each ship in sequence. After a brief pause the XO spoke again.

"All units, this is not a drill. We have a possible threat incoming and we're going to check it out. Today's squadron designation is Wasp. We'll be running three ship flights today, Captain Martin will be back on this frequency as soon as he finishes up coordinating with the other squadron. Sinclair, Terns I want you to take sections three and four. I will take section two, Captain Martin takes section one. Break and reform into sections."

An intricate dance began as the ships left their launch formation and reformed into three ship elements, the typical strike formation they'd used since early in the training process. For the Wasp squadron, this was not a difficult task. Captain Jamal Martin had trained his squadron well, and as the senior class of pilots at Saturn Base they'd had the most simulation and flight time.

For the neighboring squadron it posed some challenges. These pilots were barely into flying outside of simulators, and they'd rarely flown together. As they tried to break and reform, it was painfully obvious that nerves and inexperience were going to be a challenge. After five attempts, they eventually settled into a loose formation, the right spaceships where they were supposed to be, even if the formation looked awful.

Kimmie sighed to herself and keyed a private channel to Lieutenant Hopper. "Hey Doug."

"Yeah Kimmie?"

"Why are the rooks out here instead of the second year squadron? Also, why is G-LOC not up here with us, she's hanging back there with the Angels for some reason."

"Wish I knew Kimmie, I think they were specifically ordered to hold on their launch until we made contact. Doesn't make sense to me unless we're being used as bait."

"Or cannon fodder maybe."

"Yeah, or cannon fodder. Not like that never happened during the Chinese war."

"Usually worked far too well, got my ass shot down anyway."

"Yeah. Keep the channel clear. Martin should be back on the line any moment, he'll share if he knows why."

"Copy," she replied, killing the channel. Kimmie rolled her Mongoose, rotating the tines so she could look out over the formation. On a sudden whim, she pulled up the flight experience information on her two wingmen.

On her left wing was Steve Capson—minor combat experience during the African wars, rarely against airborne foes. Scored modestly well on his training segments. Was held back from a previous class after he bounced his fighter into the hangar wall due to an inflight failure. She checked the date, and frowned. He had been in the infirmary for over a year, until a few months ago when he was brought back in to replace a pilot who'd been seriously injured during a weapons test. Her eyes narrowed in thought. She'd been the replacement pilot on that test. She shook her head. He had no medical exceptions listed, but still.

On her right wing was Rashad Jackson. He was from her original class, they'd flown on the same freighter out. He'd been at Osan AFB when the last war kicked off, barely managing to get his plane in the air before the missiles hit. His flight jacket showed he'd been shot down twice during that conflict, once over Korea and once by friendly fire when he was approaching a temporary air station in South Japan low and fast. Reasonable scores in training, but they hadn't spent much time together.

With a shrug she began setting up their battlenet, pulling them into designated frequencies and networking their sensors together. She looked down at her blue-force tracker and identified the Angel that was assigned as her support asset, and pulling their data feeds into her battlenet she checked to see who the pilot was.

With a surprise, she saw it was Lieutenant Lori Adams, an old friend who had been part of the British SAS helicopter support units they had worked with during the last big war. Usually she was running a troop transport, not an electronic warfare Angel. She keyed her into a private frequency.

"Hey Lori, looks like you're my overwatch today."

Lori's voice boomed over the encryption, a bad connection fouling her response with static, but there was no mistaking her laughter. "Yep, I conned Master Sergeant into letting me fly on your wing since we're short support pilots right now. He said I could go, but I had to bring a SARine along to run the top turret and report back observations."

"He can fit in the top turret?" Kimmie asked curiously.

"Not very well judging by all of the banging going on back there," Lori said wickedly.

"Either way, glad you're here. Any idea why they held the other vets back from the first wave?"

"Yeah, they're worried when you guys trip into whatever this is, the first wave might get wiped. So they held them back in reserve."

"That's not very comforting."

"That's war!" Lori said with a chuckle.

"What else do you know?"

"Not much, heard the SARines scrumming before we loaded up, by the sound of it, they don't know what it is either. But they are assuming some kind of alien."

"Yeah, right."

Kimmie's HUD showed the main squadron frequency pulse quickly three times with an alert, so she swapped back to that channel and pumped up the volume with a few rapid blinks.

"Wasps, this is Wasp 1-1. Primary assignments are as follows. Wasp 1-1 is myself, Wasp 2-1 is Lieutenant Hopper, Wasp 3-1 is Lieutenant Sinclair and Wasp 4-1 is Lieutenant Terns. We're going to modify the original flight plan a bit. The Deputy Director has decided the original plan to fly in two pincers toward the predicted intercept point was too clearly a threat and that the enemy might detect that threat and react before we're ready. So instead we're going to form up into a loose wing and approach the intercept point in a long looping, low energy orbit. We have two C2 Angels out here who will be sending target data to you via your training simulators, so don't turn it off when it triggers. Whatever is out here has very good stealth, so we'll be firing guns at the simulated target until we hit something. Then adjust when it reacts."

"Like two squadrons of fighters launching at once isn't also an easily spotted threat," Kimmie mumbled to herself while she was on mute.

"Once we engage, we'll operate independently by section—try to stay within range of your support Angel. We have a few missile boats in the back, one squadron sitting in reserve. G-LOC is also out here with a support section. Any questions?"

Silence greeted him, so he cleared the radio and instructed them to stay off the squadron frequency unless it was important.

Kimmie watched the blue-force tracker intently as the wing made a sweeping right hand loop out away from the base. Her squadron, Wasp, tracked cleanly in formation, both her section mates staying in proper formation through every turn, using the minimum amount of fuel required to complete the maneuver. Rook squadron tried to mimic that turn, but was having some difficulties, over-thrusting through the turn and bouncing around in their section formations. The section leaders were allowing them a bit more space than normal due to their inexperience, but the BFT still occasionally indicated a near miss within their formation. Inward from them, toward the base, Major Sirano rode herd on the support and missile Angels. She was the only protective barrier between the unseen enemy and the troop transports of the quick reaction force far to the rear.

As they completed the loop to the right and turned back to the intercept point, the Angel flight cut across behind them, moving from behind them on the right to behind them on the left, and spreading out to present less of a target as they approached the intercept point.

Finally, with fourteen minutes to go, the simulation software kicked in, showing an oblong smear on Kimmie's HUD. The center of the smear glowed brightly, indicating the high probability of an object occupying that space, the rough edge almost transparent and not smoothly shaped. The sensor image repeatedly smeared and the resolution faltered as new data came in.

"Captain Martin, my target basket keeps changing shape and jumping around. How sure are we that this is accurate?" she asked over the squadron frequency.

"I know. Some idiot in the research center cut the power to half the sensors along the rim. They've restored power, but it takes a while for the radars to fully reload system software and regain track on the ephemeris. We expect that sensor section to be back online in five minutes or so."

"Cutting it close sir."

"Yeah, it's going to be tight."

Brenner leaned forward from the observation bridge and looked down into the sensor pit. "Higgins, SITREP on those downed sensors."

Higgins, who was typing rapidly in the UNIX terminal she'd brought up on her screen, grunted back at him, but made no other reply as her fingers scuttled across the keyboard. Lines of code flew by as she searched for the features she needed. Eventually she keyed in her final sequence and turned to face Brenner, who was nervously looking up at the countdown clock for intercept, watching it pass the five-minute marker.

"I had to reload the software to do launch-on-remote, and then recompile the whole system code to make it merge tracks from all of the sensors. In about two minutes, the C2 picture will hiccup and when it comes back on line, we should have a better picture of the ship."

"Wait, you're going to bring it down?"

"I have to, we didn't put any hooks in the system to bring new systems into the calculations. If we don't bring it down the sensors we brought back online won't be able to contribute at all, not even after the intercept. I figured you'd want it fixed before the fight kicks off," she said with a slight shoulder roll and shake of her head.

Brenner cursed under his breath as he turned to look back at Hatfield. Hatfield was sitting with his chin on his fist looking down at the combined sensor picture. Without glancing up he spoke to Brenner.

"You'd better warn them. Otherwise we're likely to have some very unhappy pilots."

Brenner savagely keyed his radio, speaking urgently to G-LOC in short clipped sentences. He sent an annoyed glance at the sensor technician.

"G-LOC wants to know if they can freeze the previous location into the displays and shoot on that, just in case your reboot takes too long."

"That would work, but you should know that significant portions of the estimate are probably wrong because of the lack of radar resources and the viewing angles."

"It's going to have to do," Brenner said as he swapped back to G-LOC. After several tense moments of conversation he was done. He turned back to Hatfield.

"G-LOC is going to have them fire shorter bursts during the initial probing fire, to conserve ammunition. Even at the rate of closure they'll be at, it could be very hard to react by the time the first rounds hit."

"Yes, that had occurred to me. Have the rookies take the lead position and fire their bursts at the high probability area. Maybe they'll hit first and the second squadron will have time to adjust fire with more precision," Hatfield said thoughtfully.

Brenner relayed the message, sending a fierce look down at Higgins who was once again typing into her terminal. A thin sheen of sweat had begun to form on her forehead as she bit her lip and tried to will her program to work faster.

<hr />

"All sections be advised you will see a hiccup in the data feed momentarily... " Hopper began over the squadron battlenet, right before somebody began viciously swearing in the background. "Capson, turn your radio off. Keep the comms clear," Hopper chastised him angrily.

"Sorry sir, I've lost my target picture completely, it just van... oh there it is again. Well sort of, it's not updating."

"As I was saying, they're rebooting the sensors fast. The plan is to fire short bursts at the last known probable target volume. If we're lucky, we'll get updates to that target prior to intercept, which is in ninety seconds. Stay focused."

"LT, the Rooks are pulling ahead of us," Terns reported over the frequency.

Kimmie broke from her visual scanning and glanced at the BFT. Sure enough, the other squadron had increased speed and was spreading out. They were moving into a position that put them more or less directly into their firing lanes. She gave an exasperated sigh and looked up at Lori's Angel, which was moving into position just to the aft of them. As she watched, the SARine rotated the top turret all the way forward and started tracking the expected target envelope as they approached. Lori tilted her Angel so she could look down at Kimmie and threw her a quick salute before turning her glass opaque and regaining her attitude with the formation. She tuned back into the squadron conversation, glancing at the countdown clock as it passed forty-five seconds out.

"They're proceeding with new orders from command. Don't worry, they will clear out before we open fire," Captain Martin said calmly over the radio.

At thirty seconds to intercept, with the Rooks nearly fifteen seconds of flight time ahead of them, the first rounds left their guns. They arced out, briefly visible on the BFT tracker, as they pulled away from the formation and kept on going. Clear misses all around.

A red flashing beacon lit up Kimmie's HUD, she blinked at the icon and watched the update flood her targeting screen as the second firing sequence headed toward the target. The far right edge of the Rook squadron fired, their rounds darting into the void and then flashing into brilliant light as they made contact with something. The rest of the squadron's rounds passed into space, with no contacts.

"All sections roll right and engage those impacts, drop previous firing pattern and push to full military power," Captain Martin's command punched through over all frequencies.

With clean precision Wasp squadron executed a half roll to the right, burning hard with their maneuvering thrusters to shift vectors like a school of deadly fish darting to the side.

The Rook squadron used their maneuvering thrusters to turn sideways, still flying in the same direction, but facing their guns toward the impact point. They all fired long bursts towards the new target area. With every round that hit the object, the radar picture sent to the second squadron became clearer and clearer.

Secondary flashes were seen as flares of gas, seemingly erupting from nothing, burned briefly before the expanse of space swallowed and extinguished them like candles in the abyss. The fighters continued to turn with their target as they swept past, firing back at the target volume, stitching it down its length with impacts and explosions.

Kimmie watched the radar picture solidify based on hits and misses, looked for an area with large numbers of flashes from secondary explosions and locked it in. "Three section, concentrate on my target, guns first, dumbfires on command. Fire with me."

They closed in, diving for their designated target as the fourth section aimed for an area further astern. Lori's Angel hovered above them, blasting the expected target area with every erg of energy her electronic jamming system could emit. As the energy emissions washed over the target, the radar picture suddenly resolved with crystal clarity in the section Lori was targeting. Over the length of the target volume the optical cloak began to fade away. Grimly gritting her teeth, she focused on the target in the HUD and pulled the gun trigger.

"Section three, GUNS GUNS GUNS!"

Both of her section mates joined in instantly, pumping out three rounds at a time in a nearly synchronous barrage of explosive, fragmentation and kinetic rounds. With almost no recoil, there was barely any indication they were firing the deadly rounds other than a slight vibration in the hull on three sides of her titanium cockpit as the magazines fed fresh rounds into the guns.

The rounds slashed in, leaving a trail of briefly flaming embers behind them before they struck the ship around Kimmie's designated target area. Instantly debris flew outward, sheathed in flames and electrical discharge. After one hundred rounds had slammed into the ship, she reached down and flipped the master arm switch for her dumbfires.

"Pickle two, Fox two." She held the release trigger down halfway until she saw a green light on both of the missile icons on her weapons loadout display. Without hesitation she pulled the trigger the rest of the way, causing the two semi-guided dumbfire rockets to rip off the hardpoints along the inside of her weapon tines and streak away. She pulsed her maneuvering thrusters twice to push her starfighter upward quickly, in case the enemy attempted to shoot the missile down, the fire wouldn't continue on and hit her.

A quick glance at the BFT confirmed her section was still with her, and looking up she saw Lori's Angel holding formation as the top turret gunner wandered rounds all over the hull, hitting strange protrusions and panels, leaving behind gouts of flame where they punched through.

With a satisfying fireball, the six dumbfires from her section slammed unhindered into the target area, penetrating deeply into the hull and exploding. A large object was blown into space to arc toward the far side of Phoebe, trailing gas and debris as it went. Kimmie flipped her Mongoose around and fired a few quick bursts at the ship as they pulled away. She watched the rounds head in, their fuel burning brightly as they accelerated.

The first burst impacted along the far side of the ship, but the last three bursts never made it. Something vaporized them some distance from the hull in bright flashes of light. As she watched, a section from the Rook squadron cut back across the ship's hull, firing along the length, some rounds penetrating, but most of them destroyed. Passing the ship, the far left Mongoose flashed a brilliant shade of green as its leading tine was hit by a ball of energy and vaporized, its mass converted to energy in an instant.

The Mongoose wildly corkscrewed away, narrowly missing the section leader as it sparked and outgassed. All of the maneuvering thrusters were firing on full power and the main engines were dark, whipping the ship around in a tumble that tracked in toward Phoebe at an alarming rate. One of the SAR Angels broke from G-LOC's flight element and accelerated toward the heavily damaged Mongoose, pushing its engines to full afterburn and extending a gravity control grapple.

Kimmie tore her focus away from the damaged Mongoose as her two wingmen started yelling all at once.

"Did you see that? Something just smashed his Mongoose, just vaporized half of it!" Capson said with panic creeping into his voice.

"Enough, yes, I saw it, pull tight into formation. We'll loop around for another pass. He was less than twenty-five meters away. Let's keep it at five hundred meters, full power. Try not to bump into anyone," Kimmie said as she checked her immediate airspace.

Lori was still with her, section four had peeled away earlier and was now unprotected by the Angel's softkill systems, conducting longer range gunnery runs on the ship which had now fully emerged from cloak. As she watched their rounds vanished in a series of flash vaporized metal and explosive.

"You seeing this Lori?"

"Yes, some kind of defense system. We're trying to see if we can detect it, right now I think it's more a point defense system than an energy shield."

"Can we get through it?" she said, as she took her section into a looping orbit that brought them toward the rear of the ship.

"Well, the closer you get, the less time it has to track and shoot at our weapons. I'd guess that's why that Rook's flight section landed some hits. But they also seem to have something nasty close in, whatever it is, I doubt a rocket has a chance in hell of getting by. The only weak spots seem to be where you targeted and where Captain Martin targeted. Looks like you guys wrecked enough of the weapons systems that there are gaps in the defensive screen there. I guess. That's all I have for now," Lori said, excitement causing her British accent to obscure some of her words.

"Great," Kimmie said, switching back to her section radio. "Ok, looping orbit, only shoot at our previous target for now. Short bursts until we have a better plan, go easy on your fuel."

"Son of a bitch," Brenner said as the ship started to decloak. "That is definitely not from around here."

The ship slowly came into view, coated in a bright reflective metallic finish that almost shimmered as explosions rocked it. The main hull was a long, flattened teardrop with a narrow blunt tip for a bow and a raised portion on the top and bottom of the stern. The stern ended in a bowl shape, four large engines protruding from the rear and a string of smaller engines lining the rim of the bowl. The large engines were dark and cold, with no sign of recent use, and the smaller engines were starting to emit significant amounts of energy as the ship accelerated toward the base. Near the bow, two protrusions stuck out from the centerline of the oval, curling around to face forward and obscuring the view of the bow of the ship. Smoke and debris leaked from several sections of the hull, with most of the damage directly forward of the raised top deck. This was where one section of Mongoose had focused their fire, deeply pitting the hull and exposing the inside of the ship to vacuum.

"Is it just me or does that look like a scorpion that somebody clipped the tail off of?" Erik said as he manipulated his screens to show him a variety of views. Pushing Molly aside he commandeered her screens too as she looked on wide-eyed.

"I think that might be a good way to . . . ." Brenner started to reply when Sloan interrupted him.

"Contact! One of the Mongoose from the Rook squadron just made contact with something near the bow. It vaporized a big chunk of his ship in an instant. He's tumbling out of control toward the north pole of Phoebe. One of the SAR birds is already en route, medical team is alerted in hangar seven," Sloan reported, urgency in her voice. "I think it was some kind of energy weapon . . . "

"Confirm large volume of short-range weapons fire coming from that ship. It's energy based and only visible in the IR spectrum," Higgins interrupted as she brought a new view up on the main screen; the enemy ship with a complex web of energy weapon discharges emitting in all directions.

Brenner spoke to G-LOC over the radio. Hatfield looked at him, eavesdropping briefly before turning his attention to Higgins.

"Higgins. Are there any weak points in that energy web they're putting out?"

"Yes sir. Near the damage that Wasp 3-1's section did. Right there at the base of the uh, raised portion on the topdeck. Well the thing we're calling the top I guess. Most of the rest of the damage seems to have only caused localized disruptions in the defensive set up."

"Any areas that are more heavily defended then the rest of the ship?"

Higgins stared at her sensor displays before hesitantly responding. "Yes, I think so sir. The bow area is protected by what is essentially a wall of fire. Nothing gets close to it and those two, um, claw-looking things serve as additional protection. Actually they bulge out enough that they provide significantly better protection than even the undamaged sections toward the rear."

"Anything else?"

"Well, the shape toward the stern, the lump that's mirrored top and bottom of the hull of the ship. It had significant defenses on the top, but 3-1 vaporized most of it during their attack run. The bottom section of the hull is still intact and shows defensive fixtures in that area. I think the stern in general is more heavily defended than the bow."

"But that one area was damaged before their camouflage was fully down?" Hatfield prodded.

"I think so, we'll know more later when we can analyze the data carefully."

"Know more now, Higgins. It may be the key to this fight. Also, bring the one-five-fives into the game. I want them shooting at that ship." Hatfield looked over at Brenner and interrupted his communication with G-LOC, breaking into it so they could both hear him.

"G-LOC, Director. One of the Wasp Sections did significant damage to a portion of the hull on the top, so to speak. I want you to direct everyone to keep pounding that area. Focus on it, I want the defenses in there eroded further so the gap is bigger. Then I want you to park your special in the hole in their point defenses."

"Copy Director, we were just talking about that," G-LOC responded over the radio, her voice booming with static.

Brenner turned to meet Hatfield's gaze. "Got it covered boss."

"Brenner. Capture that ship," Hatfield said softly.

Kimmie wheeled her ship around in a tight arc, taking a few potshots at the enemy ship below them. Nothing was getting through and she was starting to feel like this was a losing battle. The ship had accelerated and was heading straight toward the shipyard on Phoebe. There wasn't anything visibly stopping her rounds, they just flashed into a bright light and disappeared. She looked at the BFT, noting that two of the Rooks were limping back toward hangar seven, shepherded by a SAR Angel, ready to grapple them if they should lose control. That made three Rooks down already and they weren't even scratching the ship any more. She looked at the icon for her squadron in the upper right corner of her HUD, blinking twice fast. An image of the squadron health and status hovered in front of her eyes for a few seconds, color-coded to indicate how much fuel, ammo or damage they had. The Wasps were mostly green, for now, with just ammunition creeping into orange levels.

G-LOC's voice broke into her thinking as it went out across all battle frequencies. "All callsigns, adjust cockpit filters to IR channel kilo-two, laser protective visors down and retarget to my designated target, marker Yankee Six. Say again Yankee Six."

Kimmie reached up and slammed her protective shield down over her faceplate with a curse. She hated these shields. She toggled through the options of her right thigh control panel and modified her sensor view modes with the interface. Abruptly, the view before her changed. What had previously been a chrome ship with small black battle scars on it had morphed into a black-tinged shape with hot spots where recent detonations hadn't been cooled by vacuum's chill, surrounded by a web of violent purples and pinks criss-crossing the immediate area around it. She reflexively jerked the stick slightly, causing her to juke sideways as she struggled to stifle a curse.

"God that thing has a mean point defense system . . . " her wingman Jackson breathed into the radio.

"No shit. New plan, don't fly through that anymore. I have no idea how we've survived as long as we have," Kimmie said as she thought back to the close passes they had made on the ship early on. She had felt something a couple of times, almost like the ship brushed up against a feather, just sliding along the hull. With a slight shudder she swung her formation wider, away from the vessel.

Abruptly, her HUD was flooded with new data, the map application chirping as it updated to show bright red cones emanating from the base with orange cones enveloping them. Probability of impact cones, she thought. They started blinking with black text. *Danger, no fly zone.* Before she could key her radio to ask what that was about, a new target designator appeared on her display, Yankee six pulsed beside it, centered directly over the point in the hull they'd hit with their first pass.

"Wasp 3-2, Wasp 3-3, Wasp 3-1. Be advised, we have outgoing artillery coming from Saturn Base. Stay away from the no fly zones or take an express elevator to meet your ancestors," Kimmie said as she deciphered her new display information.

The BFT displayed an update, showing twenty outgoing 155mm artillery rounds heading for the alien ship. Ellipses formed around the trajectory, with a predicted impact point shifting around on the hull; a countdown clock began ticking down at the point of impact. Thirty seconds later, another round of twenty outgoing left the base.

"Section three, on my wing. We're going to do a gunnery run on the target between salvo one and two, watch the point defenses and try not to run into the damn thing. Follow my lead in."

Her wingmen snuggled up near her Mongoose as they waited for the clocks to tick down. At thirty seconds to impact, all of the Angels bathed the alien ship with the full power of their jamming systems. The artillery rounds raced toward the target area, but at the last second the ship rolled ever so slightly, changing the impact point to somewhere more heavily defended. The rounds vanished in sequence as the point defenses reached out and vaporized them.

Kimmie heard Lori swear over the radio. "G-LOC, be advised, our EW has limited impact on their point defense system!"

"Here we go fellas," she said as she nosed over and dove at the ship below. At two hundred meters out, they unleashed their guns in one long burst, then swapped over to missiles and launched one a piece at the target designator. They broke like water flowing over a rock at the one hundred meter mark, diving past the alien ship on both sides. Kimmie felt her ship shudder as something banged against the underside of her cockpit, but her board read green.

"Lori, ADA please?"

"Damage assessment is negative. They were able to shoot down all your missiles, some of the rounds leaked but not enough to do much. None hit the target, the ship was still rotating."

Kimmie snarled in frustration as she pulled her section through a long loop for another pass. Terns swept past them followed by two of the Rooks flying as a pair. The lead Rook fired a dumbfire between Wasp 4-2 and Wasp 4-3, and followed it with a long stream of gunfire, causing Tern's section to scatter urgently The two Rooks hesitated as they approached the ship, unsure who to follow. The trailing Mongoose was hit by a purple beam of light from the ship near the cockpit. It shuddered and began a long slow bank back toward the base, one engine flaring to a higher power level before blinking out, the other two engines throttled back to compensate.

Unexpectedly, the single missile the rookie Mongoose pilot fired managed to penetrate the defensive screen and slammed into the alien hull just meters from the damage they'd caused on their original pass. The missile penetrated deeply causing gouts of flame to erupt from the hull.

Kimmie licked her lips as she watched the events unfold below her. The Rook who had been damaged was drifting into the no fly zone from the base, while a SAR Angel desperately tried to regain control of the damaged fighter and avoid flying through the area. More importantly, the volume of fire defending the damaged part of the hull dropped dramatically immediately after the explosion.

"Stay close and follow me in, Wasp 2-3 I want you to fire a three second burst with guns, at the halfway point, Wasp 3-3 I want you to fire a dumbfire. Then I will fire guns for three seconds and Wasp 2-3 will fire a dumbfire, then Wasp 3-3 fires three seconds and 2-3 fires a dumbfire. Got it?"

"Got it," Lori said over their channel, startling Kimmie. "Start your attack run. I'm feeding your HUDs the timing."

Kimmie opened her mouth to tell Lori to back off then stopped. She smiled to herself and angled in on the ship, dropping down from above on a bee-line for the damaged section. Another round of artillery fire from the surface was coming toward the alien ship, three Rooks did a sweeping high angle pass on the damaged area as they approached, doing no damage and taking none. Then they were in range.

Like clockwork, the HUD told them when to fire, when to rest or when to release a missile. As they finished the firing run, Kimmie barrel-rolled them up away from the alien ship, watching her BFT to see the missiles track in. The point defense system sputtered several beams of light up at the first string of cannon rounds, vaporizing most of them but letting six through to slam into the hull near the designated target point. A single beam of energy reached out and destroyed the first dumbfire before shifting aim to the next group of cannon rounds coming in. This time, it was overwhelmed and only stopped two of the rounds, the rest of them punching holes in the hull again. After that, it was over. The next two dumbfires and over fifty cannon rounds pounded the area, digging deep into the hull and venting gas and energy into space in a rapid series of flashes.

"Damn nice shooting section three," Captain Martin's voice came over the radio tinged with excitement. "Section two follow me in, we're going to repeat that attack mode. Angel two, give us the timing."

"Copy that Wasp lead. Five seconds."

Kimmie flipped her Mongoose over on its back, her section following her through the turn. She scanned the squadron health and status briefly and frowned. Her section was down to less than a hundred cannon rounds between them and some dumbfires. They weren't going to be able to repeat that tactic. She glared at the starfield ahead of her, angry to be nearly out of the game right when the front door was cracked. As her section orbited the ship they watched the Captain's approach and gunnery run. He managed to score several more hits, but took a glancing blow of his own, losing his portside engine in the process.

"All Wasps, Wasp Actual. I've been hit, systems stable, but heavy damage. I am RTB. Wasp 2-1 is in command. Good hunting." With that he sluggishly banked his Mongoose in a sweeping turn to avoid the ship and headed for the base.

"All Wasps, regroup and prepare for another run," Hopper's voice came over the radio.

"Break break. Wasps form on G-LOC," came G-LOC's voice as she powered her blood red Mongoose into the fray, three Angels tagging along behind them.

Kimmie heard Hopper's disappointed sigh softly over the section command frequency before he acknowledged the command.

"Form on me and fire off short bursts of cannon fire at Yankee six. At my command, you need to break hard away and gain distance. Do not hesitate."

The eleven remaining Wasps formed up in a protective cloud around G-LOC's section and the Angels. Diving toward the ship, Kimmie looked at her BFT as it began chirping like mad; the reserve squadron had just launched and was thrusting toward them at full power.

G-LOC dove the squadron down toward the alien ship. At two kilometers out, they began firing. Kimmie winced at the ammo usage—there was no hope these rounds would close the gap between them without running afoul of the point defense system. At seven hundred and fifty meters, she had them all fire one dumbfire. What was G-LOC doing?

"All Units BREAK BREAK BREAK, get clear of the ship!" G-LOC's voice echoed through the command frequency. With clean precision the Wasps, G-LOC's section and the supporting Angels peeled away. She continued on, diving toward the ship, following the dumbfires in like a lawn dart. As she passed the three hundred meter mark, she fired a short burst of cannon fire and let loose one oversized missile. As soon as it was away, she flipped her ship at a forty-five degree angle to her previous vector and smashed her afterburners.

The rounds fell like rain on the top deck of the alien ship. Many were vaporized harmlessly, some were killed so close to the ship that the point defense weaponry was hitting the hull and being reflected from the polished chrome surface back into space. But dozens of rounds hit the scarred top deck of the ship and sprayed material from the ship into space. As debris clouded the area, the point defense system began losing accuracy, hitting the debris more than the incoming dumbfires and cannon rounds. Explosions and secondary explosions erupted from the area, engulfing G-LOC's larger missile, detonating before it reached the ship.

As the explosions vaporized the inert compounds within the warhead, the gravity particles collided and produced a wave of energy that disrupted the surrounding molecular structure of nearby materials. Debris and stray gas were blasted out like shrapnel in all directions in a flash of ultraviolet light, slamming into the nearby ship and tossing G-LOC's Mongoose away from the scene violently.

The wave proceeded outward, riding a ridge of compressed gases and energy, overtaking the fleeing Mongoose and Angels, tossing them about like dice on a gaming board. One of the Rooks, flying too close to the ship, was hit by a piece of hull and instantly demolished, his spacecraft reduced to small fragments of the titanium pilot tub and shards of shattered hull material.

Kimmie felt her Mongoose buck wildly beneath her, the gravity compensation fluctuated madly for a few moments and her displays flickered, before producing a steady stream of error messages. She fought to regain control of the stricken fighter as it tumbled down toward Phoebe. After several agonizing minutes, she managed to regain control and get her ship pointed back at the base. She was sweating bullets inside her spacesuit as she reached a gloved hand up to push the emergency button at the top of the cockpit window. She pulled the safety cover off and pushed it.

The cockpit vibrated sharply before a green light lit up on the display. She felt the return-to-base emergency system kick into operation. A small solid rocket engine pushed her back toward Phoebe on a low energy return, while a backup communication unit broadcast her distress on the SAR frequency.

She took her hands off the sticks and looked through the viewport at what remained of the alien ship.

"What the hell was that?" she said into the dead radio.

CHAPTER 6

Christie leaned in to whisper in Kyle's ear. "Well, they certainly seem less revolutionary now."

"Yes. Two armored Marines with murder in their eyes will do that," he said softly back as he studied the screen intently. So far it was just showing the hangar row—a very boring view of the hangar row.

Sam's wrist interface pinged, and he glanced down at it. Reading it quickly, he spoke to Winters. "Stand by."

"For what?" Christie asked curiously.

The screens abruptly shifted views. No longer showing just the hangars, the main screen now showed a blown up view of the ongoing space battle overhead. The battle was chaotic, small black shapes buzzing around a chrome ship of foreign design, a rainbow of colors erupting from it as it fired away at them.

The room collectively gasped as the reality of space battle sunk in. Even the Marines looked somewhat shocked as they turned to face the monitors. The girl who had first seen the Mongoose launch earlier suddenly pointed at the approach monitor with silent excitement on her face.

Approaching slowly, with a slight tumble, was a black shape with an Angel hovering nearby trying to stabilize it. The ship looked like it had hit a wall and sheared off one of its tips, exposing the cockpit to the view of the camera. The Angel was clearly attached to the ship somehow and was using its engines to guide it in towards one of the hangars. As they watched it approach, clouds of dust billowed away from the center of the hangar group with a brief flash of light.

"What was that?" Christie whispered to Kyle.

Kyle shook his head in confusion but Sam answered. "That was outgoing artillery rounds. Looked like pretty big guns too."

Several of the nearby researchers looked sharply at Sam but said nothing, shooting sideways glances at the Marines nervously as the room became tense watching the battle unfold. The view of the battle on the hyper-spectral display shifted to the main screen as Christie nudged Sam.

"I am assuming you got that put on the screen?"

"I told Erik that if we didn't get an idea of what was going on soon, we might have a problem down here. He talked to the Director. This is the view we'll get."

"Is that a Chinese ship?" Christie whispered.

"I doubt it. That thing is huge, almost the size of one of the tugs. We would have seen that coming. Even if it flew out here during the radhaz, which I doubt, it couldn't get here in time from Earth. No this is somebody different. Maybe the Russians had something out here we didn't know about."

They all watched intently as half of the little fighters formed up in a big ball over the top of the unknown ship and paused, before diving down in formation to attack the top of the ship. Weapons fire flashed in the distance and was met by pink and purple light rippling up from the ship.

Dr. Winters sighed as he watched. "That doesn't look particularly effective."

The Marines exchanged a look and started checking each other's gear in preparation for combat. Sam began checking his suit and going through a final check of Christie's, just to make sure everything was properly sealed up. While none of them were in a rush, a nervous current began to run through the room.

Motion by the launch tubes at the edge of the crater drew everyone's attention back to the main screen as twelve more fighters left the launch tubes in rapid sequence. A bright flash of light near the foreign ship caused the crowd to switch to watching the hyper-spectral screen intently. For just a moment the light seemed to pause there, like a sun just grazing the surface of the ship. Then it exploded. The hyper-spectral sensor blinked off immediately as the system detected an overload and threw itself into safe mode. The other monitors became fuzzy and the screens bounced as an energy wave suddenly washed over the base. Mostly invisible to the human eye, the energy wave was a silent killer blowing through the base swiftly, kicking up dust and frying unprotected equipment.

The lighting in the SIP dimmed as base power blacked out before coming back online. The cameras capturing the event shuddered and vibrated under the stress. As quickly as it had happened, it was over. Christie looked up at the secondary monitor, the optical view of the space battle. Small fighters fitfully tumbled through space at random. Several Angels seemed to be without power and adrift. The foreign ship appeared to shudder a few times as internal explosions rocked it, before the power gradually went out, lights and defenses shutting down throughout. The engines faded as the power died away, the ship itself drifting slightly off its normal course from the impact of the explosion. Several smaller explosions rocked it as the effects of the explosion continued to play havoc with the systems. One explosion resulted in two strangely shaped objects being ejected from a section of the hull and sent hurtling down toward Phoebe.

The hyper-spectral sensor gave a series of short beeps, trying to restart, but the image was heavily distorted, the damaged sensor reeling from the blast. The optical view sluggishly shifted, the operator panning the camera around to look at the fighters and Angels in free-fall.

Another dozen Angels left the hangars at the end of the crater en route to the combat zone at full military throttle. Five of them split away from the main formation to track down individual fighters that were adrift, while the rest headed for the cluster of ships that had followed G-LOC in.

The last group of fighters had launched seemed relatively unaffected by the explosion and continued to climb toward the foreign ship, now nearly dark with no signs of life.

Christie reached over and gripped Sam's hand. "I hope we did that."

"Yeah, me too. Me too," Sam said soberly.

"John, Graves just left the hangar in an Angel, he said he was going to SAR for G-LOC and left Karl in charge. I'm activating Chief Stokes and sending him over to support, he's taking a rover from hangar four SIP. ETA five minutes," Brenner yelled over the commotion to the Director.

The Director looked up from his display calmly, absorbing the fact that his main Hangar Operations Chief had just abandoned his post, nodding his acknowledgement. He looked over at Erik, who was frantically typing into his console, shifting views between six monitors, trying to track the spacecraft as they floated away from the explosion in various states of distress.

The Director watched him for several seconds before speaking in a soft voice that projected across the room.

"Erik." He waited for Erik to respond. "Erik. Erik. Dr. Bilks!"

Erik swung around in his chair, looking at the Director, eyes wide with tears forming in them. Blood dribbled down his lip where he had bitten it while trying to figure out what had happened.

"Erik, calm down. All indications are that there were no casualties. Just a bunch of disabled birds. I need you to take a deep breath and relax."

One of the Marine medics stepped forward and spoke up to the Director. "If you want sir, I can give him a sedative."

"No, absolutely not. I need his brain sharp for the next couple of hours." He paused and looked at the medic, pondering which orders to give. Off to his right, he heard Molly Caan, speaking for the first time since combat had begun.

"Hey Erik, its Molly." She reached out and grabbed his hand and shoulder quickly, tugging on them to try to turn him to face her. "Erik, it's me. Molly," she said, looking intently into his eyes before glancing past him to Sloan. Sloan met her gaze and looked at Erik, her lips pursed. She looked back at Molly and mouthed to her silently, *"Please help him,"* before returning to her screens, sending out orders to her operations crews.

Molly gripped Erik's hand again, getting his attention. "Hey. Nobody died. They won, they took the ship out. Nobody is shooting anymore."

Erik looked back at her, a tear slipping down his cheek. "I told them not to use it yet. It wasn't ready . . . not ready at all."

Brenner looked at the two of them awkwardly posed over Erik's monitors, grimaced and leaped up the stairwell to stand next to the Director's chair.

"Graves had almost all of the remaining SAR birds in full standby, with crews at the ready. They banged out of the hangar as soon as they realized the strike team had been disabled. Scorched some paint too, I think he's in Hound Seven, but that isn't certain. There's been a breakdown in comm discipline."

"Don't worry about Graves. His job is to make sure that the hangar operates efficiently and that people who crash get rescued. I'm willing to cut him some operational leeway on what that entails. If he thinks he needs to be part of the rescue to prevent loss of life, I'll take that under consideration," Hatfield said, while he worked his computer terminal generating computer models of the alien ship's trajectory.

Brenner opened his mouth to respond, thought better of it and shut it with a snap. He gestured to Sloan to join the command net and pulled his helmet on so he could view his displays better. "Ok, we have SAR birds en route to rescue those who are disabled; some are more disabled than others. Only one confirmed KIA at this point," he said into the microphone, making sure Erik wasn't hooked in to the net.

"The artillery gunnery platforms are down for repairs.

ETRO is about two hours. The targeting sensors got walloped by whatever that energy wave was. We lost power to the civ side for a moment, but it's back and appears stable right now. Not much else in the base was damaged. There was some dust intrusion past the baffles on hangars seven, eight and nine, a little energy bled through as well. Two possible injuries with the ground crew, we won't know until they move the Mongoose jig that shifted into them when the blast wave hit."

"We're functional enough. I'm more worried about the ship," Hatfield said as he gestured at his screen. "What do we know?"

"Sensors are still coming back online, but it appears that we seriously banged them up. Power systems appear offline, there are some rather large holes that penetrate almost through to the other side of it. We saw some ejected material heading toward Phoebe, nothing that I would say looked like a body. At least not a human one."

"Maybe the ship is a drone, uncrewed," Sloan said thoughtfully.

"Speculation—let's deal with what we know right now," Hatfield said firmly.

"We have some debris raining down. The entire ephemeris database for near-orbital objects is probably going to need to be redone, that blast wave disturbed everything. We saw no long-range weapons on that ship the entire time they engaged us. Everything was engaged under seventy-five meters away and seemed to be defensive in nature," Brenner said, quickly scanning the reports coming in from his analysis team in the next room.

"Yes, but I'm more concerned with the ship. More specifically where it is going," Hatfield said tensely, as he typed in more equations into his display.

"It's not going much of anywhere right now, we appear to have blown the engines and power systems," Brenner said hesitantly.

"Inertia Brenner. Inertia. It's more or less on the same vector it was before we nailed it right?" Hatfield said soberly. He loaded the results of his calculations onto his display monitor and shared it with them.

"Aw shit. It's still going to hit us," Brenner breathed, looking at several possible trajectories arcing in toward the hidden shipyard.

"We slowed it down significantly, changed its path a very small amount. But it will still hit the moon. If it hits the moon, we lose the ship, we might even lose the base. We need that stopped," Hatfield said calmly, without a trace of panic. "I want that ship. I want its crew. We need to know where it came from and why."

Brenner exchanged a quick look with Sloan and they turned back toward the main displays.

"Show me the Quick Reaction Force Angels on the big screen," he yelled down into the sensor pit. Higgins looked up at him and nodded, before bringing the display up.

Brenner studied it for a moment. "They're doing SAR assist on the damaged birds but the QRF is still in the game, still functional. I say we board the alien ship and try to commandeer it."

Sloan sighed with exasperation. "Assuming you board it and find where the controls are, they might not work, you probably won't be able to figure them out and if it doesn't work you just have a couple units of Marines riding that lawn dart in as it cracks Phoebe. It won't work."

"All true," Hatfield said. "But just the same, send the QRF in. Orders are to secure and exploit as quickly as possible. In the meantime, get me Jacobs."

"Jacobs?" Brenner and Sloan said in unison with mirrored surprised.

"Yes. He told me once he could tow anything, anywhere, anytime and save me fuel doing it. I want him to hook up to that thing and stop it."

"You want the *Atlas* to hook up to an alien ship? What is he going to hook to? Or more importantly, what do we do if the people or whatever are inside it decide they don't want to be towed? Or..." Sloan stopped as Hatfield raised his gloved hand in her direction.

"Get me Jacobs on the line. The QRF is responsible for securing the ship. It's a risk. As for hooking up to it; that poses some interesting challenges."

Brenner glanced at the Marine guarding the door who was watching the conversation like a predator, alert. His eyes locked on Hatfield—there was no fear, just anticipation on his face. Brenner remembered the conversations he'd had over the last year with the Marines stationed out here; bored and displeased they missed the first fight with the Chinese. Now he saw hope in the Marine's eyes, hope for action. He reached down to the console in front of him and selected the *Atlas* frequency.

"*Atlas, Atlas* this is the CIC, respond."

"*Atlas* here, how you guys holding up?" Jacobs voice came over the radio heavily distorted.

Brenner transferred control over to Hatfield and leaned back against a rail to listen, his armored suit grinding against the metal loudly.

"Director here. We're fine for the moment Jacobs. I need you to get your ship spun up and ready to move as soon as possible," Hatfield began, pausing to look down at his console.

"Yeah, I started prep for maneuver when you guys started firing surface artillery at that thing without checking to see who was behind it. The engine chamber pressure is up and we're about to start moving now. We should make the Titan shelter orbit in about seven hours I'd guess," Jacobs said as the static pulsed to varied intensities as he spoke.

Hatfield looked over at Brenner with surprise written on his face before interrupting Jacobs. "No I need you to start heading this way, as soon as possible. I need your probable ETA at the intercept course I am sending you now." He reached down and punched several keys on his keyboard and waited.

Seconds passed before Jacobs responded. "Say again, you were breaking up. It sounded like you were asking me to head back toward Phoebe?"

"Roger, on the intercept course I gave you." Hatfield leaned back from the microphone and got Brenner's attention. "Can you clear up this interference?"

"No, it's persistent. Probably a left over from that weapon going off."

"CIC this is *Atlas*, I copy your last. But are you sure it's a good idea for me to come in that close with nukes cooking off?" Jacob's voice came back over the radio, worry creeping in as he spoke.

"No nukes have been used yet. I need you to get in here and hook your tow system up to that ship and slow it down. It's headed right for the base. We need to stop it, or else you may not have anywhere to put your pillow in the coming months."

"That wasn't a nuke? It damn well looked like one. Alright, uh, *Atlas* understands. We're inbound as soon as I can course correct and redo some calculations. ETA to follow. *Atlas* on standby."

Hatfield gave a satisfied nod in the direction of the radio and turned to Hatfield and Sloan. "Ok. Get the QRF to penetrate that ship right at the big hole. Make sure they're careful which bulkheads they pop, and tell them to seal the holes they make behind them. We'll use two Angels on the initial penetration, so ten Marines and three SARines. Have another Angel dump their troops at the hole then stand-off. Those Marines will guard the two Angels at the hole. Marines to clear the ship, SARines to exploit it. Priority on identifying who this is, secondary priority to secure the ship. Brenner, get Major Stringer up to speed, I want the orders for the boarding party to come from him."

Brenner nodded as he turned away, sealing his helmet and

contacting Major Stringer to let him in on the plan. Hatfield turned to Sloan.

"I need you to make sure we didn't take any more serious damage during that energy pulse. Get me a list of stuff that can be repaired, in order of longest lead time to shortest, and a list of the destroyed gear to look at later."

"You don't want to know the destroyed stuff right away?" Sloan asked curiously.

"Right now, either we have it or we don't. We still have the capacity to shoot, transport and communicate, so by definition the wrecked stuff wasn't critical." Hatfield paused, his eyes narrowing. "Also have somebody check in on the SIPs in the civilian side. I don't want to find out one of them lost radio contact or air while we were fighting, and after we win we have a box full of bodies."

"On it!"

Hatfield leaned back in his chair to wait. He looked over at Erik and Molly and pondered what to do about Erik. He clearly still had some serious issues with what had happened during the last couple of weapons tests. Today hadn't helped. Maybe it was time to give him a break. Hatfield thought for several minutes before reaching down to his wrist interface and tapping out a message to Sasha Reynolds, the manager of the Eden cave project.

"*Sasha, please make one of the rooms ready for a visitor. Dr. Erik Bilks will be coming to stay with you for a while. To recover.*"

He sat still, listening to the commotion in the CIC as damage reports flowed in and the SAR efforts progressed. The Eden cave was still a secret to most of the base and as far as he knew, the leadership of the KaliSun Corporation back on Earth. Erik was a trustworthy person generally, although who really knew in his current mental state. He decided it was worth the risk to get Erik right with the world again.

He looked back at the two of them. Maybe he'd send Molly there too, to keep him company.

CHAPTER 7

Will Forsythe, commanding officer of the KaliSun Corporation's Moon Base Training Center, leaned back in his chair running his hand through his thinning hair. He watched his opponent study the chessboard in front of him intently with a grim look on his face. He'd boxed him in rather neatly.

"You know, for the CEO of one of the larger corporations on Earth, revered for your duplicity and scheming ways, you sure were easy to trap this time," he said to his opponent Ed Stokes, just recently up from Earth.

"Hmm, yes I've spent too much time playing a computer instead of an irrational human," Ed replied with a grimace as he tried to extract his queen from almost certain defeat. "On the plus side, now that I'm at the MBTC, I'll have more time on my hands."

Forsythe laughed at him, but understood the bitterness underlying his comment. Given the current state of affairs, they couldn't risk much direct communication with Earth, so Stokes was relying on his surrogates while he kept a low profile at the MBTC. It must be frustrating for a man who had spent the last seventeen years being in complete control to become, essentially, retired, but still responsible for the company.

"You left the company in good hands. Take this as an opportunity to refresh your brain and figure out how we can leverage the mess Earth is in," Forsythe said.

"Leverage. Yes, I'm sure there are opportunities to make truckloads of money. I'm not sure it's a good idea to pursue them. At least not in an obvious way."

"You mean because we were directly responsible for most of the damage due to Hatfield's experiment?" Forsythe said with a smile.

"Our experiment. But yes, I think right now we could probably avoid serious repercussions if we're careful. If somebody discovers we destroyed half the computer-based technology on the planet and then decided to profiteer off the rebuilding efforts...well it's tough to spin that. I'm sure some of our subsidiaries will get in on the action though."

Stokes made his move on the board, sliding his bishop over to take one of Forsythe's pawns. Forsythe leaned forward, frowning.

"What are you up to? That made almost no sense."

"Loose lips sink ships," Stokes said with a smile.

Forsythe was staring at the board trying to figure out Stokes' move when there was a loud chime from the communication terminal built into the table. He looked at it with an annoyed glance.

"Yes?"

"OPS for Commander Forsythe sir, there's been a development."

"Something went wrong with the Badger squadron strike on that Chinese convoy?"

"No sir, we are picking up sensor data from Saturn. It looks like a major battle is going on."

Forsythe sat bolt upright and looked across the chessboard at Stokes. "Say again OPS? What kind of battle?"

"Space battle by the look of it. We're picking up significant Angel jamming, something that looks like explosions. It's too far for radar to get any good readings on something that small, but optics has some imagery we were able to clean up."

"Push it through, now."

He pulled up the data and moved over so Stokes could sit next to him on the bench. The image was quite dark, a spectrum analyzer showing nothing out of the ordinary with the EM spectrum. Then the image skipped forward in time, this time showing increased encrypted radio traffic from numerous sources. It skipped ahead again, showing a massive increase in jamming frequency usage, as well as some other oddities. Forsythe reached forward and slapped the pause button, scooting close to the screen.

"OPS, what the hell is that bright object in quadrant thirty-one?"

"We don't know. It doesn't match anything in our database, it's pretty big and spewing IR coherent light." The analyst abruptly broke the connection without explanation.

Forsythe played with the controls, trying to zoom in on the object, the computer trying to keep the image as sharp as possible. It was coming from a backup telescope that had survived the radiation event that Hatfield's interstellar drive test had caused, and was not as effective as the main telescopes.

The analyst came back on. "Sir, we just witnessed an event. Analysis is coming through any moment."

Stokes and Forsythe leaned forward as a short video clip played on the screen. The EM spectrum was fluctuating steadily, with a designator next to the waveforms indicating structured jamming from an Angel. A point of light briefly shone on the top of the white object before a massive flash, causing the telescope to white out its image in protest. The EM meter on the screen continued to read however, showing normal measurements before rapidly shifting to massive fluctuations as the wave reached the sensor.

"Sir, we're seeing gravity fluctuations, significant flashing in the IR and UV spectrums, as well as optical distortions caused by something we don't understand. We can only observe that things are behaving oddly. It looks like something huge just exploded out there."

The EM spectrum showed several minutes of disruption before dropping back to what would be considered a normal level of radio traffic. No jamming, no major fluctuations in the measurements.

"OPS, was that similar in any way to when that plasma comet came through?"

"Uh, maybe sir. That displayed some gravity shift as well, but nothing quite like that, no."

Forsythe muted the communications terminal and turned toward Stokes. "Any other projects out there we should be aware of, now is the time to speak up."

"Not that would cause that. That thing looks like a ship, but not like any ship we designed. I'd say that's not a KaliSun asset."

"What do you mean? All the Chinese are duking it out with us here. The Russians haven't had a plus Earth orbit asset in years, and what they did have got fried by the plasma comet. Nobody else has anything remotely close to that size."

"Nobody else, right." Stokes gave him a cautious look.

Forsythe closed his eyes and swore to himself viciously. He mashed the mute button.

"OPS where is Badger strike force right now?"

"About twelve minutes out from intercept. He's on radio silence right now as they commence final approach."

"Is that flash and gravity wave likely to cause any problems here? Anything like the disruption to communications and navigational aids we saw during the plasma comet?"

"No sir, we don't think so."

"Warn him anyway and tell him to hit the Chinese fast and get back. Who knows if there are more of these things out there."

"Yes sir." There was a pause before the analyst spoke again. "Sir, we just did a rough estimate for the force of that blast. The shockwave would be equivalent to a roughly ten kiloton nuclear warhead going off. The gravity wave would add damage, but we have no way to calculate something like that. There was radiation in the explosion signature. But..."

"But what?"

"Not in the amounts you would expect from a blast that big."

"We're on our way," Forsythe said into the radio before dropping the connection. He walked over to the wall closet that held his armored command suit and began putting it on, piece by piece. Stokes followed behind him, speaking into his personal radio to his bodyguards, then donning his own command suit.

"Guess things aren't going to be so relaxing after all," Ed said calmly.

"Yeah, we really put our foot in it with that little flight test."

"We're not sure they're related," Stokes said patiently. "Let's not jump to conclusions and make bad assumptions."

"We live or die by our assumptions. Right now I'm assuming whatever is throwing nukes around is dangerous. I'm assuming whoever that shiny ship belongs to is dangerous, and more importantly, I'm assuming there are more of both incoming," Forsythe said grimly.

Captain Wilks kept his hands gripped loosely on the twin control sticks of his Mongoose as he led Badger squadron and its support elements across the lunar surface at a stomach churning altitude of fifty meters. They were approaching a Chinese convoy that was trying to sneak into position closer to the Moon Base Training Center. Four gunships were providing point defense for two large transports and the main target, a mobile command post that was designed to be deployed as an instant base. Once grounded, it would spin up an internal reactor, burrow down slightly into the regolith and activate its weapon systems.

In the time since the plasma comet had completed its pass of Earth, Wilks had participated in the destruction of four of these command posts. Acheron squadron had picked off two others during a single patrol. The Chinese kept flying new ones up from Earth and trying to place them closer to the KaliSun base as forward observation posts and anti-space batteries. Once they were dug in, it took ground troops to root them out, something they had learned at no small expense last week.

After that fight, Forsythe had ordered all of the bases be destroyed immediately upon detection. So with the Badgers being the only full strength squadron, Wilks had been given pest control duties. At least this convoy didn't have a large fighter escort.

He blinked his eyes at the corner of his HUD, bringing a squadron formation graphic onto his helmet faceplate and studying it for a moment. He had twelve Mongoose, his main force, their normal pair of support Angels, and a solo Angel that flew high above the lunar surface scanning for enemy activity. His assaulter group consisted of a single platoon of Marines split between three Angels and another Angel carrying three SARines. Backstopping the entire flight were six Angels packing anti-space missiles and one tactical space attack missile a piece.

All units were holding formation with no faults detected. He blinked the display away and pulled up the overwatch Angel's sensor picture of the target convoy. If this convoy was like previous ones, the four gunships would be a real pain to deal with. Heavily armored with between thirty and sixty gun stations, they could take significant punishment before they went down. Their engines we nestled in among armored plates amidships, and they could both rotate and thrust vector, making it difficult to get in behind their weapon fields of fire. While most of their weapons lacked the punch to down an Angel or Mongoose, they could easily make short work of an exposed Marine unit or incoming missile fire.

Wilks frowned—with four of them in this convoy, getting a good angle for the opening salvo on either the transports or the command post was going to be difficult. Once they were aware of the KaliSun fighters it would only get rougher. He looked past the feed and dodged a rocky rise from the lunar surface, settling back into terrain-following mode. He glanced at the mission clock—fifteen minutes to go, decision time.

"Badger Strike Force, we'll do a slash attack on the left side of the formation. Strike Angels hang back behind grid 28, hill 2321. Commence jamming on approach, we'll ripple fire into the nearside gunship before circling around behind them and trying to draw fire. Once we've done our approach, Angels pop over the hill and launch on the overwatch Angel's sensor track with TSAMs. Focus fire on the left side gunship. I want Angels five and six to retain their TSAMs for the command center. We'll reassess then. Angel Strike leader if you have a shot, try to get some ASMs on those transports. If we can down one early, they'll be torn between staying together as a convoy or splitting up. Strike units confirm orders."

"Strike Angel Lead confirms."

"Overwatch Angels confirm."

Wilks looked up at his squadron display and watched as his pilots acknowledged the command. "Alright, comms black out starting now."

"Standby Badger Actual, communication coming in from Ops," the overwatch Angel interrupted him as they passed the ten mark.

"Actual, Ops says *"Attack detected at Saturn base, destroy command center and pull back to base. Best possible speed. W.F."*. How copy?" the overwatch pilot repeated.

"Alright. I acknowledge. Kill it and come back. We'll scratch the intel exploitation. Going silent."

"Overwatch copies."

The next eight minutes passed slowly for Wilks as he wondered what could have happened at Saturn for an attack to be visible from Earth. Even the best telescopes had to strain to pick up much from that area, it was one reason they'd put the base out there. He pushed thoughts of friends and happy memories of the base from his mind and focused on the task at hand.

The squadron approached the final ridge separating them from the Chinese, the Mongoose accelerating to full speed as they approached, the trailing Angels popping their retros to slow down, hiding behind the ridgeline as the Mongoose exploded over the edge. The fighters fell on the convoy by section, firing bursts of cannon fire followed by dumbfires as they raked the closest gunship. The gunships immediately responded with a wall of lead, sent toward them in a grid pattern that didn't rely on tracking or sensor feeds. It seemed the Chinese had learned how to deal with the Angel's jamming.

The Badgers bounced around in their assigned flight paths, pumping their maneuvering thrusters at random as they tried to take out the gunship's weapon blisters. Heavy cannon fire tore into the gunship, gouts of fire and debris erupting from the hull as they passed. The first dumbfires impacted in a wave down the length of the ship, staggering it and causing the starboard engine to explode in a bright flare as the Mongos continued past.

Section four flipped their ships around and fired bursts at the rear gunship, peppering its stern and damaging some of the sensors on the top deck. The other three gunships sprayed fire out in all directions, but one entire quadrant of coverage was no longer being defended as the flaming ship drifted out of formation.

Wilks gritted his teeth as some gs leaked through his ship's compensator and watched the scene below him. As soon as the gunships began to reorient their formation to cover for the downed ship, he ordered the Angels to attack.

Waiting behind the ridgeline, they rose up like silent predators about to strike. The camouflage scheme writhed, obscuring the outlines of the Angels, confusing optical sensors from detecting them. With the one gunship out of action, the Angels were free to fire into the heart of the formation as it approached them. With the Badger support Angels' jamming their sensors, the only hope the Chinese had in detecting the Strike Angels was if they looked out the window and saw them.

The Angels hovered over the lunar regolith, turning in unison as the convoy slipped past them before unleashing a torrent of TSAMs at the formation. The first heavy missile struck one of the transports amidships, cracking it like an egg and blowing its contents into vacuum. Small figures in spacesuits flailed about helplessly as the atmosphere from their spaceship combined with the explosive force of the missile to fling them into the abyss beyond.

The next four missiles slammed into the command and control post in the center of the formation. It shuddered violently, driven sideways and down by the impacts, sliding toward the lunar surface just a few hundred meters below. The command post had thicker armor, intended to handle airstrikes and ground attacks, but the combined force of four heavy missiles caused its armor plates to peel back like a tin can. It ponderously slid under the far side transport as smoke and debris spewed out of the rents in the hull. A final missile arced into the far transport, and the gunships began to react, firing through their own formation in an effort to hit the TSAM. The missile took several hits but still managed find its target, hitting the transport just forward of the engines. With a violent explosion the transport broke up, its engines driving it down toward the surface of the moon.

The Angels showed no mercy, unleashing a torrent of ASMs at the gunships and the command post. As the missiles stalked their targets, the Badgers cut a brutal path across the top of the formation, firing down at weapon blisters and sensors with cannon fire and dumbfires. The command post shuddered under relentless missile strikes before finally succumbing. The rear section of the module exploded violently, its fuel tanks ruptured, sending shrapnel in all directions and driving its bow down into the moon's surface

Captain Wilks watched with satisfaction as the convoy

struggled under the onslaught. He wondered if this was how his ancestors had felt when they had tried to attack American convoys during World War II. A thin smile crossed his lips. This wasn't quite like attacking a convoy on the open ocean with submarines, although they had adopted the old wolf-pack tactics to tackle these heavily defended convoys. It was more like jumping an old B-17 box formation and hoping that one day they wouldn't put bigger guns on the ships. He glanced up at the mission clock in the corner of his HUD, six minutes after first contact they had taken out the primary and secondary targets. They were getting better at this.

"Ok Badgers, this was a slash and dash. We need to get back to the barn. Break contact and form on me. Save your missiles and avoid any more damage."

Badger squadron broke hard away from the remaining ships in the convoy, reforming out over the ridge where the Angels had hidden. The Angels rose from their ambush location and rejoined the formation. As they flew away, the gunships continued to pound hopelessly away at them while the debris from their formation fell in slow motion to pepper the surface with fresh craters.

CHAPTER 8

John, QRF is almost ready to grapple and board," Brenner said as he looked down at the screens in front of him. "I'm still not sure if we're sending enough to clear that ship. It's a pretty big target to sweep."

"Any sign of life?" the Director asked calmly, ignoring the question on troop strength.

"Some residual power sources functioning deep within the ship, possibly something on batteries. All weapons are dead cold at this point, the engines in about the same condition. Occasionally, we see some gas venting, it's not having a big impact, though it did change the vector a bit on the ship."

"What kind of vector changes?" Hatfield asked intently.

"Fairly minor, it induced a slow change in the direction of the nose. The ship is still proceeding toward the specialty hangar. Think of it like a skid," Higgins reported from the sensors pit.

"Where is the nose pointing now?" Brenner asked.

"More or less towards the base crater," Higgins replied.

Brenner and Hatfield exchanged alarmed looks, before Hatfield spoke. "Higgins, the moment any further venting occurs I want to know. The same for any activity with the weapon blisters we've identified, or the engines. That venting may not be as innocent as it appears."

Higgins acknowledged the order, but before Hatfield or Brenner could discuss it the communication board lit up.

"*CIC, this is QRF. We are grappled and are preparing to board through penetration two-alpha. Once inside, we'll pop the nearside bulkhead to make some space, enter and seal it behind us. ETA to first penetration is about three minutes. We'll hold on this channel. Phoenix Six out.*"

"Last chance to change your mind John," Brenner said quietly to Hatfield.

"This might be our only chance to secure this ship before it becomes a kinetic weapon. I don't want to tie *Atlas* to something that could pull them down here with them. We need to clear the ship out."

"But just thirteen guys, that's not a standard attack force by any standard."

"It's risk mitigation. If I put my whole QRF on there and they get wiped, we've got nothing in space to make a second attempt. That could prove fatal. We wait for them to recon the ship and respond accordingly. Even if all they can do is secure tow points so we can stop the ship, it will be enough."

"Point taken. I just don't like exposing them like this."

"Don't let your personal feelings for them hinder your tactical mind. They are Marines with the best gear we can provide, trained as well as they can be trained. We hired them to deal with the non-perfect situation. We aren't throwing them away casually; there is logic defining the reason for this course of action."

"Yes, I know," Brenner responded somberly.

"*CIC, QRF is claws down on the exterior of the ship. Ships are secure to the hull. Egressing now.*"

Hatfield looked over at his aide Ed Styles who was sitting nearby, quietly preparing. The first boarding of an enemy ship by the KaliSun Corporation needed to be recorded so they could learn from any mistakes.

"Give me their HUD displays and helmet cams on the observation screens, with a real time track of that ship's expected trajectory and an IR view of the exterior," he said, pointing at the various overhead displays.

Hatfield's aide Ed Styles nodded once before bending to the task, pulling up the data feeds being boosted back to the base by the two support Angels. The main screen was dominated by Alpha squad leader waiting for the Angel door to open.

The pressure equalized between the Angel and the vacuum beyond to prevent the Marines from being blown out into space and the door slid back. The Angel extended its gravity field down to the ship until there was partial gravity on the exterior, while the lead Marine scanned the hole in front of them, before dropping down on the hull with a crunch.

The crew in the CIC stopped working to look up at the overhead displays, and as the Alpha squad sergeant panned around the hole inspecting it for danger, the crowd caught glimpses of the damage. A multi-layered hull segment was peeled back, exposing conduit and wire to open space, occasional sparks arcing in the vacuum as ship systems continued to short out. The laser reflective coating on the exterior of the hull was crumpled and crushed by the oversized front landing claws of the Angels.

One of the SARines silently stomped through Alpha squad leader's field of view to crouch by the hole, releasing his eyebot personal drone from his suit and sending it into the hole. On another screen, an interior map of the ship began to develop as the drone mapped the room below. His armor shifting to match its surroundings in a dizzying display of morphing colors, the SARine tilted his body back, lifting his opaque face mask to look up at the Alpha squad Sergeant and give him a five count on his gloved hand.

His hand closed into a fist as he counted down to zero, and Alpha squad stepped off into the hole, using small thrusters in their suits to drive them down through the weak gravity of the Angel and into the ship. They landed in a compact cluster, weapons pointing in all directions. The room itself was actually several rooms interconnected with hatchways; the ceiling was about three meters high, allowing them to move around easily, occasionally reaching up to adjust their position with a push off the ceiling. Damage was evident everywhere, and it was difficult to tell what most of the intact features of the room were intended to do. No bodies were present.

They spread quickly through the room, giving SARine Phoenix Six space to drop in. He landed with a thud and slowly panned around, integrating the map image from his eyebot with his own POV camera imagery. The eyebot started another scan of the area, this time using hyper-spectral sensors overlaid on LADAR imagery, sending a complete picture back to the CIC.

The defining feature of the room was a doorway that entered from one end and ran down the ships lateral line, with a second doorway leading into the ship forming a T-junction with it. The doors were four meters across by three meters tall. The SARine analyzed the data from his eyebot, communicating with his two comrades waiting above with Bravo Squad. After a short consultation, he walked over to one of the hatches that ran laterally the length of the ship, selected a combination of breaching charges from his pack and carefully packing them against the hatch.

The Marines took shelter behind the wrecked contents of the room as the SARine gave a silent count with his gloved hand then mashed the detonator. The CIC feeds showed a brilliant flash as the explosion blew the door away, allowing the atmosphere beyond to vent into space. As soon as the explosion was cleared, the Marines pointed their weapons into the new hole, waiting for any response. They were met with nothing. A few scraps of metal blew out and then it was still as only vacuum could be.

Phoenix Six signaled his team, who proceeded to drop down and take up positions on either side of the breach. Six sent his eyebot into the neighboring room and waited as it scanned. When the image was completed they all studied it intently, looking for traps or hidden danger. Satisfied, he signaled Alpha to proceed.

The Marines approached the hole, sending two inside, the other three covering them. Getting no response, the rest ducked inside followed by Six. As they were filing in, Bravo squad dropped into the room and took over their positions, covering the other two doorways. They inspected the neighboring room, noting it had another doorway leading into the ship and that the lateral path continued ahead. The team spread through the room, looking for any sign of the inhabitants, noticing the majority of the features seemed automated, with no visible chairs or benches for an operator.

Six looked around the room once more, confirming it was clear of danger and called in the third Angel. This Angel hovered over the hole without locking on to the hull, the side door opened and ten more Marines dropped down. As soon as they were clear, the Angel pulsed its maneuvering thrusters to pull away from the alien ship.

Once Bravo and the rest of Phoenix triplet were inside the second room, they applied a flimsy vacuum sealant over the hole, regaining the room's airtight integrity.

"Phoenix Six to Chalk two."

"Go for Chalk Two."

"Maintain security around the Angels. Watch the doors and keep an eye out to make sure nothing sneaks up on the Angels along the hull. Stay on our battlenet and follow progress in case we get into some shit. I'm taking Alpha and penetrating into the ship through one of the doors and sending Bravo down this lateral line toward where we assume the bridge is. Phoenix Seven and Eight will go with Bravo."

"Copy Six. Good hunting."

"CIC, Six. With your permission we'll proceed."

Hatfield's voice came distorted with encryption and static, booming through the speakers. "Get cracking Six, forty-five minutes from now *Atlas* will be in position. Sweep and clear, don't hang around long for the sightseeing and keep the damn mapper going so we can try to get a handle on the mass characteristics of this thing so Jacobs doesn't get smeared trying to hook up to it."

Six acknowledged and the three SARines began putting breaching charges on the next two doors. Six pulled his eyebot into cover and tripped the explosions. The doors ripped open, blowing away from the men. The two squads of Marines split up, pushing into the tunnels beyond with an eyebot leading the way to map and detect threats. Six shot a final look over to his two teammates and pulled out his shotgun, then with a nod he headed down the tube that lay beyond the portal to the next room.

Brenner pinged Dr. Bilks three times before he saw him stir. With a sigh he walked over toward Erik as he sat slumped in his chair, Molly Caan sitting very close to him trying to comfort him. Brenner nudged him with his boot.

"Erik. Reports indicate no casualties from the weapon discharge. It just banged a few pilots around who were too close. Ava isn't even blaming you and I know you two get into sometimes."

"Yeah."

Brenner squatted down so he was at eye level to Erik. "Hey, we're boarding an alien ship right now. It's full of strange things and I could really use my best weapons expert to look at the data coming back so we can spot whether or not the thing is a trap or not. You could save the lives of the Marines we have in there, maybe even discover entirely new things about the aliens."

Erik stirred slightly. "How many Marines went in?"

"Ten Marines and three SARines are doing a sweep. Ten more Marines and two Angel crews are holding at the insertion point."

Erik's lips pursed. "Nobody died from the missile explosion?"

"None of our guys anyway."

He sat up, shrugging Molly's hand off his shoulder in the process and leaning toward his consoles. "Guess I better get up to speed before one of you noobies gets somebody killed." He began setting up his board with feeds from the two squad leaders and the SARines.

Brenner stood up and shot a look at Sloan who shrugged back. *Maybe he's ok, maybe he's on the edge of losing it.* Brenner walked back to his post, mentally reviewing all that had happened to Erik in the last few months. First the weapon test had gone south on him, nearly incinerating his assigned test pilot, then the *KaliSun* had come back from her flight test spewing radiation and sending a ball of angry plasma ricocheting through the solar system. It had done a number on a couple of the SARines and Marines who had been exposed at the base, killing three and severely injuring several others, before continuing to emit pulses of electromagnetic interference that fried space satellites and knocked out sensors system-wide. It made a close pass of the sun causing significant solar activity and some major coronal mass ejections to flow out and hit Earth, in the process knocking out electrical grids and other technology.

Several cold wars erupted into hot wars, there were food shortages; it permanently ruined some technology and gave the Chinese a perceived opening to attack the KaliSun Corporation's Moon Base Training Center. The dense mass of plasma continued on past Earth and struck a number of asteroids near Jupiter, before emitting one final gamma ray death cry to fry what hadn't been destroyed already. Now, Erik's new warhead had managed to knock out over two squadrons of fighters.

It was hard not to feel a twinge of sadness for him. While he wasn't solely responsible for the *KaliSun*'s flight test, the fact that millions had died and the number continued to rise would weigh heavily on anyone's soul. In fact, it wasn't hard at all to understand Erik's fragile state, it seemed every project he'd started recently had ended in disaster. Brenner looked up at the main display at Phoenix Six blasting his way through hatches on the way toward the bridge. Perhaps some redemption would come out of this for Erik.

"Brenner," Hatfield called to him.

He turned back to the Director. "Yes?"

"Bravo is getting closer to the bow of the boat, do you notice anything different? Something about the rooms, but I can't quite figure out what it is."

Brenner looked at the mapper data and rewound the helmet camera data several minutes. Nothing immediately jumped out at him. "I dunno, the ship volume narrows as you get to the bow before it splits off into those two pods that look like claws. Other than that, I don't know."

"There are no more cross-tunnels," Erik said from his terminal.

"What do you mean?" Brenner asked.

"The tunnel Alpha went down is most likely a cross-tunnel; an access hatch to get from one side of the ship to the other. The tunnel Bravo is in looks like a similar tunnel that runs the length of the ship. Alpha has seen three crossways that run bow to stern as they've gone down their tunnel. There's also a strange dead-space located near the middle of the ship we can't get a solid reading on. They've just entered a room with a T-intersection in it. If you overlay the mapper data with the external measurements, they've cut through the ship to the far side completely. It's a grid. The problem is near the bow, where there are no cross-tunnels. It's almost like there's something running right up the middle of the ship that you can't put a tunnel through. I would guess, based on the three eyebots' data, that whatever that is, it's probably something we don't want to get too involved with."

"Why do you say that?" Molly blurted out, before covering her mouth in embarrassment.

"Because, if they don't want the crew to access it, it's probably pretty dangerous," Erik said before pausing. "Assuming they think like we do that is."

Sloan leaned back. "So let's think. What things do we not want people to easily access here?"

"Power cores, toxic or radioactive material, officer country..." Brenner started down the list ticking it off his fingers.

"Weapons. It could be a big weapon," Erik said softly.

Hatfield looked at them and changed the view on the main screen so it showed the ship's orientation toward the base. "It's pointing more or less right at Phoebe, slowly turning to point right at our main military side base...."

"If it's a weapon, maybe they only have the energy for one shot," Erik said.

Brenner reached down and keyed into Bravo's communications. "Phoenix Seven, proceed with all possible haste to the bow. Immediately. We need to know what is up there right away."

"Seven acknowledges."

They all turned to watch the screen as the lead SARine accessed the portal ahead of them. The bottom was slightly cracked open. Rather than risking another explosive entry, he pulled out a device known on Earth as the 'jaws of life' and jammed it in the crack. With a hum the machine started spreading the portal upward, metal shrieking as it went. When the portal was half open, one of the Marines cracked a glow stick and threw it in.

The eyebot slipped through the opening beeping repeatedly as it scanned the room. The SARine backed away while the rest of the team pointed their weapons into the doorway. The Marines slowly scanned the room; there was nothing out of the ordinary.

"CIC, Phoenix Seven. My eyebot has detected a stronger than typical concentration of gas in the next room. Mostly nitrogen and hydrogen, with very low levels of oxygen. This density of the gas is significantly higher than in previous chambers. There is almost no gravity present."

"Any sign of occupants?" Hatfield asked.

"Nothing we can detect, just higher gas levels. It's very bright in the IR spectrum, but visible light is almost nonexistent. There are some areas we're having issues getting a clear picture of," Seven reported as he used a remote to steer the eyebot's view around.

"Director, the ship is almost in line with the military side of the base, still no signs of any activity," Higgins reported from below.

"Can the Angels use their thrusters to try and steer it?"

"No sir, it's too massive, they'd rip their landing claws off trying."

Hatfield grimaced. "Seven, CIC here. Continue through the tunnel with caution, we need to know what's in the bow."

"*Seven copies.*" The SARine looked over at one of the Marines near the entrance to the neighboring room and motioned him forward, steering the eyebot deeper into the room and toward the ceiling to get it out of the way. He spun the bot around to look back at the Marine as he entered the room, the glow stick throwing strange shadows off his armor.

The Marine aggressively entered the room and knelt down out of his comrade's line of fire to scan the space one last time. Just as his knee touched the floor, a shadow passed over his faceplate. He looked up, tilting his neck back to look toward the ceiling, and froze. A dark shape lunged down from the ceiling, splitting in half as it got closer. The Marine raised his weapon in an effort to shoot it, but it was too late. The two halves of a massive claw settled down over his torso and squeezed.

Reflexively he fired a short burst into the wall and floor as the claw sheared completely through his armor and split his body in half. A gurgle of surprised pain went over the radio link, cutting off as the claw twisted and sheared through his body and launched his now limp form through the low gravity into the corner, narrowly missing the eyebot as it hovered passively nearby. Crimson blood sprayed outward from the corpse as it caromed off the wall and settled near the ceiling in an expanding ball of gore. With just a moment's hesitation, the Marines in the neighboring room leaned through the doorway and blind-fired toward the ceiling above.

The creature retracted its pincer claw and tightened up into a protective ball as the weapons hammered its exoskeleton to no effect. Two Marines leaned back into their room, getting clear of the doorway as they performed quick reloads. SARine Phoenix Eight stepped to the doorway and stuck his shotgun into the room, his HUD displaying the image from his gun's optics, directing his fire around the corner into the strange creature above the doorway.

The first three shots only pushed the creature around the room, but the fourth snuck through its defenses. A gush of blue liquid sprayed out from the wound forming into globular masses, sticking to the walls and hardening darkly on exposure to the atmosphere.

The creature reacted violently, a blast of focused compressed gas leaving its rear section and propelling it toward the door leading from the room and escaping into the darkness beyond.

"Shit, what was that?"

"Something big," Phoenix Seven said as he gingerly stepped into the room.

Hatfield broke into their communication loop. "Seven, CIC here. We're pulling up your eyebot's data now, give us a minute and we'll try to assess what that was. Say status of Bravo Three, he shows off the board here."

The SARine turned his hulking command suit slowly toward the tumbling body of the dead Marine and shone a light on him. Frost was forming over his body as the low temperature of the room cooled the blood spattered across his armor. The body slowly rotated, giving the SARine a clear view of the Marine's face, locked forever in surprised agony. He panned the camera feed and light down to view the massive damage done to his chest and shoulder.

"Bravo Three is KIA," he said somberly into the radio, before muttering under his breath. "Poor bastard . . . "

———

"Brenner, what the fuck was that?" Hatfield said calmly but quickly as he leaned forward off the observation deck.

Brenner had uprooted one of the technicians from their chair and was working on the keyboard in front of him, sparing just a moment to hold his finger up at Hatfield, silently begging for more time. He looked up at the screens and hit a button on the console.

Instantly, several of the screens swapped to a new view, an animated image showing the attack from the point of view of the eyebot, and a series of still captures taken from both Bravo Three's helmet cam and the eyebot. As the crowd squinted up at the screens he hit another button and a series of lighting filters were applied, converting the underlying IR data into something they could better view with the human eye.

"That, is...uh...Not from here," he said softly.

"Meaning what exactly!" Molly interrupted urgently.

"It's an alien, a real live alien," Sloan said in quiet wonder.

Hatfield glared at the image on the screen. What he saw before him looked part of some malevolent nightmare from his childhood. The main body was a heavily armored teardrop, the narrow end pointed forward toward the Marine, two large claws on either side of the tip, held like a boxer's gloves in an apparent attempt to protect it. Smaller legs were tucked up under the shape, and there was no apparent head on the thing. But the part of the creature that drew the eyes of the room was the tail, which looked like a scorpion's tail with a claw instead of a stinger. It was that claw that had whipped down from the ceiling and clipped Bravo Three in half like a giant pair of tin snips. Once finished with the marine, the tail claw retracted into a protective pose along the top of the shell.

Brenner looked back at Hatfield. "John, look at it. It looks like a stone crab with some kind of flexible tail claw as well."

"Sure does, looks just like the ones we have down in the aquaculture area. Well except for that big shearing claw," Sloan said, pulling up an image of a stone crab on her screen and looking between the two of them. She squinted down at her screen. "Well, ok. Not just like it. The head area on our alien here is a lot more heavily armored, can't see well enough to spot eyes or anything, but look how well he protects that area. It must be his head."

"It's too early for that kind of assumption," Hatfield said. He reached down and pinged Phoenix Seven. "Seven. Secure that room. Find some of that blue stuff that spurted out and get me a sample."

He sent Sloan a sideways glance. "Can you do a DNA trace on the blood they're collecting remotely?"

Sloan bit her lip. "Maybe. We should be able to use the data collection tools we use to take blood samples from enemy KIA in situ. But speaking of making assumptions, we shouldn't assume it has DNA either," she said with a quirk of her eyebrows and a frown toward Hatfield.

"Noted," Hatfield said and keyed the radio again. "Seven, use your DNA collector on it and send that data out as soon as possible."

Brenner continued to manipulate the screen images, overlaying the hyperspectral data from the eyebot with the visual image of the creature. He looked up. "I can't see where they shot it the first time or if any damage was inflicted, but I can tell you what happened when they shot it in other places." He zoomed in on the claws and pulled a video clip onto the main display.

"This is a full burst from one of the Marines," he said as they saw a stream of small caliber frangible ammunition enter the screen from the bottom, slamming into the left front claw. The rounds impacted and shattered as if they were hitting a steel plate. Brenner let the images replay several times then swapped to another view, this time of rounds hitting the body. The creature's shell seemed to form into a different shape after the first round hit, causing following rounds to ricochet away harmlessly.

"What about the one that got through?"

"No good angle on it. I think he might have hit the joint for some of those small legs on the bottom. The little . . .

T-rex claws that are tucked up tight to the body."

The crew was intently staring at the screens when Dr. Bilks interrupted them. "You notice anything about the creature that looks familiar?"

"Yeah it looks like something we eat on date night," said Sloan.

"The ship. The ship looks just like this thing. They modeled the ship after their own body design. That implies that whatever is in that part between the two pods of the ship is probably very important to them. It could mean that... "

"Sir! Major gas ejection from the ship and a partial firing of several thrusters has caused it to start swinging to line up with the military side of the facility. We've also just been actively pinged with some kind of energy wave come from the bottom spar of the ship, that lump on the underside," Higgins shouted out urgently, pulling the exterior image of the ship up on the main screen.

"CIC, QRF Angel reporting ship is shuddering and shifting vector... " a tech called from the bottom of the pit.

"Sir! Sir! Those pods or claws near the front have rotated away from their previous position and it appears that the nose is opening up. I'm detecting an increase in IR emissions near the tip of the... "

Alarms began blaring from all corners of the room. Depressurization alarms, damage alerts and collision alarms. Everyone in the room scrambled to slide their helmets on and lock them in place as their ears were assaulted by the shrieking base alert system.

Sloan slapped her helmet in place and toggled it down with one hand while bringing up the alerts on her main board and reading them quickly. She prioritized as quickly as she could, localizing the impact points on the display and pushing them out to the main screen so everyone could see.

"We are taking fire in the vicinity of Broadway, many sensors in the area are disabled or destroyed. We are getting indicators of a major pressure loss penetrating deep into the base."

"Why aren't the damn pressure doors down?" Brenner yelled over the radio.

"They were!" Sloan said, her eyes widening as she reviewed the last moments of the security cameras in Broadway. "They're gone, something shot straight down Broadway and vaporized the doors. Broadway is now open into vacuum!"

"Seven, Six or any Marines in the QRF. We are taking heavy fire from the ship. Find the power source for that gun and kill it. *Now!*" Hatfield yelled into the radio, the first signs of fear entering his voice.

"Sir! Those two pods on either side of the nose just detached and are heading in the direction of Broadway.

Hatfield and Brenner exchanged a long look before Hatfield spoke somberly. "Prepare to repel boarders."

Phoenix Six heard the radio call and frowned. He'd never heard the Director sound fearful before. "My team, push toward the stern. Phoenix Seven, push toward the bow. We destroy anything that looks like it has a lot of power going through it."

They charged down the access tunnel toward the rear of the ship. As they approached the end of the tunnel, the ship shuddered twice, lifting them momentarily off the floor.

"What was that?" he said over the primary battlenet for the QRF.

"Two objects just detached from the ship sir," one of the pilots reported to him. "They're headed down toward Phoebe, we are moving to engage."

Phoenix Six dropped back into the squad channel. "Push," he said, motioning them forward.

The Alpha team leader breached the hatch at the end of the tunnel. They found themselves in a room with a long series of cylinders. Cabling ran from conduit in the wall down into the cylinders. Most of them appeared cold and dark, but several were softly vibrating.

Six raised his fist and the team backed up into the tunnel as he placed several large explosive charges around the conduits. He raced out into the hallway and mashed the detonator. With a muffled bang the charges went off, severing the conduits and shattering several wall panels. They waited for a half minute as secondary explosions ripped out of the cylinders. Abruptly the vibrations stopped.

"QRF, CIC. Whatever you just did killed the weapon. Good job, secure the ship. Hatfield out."

Six breathed a sigh of relief silently into his radio before trying to raise the other squad. "Seven, how is it going?"

"Oh we're just great. We pressed forward toward the bow. I think the thing we shot is holed up in the room ahead of us. We can't get this door open, it's resisted four breaching attempts. Whatever's in there, it's not coming out without better tools. We got another crack at downing it, but the armor it's wearing is pretty intense. Don't even bother shooting at their backs or tops. It's like shooting a foot thick plate of steel. Tried to use a cutting laser on it too, but its shell seems impervious. The heat from the laser just absorbed into it, I think I scorched it a little and that's it."

"A cutting laser? How close did you get?"

"Too close. It wrecked my shotgun, broke my wrist and used its tail to beat Bravo Four senseless. We think he'll be ok, but it managed to dent his armor..."

Six stopped walking and used his HUD to pull up Seven's video feed. He rewound the feed to the moment before they entered the room and let it play. He watched in silence as the Bravo squad piled into a room and came face to face with the creature. The creature pulled its main claws up to protect its face and began whipping over the top at them with its over-claw. Six watched as Bravo Four caught a swipe which bounced him hard off the wall and then he saw Seven stick his shotgun close to the creature's rear area and fire. The round fractured the shell, small shards and flakes of armor spattering around the room, but it did not penetrate. The creature spun around and bashed the barrel of the gun so hard that it snapped it off, shattering the receiver, before it zipped out of the room and the hatch shut behind it.

"Seven. Don't get that close to it again."

"No shit, sir."

Lieutenant Jasper Wilcox led his Mongoose squadron in a lazy orbit around the enemy ship. They had been the last squadron to leave the hangars and with so much confusion they had only recently received their squadron designation for the day—Hornet. As a result, he was still trying to get the flights organized, and the pilots were a bit sluggish from their time in the MIC.

"Hornets, assume three ship formations and keep your distance from each other while the Marines capture the ship." He watched as the squadron reformed into new flight elements and broke off.

The QRF had been aboard the ship for a while now. Occasional reports had indicated the ship was mostly empty up until a few moments ago when one of the Bravo Marines was killed by a creature of some sort. Jasper mulled that word over in his mind; creature. It implied something non-human, maybe something alien. A shiver shot down his spine.

Suddenly the battlenet came alive, one of the Hornet pilots calling out observations.

"Hornet Actual, Hornet 3-2 here. I think those pods are mechanically moving away from the nose. It's hard to tell, but it looks like they're uncovering the tip."

"Copy Hornet 3-2, I see it. Hold your fire, we have Marines in the ship."

"Hornet 3-2 cop . . . ." His voice went silent as a brilliant beam of light shot from the nose of the ship and impacted the crater wall. Visible only in the infrared spectrum, the beam pulsed brightly as it melted through the crater's rock walls and into the underlying metal of the base below.

The Director's voice came over the battlenet using the command override. As he was blistering out orders to the combined space forces and boarding party, the ship continued to fire, sending punishing energy bursts into the facility below.

"Hornet Actual, this is Hornet 2-3, I just observed the left... wait, both of those pods have separated from the ship and are firing thrusters. They're maneuvering toward the base!"

Hornet Actual flipped his ship over so he could get a better view and saw the two pods diving down toward the base. "All Hornets, intercept the pods. Keep your IR filters up and don't fly through the beam!"

The Hornet flight elements flipped around and punched their thrusters to max, speeding after the drop-ships. By fortune, the lead flight element was the closest to their path and was rapidly closing the gap.

"One flight, short controlled bursts. Remember, if you miss, you hit our base. Watch out for any kind of rear turret or defense mechanism. Engage at two hundred meters."

As the range finder gradually ground down to engagement range, his heads-up display kept constant track of the predicted intercept point if he fired. It was a tail chase, even from their advantageous starting position, and the base was starting to get very large through the cockpit glass.

"Focus on the right target, designated A on your HUD. I want to make sure it's downed before swapping to target B. Hornet 1-2 bracket him to the right, Hornet 1-3 bracket him to the left. We'll see if we can prevent him from slipping the killbox."

They acknowledged him and continued their dive. At five kilometers above the surface the HUD indicator finally lit up green. He centered his gun pip on the nose of the drop-ship and caressed the trigger. Cannon rounds were fired electrically, igniting the fuel inside and sending them shooting out like wicked fireflies in the darkness of space. The noise reverberated through his ship, tingling the palms of his hands through the control sticks as he fired quick ten round bursts of cannon fire at the right pod. He watched as his first burst raced out toward the dropship, noting when the last of the internal fuel burned out, his wingmen firing bursts aimed at the edges of dropship as it tumbled.

Wilcox watched in dismay as burst after burst slammed the ship, chipping away at it, but doing very little significant damage. He checked his rear sensor displays; the rest of the squadron was too far away to help. With Phoebe rushing to greet them from below, he made a decision.

"One flight, swap to dumbfires. Fire by pairs, one salvo. Make sure they lock before you let them loose," he said before swapping to the command battlenet.

"CIC and all elements, we are engaging enemy ship with dumbfires, shelter in place in case they overshoot!"

He had closed to within sixty meters of the pod now, and it was streaming small particles and leaking atmosphere. He reached down and flicked his master arm switch to the on position and settled the lock icon directly on the top of the nose of the drop pod. He depressed the trigger until he heard the lock tone start to beep in his helmet. When the beeps finally got so close together they became a solid blur of sound, he triggered the launch. Two dumbfires ripped off the rails and raced toward the target. His wingmen promptly followed suit. At 500 meters off the surface of Phoebe he made the call.

"PULL UP, turn and burn." Using his maneuvering thrusters he flipped his fighter and pointed the nose away from Phoebe before hammering the throttle to its max and struggling mightily to slow his descent. The first two missiles, fired by Wilcox, impacted the nose with a heavy explosive force, causing the ship to tumble erratically. The four missiles directly behind it tried to compensate for the change, but only two were able to make contact, the others continuing on to impact just inside the still smoking hole where the enemy ship had melted the surface of Phoebe.

The dropship fired thrusters to try and regain control, just barely getting reoriented before it plowed nose-first into a pile of gravel leftover from the construction of the base. It split like an overripe grape, littering the surface with debris. There were no survivors. The other pod landed just inside the smoking hole, setting down on retro rockets before firing a metal rod into the surface as an anchor. The top popped open and four shapes darted out, immediately proceeding deeper into the hole. The rest of the squadron darted past the lead flight element firing a few short bursts at the downed pod.

"HORNETS HOLD FIRE!" Actual shouted into the Battlenet. "If you shoot in there, you will damage the base further. Assume combat space patrol between the ship and the base."

The rest of the Hornets sheepishly pulled out of their gunnery runs and took up defensive positions. Hornet Actual looked back at the impact crater of the pod they'd shot up— they had barely managed to escape impacting right next to it. He shook his head slightly as a shiver went up his spine.

The room was silent as they watched the main display, an optical camera feed from the science side of the base. The Mongoose were chasing the two pods down toward the surface, sending spirals of tracers that glowed hot in the infrared spectrum. Occasionally a round would shoot past the pods to continue on into the moon. The ventilation system echoed with the impacts, causing Molly to flinch reflexively while looking up nervously toward the ceiling.

"Compliments to G-LOC. Her pilots are very accurate," Brenner said tightly.

"Not that it's doing any good. Whatever those ships are made of, they're armored to the hilt. I think our initial expectation was correct, they were placed the way they were on the ship as protection for whatever is in the nose. I'd guess we're going to need to up our game if we want to have any chance at all . . . of stopping them," Erik said as he watched the screen intently.

Hatfield was reaching for the push-to-talk button on his console when he heard Hornet Actual give the weapons free command for dumbfires. His hand paused awkwardly over the switch as he watched the screen. The impacts flared brightly on the screen, before several of the missiles swept past. He grimaced and moved his hand to a different communication panel.

"ALL HANDS, BRACE FOR IMPACT," he broadcast to the military side of the base, right before the first missile streaked into the surface of Phoebe.

A low long rumble shook the room as the rock above their heads compressed downward, impacting the modular base sections that had been sunk into Phoebe's skin. Each module was the size of a freighter's cargo cell, connected to its neighboring modules with passageways and supported from all directions by springs and gravity compensators. The structure was designed in much the same way that the United States had built nuclear bunkers for its command and control assets during the cold war, and as a result the missile impacts had a very limited impact on the structural integrity. But they were still loud and nerve wracking for those who had not been in combat before.

Hatfield watched as the pod spun out of control, slamming into the surface. He swapped communication circuits to Major Stringer's battlenet.

"Major, Hatfield here. We have an intrusion in the topside portion of Broadway. I believe we saw four or five creatures enter into the damaged section. Contain and detain them. Also, send a SARine triplet with one squad of Marine backups to the crashed pod section at my coordinates and have them confirm the kill, collect what data they can. Acknowledge."

"Stringer acknowledges, contain and capture enemy boarding party. Secure crash site. Do you want us to send a detachment over to the pod that landed safely?"

"Send a platoon and another SARine triplet to deal with it. I want that ship intact if possible. But I don't want casualties."

"Roger. Be advised, most of the doors leading into Broadway were sealed shut by the weapon fire from that ship. My scouts report they are effectively welded. We'll have to breach down by the last functioning bulkhead and defend from there. Order of Battle update on the way to you in moments, Stringer out."

Brenner looked over his shoulder at Hatfield. "We could also send a unit to approach them, going down Broadway from behind, pinch them off."

"No, bad tactics," Hatfield said, focusing on his screen. Brenner canted his head to the side and stared at him a moment before glancing at Sloan who shrugged.

The interplay was not lost on Hatfield who continued to focus on the displays in front of him while speaking to Brenner. "If we approach from the rear, when we make contact, we'll risk shooting each other. We've seen no ranged enemy weapons at this point, so all our guys have to do is maintain their distance and they should be safe. Unless, of course, they get shot by friendly fire."

Brenner grimaced but said nothing, turning back to his console.

Hatfield watched the blue-force tracker for several moments, before turning to Sloan. "Sloan, do we have any idea where those creatures are?"

"No, not really. Most of the security system got slagged by whatever they shot at us."

He turned back to the tracker, a sour look on his face.

One of the communication techs patched in the Marines battlenet over the room speakers so they could all hear. Hatfield looked up, started to say something, before he saw the attentive look on the faces of his subordinates and subsided.

Master Chief Gene Marin's voice crackled over the speakers. "Alright, this is the extent of the damage from that gun that shot us. We'll press forward about ten bulkheads and make a fighting position as best we can. I want to have room to give ground and maneuver if we need to." There was a period of heavy breathing as they clambered along the walls toward their target destination before he spoke again. "Phoenix Thirty-Two, can you remote access the section behind the pressure door we just left?"

"Yes, but I don't have a way to make sure what I tell it to do works. The door was partially melted, heat transfer could have baked the room," she replied.

"See if you can pump it down to vacuum in there, so the pressure is equal. If we take fire from these things, I don't want that door blowing into us from behind."

"Yes sir. I think the area is intact enough for that."

"Sir," the first squad leader spoke as they settled into their designated positions. "We may have a problem."

"What's that?"

"We don't have a clean line of retreat. We can pull back to that pressure door, but after that we're going to be at risk of losing containment on them."

"We won't be retreating past the pressure door." Gene turned a speculative eye back toward the melted surface of the door. "It's only a few bulkheads farther to the cooling coils for the base reactors. If we don't stop these things, we'll be glowing by dinner. We hold or we die."

"Yes sir," the squad leader said gravely, before switching to his squad battlenet to explain the situation.

Marin made a small hand signal to the leader of the Phoenix SARine triplet. Phoenix Thirty shook his head in acknowledgement and released his eyebot. It hovered in front of his faceplate for a few moments while he gave it instructions then bolted down the length of Broadway, dodging floating debris and mangled equipment

CHAPTER 9

Dr. Elliot furiously typed commands into the console, trying to gain access to any of the base security cameras on the military side. They had all seen the two pods streak into the dusty hole in the rimrock surrounding the crater, and now there was an eerie silence in the room as they considered what it could mean.

"More Marines heading toward the impact point. I think there are some of the big ones with them too," one of the grad students in the back spoke softly.

Christie looked up to see one of the Angels lift from a hangar and swing toward the impact point with its main door open, Marines hanging out with their weapons at the ready. She squinted at the Angel and frowned. It was one of the ships they used to transfer equipment on the freighter run, an unarmed Angel. She took a breath through gritted teeth and went back to querying the security system. Sloan had given her access to a few small sections of the military side months back in case something happened to her, but her access wasn't working.

"What exactly are you doing?" Sam whispered over a private channel to her.

"Trying to get access to the Broadway security cameras. That impact point looks like it could have been near where Broadway's big cargo hatch leads to the surface. It's also the same point where the explosion happened a few minutes ago and we saw the IR flashing."

"Are you being denied access? I thought Sloan gave you clearance?"

"No, it's like they're just gone. Maybe they have a power outage and are just offline."

"They get power over the datalines for those cameras. That system has triple redundancy, it would take a hell of a power outage to drop it." Sam said as his voice trailed off.

Christie was in the middle of typing the access code for another set of cameras when Sloan messaged her. "What are you doing Christie?"

"Trying to figure out what just happened to you guys over there!"

"We're fine, but I need you to stop hammering the access server right now. There isn't anything to look at, sensors are gone."

"All of the sensors are gone?" Christie said with alarm.

Sloan hesitated before responding. "Hold on a second." A minute passed then she was back. "Ok, is it just you and Sam in the SIP?"

"We have a bunch of researchers in here too."

"I mean KaliSun employees."

"Yes, and a couple of Marines."

"Give me their ID numbers."

Christie walked over to the Marines and scanned their nameplates with her reader. They stared at her quizzically, but said nothing. She nodded at them and sent it to Sloan. Seconds passed before she popped back on.

"Team member eyes only. Stay off the net right now, Sloan out."

Christie furrowed her brow in confusion as she tried to figure out what Sloan was talking about. A remote video feed pinged for her attention at the edge of her HUD. Out of the corner of her eye she saw the two Marines stiffen sharply before they settled into a state of attentiveness. She activated the feed, giving it nearly eighty percent of her display space.

She blinked rapidly and tried to process the image on her screen. Broadway was zipping past at high speed as an eyebot sped through the corridor, weaving in and out of debris. It was approaching an odd lump that was gliding down the length of Broadway, bumping debris out of the way. As the bot approached, it pinged the lump with its sensors, her view changing from normal vision to IR to ultraviolet rapidly as the eyebot tried to assess what the objects ahead were.

Christie squinted hard at the image, wishing she could get the bot to stop darting around so much and focus on the strange shape. Abruptly, she realized it wasn't one shape at all, but four shapes that were gliding down the hallway hooked together, using small legs tucked tight to their underside to occasionally propel themselves faster. She took an involuntarily breath, her pulse quickening.

The eyebot made a near pass above them giving her a view. It was a nightmare of armored and mottled exoskeleton, heavy claws, and a strange claw lying along their back. The long, articulated claw on its back consisted of one big pincer claw, with two little claws covered with sharp spikes tucked into its armor. As the bot passed over, one of the creatures took a swing at it with its over-claw, missing and slamming into the nearby bulkhead, leaving a dent.

The bot accelerated away before turning and hovering in the tunnel. Once the creatures resumed their path toward the reactor, the bot fired a sticky dart at the back of one of the creatures, landing it at the base of its over-claw. The dart stuck to the overlapping armor plate and began transmitting its location data to the blue-force tracker. The bot repeated the procedure multiple times, making sure each creature was stuck at least twice before it followed them as they went deeper.

"That's not good," Sam spoke in her ear.

"Don't let the researchers know," she said with fear in her voice.

"I'm sure they know something's up."

"Why do you think that?"

"They're all watching us instead of the exterior feeds now."

Christie stole a glance toward the Marines and sighed. They were setting up a firing position to shoot anything coming through the door, one of them flipping a table up on its side and clamping on the mounting mechanism for a machine gun. They were moving with the calm cool of professionals who knew they were about to be in a fight. It was hard sometimes to remember they were all trainees, and that while they had the polished edge of a veteran they still lacked some experience in the finer details of the environment.

She pulled a channel to the two of them. "You are going to scare the civilians." She spoke evenly.

"Noted."

"Maybe barricading the door will be sufficient," she said helpfully.

"That's next on the list. If they come here, we'll be ready for them."

Christie looked back over to the researchers who were numbly watching the Marines get set up and bit her lip. *We*, might be a strong a term, she thought to herself.

<hr />

"Are you seeing what I'm seeing Mark?"

Phoenix Thirty shook his head affirmatively. "Yeah, the crabs are advancing with two facing front and two facing behind, covering up with those big claws."

"Damn Roman Testudo," Gene said softly. "Thoughts?"

"I say we throw some grenades under them and hope for the best," the Marine squad leader replied.

"We'd have shrapnel everywhere, but that is an option," Gene said pensively.

"We could smack them with some breaching charges, even if it doesn't kill one it should ring its bell pretty good," Phoenix Thirty said as he watched the eyebot's footage. The crabs were only fifteen bulkheads away, their dark outlines just visible in the darkness of Broadway as they advanced under the eyebot's spotlight.

"Method of last resort. What if you miss or they flip it back at us? We need a better option."

"We could lay some shaped charges on the floor and blow

them when they pass over them. If we miss they're going to tear up the ceiling, but if we hit, it might clean them right out. I'm pretty sure small arms fire isn't going to slow them even a little."

"I think we'll do . . . " Gene was interrupted by Brenner, breathing heavily into his mic over the battlenet.

"Hold fast, we're coming."

Gene shot a quizzical look at the SARine Commander who shrugged back at him noncommittally. He sighed with impatience. He liked Brenner and respected his engineering prowess, but now was not the best time to come chat.

Phoenix Thirty saw his expression. "Any reinforcements he brings would help. Besides, Brenner has deployed with us a couple of times during exercises, he's no slouch with a weapon and has some interesting insight at times."

Gene grunted a response back to him and watched the eye-bot's footage. The crabs had tightened up their formation, hovering a short distance above the floor as they scooted along using compressed gas ejected from somewhere along the rear of their shells. The over-claws were tucked down over their heads, the big claws nearly completely blocking the view from the front.

"Mark, give me three rows of shaped charges on the floor pointing up and down the hall a bit. We can't wait for Brenner to get here to deploy them, otherwise they'll see us plant them. Worst case they are just in the way for whatever he has in mind."

"Yes sir," Phoenix Thirty responded, darting forward with his team carrying three strings of explosives.

Gene watched as the three SARines expertly attached the explosives to the floor, using their maneuvering jets to hover in Phoebe's weak gravity. The floor was a mangled mess in the area they were working making it easier to conceal the explosives. His blue-force tracker chirped, showing two command suits approaching from the rear, one with an asterisk next to the pip. Brenner was coming.

Brenner paused at the end of the hall, inspecting the last pressure door that had been damaged but not breached. The suited figure with him pointed at several different areas, discussing something with Brenner before Brenner turned and used the debris to pull himself quickly up the hallway. The other person followed behind dragging a bulky container.

Brenner glided down the hall to land next to Gene softly with the skill of significant time spent outside the controlled gravity of the base. The other command suit crunched into two of the Marines along one of the walls as he tried to control the container unsuccessfully. Gene flicked a glance in his direction and saw one of the Marines reach up and haul the container down to secure it to the deck while they untangled themselves.

"Who is that?"

"Erik. We went to his lab and got something to try on these guys. Damn thing is unwieldy though."

"Hope it wasn't fragile."

"Yeah, it's crude, but built to be pretty strong. Give me a SITREP."

Gene fed him his eyebot feed before responding. "I've got my eyebot Scout down the hall shadowing the crabs. They're approaching in a tight formation with their legs tucked up under and those claws covering most of the top of them. We're laying explosively formed penetrators along the floor, when they fly over them, we're going to splatter them." He pointed to the SARine triplet a short distance away. "Have you guys learned anything else about these things? So far Scout has been relatively unsuccessful in getting much of a reading on them. It can't get close enough to run an x-ray. They're almost non-emissive in the infrared spectrum and their shells seem to absorb visible light and mottle in a rough approximation of their surroundings. Almost like our lunar camo actually, it's very effective."

"We don't know much about them. Expect them to be very tough, that's all Phoenix Seven could tell us. He shot one at point blank range with a shotgun to little effect. Their underside seems to be their vulnerability, so putting the EFPs on the ground was a good start. Have you tried to hit them with a hyper-spectral scan yet?"

"Yes, mixed results. We pulsed one with some thermals and took a few pictures," Gene said as he forwarded the images to Brenner and Erik's helmets.

"Ah nice," Erik said.

"Nice what?" Brenner prodded.

"Well, it's basically behaving like a black body. We're in vacuum open to space right now so the creature is basically behaving like an inert object, neither absorbing nor emitting heat. So that weird halo you see is its black body radiation spectrum. Look at image three," Erik said.

Silence fell over the battlenet as Erik manipulated the image to a clearer view. "Look at the emissivity of their shell, it's .93. That's almost to the level of, say, graphite. Those little strange lit up places are where some heat is escaping the body, mostly around the joints. I'd guess that it operates some kind of organic mechanism to allow external radiation in as needed to maintain its internal temperature. Basically, it loses a little heat energy through its joints and probably face, so it absorbs external energy to replace it, and when it has enough, it turns coal black."

"That's very interesting Dr. Bilks. However, they are about fifty meters away, so if you would like to get to the point soon, I'd greatly appreciate it," Gene said patiently.

Erik chuckled. "I wouldn't try to shoot a laser at it."

"Why is that? And Doctor, we're on a timeline here…" Brenner said with some urgency as the faint outlines of the crabs became visible, drifting down the hallway towards them. The three SARines scrambled back and assumed firing positions, one of them clutching three detonators in his hands.

"The number up in the upper left corner of the image indicates a reference file. To summarize the file, their outer

shell seems like it can morph its internal structure. Right
now it's in a configuration that follows Lambert's cosine law;
you shoot a laser at it and it's likely to diffuse the beam and
reflect it back at odd angles. It could potentially morph into
a new crystalline structure which changes it to a specular
reflector, in which case it could nearly perfectly reflect the
laser beam right back at you at full intensity. So lasers are
probably dangerous with these things, in fact they look like
they were almost designed to deal with energy weapons . . .
hmm, yeah. I need to get the device ready." Abruptly, Erik
cut out of the battlenet and wandered back over to his case,
opening it and handing pieces of pipe to the confused Marine hovering nearby.

"Director, is Erik ok?" Gene asked as he watched him work.

"Not really, I think he's starting to lose it. As soon as this
is over, he's getting some R and R. Just make sure you point
the right end of the tube at the crabs, if this thing backfires
and kills one of your men he'll never forgive me."

Gene turned to face Brenner. "What is going on?" he asked
in a quiet tone.

"Those are some replicas we made of Von Tremel's zip gun.
He objected to using them and then he got real quiet and has
been lecturing me ever since. When we entered Broadway he
was explaining to me how the metal in the doors had been
fundamentally changed by whatever they shot us with. Said
it was like all of their subatomic particles got realigned."

"You copied that damn zip gun?"

"Yeah, well, we can't seem to penetrate their armor, so I
brought a backup plan. I have faith in your EFPs though, just
time it right," Brenner said. He pulled his assault shotgun off
his back armor plate and checked the load.

Gene watched him carefully. Brenner had been on numerous training operations as an observer and occasional
participant, but he was still an engineer with a gun. His eyes
narrowed and he reached over and spun Brenner around

abruptly, looking at the back of his armor. Slung across the back of his armor was a bare blade with a wicked forward bend in it.

"What the hell, sir?"

Brenner shrugged. "I'm better with a sword than a gun, holdover from college. Ammo was too pricey to practice enough, but you never have to reload a sword."

"You are *not* permitted to get that close to those damn things. Hatfield will rip my entrails out through my ears if I let you!"

Brenner chuckled back at him. "So noted, I guess you better stop it before it gets here." He forcefully pulled Erik back into their channel.

" . . . .see the key thing here is to make sure you point the right end at them. See the little designator laser on the end, don't use that. I don't think lasers are a good idea on these things. Just aim for the center of mass, pull this pin out and then mash the button. Shouldn't kick much . . . wait. Brenner, damn it I was in the middle of explaining how to use these things."

"They're Marines, you gave them a weapon, I'm sure they can figure it out," Brenner said impatiently before softening his voice. "Gene, please instruct your men about Dr. Bilks' instructions for use."

"Yes sir."

"Erik, I want you to bring me a couple of the zip guns and then pull back to the entry."

Erik pushed himself off the wall and drifted over to Brenner, handing him two zip guns. "No."

Brenner took the guns from him and looked at him curiously, his face showing concern through his murky faceplate. "What do you mean *no?*"

"No, I'm not going to leave. If they can't get them to work I intend to be right here so I can help. I'm not going to have somebody killed by my invention because I ran off and hid."

"Von Tremel invented these things, not you. You have no

responsibility here, it's all on me, now please, pull back."

"All the more reason to stay here, that man is a nutcase and you're trusting his design to save you."

Brenner looked nervously down the hall. The crabs were definitely closer now, approaching at a sedate pace as they struggled to maintain their defensive posture while navigating the twisted metal in the hallway. "Fine, pull back a few bulkheads so you aren't under foot if we have to move quickly. You don't have enough combat EVA time in that suit to risk trying to move at our speed. Please."

"Fine," Erik said as he drifted farther down the hall, weaving in and out of the remains of the hallway. Gene pushed off the wall and shot over to Brenner, settling in next to him and taking one of the zip guns.

"I took something like this off a kid in Nairobi, after he blew his damn hand off using it. You have tested it right?"

"Von Tremel did."

"We trust him?" Gene asked quietly.

"I do, he may be a completely crazy, but he was a good engineer. I trust his device because he made it with the express intent of penetrating Hatfield's armor and killing him. He *hates* Hatfield. I trust in hate."

"What? When did you learn this?"

"Joe, the SARine interrogator, managed to break through the firewall on his diary. Well, part of it."

"Damn..."

Brenner nodded as he peered over the piece of metal grating he had hidden himself behind. The crabs were almost to the EFPs but they'd stopped and were floating in the hallway. They drifted tighter together, using the smaller pincer hands on their underbelly to hold on to each other.

"I think they see us or maybe your EFPs," Brenner said.

"Yeah. I was hoping they would just fly right over them. Guess it's time to see if we can draw them in." Gene broke into the local battlenet, speaking rapidly. "I want squad one to engage the enemy, aim for the legs and the joints, three round burst only. Squad two hold fire, SARines stay hidden."

Brenner hugged the tangled remains of the floor tighter and brought the eyebot's data feed back on his display. Swiftly, five of the Marines rose from their hiding positions and fired at the crabs. The rounds left cheerful looking streaks through the compartment before impacting against the crab's armor. The formation shuddered backward briefly as the impact pushed them down the hallway, but they were back in control quickly. Looking at the data, he could tell nothing significant had happened to the armor, although zooming in on the top of the bigger crab he could see a long streak where it appeared to have been grazed. He upped the magnification and swore under his breath.

"Gene, instruct them to try to shoot at the crabs for glancing blows. Hitting it straight on is not effective, but when they get hit with a shear force it seems to work better."

"It's a rounded surface, we might get a lot of ricochets."

"I know, but they aren't moving. We need to convince them sitting there safely isn't an option."

Gene gave the order to the first squad again. This time they started shooting at the angled surfaces on the crabs. More gouges appeared, but no significant damage was being done. Still, they sat there. The veteran Master Sergeant swore under his breath and ordered SARine Thirty-Two to fire a sticky grenade at the crabs.

It zipped out from the Marine's position and stuck to the larger crab's big over-claw as it hovered over its head defensively. With a brilliant flash the grenade exploded, driving the crab down into the deck and breaking the testudo.

Instantly the Marines responded, shooting the remaining forward facing crab repeatedly in the underbelly. As it tried to right itself, the SARine got another grenade off, this time sticking to the T-Rex claws underneath. The crab reacted, moving its big claws out of the way as it tried to get the sticky grenade off the smaller ones. The grenade went off causing everyone to duck, blowing most of the claws off the underbelly and driving pieces of them through the creature's shell and into its interior. Spurts of bluish goop erupted and flash froze in the vacuum of the tunnel as the creature thrashed around, its insides being pulled through the holes in its shell. The goop hardened, sealing most of the holes, but not enough to stop the bleeding.

The thrashing crab floated back up the tunnel, narrowly missing the eyebot. As its lifeblood drained into the hallway, the exterior of the crab turned a salt white color, its limbs slowing. The body bounced off the bulkhead and continued on up the hallway at a very slow pace. The first crab that had been hit was tangled in the debris along the floor now, its thrashing wrapping it up in the power and data cables under what had been the floor in the hallway.

The other two crabs spun around towards their attackers and raced forward at high speed, claws protecting their faces. As they passed over the EFPs, the SARine mashed the detonation keys, but he had misjudged their speed. Only the left crab was hit by the last line of explosions, the liquefied copper piercing its shell and spattering around inside. The force of the impact drove the crab into the ceiling with a wet splatter as its blood squirted out of the multiple perforations in its shell.

The remaining crab charged through the onslaught of concentrated gunfire, the impacts slowing its approach and requiring the alien to dip its under-claws down to grab the deck for added propulsion.

"Don't fire until you see the whites of their eyes..." Gene mumbled as the crab closed in on them.

"NOW!" Brenner yelled into the battlenet.

As one, they rose and fired right for the head with the zip guns. The creature instinctively covered his face with both big claws and his over-claw. The shots hit the exterior of its claws, but didn't seem to slow it down. Then it halted and started spinning in circles, banging into the walls and floor as it scrabbled at its own head like a child trying to get a spider out of its hair. Its movement slowed and became erratic, then gradually its shell turned white and it stopped moving all together.

Brenner hovered in the hallway watching, his spent zip gun clutched in his hands. The three creatures that had been killed were slowly tumbling in the hallway. The fourth was tangled in the debris on the floor, virtually immobilized. Whenever it struggled one of the power lines would short out and zap it, so now it sat very still. Brenner patted Gene on the back and gave Hatfield a call.

"John, I think I have a present for you."

CHAPTER 10

Major Ava Sirano drifted through space, her Mongoose mortally wounded, tumbling away from Saturn toward the vast emptiness of the outer solar system. She lay back in her seat, feeling the Gs sit on her chest as she worked the hand crank generator next to her pilot's chair. Her heads up display was dead, most of the indicators in the cockpit were dead or a dull orange color, the sticks unresponsive. As the ship tumbled the view out of the cockpit changed. One moment it was the depths of space, an infinite starfield with galaxies and nebulas, the next it was the vibrant weather patterns and rings of Saturn shining through the cockpit glass.

She breathed slowly, staying calm and focused on cranking the generator. As she neared five hundred cranks, the orange indicator in the center of the console changed to green and a small diode on her control stick lit up weakly. She smiled to herself and gingerly took the stick, still cranking the generator with her other hand. She'd have a very small margin for this to work, otherwise she could end up heading to parts unknown and cold, lonely death.

As Saturn slowly came back into view again, she tapped her thrusters slightly, working against the tumble and trying to orient herself toward the heart of Saturn. The tumble slowed, but didn't stop. She took pressure off the thrusters and kept cranking, waiting for Saturn to come back around. Again, she popped the thrusters to slow the tumble and again she slowed but couldn't stop. The green light on the console started to dim and turn yellow. She carefully took her hand off the control stick, cranking again and giving her other arm a rest.

As the console light gradually regained its green color, she released the generator handle and waited for the next revolution. Now her tumble was so slow it took a full three minutes before Saturn came back around, and this time she used a longer burn from her thrusters, steadied out with the three tines of her Mongoose all pointed within Saturn's face. The G-load gradually lifted off her chest as the force diminished. With a nervous sigh she took her hand off the stick and reached forward to the button labeled 'RTB' on the center of the console. The indicator showed it was green and good to go. She armed it and slowly pressed the button down.

In theory, the 'Return to Base' feature of a Mongoose was foolproof. A small, heavily shielded chip used inertial guidance to determine where the ship was in space, and would actuate a long impulse thruster in the back of the ship. Even with limited instrumentation, testing had shown that the RTB feature could bring a damaged bird home, as long as it didn't have to maneuver too much.

In Sirano's case, she was hoping it would keep her near enough to Phoebe that a SAR Angel could rescue her. She waited for the vibration to start, indicating the engine was spinning up. Nothing happened. She pursed her lips in thought and started cranking the generator again. With her off hand she flipped open an emergency panel down by her thigh and poked a finger in. She felt around, finding the CPU restart button for the Mongoose's main systems, and paused. Right now, she could crank up enough juice to use one thruster at a time, and her suit was getting power from the backup batteries in the chair and the energy recovery system, but if she restarted there was no way to be certain the status quo would continue after the attempted reboot. It could improve or she could be even worse off than she already was.

She took her hand out of the panel space and reached up to toggle the arming switch on the RTB button, then tried it again. Still nothing, not even a ragged start to indicate it had been damaged. She closed her eyes and said a quick prayer before punching the system restart button on the

Mongoose's CPU. All the indicators on her console went dark and the suit showed a brief flashing icon meaning exterior power was lost, leaving just the soft glow from Saturn to illuminate the cockpit.

After a moment, the restart kicked in and there was a brief flicker of activity on her display. The command prompt appeared and started running through the system start functions. A message indicating a bit error crossed the screen, and the system rebooted all over again, slowly working through its processes before it reached the same point and crashed again. After the second crash, the console remained dark, the indicator's dull pips staring back at her morosely in the dim light.

She gave up cranking the generator and opened up her wrist interface, poked at the HUD controls and cursed to herself. That weapon of Erik's had fragged pretty much every piece of electronics she had when it went off. She flipped the dip switch and tried a fresh restart on the HUD in her helmet. For a moment it blinked on, displaying icons along the top of her glass view and struggling to update her location against the map. Before the update could complete, it locked up and crashed, leaving nothing but a spinning KaliSun logo in the corner as its software rebooted.

She kicked her control pedals in frustration and leaned back in the pilot's chair, staring at Saturn with the beginnings of tears in her eyes. Taking a deep breath, she closed her eyes and tried to calm herself. Listening to the soft ping of micrometeorites against the hull armor and the nearly inaudible hum of the helmet systems restarting, she almost missed what happened. She opened her eyes with a start as a shadow passed over her face. She struggled to see through the tears. There, framed in Saturn's glow, was a shape that made her heart soar.

Descending toward her in full profile was an Angel, its humped wings silhouetted against the swirling oranges and yellows of Saturn. In the doorway of the Angel stood a man wearing a command suit with a recovery grapple in hand.

She shook her head to fling the tears away and squinted at the Angel as it approached. Her helmet HUD finally rebooted and populated the fields around the rim of her display. A glowing triangle formed over the ship's nose with a name designator next to it, *Hound 7*. She smiled, and carefully disarmed the RTB button before settling back into her chair with her arms crossed, waiting.

"Hornet Actual, this is Hatfield."

"Go for Hornet Actual."

"Sensors detected several shapes eject from the ship during the first series of gunnery runs. We've found them with Skysearch, CIC is forwarding the sensor track to your support Angels. Detail a flight section and support Angel to track down whatever it was and secure it," Hatfield said.

"Solid copy. Find the objects, secure and return to hangar with them. Hornet Actual out."

Hatfield leaned back in his chair and looked over to Sloan and Molly who were sitting in conference to his right. "SITREP Sloan."

"Civilian side is reporting no casualties, no contact. Sensors pretty much back online after the surge from Erik's firecracker. Hangars are in good shape. Space defense artillery is still down, ETRO is about sixty minutes, rough estimate. Mil side took most of the damage. Broadway is being sealed internally so that we can pressurize some of the rooms nearest to it and get to work on sealing the tunnel. Sergeant Marin did some additional damage to the section of Broadway where they interdicted the ... creatures. Nothing significant, however there are intermittent power outages on sections twenty and twenty-one, the two modules closest to the surface of the moon. We've extracted those employees who were sheltered there and are working alternate power to the area so that life support systems don't suffer too greatly."

"Do your engineers have any idea how to extract our prisoner out of the floor?" he asked Sloan.

"Uh, no. They work mostly with pretty docile creatures. The worst they've had to deal with is a horny goat. We're trying to work something out now, but they're pretty stumped. In the meantime, I'm turning the large room we were detaining Von Tremel and Senator Hernandez in into a cage for your pet crab. I've got thirteen people working it, but every minute they're over there is another minute Broadway stays exposed to space."

"You can't repair Broadway without getting the crab out of there. So it is what it is."

He leaned back down to his radio, paused and looked back at Sloan. "What is the unit designator for the team exploiting the pods?"

"Uh, not sure we gave them one."

"Thought so." He keyed the communications unit and spoke into the receiver. "Surface security team, CIC please respond."

"Phoenix Twenty-Seven here."

"Send me a data dump on what you've discovered, and give me a status report on the hole in the base. Make sure it's encrypted."

"Copy, stand by for data dump. Hole is problematic. The weapon cut through fourteen meters of rock before hitting the module wall. All local electronics have been disrupted by either the alien weapon or the large detonation we observed near the alien craft. Whatever the weapon they used was, it cut through the metal like it wasn't even there, no jagged edges left, just a hole big enough that none of our meteorite patches can remotely cover it. I think we're going to need to make a plug for the metal, excavate a bit more of the lunar soil around the wall, and patch it that way, then backfill the area with additional lunar soil. It's never going to be as strong as before. Also, to rewire security throughout Broadway is not a short term activity."

Hatfield looked to Sloan, who confirmed what he was saying with a sad nod. "We can replace it all, but it will seriously deplete our spares. The problem is that Broadway goes through the center of the mil side, so we can't ignore it. That was the densest concentration of sensors and communication gear in the base, and most of it was vaporized. The pressure doors are a different matter and that alone will take our fab team most of a month to replace, if I had to take a guess at it," she explained.

Hatfield nodded and opened the battlenet connection again. "Secure the pods for study, keep them in the open space away from the hangars until we figure out if they're safe. I want a watch mounted at the hole with a communication repeater. Let me know if anything else tries to get in. Send the rest of your team down toward Sergeant Marin and link with him—take observations along Broadway as you go. Communication checks with CIC every five minutes. Hatfield out."

He turned and looked up at the big display, studying the projected paths of the alien ship and the intercept course being followed by *Atlas*. Jacobs was cutting it close, things could get pretty interesting if this didn't go according to plan. Another eighteen minutes and the ship would be too close to the base to risk exploding. The debris would pound it like a giant shotgun blast.

Molly followed his gaze and tried to decipher the main screen before she finally asked, "Are they going to be able to stop the ship from hitting us?"

Sloan shrugged and gestured with her helmet toward Hatfield, before looking back down at her console, digging through the reports as they poured in. Hatfield sat with his eyes focused up at the display, his armored fingers drumming the console in front of him.

"Maybe, if he gets a clean grab on the first try, I'd say he has a better than even chance. If he tries to grab it and the cable snaps or the ship masses more then we think it does he might get dragged down into Phoebe with the alien ship and the Marines we have aboard it."

Molly looked around in alarm. "What's the backup plan if the tug can't grab it?"

Hatfield sat in silence, his face a mask, for several long moments. "We might die."

"Drones have begun their approach, Captain," the drone control officer reported from his station. Jacobs gave a tight smile and acknowledged him while looking up at the mission clock. Intercept with the alien ship was in seven minutes. He scrolled through the menu on his command chair arm until he found the frequency for the QRF Marines, and cleared his throat before speaking.

"QRF Angels, this is *Atlas*. Drones are in flight. I have three cables spooling clean. We've got a load spar on the way to you now, is the ship ready to receive?"

"Copy you *Atlas*. Hold for a moment, we're just about ready."

Jacobs watched his display intently as the drones flew out toward the alien ship trailing cables, while the *Atlas* ponderously maneuvered its primary thrusters—when they fired again they could pull the alien ship away from Phoebe. He brought up a view of the derelict ship, watching as the two Angels attached to its side suddenly released their landing claws and boosted clear. He saw the Marines scattered along the top deck brace themselves, grabbing onto damaged ship components and each other.

"*Atlas*, twenty seconds from ... mark."

Jacobs squinted at the image of the ship, upping the magnification as much as he could. A sequence of flashes erupted in a circle pattern on the mostly undamaged portion of the ship. The camera defocused for a moment as the change in contrast saturated its filters, coming back to show a neat hole had been blown in the side of the ship.

"*Atlas*, Phoenix Seven. Looks like a successful cut. Sorry it took three tries, this ship is tough."

"No worries Seven." He cut the battlenet and looked down to his drone controller. "Alright, let's get the load spar in place, we're running out of time."

The controller nodded his head and told his drones to speed up. Two drones in the center of the formation, towing a long composite beam between them, put on a burst from their thrusters. As they got close, they changed direction, slowly reversing course until the tow wire was taut before they applied maximum thrust and slowed to less than three meters per second relative to the target.

A SARine clinging to the surface of the alien ship fired a grapple gun at the load spar, catching the beam near one end. The drones steadied the beam, helping him bring it in to the ship. Quickly, the SARine cast the drone's tow-line away from the beam and began to slide it into the alien ship through the battle-damaged hole they had first boarded through.

Jacobs pulled up Phoenix Seven's helmet feed and watched as they fed the beam through the hole and down one of the passageways that ran from side to side through the ship. He marveled at how fast they were operating, even in zero gravity. Their actions were swift and sure, with no wasted motion. The beam protruded out the new hole in the ship, and they steadied into place so that his remaining drones could attach the two main tow cables to the spar.

He typed a query into his console, bringing up the ship's history on similar tows in the past. This wasn't the first time they'd used the spar. Usually it was to control large rocks or mined minerals that had a uniform density. This ship could be another matter entirely given the ambiguity about where the center of gravity was, and if any parts of it might shift during the thrust. He scratched his chin thoughtfully and brought up the spar's tech specs.

The data scrolled passed until he paused it on the past performance page. They'd never used one of these beams at more than forty-five percent throttle. He licked his lips nervously and ran some simulations, looked at the results and frowned. He changed several assumptions and tried again getting a slightly better answer.

Reluctantly he keyed in the CIC battlenet. "CIC this is *Atlas*, main spar is in place and tow cables are being attached. Please review my numbers in the attached data file."

A long pause followed as Hatfield and his team went over the simulation he had sent. Jacobs rolled his shoulders inside his spacesuit, trying to get some of the tension out as he checked the *Atlas'* velocity and changing vectors. He looked at the exterior camera feed. Phoebe was getting very large.

"*Atlas*, we believe your simulations," Hatfield's voice came back. Jacobs could hear the stress underlying an otherwise calm statement. "You are authorized to use any thrust setting deemed necessary at the time you begin the tow. Best of luck. Hatfield out."

Jacobs acknowledged him and cut the battlenet. He sat there staring at the simulation result before swearing under his breath. He threw his stress ball at his first officer, who was head down in the corner staring at the drone feeds. The ball bounced silently off his armor and settled in the corner, the small KaliSun Corporation logo glowing in the dim light. The first officer walked over to him, looked at his screen, grunted noncommittally and walked back to his station.

Jacobs keyed the battlenet for the QRF and pulled in his ship-wide comm system as well. "QRF, *Atlas*."

"Go *Atlas*."

"We need to start our thrust earlier than planned."

"How much earlier? We've still got forty minutes to go."

Jacobs rubbed his forehead and grimaced before responding. "Every minute we delay starting thrust operations, we increase the amount of thrust we'll need to use in order to stop the combined mass of the ship and ourselves before we hit Phoebe. If we go per schedule, we'll be looking at eighty-seven percent thrust."

"So it sounds like you have a little bit of margin then," Phoenix Six responded with relief.

Jacobs and his first officer exchanged a look before he continued. "Negative Six. The most thrust we've ever used on a load spar was about forty-five percent or so."

"Confirm *Atlas*, did you say four-five percent?"

"Copy, four-five percent. If we go much above that, the spar may delaminate. Once that happens beyond a certain point, it's likely to fail. Spectacularly." Jacobs closed his eyes and ground his teeth before finishing. "Sorry."

"Standby *Atlas*," Phoenix Six said briskly.

Jacobs transferred his calculations to the main screen. In the one corner was a clock counting down to the originally scheduled ready point. Below that was a steadily increasing thrust profile showing rates of fuel expenditure. He ran the calculation again, comparing his expected fuel mass against his remaining fuel and frowned. Before he could say anything Phoenix Six was back.

"*Atlas*, we can get you twenty-four minutes back on your schedule. Be advised, we won't be evacuating the QRF from the ship during the maneuver as planned. Six out."

Jacobs stared down at his console and accepted Six's report. They were taking a terrible risk. If the spar broke they would have nowhere to hide from the shrapnel, and there was no way to execute a rescue either, just a short ride down to the surface of Phoebe. He rubbed his nose in irritation as he felt the sting of a tear forming in one of his eyes.

"Mike, when was the last time we detached the auxiliary fuel pod from the ship?"

The first officer looked up from his screens with a thoughtful expression on his face. "It's been a while. Probably back when we were practicing taking them off, so about three years ago now? Why?"

"Could you detach the pod and have an Angel tow it away from us? In fifteen minutes?"

"We might damage it a bit, I mean, it's meant to be a short procedure, but other than routine checks we haven't looked at any of the gear in months. Maybe even a year."

"Grab whoever isn't working the tow and get to work on it. I'm going to transfer as much fuel as I can into the pod. Maybe we can cut our mass enough to buy us some margin. If I'm right, it buys us almost six percent less thrust if we cut our onboard fuel down to five percent over the predicted fuel requirement."

"You'll be almost bone dry at the end of the maneuver sir. I mean, I see your point, but what if it takes more thrust than you want to use? You'll burn through that margin in an instant. Not to mention, we'll be almost helpless at the end, no fuel left to thrust, just dead in space tied to that derelict," Mike said.

"I'm going to have the Angels remove it and then match velocities with us. The moment we get the derelict stabilized, I'll direct them to reattach the tank. Hopefully we won't get any surprises."

The first officer nodded and started through the hatch but paused and looked back at him. "Sir, *hope* has never been my favorite plan."

"There is no motivation like a ticking clock. We need to act decisively, even if it's not the best solution."

"Hornet 2-1, status report," Jasper Wilcox's voice rasped over the squadron battlenet.

"Hornet Actual, we have spotted several objects that we

believe are from the ship. They are on non-ballistic trajectories approaching the base from the far side."

"The far side? How is that possible, if they blew out from the ship shouldn't they be heading away from the base by now?" Wilcox asked, perplexed.

"I know Actual, but I have two objects, heading in from the far side of the base. My support Angel's sensors show two pancake shaped objects, in formation, heading toward the civ side. Maybe they've already orbited Phoebe and are coming back around. That could explain the trajectory."

"Whatever they are, engage them. Take a wingman down and gun them. Leave the rest of your section protecting your Angel."

"Copy that Actual. Rolling in now."

The pair of starfighters gracefully rolled in unison and headed down toward the base crater, leaving the support Angel to fly high above the base and maintain direct observation. As they leveled out two hundred meters above the crater floor, the Angel relayed a sensor picture of the unknown objects' location. The section leader made a small course correction as they flew over the line of hangars strung across the crater.

"Keep it tight 2-2, not sure what these things are, but let's be careful. High-speed head to head pass. You take the right target, I'll take the left."

"Copy 2-1," she replied, nudging in closer to her section leader. They passed over the tram line and the newly installed anti-meteor artillery as they approached the far wall. The target pips showed directly over the rim of the wall, heading on a beeline for the Promenade.

"Here we go."

They pushed up over the edge of the rim wall and opened fire. Glowing explosive rounds leapt from the guns of the Mongoose, tracking the incoming targets. Abruptly, the objects began moving, shifting away from each other as they tried to become a more difficult target. The object on the right exploded as 2-1's wingman found her target and drilled it with several rounds, a cloud of mist forming as the liquids crystallized into ice. The second object opened fire on 2-1 with an energy weapon of some sort.

For a split second he stared in confusion at the oncoming orbs of blue-violet energy, before his wingman's shouted warning penetrated through the fog and he jerked his control sticks into a climb. The hesitation cost him, the balls of energy tracking right through his path. With a jolt, his top tine was hit before he could twist out of the way. He watched in horror through the cockpit window as the energy wrapped itself around the tine and seemed to cling to it like St. Elmo's fire.

Before his eyes, the very fabric of the Mongoose seemed to break down and flake away. He shook the sticks, trying to dislodge the energy clinging to his ship, its tendrils crawling along the surface. As the maneuvering thrusters in the damaged tine fired, the force applied to the Mongoose's structure proved too much and it broke at the point of impact, leaving a trail of wire and a cloud of radar absorbent material in its wake.

With his maneuvering crippled and short a gun, Hornet 2-1 punched his throttle to max and tried to head back to the base. He lined up with the hangars using his lateral thrusters to zig-zag while the alien shot lines of energy at him. Some of the shots went into space but others impacted segments of the civilian side, crawling along the structures and damaging them in a spectacular light display.

"2-2, get this thing off me!"

"Trying! Every time I start to get lined up he flips around and shoots at me too."

Hornet 2-1 swore under his breath, looking at the growing number of indicators that were shifting from green to orange. "Hornet Actual, I am experiencing system failures, I'm RTB-ing. Hornet 2-3 and 2-4 engage that son of a bitch!"

He reached a gloved hand up and slapped the RTB button on the console. The Mongoose shuddered and then began a graceful descent to the emergency recover hangar. Grimly he gripped the ejection levers. If he got hit again, he'd probably have to bail, assuming it didn't kill him instantly.

Hornet 2-2 maneuvered behind the remaining alien as it continued toward the Promenade. Her rounds raced through the vacuum around the alien as it jinked back and forth, but she was having no luck hitting it. Her attack was limited by the real fear of hitting the civilian side of the base, and her time to intercept was running out. Soon it would be among the buildings.

The Director's voice came over the battlenet. "2-2 stop worrying about hitting the base and down that son of a bitch."

"Copy CIC," she said as she pulled a murderous turn back toward the alien, stacking up so many Gs that her compensator was overridden, pulling her face into a grim death mask. The alien spun back toward her, firing a pattern of energy orbs in an attempt to bracket her in as she moved in closer for a kill shot. The rate of fire from the alien was intense, and she ducked back and forth in a violent replay of her training on the asteroid course. She fired short bursts at the alien, trying to box it in, but it continued to duck her rounds with intense bursts of gas from its rear area, almost letting the rounds get to it before scooting to the side to avoid them.

She was less than two hundred meters away and closing fast, her gun magazines almost dry, when the creature exploded violently in front of her. She flew through the debris flinching as rapidly hardening blue goop spattered her cockpit windows.

"Splash target," the anti-meteor artillery commander said over the battlenet. "Sorry for the delay, we just got the targeting computer for the 155s back up a moment ago. Don't think it ever saw that coming."

"Hornet two section, locate remains of enemy assets and await a SARine unit to collect them. Hornet 2-2 you are

Section Lead now," Wilcox's voice came over the battlenet. "Nice shooting flak battery."

"Yeah, it was an agile little shit. But it kept repeating the same pattern. Let her rounds almost get to it, then scoot to the one side. So we just aimed for the empty space and timed her shots. Still, the damn thing was a menace."

Hornet 2-2 breathed out a heavy sigh of relief that fogged up her helmet. Looking at the weapons display in her HUD, she saw she only had twenty-seven rounds left. She bit her lip, anticipating that her future would be full of gunnery simulator time.

⸻⸻⸺

"What is he doing?" Molly demanded as she watched the fuel pod detach from the ship, pulled away by an Angel on the main display.

"Rolling the dice," Hatfield said softly.

"What do you mean? The display says that's his fuel supply, how does that help us?"

"He's lightening the load, less mass means he can try to finesse the tow more."

"Is it going to work?"

"It might. We'll know shortly."

"Might? Might! He didn't even ask permission!"

"He is the Captain of his ship, he doesn't need to ask my permission Ms. Caan. I think you'll find that people are quite capable of success without being micro-managed. I ordered him to stop that ship from crashing into the base. For men like Jacobs, that's all I need to say." Hatfield paused, pursing his lips before a sly smile crept across them and he sent a nod in Sloan's direction. "Men and women I should say."

Sloan smirked and rapped her knuckles against her helmet before leaning into her displays again, compiling damage reports and organizing the repair effort.

"And what will you do if he fails?"

"Depends on how badly he fails. We can probably survive a low velocity impact. We've taken rocks before, granted, nothing that massive."

"And a high velocity impact?" Molly asked with a tremble.

"We'll probably die." He paused pensively. "Actually we'll very likely die if that thing's power core goes up."

"Shouldn't we evacuate? We have to get somewhere safe."

"I'm afraid there is nowhere to run. This is space. Even if you avoided the impact you would die later. If that thing lands, it will take out most of the power reactors in the base. Stay here and die mercifully or run away to die in a few hours when your suit fails." He sent a sideways glance at her patiently. "Those are your choices. Life isn't fair."

"What about Sasha's cave? We could still make it there!"

Hatfield sent her an angry glance. Sloan reached over and gripped her arm, shaking her head no at Molly. Molly unsuccessfully tried to shake loose before leaning in toward her to whisper urgently.

"It could be our only chance to survive!"

"This is not the time or the place for this. Remember your role and stop disrupting the crew!" Sloan hissed back at her. "They need to focus right now, they know they can't leave and you talking about running away and leaving them to their fate is disruptive. Now grow a damn spine!"

Molly shrank away from Sloan, uncomfortable with the change from a lighthearted mood to quiet viciousness, and aware that she had just spoken of a place she had been sworn to secrecy about. She looked around the room, most of the staff was ignoring the byplay going on behind them as they helped *Atlas*'s crew get ready for the first thrust. She opened her mouth to speak, beads of sweat coating her face, but one look at Hatfield caused the words to die on her lips.

"Director, they're ten seconds from first thrust. Marines have taken shelter in the bow and are braced," Higgins reported from her sensor console.

"In the bow . . . " Hatfield muttered, as he realized the Marines had chosen to head to the place closest to the point of impact. He reached down and pushed the command battlenet out to all of the Marines and Brenner, letting them know what was coming.

"Engines lit. Jacobs has ramped it up to thirty percent thrust already, no reports of engine ringing yet," Higgins said. "Velocity already slowing. We're detecting a number of objects breaking free of the derelict and continuing toward Phoebe."

"Anything of any significant size?" Sloan asked.

"Few pieces of hull material, some small debris from the hull, some things I can't identify. Nothing of any significant mass."

"Marine surface force, if we stop the ship, send a three man fire team over to assess the debris. I want to make sure nothing, not a creature or bot, used the braking maneuver to land on Phoebe," Hatfield said as a tremor ran through the floor. He turned from his station to glare down at Higgins. "What was that?"

"One of the Wasp Mongoose just hit the moon trying to RTB. Pilot ejected. He was disabled during the special weapon discharge."

Hatfield sighed and looked back at the main display as *Atlas* continued to strain back on the tow cables hooking her to the derelict. The ship was getting very big on the view screen. Soon the exhaust from *Atlas* would be stirring the moon dust above them.

"Graves reports all disabled birds have been stabilized. One minor casualty to report—one of the Rooks got a concussion when his gravity compensator surged. He's shepherding them in now as a group. ETA about thirty-five minutes. They're going to try to fit them all in the recovery hangar," Brenner reported over the battlenet.

"How is your capture effort on the creature going?" Hatfield responded.

"You ever try to band a bull's balls after somebody poked it with a cattle prod? Like that."

"Band a bull's balls?" Molly asked, confused.

"Old school way of castrating a bull, they put a big rubber band over the nutsack. Cuts off the circulation . . . few days later it falls off," Sloan said out of the corner of her mouth.

"Where do you come up with this stuff?" Molly asked with a disturbed look on her face.

"Brenner loves his metaphors. Although, it might not have been a metaphor, maybe he found the thing's balls and he's trying to pacify it."

Molly visibly gulped and tugged at her space suit collar. "That creature should be treated with dignity and respect, I hope you wouldn't do that . . . to them."

Sloan stopped typing and looked at her quizzically. Noting the green pallor over her face she rolled her eyes. "Trust me, the last thing he's trying to do is figure out the sex of that thing. I'm not promising his efforts will be humane, but I'm betting he's focused on other things."

"Speaking of staying focused," Hatfield said sternly, trying to get things back on track. "Higgins, status of the *Atlas*."

"She's almost to the max thrust they planned in their profile, the spar has deflected almost half a meter at this point. Jacobs said they were worried about thrusting hard right now because sudden changes in force might splinter it. Assuming the spar doesn't break, in three minutes they should have it stopped."

Molly let out a gusty sigh of relief and leaned back in her chair, smiling over at Sloan until she saw the look on her face.

"What?"

"Hmm? Oh, the predicted impact time was two minutes and fifty seven seconds before. I'm just hoping they aren't stopping it with Phoebe," Sloan said, staring at her screen and redoing her calculations.

"What?"

"Ah found it. I assumed gravity was constant for the entire time. Well I assumed it would be Phoebe's gravity, but for part of the timeline, Saturn's gravity exerts more force than Phoebe. Just a minor error, I'm sure we'll be fine. Jacob's knows what he's about!"

Molly looked at her fearfully before bending her head and saying a prayer, her words lost to the chatter coming up from the crew consoles. The mated ships closed with Phoebe on the main display until the trajectory track and the surface of the moon were indistinguishable from each other. Crew members turned away from the screen, looking at each other and up toward the ceiling with fear-tinged resignation.

Then it was over, the *Atlas* hovered above the alien ship, pulling lightly on its tow lines to keep Phoebe's gravity from slowly bringing the ship in for a rough landing. The Angels were towing the fuel pod back and the derelict hung like a wounded buzzard over the base. As they zoomed in on the scene, one of the SARines could be seen poking his head out of a hole in the side of the craft to look down at Phoebe.

"And that, Ms. Caan, is why you let people do their jobs," Hatfield said softly.

CHAPTER 11

Sir, we just got a flash update from Saturn Base. It's double encrypted and requires your personal approval to access the decryption algorithm," Will Forsythe's aide reported.

Forsythe glanced over at the CEO of the KaliSun Corporation and tapped a command into the console, covering one hand with the other as he did so. A small keypad slid out of the desk, the numbered keys randomizing as it came to rest. He punched in a code and hit enter. The pad beeped and reshuffled the keys again, prompting him for his password once more. He punched it in carefully and hit enter. A small slot appeared in the console, into which he inserted the message stick. After a series of beeps it prompted him to remove the stick and displayed the message on a small reader. Stokes leaned over and read with him in silence.

"*Will. Encountered two type four entities. Hostilities commenced, currently we own the hill. Unknown origin. Second entity did not engage. Suffered casualties; minor. Tech level eight. We had to pop a firecracker to knock them off the mountain. More to follow. They can chameleon. John, out.*"

"Let's move to the secure room," Will said, clearing his screens and locking them down. He hastily left the command deck and entered one of the intelligence analysis cells off to the side.

"We need the room. Clear out for twenty," he said to the intel analysts inside. They looked up and filed out wordlessly as two of the most powerful men in the company walked in and took a seat.

"Before John left to head out to Saturn Base we developed codes for conversing between us. The idea was that we would use one code, then when I got the information to you, we'd use a second code. That way even if his encryption was compromised, they would still have to break the codes we used to communicate within the message."

"A reasonable precaution, although it would have been nice if you'd let us in on it," Ed said with a smile.

"The more people who knew, the more chance there was for an OPSEC failure. It was necessary."

"Don't worry, I agree. So what does the code he used mean?"

Forsythe took a deep breath and furrowed his brow. "Hopefully not what I think it does. We have four entities. American, Chinese, Russian and well, alien, in that order. He said he saw two type four entities. That means two different alien things, either ships or somethings. That also presumes that he can tell they're not the same."

Stokes leaned back into his chair and stretched. "Aliens. They fought aliens."

"Well it sounds like they fought one of the two and were victorious." Forsythe rubbed his hands down his pant legs nervously. "That's what 'we own the mountain' means. King of the hill. But let's assume, if they don't know where they came from, they most certainly didn't come from Saturn. Which means that anything they fought could be just the beginning."

Stokes took a deep breath and carefully considered his words. "We haven't seen any aliens to date, correct?"

"Just a few things that might be microbes and those mushroom looking things on Titan that ingest the nasty stuff in the atmosphere and releases heat and trace gases. We're not even sure if that's not just a weird chemical reaction, it has no visible cell structure."

"The tech eight stuff, what was that about?"

"We needed a way to assess an opponent's tech. So we created a scale. We are five. Below us is less capable, above five is more capable. Eight would be very challenging. Better weapons, defense, troops, it really could mean a lot of different things. The fact he said they had to blow a firecracker should mean he used a nuke. But we didn't see any radiation equivalent to the nukes he has. So unless he's been making his own very clean nukes, it's something else..." Forsythe looked at Ed expectantly.

"The signature of the explosion matches a large version of what could happen when a lot of the gravity particles that run that ship's engines interact. High energy output and gravity fluctuations..."

"Honestly Ed, do you think he weaponized the fuel for that space ship?"

"Yes, it sure looks like it."

"Did you authorize it?"

"No, he was restricted from making weapons of mass destruction," Ed said carefully.

"I think whatever they popped off qualifies."

"Agreed, but not much we can do about it. We gave him that order specifically because we were afraid of a situation where he has serious weaponry we can't fight against. It didn't specifically say nuclear weapons, but that was to prevent him from making chem and bio weapons, not whatever that is." Stokes gestured vaguely in the direction of Saturn. "If I had to guess at how he'd justify this, it's probably a mining device or something for breaking up asteroids."

"Either way, it effectively means he's a nuclear power. If he keeps blowing those up, we're going to have a lot of explaining to do."

"The arrival of aliens should make that a moot point." Stokes paused, glancing around the room as though he was checking to make sure they were alone. He leaned closer to Forsythe and spoke softly. "Hatfield likes his secrets. If he decided to use one of those, it's because he had very little choice. It's possible he was about to lose. If I had to guess, that warhead was designed to one-shot an incoming freighter if it turned out he didn't like the cargo. I'm not sure he'll have a lot of them if that's the case. It could have been his only hole card, so we need to think about what happens in that case and plan accordingly."

"What do you have in mind?"

"Well, if the aliens came in one ship they will be expected to report. If they don't come back, we can expect more company. If more than one ship came, he might not have detected them all. There are a lot of blind spots in the Saturn system where our sensor coverage is very low. He also referenced a chameleon function, which makes me think it can cloak. Either way, we need to deal with the fact we may have additional contact with a hostile force he had to defeat with a nuke. Something I might add doesn't seem to have disintegrated that ship we could see them trying to hump with the tug."

"We have a very small nuclear arsenal here. Ten warheads, twenty deployment systems, all designed for use by the Angels. So we're limited. Not to mention, a NUDET right above the base could be more damaging then the attack itself. I have a fair bit of heavy artillery stashed and the space forces, but we were expecting small combat, not interstellar nuclear war," Forsythe said. "More importantly, we have to deal with the Chinese, who despite the best efforts of the space forces have been gradually encroaching on us."

"Yes, the Chinese. I think it's time we did a recon in force. You said the Chinese were encroaching?"

"Yeah in sector 91, they snuck a firebase in and have set up a pretty intense defensive fire grid. We can't get standoff weapons through their point defenses and we can't use vertical lift in there. So basically the only way in is on foot or rover. The base is set up on a low ridge with a crater in front of it. Coverage in all directions, but there is an area under the ridgeline they can't get line of sight to fire on. The problem is getting close enough to do anything about it. It's a long way across open terrain before you're under the line of site for their guns and they could still get at you if they stepped outside."

"So we run a polar recon with some Angels at the same time you hit the Chinese base with a ground assault. Tell the ground commander to focus on minimal casualties and make it very loud once it goes, we want them focused on the ground pounders. When we get a picture of the Chinese Base structure... well we'll be better off than we are now. I just don't want to lose too many assets for a bunch of pictures."

Forsythe sighed in resigned tone. "I'll have Colonel Davis and Captain Spears work something up. These polar recon missions are high risk. They have to get high enough up to do their sweep but then they're sitting in the crosshairs of every anti-sat system the Chinese have."

"Better put some sharp knives on it then. We need to know what the Chinese have so we can tell the difference between them and whatever this alien threat ends up being."

"Do we warn Earth about the aliens?" asked Forsythe quietly.

"Warn who? Right now most of the big players are so disorganized they can't keep their own people from rioting. If we tell them, somebody will leak it and the panic will get worse. We need to tell them, but we have to find somebody with their emotions under control or else they might start slinging nukes at every Angel that buzzes Earth without telling them."

Forsythe turned to look at the map of the moon on the wall display and studied the disposition of the enemy positions arrayed before them. Significant blank spots covered much of the map, with low confidence appraisals scattered everywhere else. He took a breath as he turned to leave.

"It's going to take two passes to hit everything. We'll get it done. I can't promise there won't be losses."

"It's war," Stokes said simply as they walked out of the room.

Captain Jamie Wilks slammed down the launch tube and out into space. Calmly he reached down and took over from the computer, beginning a lazy spiraling climb to a higher orbit. Checking his blue-force tracker, he confirmed the rest of his section had cleared the launch tubes cleanly and was ascending with him toward the rendezvous point.

With Talon Squadron effectively still out commission after the first Chinese attack on the MBTC, and the new Wing Commander leading the attack on a new Chinese forward operating base, the Badger Squadron had been assigned combat space patrol over the base. Well most of it anyway. Wilks led his section over to the waiting Angels and support refueler on a mission of their own. Normally he would be the squadron leader of the Badgers, but early this morning he had been assigned a new task, one that would take careful timing and precision to pull off.

He approached the refueling ship, flipping his Mongoose along its back in the process, exposing the refueling port in the belly to the probe extending toward him. With a jarring thud the two ships were mated and he topped off his fuel reserve. They were going to need every flake of fuel to pull this mission off, and even the limited amount they had burned during the launch and escape from the Moon's gravity was too much to spare.

He pulled away from the ship gently, using only the maneuvering thrusters located in the three weapons tines that extended beyond his cockpit. As he cleared the ship, he pulsed the main thrusters slightly and slid into formation with two nearby Angels, their wings full of recon pods instead of weapons, the top turret removed for additional optical equipment.

"Oracle Lead, this is Tick, refueling complete. Forming up now," Wilks said softly over the point-to-point laser communication system.

"Copy Tick. We're good to go, waiting for the mission timeline to kick off and we'll head downrange."

Wilks pursed his lips and looked down at the MBTC, nearly a hundred kilometers below. If he stared long enough, he thought, he could catch glimpses of the rest of his squadron doing an endless orbit over the base. The base seemed so large at ground level, but from his current vantage point it looked like a few specs of sand in the vast sea of grays and blacks that was the Earth's Moon. The rest of his section had completed tanking off the support ship, and it flashed its running lights and peeled away, heading to its secondary staging location. If things went well, they'd tank once more as they came around for a second orbit. If they made it through the first time, Wilks thought grimly. He checked his tracker and saw that the rest of the section had joined the formation smoothly. These were his best pilots; light hands on the throttle, steady nerves and experience in both space and air combat.

"Ticks, this is Tick actual. Remember to snuggle in close on this flight and keep your nose pointed at any search radars that try to find us. Oracle flight will be spotting for us, but we're trying to minimize active jamming, so we'll need to keep the RCS as low as possible. Commence final system check and hold thrust until the timeline starts. Good luck." Wilks began his own preflight check.

No missiles this flight, just chaff pods, flare dispensers and a short range soft kill pod that was supposedly good enough to down incoming anti-sat missiles well short of them. He didn't recall seeing any record it had been tested.

It was a simple enough mission—wait for the ground strike to start, thrust hard for the first twenty minutes to get some velocity, then go cold and let gravity pull them around the moon. The recon Angels would record as much data and imagery as possible, only lighting their thrusters again if they got spotted. After that, all they had to do was try to make it home without running out of fuel. A simple plan but complicated in execution. If they managed to pull it off, they'd refuel from the tanker and make a second pass over a different area.

"Probably better than flying the CSP all day anyway," he mumbled to himself. He just hoped his under-strength squadron didn't get jumped while he was gone.

Captain Mike Spears looked out over his assembled men and women and smiled inside his helmet. As Commander of the 3rd Company First Space Marines, he was the primary offensive commander in the KaliSun Corporation. The other four companies at the MBTC had important duties, but were primarily focused on defense of the base. For this mission, his company of one hundred and twenty Marines was supplemented by a scout unit with their fast rovers, a pair of mobile artillery units from 1st Company and SARines along to exploit any intel they could find at the site.

He smiled confidently at his XO standing nearby, even though it was doubtful she could see him in the shadow of the crater wall. This would be their seventh major operation in the short weeks since the war had started. So far they hadn't lost a single Marine to enemy fire. A combination of superior equipment, surprise, and local force superiority had allowed them to smash organized resistance before the Chinese could mount a credible defense. His smile faded as he pulled up the layout of the enemy base on his HUD. This time was likely to be very different.

The Chinese had perched their command module on the lip of a crater overlooking the area in front of them in a perfect enfilade position. Anyone charging through the crater would be eating radar controlled weapons fire the entire time. Any approach along the top of the crater rim would be picked up by a sensor net that enabled them to see approaching Kalisun rovers dozens of kilometers away.

It was a problem straight out of the training they had received at Saturn Base when training in the Pit, except this crater was a lot larger and wasn't shooting targeting lasers. They were sitting behind a collapsed wall in the crater, waiting for everything to be in place before they ran the gauntlet through the crater. He glanced over at the SARine leader, Chief Morris, and pulled him into his battlenet.

"How's it lookin'?"

"Should work, provided they didn't seed the crater floor with mines," the SARine said quietly.

"Nobody has used minefields yet on the Moon, not sure why they would here," Spears said thoughtfully.

"Nobody has seen one of these firebases fully operational before either, Captain. Usually the pilots dust them before they're set up. I can't promise they won't have mines, then again with the amount of fire they intend to dump into the crater if anything is detected, I'd be surprised if their own mine field didn't get wacked in the process."

Spears thought for a few heartbeats and nodded. "Let's go then. We'll start the timeline when you initiate the decoys."

"Yes sir!" the SARine said with a tinge of excitement as he took bounding leaps over to the waiting scout rovers, raising his clenched fist above his head as he went.

The waiting scout troopers looked up and eagerly jumped into their vehicles, lunar versions of special forces dune buggies from the Earth Wars. Spears watched his blue-force tracker display suddenly come alive as the rovers came online. A predatory grin crept across his face; this was much better than the first time they hit the Chinese when he couldn't even talk to his detached units due to all of the ambient radiation.

The rovers lined up on the edge of the wall debris and paused, like greyhounds waiting for the mechanical rabbit to race out in front of them. Each one had three scout Marines in it, a special group chosen more for their ability to handle the nauseating high speed transits across the moon's surface while still accurately shooting their weapons than they were for their technical skills.

Convinced they were good to go, he licked his lips and entered into the support Angel's battlenet. "Hemingway."

"For Whom the Bell Tolls."

He muted his connection, mumbling under his breath, "Here we go . . . "

Commander Zhao looked up from his report at the urgent sound in his subordinate's voice. He stood from his desk and strode across the cramped space of the command module.

"Yes?"

"We picked up a single exchange from the Americans."

"Was it encrypted?"

"Yes, using one of the codes we got from the Intelligence Directorate."

Zhao smiled to himself, careful not to let his subordinate see that he was pleased. For months now, the Intelligence Directorate had been promising that they would crack the American Government systems again and scrape some useful information to use against the corporate war criminals. For the first few weeks their lack of success was understandable; half the infrastructure between them and the United States was damaged in the strange radiation event, and the groups they were targeting didn't seem to know what was going on any better the Directorate did. That lack of knowledge had come at a terrible price when they had launched what should have been a successful attack against the enemy moon base.

Instead of rooting them out of their underground caves and venting them into space, their space forces had been pushed back with serious losses. Fortunately, Senior Command on the moon had had the sense to hold back with the initial attack. He clenched his fist at the memory, causing the nearby officers to avert their eyes. But now, the Directorate had finally come through.

"The enemy will attack soon. Ready our defenses and get the reserve mobilized," he said with a fierce glare. They had known putting a base this close to the Americans would be intolerable, and knew they couldn't resist attacking.

He walked back to his command chair and sat down, pulling up a video display of their reserve. A full company of their best space defense troops was scrambling to get suited up and ready. When these company men tried to swoop in with their fighters, his men would be ready to light up the skies with chemical lasers, missiles and exploding flak. He smiled secretly, patting the locked box to his right. Yes and if they were starting to get overwhelmed, he could always detonate the nuclear weapon sitting just under the surface.

The EMP alone would be enough to destroy most of the enemy spacecraft in one fell swoop. One way or another, the balance of power was about to shift in their favor.

"Sir, we're detecting incoming missiles come from sector 12!"

"No jamming? Initiate point defense system."

"No jamming detected. Point defense system is tracking and will engage in moments."

He leaned back in his chair to wait, watching the displays on his console. There was something strange about what was going on, nothing specifically out of place, just a sinking feeling in the pit of his stomach.

"Are any ground troops visible?"

"No commander, no troops, no spacecraft . . . wait, SIR!" the sensors officer screeched while pointing up at his display.

The missiles split into dozens of objects just as they entered weapon range. As they watched, some of the objects seemed to spawn more objects from progressively smaller packages, like a Russian nesting doll. The sensors chugged as the number of targets to shoot at increased exponentially.

The sensors officer looked down at his display in horror. The sensors were being blocked by a wall of debris and they had no idea what was following behind. With a roar more felt than heard, the point defense weapons started firing, spraying tracers and exploding rounds into the oncoming debris field in a light display to rival any in history.

Zhao leaned into his microphone, screaming for his reserve space defense unit to deploy and engage anything hiding in the debris. Collision alarms began to sound as the sensors intermittently picked up heavier objects among all the chaff, flares and decoys.

Zhao swore viciously and ordered the manned turrets to fire through the chaff. Whatever was trying to sneak in behind this wall of junk wasn't going to see his outgoing fire any better than he could see them.

⟫

Henry Adler saw the missiles streak overhead and tightened his hands on his weapon grips. The waiting was the hardest part, the missiles had to travel almost four more kilometers before they reached what was presumed to be the edge of the enemy engagement volumes. If his scout unit left the jump-off point too soon, they'd be visible before the chaff bomb exploded and the enemy would have time to react. Leave it too late and the chaff and other debris would have arrived at its destination and their cover would be gone before they could get close enough to drop their package and escape.

Looking to his left he saw the loaned artillery units and two armadillos waiting to engage the enemy. He chuckled—the armadillos were the complete opposite of his nimble little rover platoon. Heavily armored and packing several star-fighter gun systems on top, they were intended to supply heavier weapons fire in support of the infantry.

The designers had struggled with how to make them move effectively over rough terrain. So after a few different aborted designs they had come up with the armadillo concept, a heavily armored shell that could use pistons in legs to leap along the ground like a scared armadillo. He'd heard that riding in one when it was at high speed was a full contact sport.

The countdown approached zero on his HUD. Finally, after five days of sneaking up on this position through the stark lunarscape, they were ready to go. As the counter ticked to zero he flashed his beacon strobe once. As a group, the scout rovers leapt up over the lip of the collapsed wall, soaring through the vacuum before bouncing down on the surface. After that it was a race. Individual rovers left to follow the best path available to them, bouncing and skidding across the surface in a flash of dust and rock.

He risked a glance upward at the decoys heading toward the base; enemy anti-space artillery was spraying out in continuous streams of light at the oncoming mass of debris. Occasional flashes erupted within the cloud when larger objects were obliterated, but the cloud continued on. He looked along the rim of the crater and upped the magnification on his HUD. To his amazement he saw that the entire crater rim was crawling with Chinese, far more than they had been expecting, all of them firing weapons at the incoming debris. It wouldn't take much for one of them to look down into the crater rim and see the rovers ducking in and out of the pocketed crater floor; their shifting optical camouflage was good, but there was no disguising the dust they were stirring up.

He shifted his gaze toward the nearer point defense weapons as his body was jarred by the constant shifting acceleration of his driver. The barrels of the guns were glowing white hot from the constant fire. He shook his head. They must have just turned the system on full automatic and let it blaze away.

His drivers were experts at traversing the lunar surface and veterans of the first battle of the MBTC, and they quickly covered the eight kilometers to the crater wall under the Chinese base. With a rough retro-thrust they stopped at intervals along the sharp crater edge, dust settling slowing around them in the low lunar gravity. Along the line of scouts, the gunners hopped out and sprinted toward the crater wall, dragging bags of explosive shape charges behind them. The drivers climbed into the gunnery position and manned the turrets covering the crater rim expectantly.

He listened as the rasping breath of his men came over the battlenet. They worked feverishly to boost themselves up the nearly shear face of the crater wall, attaching themselves to the wall as they strung the charges up in rows.

The explosives were custom made by the SARines using lessons learned from mining on the moon. The result was strange explosion that happened in two parts—a sharp, explosive pulse into the rock, followed an instant later by a longer pulse explosion. In mining tests, the result had been a deep-penetrating shaped charge that could carve off large chunks of a crater wall to get at the material within.

Nervously, the commander looked up at the precipice, noticing for the first time that shell casings were cascading in slow motion down the cliff face. His face softened—it was really beautiful. The streaking tracers reflected off the shiny brass as it tumbled through the low gravity like a star field against the dark gray of the cliff face. He shook off the reverie as his men and women began to descend the cliff face, using their boot jets to kill their velocity before they got to the bottom.

Pulling up the objective menu on his HUD, he scanned through making sure that everyone's package came back green. He felt his driver drop down out of the top turret and get resettled in his seat as the gunner sprinted back. As soon as the driver's HUD showed the gunner's ass in the seat and strapped in, he hammered the throttle and left without waiting for the commander to say anything.

"Enemy rovers retreating through the crater!" shouted the sensor technician over the warbling alarms.

For an instant Commander Zhao hesitated before screaming back, "Retreating from where?"

The sensor tech turned around, fear crowding his eyes. "The crater rim..."

As Zhao sat staring at the display the entire base was rocked by a series of sharp explosions, followed by a low rumbling vibration that he could feel through his suit at the base of his spine. He looked across the exterior video feeds, searching for clues as to what happened. One of the feeds showed several of the space defense soldiers drop their rocket launchers and look down fearfully at their feet. Seemingly in slow motion they turned to run back toward the module. As they ran the lunar dust behind them spurted up, obscuring for a moment the fact that the face of the cliff was gradually falling away behind them.

Zhao stared in horror as they ran toward the camera's location. They passed an automated mini-gun that fell away behind them, the power and ammunition systems ripping up out of their mountings and breaking free. One of the power cables snapped and whipped through the vacuum, silently arcing out and electrocuting soldiers as it passed, before plowing through a cluster of men operating a crew-served weapon. With a flash, the high voltage sparked off the remaining rounds in their weapon, throwing parts of soldier, weapon and space suit across the lunar surface.

The ground continued to give way, racing past the outer edges of the command module as the entire hillside slid down into the crater. With an agonizing screech heard throughout the module, connections to other supporting structures and gun emplacements were ripped from the command module's walls as it slowly succumbed to the inevitable and rode the collapsing crater wall down into the pit below. The automated defense systems blinked out as the control function failed, darkening the sky again as the steady stream of trace fire ended.

As the module crashed toward the bottom of the crater, the debris field cascaded down behind them, showering the module with a fine mist of fiber, ash and metal. Before the billowing dust of the collapsing wall obscured his sensors completely, Zhao saw a much larger enemy ground force approaching, racing toward the escaping scout rovers, weapons tracking the module. He slammed the send button on his communication console once, sending a final call for help back to the main base. Gripping the armrests of his chair he tilted his head back to emit an angry scream as the front of the command module slammed into the crater floor and tipped forward, landing on its top.

A victory cry echoed through the battlenet as they watched the command module slam into the crater floor and flip over. A cascade of space-suited soldiers tumbled down the slope behind it, bouncing awkwardly off the sharp shards of rock left after the explosion.

Captain Spears held on for dear life as the APC's optical scope showed him a stabilized image of the results of their attack. Reaching up, he braced hand against the ceiling, careful not to hit any of the switches, and stared at the command module. Dust obscured his view, so he pinged it with a radar pulse.

A smile crept across his face and he beat the SARine's shoulder pauldron in the seat ahead of him twice in celebration.

"It's like a fucking turtle on its back!" he said over the command battlenet.

"Yes sir. Still have to kill it though."

"You have no faith!" Captain Spears teased before considering the statement. "Should we prep it, or do you want as much intact as possible before we get there for your intel exploit?"

"Better prep it, there were a lot more guys there than intel expected."

Captain Spears nodded and spoke with excitement into the battlenet. "Execute fire mission two-alpha!"

"Copy Captain. Two-alpha outbound!"

Spears watched the blue-force tracker in the corner of his HUD intently. The system detected his gaze and blew the image up to cover much of his helmet view, just in time for him to see a swarm of blue dots zip out of the rear area as the artillery commander fired the equivalent of a modified rocket artillery at the downed module.

The rockets zipped toward the module, exploding overhead and raining down a curtain of copper explosives on the enemy troops. The impact was devastating, dazed soldiers maimed in a violent buzz-saw of flying metal and rock. Blood and gore mixed with the dust, falling to the lunar surface in puffs of dust. The module itself was bombarded, but relatively unharmed by the anti-personnel rounds, those inside suffering through the sound of the explosions hammering the hull, but surviving.

"All callsigns, crack that egg. Breach and decompress then enter and clear. Be advised, we just dropped artillery on that thing so watch out for unexploded bomblets!" Spears announced over the battlenet as they raced toward the module's final resting place.

His tracker chugged and he saw that Angels and support Mongoose had just arrived on scene, splitting up to engage the targets that remained along the crater rim and set up a protective combat space patrol. The APC came to a skidding halt just outside the edge of the debris field. The hatch at the back opened and his squad spilled out to take up positions in the surrounding rock field.

The top gunner sent bursts of fire into a struggling Chinese soldier, dimly seen through the dust as the Marines began to advance on the module. Using hand signals, he motioned his platoon leaders forward and they advanced en masse under the watchful eyes of several hovering Mongoose CAS birds and the APC gunners. The Chinese were still dazed and struggling to get their bearings when they made contact. Those who were standing never stood a chance. The Marines shuffle-sprinted through them in a line; as targets emerged out of the dust they engaged them with short bursts, cutting a path through the confusion.

Spears led his headquarters platoon toward the main airlock of the module. One of the SARines leapt up and slapped three breaching charges on the airlock and backed away. With a sharp flash the outer door dropped ponderously toward the moon. With no evidence of decompression the SARine moved forward again, this time laying three more charges against an inner door. There was a harsh pop and the door blew out and exploded away from the module as the higher pressure inside was suddenly released.

A stuttering volley of small arms fire erupted out of the opening as the Chinese inside attempted to keep the Marines out. One of the Marines ran forward, stuck his head up into the opening briefly to get a look and then backed away quickly. The volume of fire intensified for a moment then paused. He pulled a grenade out of a case and peeled away sticky protective covers off the face of each side. The Marines reached up and pulled a secondary visor over their faces and opaqued the faceplate underneath entirely. Checking it once more to make sure every facet of the grenade was cleared, he twisted a small dial on one face and threw it in a soft arc inside before looking away quickly.

As the grenade flew through the compartment the Chinese inside tried to shoot at it. It traveled a few meters inside the airlock and activated. An intense single-use chemical laser initiated, shooting eye damaging light at a series of reflectors which emitted them through all facets of the grenade in a brilliant flash of light. The Chinese staring at the clear orb that sailed into the room were instantly and permanently blinded by the flash. With howls of pain and outrage they flailed around the room, the Marines leveraging themselves inside, shooting anyone they saw in a spasm of violence.

By the time Spears was in the room, most of the blood and gore had begun to drift gracelessly down toward the floor. He grimaced as he picked up the chem-laser grenade. He hated these things, but there was definitely a place for them in space. He tucked it distastefully in a pouch on his waist, careful that there was no chance the enemy could get hold of it if they had to retreat suddenly. He had no desire to face these things in combat, and the thought of losing his eyesight permanently made him shudder.

He entered the command deck of the module, walking on what used to be the ceiling, just in time to see a Chinese officer frantically trying to operate a locked button on the console next to his chair as he hung upside down from his seatbelt. Realizing it was probably a self-destruct button he swore and brought his close quarters weapon to bear on him. Before he could fire, the SARine to his left opened up with a shotgun, blowing both of the officer's arms off at the elbows. The blood and bone sprayed across a nearby Marine's faceplate. The officer held his stumps in front of his face, a horrified expression clearly visible through his faceplate.

The SARine took two steps forward and applied tourniquets to the man's upper arms, using his knife to cut away his restraints and drop him to the deck. He settled him on the floor, swiftly stripping him of weapons and equipment. He took a syringe out of his thigh armor and stabbed it through the man's suit to injecting him with painkiller. As the pain medication flowed through the commander, his horrified face shifted first to shock and then into an unsettling drugged gaze.

"Waste not, want not," the SARine said as he handed his captive to one of the other Marines for transport back to the APCs. With a fatherly swipe, he wiped the gore off the Marine who he'd spattered then climbed up into the Chinese officer's chair. Balanced precariously upside down, he used several suit hooks to attach himself to the chair then began inserting probes into the module's main computer.

Spears looked at him, unsettled, but drawn in like a bug to a light. The hulking SARine armor was suspended over the room, upside down, while the SARine nimbly typed into the console in front of him like nothing was amiss. Spears glanced around at the other Marines, who were staring up at the SARine instead of securing the module.

"Stop gawking and get to work. Spread out through the module, I want this thing ready for exploit and cleaned of rats in five."

"What about survivors?" one of the Marines asked.

Spears looked up at the SARine, who responded. "We got the Commander. We don't need any others."

"Clean slate. Get to it."

The Marines saluted and began clearing the rest of the module room by room. Spears listened as he watched the SARine work, hearing occasional combat noises over the battlenet. After a few minutes, the SARine looked down at him.

"Good news. I've got it all unlocked. Ripping the mainframe now. Excellent work Captain!" He looked back at the screen in front of him.

Spears looked down at his feet, nudging the commander's gloved hand, the bone protruding out the wrist, and grunted.

"Bane Actual this is Bane Angel 2."

"Go for Bane Actual," the new MBTC Wing Commander, LTC Colonel Joe Prieter said.

"Enemy contact. Range seventy-five kilometers, mixed rover and space superiority force. Closing on a bearing of 239 true," the Angel pilot responded.

"Copy that Bane Angel 2. Head to flight level three hundred and give me a wide-angle scan of the area. Let's make sure we don't miss a second force."

"Copy that Bane Actual." The pilot's Angel broke from formation and began a tight spiral ascent above the lunar surface, turning his powerful sensors on the surrounding area as he climbed. As the computers worked the data into a seamless sensor picture, complex algorithms within the programming looked for known structures, formations or RCS telltales. The Wing Commander's sensor picture quickly expanded as the Angel climbed to a higher vantage point.

The Angel reached its targeted altitude above the moon and was immediately targeted by multiple search radars from the oncoming convoy trying to get a lock on them. Within seconds the sensor officer was designating enemy radars, sending jamming signals back at them. Suddenly the total number of enemy sensors trying to get lock on them increased exponentially as several of the rovers peeled back their top protective covering to expose dozens of man carrying missile systems. The sensor officer paused, realizing that there was no way to jam it all. So she dialed the jamming down and pumped out the sensor picture they had acquired to their wingmates below before screaming over the battlenet at the pilot to dive for the surface.

The Chinese column fired a large wave of anti-space missiles at them. The sensor officer cranked the jamming to max, changing the sensor platform from search and acquisition to wide-spectrum jamming mode, pulsing massive amounts of energy at the coming onslaught. The pilot yanked the sticks hard over and put them in a dive toward the deck, rotating the ship on its axis so the top turret gunner would have an angle on the incoming missiles.

"Bane Actual! Bane Actual! We are under heavy fire, coming in fast. Oncoming force has heavy anti-space weapons throughout the convoy!" the Angel pilot reported as he lined up his HUD on the distant crater wall far below. With a vicious vibration he felt the top turret gunner pulse short bursts at the denser clusters of oncoming missiles with little success. The sensor officer managed her soft kill station, directing concentrated beams of energy at incoming warheads as quickly as she could. Occasional flashes lit up screen when the top turret gunner, or an electronic countermeasure, succeeded and an incoming missile exploded, but still the flood continued.

With a dying rattle, the top turret gunner's magazines emptied out. He dropped down into the main compartment and strapped himself in, bracing for the coming violence. The pilot punched his maneuvering thrusters hard, swerving sideways toward the protective cover of one of the low-flying Acheron support Angels. He activated flare and chaff dispensers, kicking out a brilliant series of IR and UV flares behind the ship.

Many of the missiles swerved out of line or couldn't make the turn, detonating in the evading Angel's wake, but three streaked through to plow into its right side, destroying the wing root and sending the wing spinning off toward the lunar surface. The cloud of debris and shrapnel exploded inward, perforating the sensor officer's station, killing her instantly and cutting the fuel lines to the main engine. With a shuddering bang, the engines of the Angel cut off unevenly as the pressure dropped, causing the crippled bird to enter a tight spin with a dead stick.

The gunner gripped the sidewalls of the Angel, praying to any god that would listen to let him survive the impact as they spun down sharply at the lunar surface. He saw the pilot push the sticks away and curl up in his protective titanium tub as the lunar surface rushed up and crumpled the nose of the Angel, the ship cartwheeling up into the vacuum above the moon. Dazed, he watched debris and blood float throughout the ship, bouncing off the cabin walls erratically in slow motion before the Angel tumbled down toward the moon surface.

The last thing he saw before the final impact was the slack-jawed death mask of the sensor officer showing through the shattered faceplate of her helmet. Then there was darkness.

Captain Spears had just exited the damaged command module when the battlenet exploded with calls for help—one of the Bane Angels was corkscrewing toward the crater at maximum velocity. He watched in awe as the pilot hammered the Angel in a tight evasive pattern, tracers leaping from the top gunner's position at the tiny flames racing toward them. As they neared the ground, several of the APC gunners took passing shots at the missiles with limited effect, adding to the chaos above them. The Mongoose executing their CSP broke by sections to evade any further launches and try to get a shot on the missiles as they zipped through the area.

In a final desperate move, the Angel broke hard to the east in an attempt to lose the missiles, but it wasn't enough. A bright series of flashes lit up the darkness of space and sent the Angel careening down to smash into the surface and tumble to a rest some distance away.

His command armor CPU chugged while he received a large data update on the incoming enemy forces; the map practically bled red with enemy contacts. He turned to his SARine commander and pointed at the wreck. Without a word the SARine grabbed four of his men and raced over to the scout squad, co-opting two of the rovers and heading off in the direction of the downed Angel.

"Adler, this is Spears. Attach your dismounted troops to Charlie platoon. Take the rest of your scouts and harass that incoming. I want you to force them to dismount if possible."

"Wilco Actual. Moving now!" He swapped channels with a click of his tongue and started giving orders to his men.

Spears pulled his Alpha squad leader into a private channel. "Rick, get me pre-designated artillery strike gridded up for the crater wall above us. I need it fast, focus on places they might park the rovers and sniper hides. We're going to have to retreat under fire and I want to minimize casualties and make pursuit difficult. I want a clean withdrawal but with enough crumbs behind us that they make a limited pursuit along our preferred path so we can soak them with indirect fire." Spears spoke rapidly as he watched his Alpha Squad leader nodding from his perch on top of the crater wall. He waved an acknowledgement and took off with his squad to update the maps with the new lunar terrain.

"Bane Actual, Preacher Actual. I need you to try to hold off that column for about ten minutes. I've got scouts heading to harass them, I know it's nasty, but I need some air cover for them."

"Copy Preacher, be advised, TSAM strike dialed. Execute in three minutes."

Captain Spears blinked his surprise away, causing his HUD to flicker between menus as it tried to discern his intent. "Do you have a good enough target for a TSAM strike?"

"Tell you in seven minutes. Bane Actual out."

He kicked over to his company battlenet and used his command override. "All callsigns, Preacher Actual. Line of retreat is along path bravo three. We'll set up a fire support line there and hold until the SARines finish with the downed Angel. Move in ten minutes, get cracking."

He glanced over at the SARine standing nearby and swapped to his channel. "You guys done in there?"

"Yes sir, data has been ripped, copied and we've already loaded one set of copies on Acheron Angel One. No survivors remain inside. We still have a fairly strong enemy force along the north crater rim and a few scattered survivors at the base of the crater wall fighting back."

"Our line of retreat will buy us some distance from them. Blow it."

He walked away as the rest of his Marines streamed back toward the APCs, some stopping to return fire at the occasional Chinese soldier who peeked up over the crater lip. With a last look at the command module, he turned and stepped toward the entrance to his APC. As he was about to enter, a sniper rifle from far up the crater wall flashed briefly, sending a fifty caliber round slamming into his shoulder.

The impact lifted him off the lunar surface, spraying dust as his feet trenched the ground and drove him against the outside hull of the APC. Groggily he got to his feet and was pulled into the APC as another round slapped the hull near his head, gouging the armor. The top gunner swung his turret toward the source of the sniper fire and fired off a series of short bursts to cover them.

Inside, Spears staggered toward the bench seats along the wall, trying to read his HUD display alerts and tasting blood in his mouth where he'd bit his lip. One of the SARines who had already loaded up leaned over and pushed him down toward the floor, inspecting his armor plates. He found the fractured plate and several small tears in the exterior fabric of the suit. Using his penetration repair kit he applied a thick goop over the hole, letting it settle before curing it. Another quick inspection and he helped Spears up.

"Good thing you have a command suit on sir, that probably would have broken your shoulder or killed you if you'd been in Marine armor."

"I feel like I got hit by a car," Spears said as he winced in pain and tried flexing his shoulder slowly.

The SARine laughed over the battlenet. "Well, he cracked the armor plate. That's a first time for us. Probably hit you with an armor piercing round. In that caliber, well that's a beast. On the plus side, he missed your head eh," the SARine said as he turned back to his equipment

Spears nodded and tried to bring his BFT up, but the data wasn't accurate or updating. He flipped to the diagnostic and saw that the antenna for the system had been disabled by the shot. With a sigh, he pulled a wire out of his wrist gauntlet and plugged it into the APC wall, slumping into his seat. As the picture updated he gave his orders to begin the withdrawal along their line of retreat before flipping through the status reports of his units. With a thud felt through the rover's wheels, the command module's power source exploded, throwing debris up above the battlefield and peppering his APC with shrapnel.

To think, just a few weeks ago, they could walk with relative impunity through Chinese weapons fire. The enemy had already evolved to nearly drop a command suit with a single round. Grimly he swallowed the blood in his mouth and willed it to stop bleeding. Sometimes not being able to touch your face could be really annoying.

It had been almost an hour since they had stopped thrusting and Captain Wilks was getting a little anxious. They were arcing silently above the moon, the Angels doing all the work while the fighters drifted along. They could occasionally pick up updates of what was going on with the strike force and it didn't sound like it was going well.

The initial strike had been very successful, overturning the command module and disrupting power to the other structures. But then they lost one of the Angels and things started to get ugly. Spears had blown the command module and begun a series of leapfrogging retreats while they kept their APC line between the advancing Chinese and the downed Angel. The majority of the SARines were now desperately trying to cut the Angel apart to get the two surviving crewmembers out while Spears had finally found a spot with enough cover to dismount his men and mount a defense.

The last BFT update he'd seen showed a horseshoe shaped line with the downed Angel in the middle. The problem was that the command module's original defenders had chased them across the crater floor, constantly engaging them and trying to inflict casualties. At the same time, the enemy QRF had arrived along the crater wall and was now peppering them with long-range fire, preventing close space support missions for the Marines.

Spears had been forced to send his scouts out to blunt repeated flanking maneuvers by the Chinese who knew that if
they could encircle the 3rd company they would have a very
good chance of wiping it out. The farther they got away from
his main body, the more they risked being cut off themselves.

Now Spears was attempting to use his infantry to protect
the APCs as they tried to dislodge the enemy vehicles and
snipers off the crater wall some three kilometers distant. A
number of Mongoose had already been forced to return to
base with damage or empty weapon racks, and there had
been casualties. The MBTC had begun to ferry out replacement Marines and extra ammunition as the fight dragged on,
but the situation was getting grim on the ground.

Meanwhile they were drifting in a high orbit around the
moon, approaching the site of their first battle with the Chinese. The massive base had been damaged during their attack, but they hadn't been able to get a good look at it to see
what progress the Chinese had made in repairing it.

Wilks wasn't sure what he was expecting, but it certainly
wasn't what he was seeing. As they entered into visual range
he used the optical pods hooked into his missile racks to
zoom in on the enemy base. When he had left the base at the
end of the first attack, it had been a ruptured ruin. The heat
exchangers destroyed, the surface water supplies fragments
of ice scattered throughout the lunar landscape, and rows of
ruined rovers dominating his memory of the battle.

Now, it looked like a thriving metropolis. Two-dozen command modules were grounded in neat rows under the watchful eyes of dozens of point defense systems. Rovers streaked
over the surface, new buildings were sprouting up at irreg-
ular distances, and several large hangars had been erected.
The entire base seemed to have doubled in size, with significant increases in defensive systems. Bunkers were being con-
structed, ringing the base like a modern day Maginot Line,
weapons emplacements poking out in all directions. Track-

ing radars and communication arrays were scattered around the base, occupying almost every scrap of high ground or tall building. The RF and thermals pulsed with returns when they scanned over the base.

Wilks took a deep breath and blew it out slowly. When they had first hit the base, they had swept through it effortlessly, killing at will. As he looked down at the imagery recorded by his ship he wasn't even certain how they could assault it now, even if they used everything in their inventory at once. It was a fortress, pure and simple.

As they passed the base he connected to the lead Angel over the laser communication system.

"Oracle Lead, Tick Actual."

"Go Tick."

"What do you think?"

There was a long pause as the Angel pilot considered.

"I think the Chinese have a new Great Wall to keep out the heathens."

"Yeah, I think flying in there would be suicide."

"Flying, fighting, driving. Personally I'd nuke the site from orbit. Even that might not be enough given how much we know is underground. Spears is gonna have his work cut out for him cracking that nut."

"If he even makes it out of death valley to begin with," Wilks said soberly.

"Yeah. Looks like he's up to his eyeballs in shit right now. I know you guys are mates . . . " The pilot's voice trailed off for a moment before he continued. "It's rough. But he's smart and has been to hell a couple of times already. He'll find a way out."

"Yeah," Wilks replied, cutting the link as he sat in his cockpit watching the lunar surface roll past. Soon they'd be on the dark side, where they expected to find more Chinese. He thought back to the base they'd just flown over. It wasn't possible for the Chinese to have brought it all up from Earth recently without them seeing it. It must have come from somewhere else on the moon. His eyes tracked toward the light-dark terminator quickly approaching, a quiet dread souring his stomach.

"There are monsters in the darkness…" he whispered in the silence of his helmet.

***

"Sir, we just suffered a mobility kill to APC number six," the APC's communication tech told Captain Spears. "Front right wheel, they hit it with a guided rocket. Should we blow it?"

"Not yet, they can still be a pillbox for the moment. Is the damage repairable?"

The tech swapped channels and spoke to the damaged APC. "He says maybe, but not under fire from that ridgeline."

"Tell APC eight to pull in front of them and provide some cover." Spears dropped out of the channel and looked at his blue-force tracker, mumbling under his breath. "I have a feeling we're going to need every APC by the time this is over."

The tracker told a dismal picture. The crater floor was uneven and allowed them some cover for the APCs and dismounted Marines, but they were still being fired on from above. The initial TSAM strike had destroyed some of the heavier rovers and dropped some cluster munitions on the open tops of the rear rovers, but hadn't diminished the enemy forces enough. So now they were pinned down, being pressed from the north by the original garrison of enemy troops on the crater floor, and taking fire from the west from the enemy QRF that had taken position along the crater rim. Fortunately most of their heavier rounds seemed to be ill-suited to hitting moving Marines, but they were still taking casualties from sniper fire and the occasional surface-to-surface missile.

Ferry flights from the MBTC had brought ammunition supplies and some fresh troops out, but this was a game of at-

trition and they were a long way from home. The only bright
spot so far was that the enemy hadn't brought any gunships
with them this time, so they didn't have take direct fire from
those. He paused and swapped views on the tracker, pulling
up the space view. The Mongoose had finally gained space
superiority over the field, driving off the lightly armored
enemy fighters. He squinted at his HUD—they were definitely short a few birds from what they'd started with.

"Acheron Actual, this is Preacher Actual. Say status."

"Acheron here," the Wing Commander's tired voice came
back. "I'm rotating sections back to the MBTC for re-arm
and refuel now. The enemy fighter support bugged out about
ten minutes ago, low on fuel if I had to guess. We've been
pretty fortunate, some birds damaged, none downed. The
AAA over the enemy infantry is intense, several of their
rovers are designed purely for space defense and they can
put out a lot of damage very quickly. High damage, mix of
proximity bursting and armor piercing; the bursting rounds
tend to strip all instruments off the hull like a knife through
butter. Close ground support missions are pretty dicey."

"Copy that, any additional ground troops inbound?"
Spears asked, dreading the answer.

"One second." Acheron Actual went silent for a moment
before pulling in an Angel Pilot. "Acheron Two joining us."

"Detected dust indicators to the west, make it thirty klicks.
Size unknown," Acheron Two spoke up.

"Rate of closure?"

"I've been tracking them about five minutes. I think the
terrain is giving them some issues. The previous column
plowed through there. This might be heavy armor."

Spears didn't speak for several long moments, staring at
the wall dejectedly. "Let me know when you get a visual on
them, we're trying to extract soon."

"WILCO Captain. Good luck." Acheron Two bounced
out of the channel.

"Everything going ok Captain?" the Wing Commander asked.

"We're getting hammered off that ridgeline. We're not taking many losses, but some. Problem is we can't get a good angle on them, we keep hitting the crater lip. Artillery is transitioning to a new firing location. We need indirect fire to scatter them or we'll take losses when we try to extract. This is starting to feel a bit like Custer's Last Stand down here."

"I'm plus four klicks above you, I can see the problem. Let me see what I can do, most of my sections are low on ammo and need to save it for any more bandits."

"Thanks, good hunting. Preacher Actual out." Spears dropped off the battlenet and leaned back against the wall. His whole body felt sore and there were shooting pains coming from his shoulder every time he leaned forward. He could feel the vibrations of small caliber weapons fire impacting his APC and the responding top turret gun firing sparingly back at them. The Angels had brought a large pallet of ammunition for the APCs on their last trip, but the intensity of the battle was burning through supplies at a rate he hadn't seen since Kenya.

"Rescue team, say status."

"Need another two-five mikes at least. We got the gunner out, but the pilot is really in there tight," Chief Morris responded.

"Is he still alive?"

"Yes. Minor injuries, but the titty tub bent around his lower half. We're having trouble cutting it free. Angels are built tough, sir."

"Understood. Be advised possible enemy armor column inbound from the west."

"Copy. We can speed it up a little if you need us to. Risk to the pilot."

"How?" Spears asked, his voice tinged with curiosity.

"Shaped charges to separate the tub from the rest of the Angel, then we load him into a new Angel, still in the tub."

"What's the risk?"

"His hips are trapped. Big enough bang, might break them."

"Prep to execute, but proceed with normal extract until we get confirmation on the armor. Preacher out." Spears cut the connection and turned back to the tracker data.

He zoomed it out and changed the filter to show detected enemy assets, and pondered the combat picture. While some of the red dots faded in and out of view, the rovers had settled into an area behind a small rise past the crater lip, infantry spread along the lip firing down on Spear's company. To the south, he could see the scout unit with what was left of Bane squadron performing repeated envelopments on several units of Chinese troops in rovers that were trying to flank their position.

Each time the enemy began to break out around the flank, the scouts would circle their column and riddle them with light arms fire. Once they managed to disorganize the column enough that they'd lost forward progress, the Mongoose overhead strafed them. The enemy force outnumbered the scouts almost eight to one, but they were making no significant progress against the little buggies. He made a note to recommend Alder for a medal.

As he was checking on the progress of the armadillo's retreat back toward the MBTC, he noticed another flight of Angels enter the crater with two Mongoose and frowned. The Mongoose sections always came in three or four ship flights; just two was strange.

This close to the base, the Badgers' combat space patrol had been extended outward, so there was no reason for them to be running with an escort. Confused, he watched them track in toward the sheltered spot they were using as an LZ near the APC line. As they approached it, the two Mongoose split off to the north, ducking down toward the surface and weaving in and out of rolling hills left over from ancient impacts.

As they circled around the northern Chinese flank, the tracker finally updated with their squadron identifiers. With surprise, he saw that it was Talon Six and Talon Ten, part of the squadron that had defended the MBTC against the first surprise Chinese attack. Most of them had been so badly damaged as to be practically unrecoverable after that. He watched as they lined up on the eastern crater rim and accelerated.

Realizing they were about to start a strafing run he raced to find them on the battlenet; they had no idea that the whole area above the rim was a no go zone due to the volume of AAA the enemy could throw up. But they didn't have the comm. codes and he couldn't talk them. Instead, he watched in horror as they came in just meters above the ground straight for the infantry lining the rim and the rovers parked beyond.

At two hundred meters out, they began firing in unison toward the infantry sitting oblivious along the crater rim. After having been sheltered from the majority of the Marine's ground fire for over an hour, they had grown lax. No swarm of air-to-space missiles greeted the incoming Mongoose, no streams of tracers from the flak batteries. Instead, the two pilots cut velocity and leisurely chewed up the infantry as they passed overhead. When they reached the midpoint of the Chinese position, they used their thrusters to shift direction, maintaining their forward velocity. Long streams of heavy rounds and dumbfires slammed into the tightly packed vehicles.

The rover formation, which had been packed tight to help defend against the previous TSAM attacks, erupted in flames as the rounds pounded into their sides, exploding and throwing debris high into the lunar sky. Brief flashes dotted the debris as fuel sources ignited in a spasm of oxygen fueled fire before being choked out by vacuum.

The two Mongoose pulled out of their slide and poured on the throttle, heading west toward the approaching enemy column. Spears watched them leave the crater area and turned his attention to the damage assessment reports flooding in from the Angel overhead. The single strafing pass had covered only thirty percent of the ridgeline, but the parts it had covered were almost devoid of enemy troops. The slow, precision pass had proven devastating to the troops who were sprawled out in the open. With no atmosphere to transmit sound, many of the soldiers had never been aware they were being fired at until the lunar soil around them had erupted in chaos.

Captain Spears felt a pang of fear, the thought that one day, he might be on the receiving end of a strafing run like that that gripping at his senses like a childhood terror. He shook it away and looked at the data from the rover strike. Most of their transport rovers were gone, but the AAA rovers had apparently been dispatched to the south in an effort to help with the flanking maneuvers. The strafing run had missed them, although the more he thought about it, Spears wondered if the attack would have been successful at all if they had been there. He studied the display for another couple of heartbeats before coming to a decision.

"All callsigns, Preacher Actual. Prepare to extract, oscar-mike in ten."

He swapped battlenets to the Adler's scout group. "Shank this is Preacher Actual. I need you to try to draw them further south and disengage in twenty mikes, how copy?"

"Shank Actual Copy. Confirm general withdrawal initiated?"

"Confirm, meet at waypoint Zulu via the southern route. I need you to keep the flankers off us until we get organized."

"Understood, don't slow roll it. We're almost winchester. Shank Actual out."

He leaned forward and shook the shoulder of the comm. technician. "I need a status on APC Six now!"

"They can move, but only at thirty percent throttle. Level grade sir," the tech replied without hesitation.

"Get them heading to waypoint Zulu, now, best possible speed. The rest of the column will catch up as we disengage." He pulled the driver into their channel. "Driver, squad recall and get me back to the downed Angel ASAP!"

The driver nodded back over at him and began initiating a squad recall. Almost immediately the APC's cargo tumbled in through the back doors, piling into the benches and belting in. Before the door was even fully cycled closed, he had them rolling east toward the downed Angel, carefully weaving in and out of the other Marines as they scrambled back to their rides.

It was far from a chaotic retreat, the Marines carefully collecting their gear before retreating back to their individual APCs. Each APC pulled out of the line as they filled up and formed a slow rolling wedge that pulled back toward the downed Angel, moving in reverse with their noses pointing toward the enemy. The top gunners opened fire on anything that tried to pursue them as they plowed through the dust and rock that had been churned up by the many explosions.

Spears climbed his way through the crowded APC to the rear door and waited at the back. He looked back at his Marines and smiled through his helmet, making sure it was transparent so they could see. They were dirty, dented and looked worn out, but they were still in the game. Several of them had visible goo marks on their armor from PRK usage and one was holding fragments of what used to be her weapon. As he watched, they reached under the benches to pull out extra ammunition, passing it around in case they had to dismount and fight again.

With a lurch they stopped and he cycled the rear door, stepping out carefully, the APC between him and the enemy held crater lip. He turned toward where the Angel had crashed and stopped dead in his tracks. There was a deep gouge in the surface of the moon, scattered bits of metal and composite materials, and a cluster of SARines hovering over a spot. But no Angel.

Confused, he sprinted over to the men, jumping into the SARine battlenet as he did so. "Report!"

"Almost got him sir."

"Where the hell is the Angel?"

The lead SARine turned his hulking command suit to face Captain Spears, making his faceplate transparent in the process. "We disassembled it Sir. Ferried the pieces back on the last couple of Angel's that resupplied you."

"The whole thing?" Spears said in utter amazement.

"Yes sir, standing orders from the Commander not to let any spacecraft be captured. We used most of our explosives taking out the command module. So we had to take it home, piece by piece."

Spears just stared at him aghast. "What were you some kind of chop shop artist back in the real world?"

"Something like that. I grew up in south Boston," the SARine said with a smile before continuing. "We would have had the pilot out a lot sooner, but the damn titty tubs are meant to resist being disassembled and his got bent, making it even harder."

Spears swore under his breath and looked back at the advancing APCs. "Five minutes. We need to get the hell out of here before their reinforcements come. That Mongoose strafing run bought us some time to get distance on these assholes, but it's limited. Hustle it up."

"On it sir," the SARine said as he turned back to supervise his men. Spears sighed and jogged back the APC.

Lt. Raynes sat in the reclined seat of his artillery rover and watched the optical feed from the overhead Angel intently. Sitting six hundred meters above the lunar surface, the Angel was inverted so that its more powerful optical scopes could peer down at the retreating APCs of 3rd Company. The Angel was almost motionless against the darkness of space, its paint absorbing the sun's rays and shifting in color and tone to keep the Angel nearly invisible to casual observation. Only a focused search using a hyper-spectral sensor would pick up the shimmer along the edges. The pilot was good, settled into a near perfect hover with occasional random maneuvers to stop anyone from shooting at them from below. The optical view was rock steady.

Raynes watched as the APCs raced for the nearside of the crater, heading for a small collapsed area that led into a narrow canyon. That canyon was their way out, another kilometer along it and the column would catch up to the artillery. Three kilometers further and the canyon opened out back on the lunar surface. It was the best cover for quite some distance in all directions and the obvious line of retreat. In the distance, a dust cloud could be seen approaching the collapsed crater rim where the command module had been.

He sent a request to the overhead Angel, asking for a secondary view of the oncoming enemy column. After a brief pause, the imagery flickered into view at a much higher magnification. Racing across the lunar surface were nearly thirty rovers. Not the squat, man-transporting rovers they had seen to date from the Chinese, but sleek, grey armored tanks rolling on treads instead of big wheels. They were covered in reactive armor blocks and carried numerous weapons. As they rolled into view approaching the lip he looked at the weaponry of each variant. Some were clearly big bore cannons, meant for shooting a large caliber round on a flat trajectory. Several others had multiple barrel cannons that looked like they were intended to pepper a target with smaller rounds, possibly infantry, possibly anti-spacefighter.

They cut deep into the lunar gravel as they passed, stirring up dust and pulverizing rock. The lead elements approached the collapsed lip above the command module slowing so they wouldn't tumble down the hill and drove off edge. Even in the reduced gravity, the weight of the tanks kept them in contact with the loose gravel of the newly formed slope as they slalomed down the hill at breakneck speed, scattering their own infantry in front of them as they tried to avoid being run over.

Raynes sighed. None of their ground vehicles had nearly that kind of mobility on the moon. They had to pick and choose how they advanced. There were weaknesses to the heavy-treaded tank concept, but fighting on flat terrain wasn't one of them. They sliced through their former fighting positions like so many sharks in a feeding frenzy.

"Load anti-armor rounds," he called over the battlenet. They'd get just one shot at blunting this thrust before they'd be crawling up the column's ass, too close to fire on. He swapped back to a view of the canyon opening just in time to see Spear's column race in. The last APC traveled less than one hundred meters in before sliding to halt as the back hatch opened and several SARines ran out.

He watched them frantically digging with hand tools along the edge of the canyon wall, staying mostly in the shadows. A countdown clock appeared on his screen designating time to arrival of the Chinese armor. His breath caught as he saw it was less than six minutes and rapidly counting down. He felt a slight shudder; if the Marines had pulled back any slower, they would have been caught in the open against these things and slaughtered for sure.

The SARines were sprinting back to the APC now, which had already started to creep forward slightly when the first enemy tank had entered the canyon. The APC rumbled ahead, desperately trying to get around the corner before the tank got the angle on them, barely making it before a 150mm shell impacted on the canyon wall just past them. The tanks formed a single file line and chased, speeding ahead with reckless abandon, bumping into the walls and hopping over small lumpy areas.

As they reached where the SARines had been working, the call finally came.

"Rain, Preacher Actual. On your best judgment. Danger close authorization given. Spears KILO-MIKE-MIKE-OS-CAR. On grid one-nine, engage on contact. Good shooting, out."

"Rain acknowledges, tell everyone to pucker up, this is going to be close."

The blue-force tracker updated as Spears had the SARines activate their explosively formed projectile booby traps, a line of icons appearing on the map display closely tracking the canyon wall. As the first tank approached, the mines toned, but did not explode. Raynes flexed his hand and flipped up the arming guard over his fire control initiator. The second tank passed the leading edge of the mines and there was another tone. As the third tank passed the sensor eye of the first mine, the third tone sounded and then all hell broke loose in the canyon.

The first tank was nearly twenty meters ahead and passing through one of the final EFP mines when it detonated, shooting a stream of liquefied copper laced with tungsten BBs into the side of the tank. The copper was propelled by a special shaped charge, allowing it to bypass the reactive armor, detonating it but continuing unhindered to slash through the armored wall of the tank like a knife through butter. The copper blazed a trail for the small tungsten BBs to follow.

Once inside they began to ricochet around, shredding the commander of the tank column and smashing equipment. The tank lurched sideways into the wall, smashing into the crumbling façade with a sickening impact that detonated several more reactive blocks. They blew outward from the tank, penetrating the rock face and causing a small, slow motion rockslide to cascade down over the killed tank.

The second and third tanks suffered similar fates as Raynes watched. With grim satisfaction he pressed the fire button. Instantly, his artillery battery launched a series of rockets toward the opening of the canyon. The rockets raced toward the tanks as they tried to stop in the tight confines of the canyon. The fourth and fifth tanks, blinded by dust and rock, slammed into the third tank at full speed. The fifth tank going so fast it climbed up the back of the third tank before slipping off and landing on its side with a puff of dust.

As the Chinese column tried to get organized in the dust hanging the canyon, the artillery rockets arced overhead and detonated. A rain of anti-material fletchettes belched from each rocket, spraying downward into the top armor of the tanks.

The tanks never stood a chance as the steel rain descended on the stalled armored column. Reactive blocks exploded, spreading shrapnel throughout the canyon in a haze of high velocity death that peppered everything in the kill zone. When the smoke and dust began to clear, it was a scene of devastation.

The twisted remains of twenty enemy tanks lay contorted and smoldering in the canyon, the last of their oxygen consumed by fire and space itself. The remaining tanks hadn't yet entered the canyon; seven were able to withdraw out of range, spreading out to avoid any further artillery strikes. But three tanks rested where they had stopped, treads off the track and smoke leaking from the rents in their armor.

"Preacher Actual, Acheron Angel Two. I have roughly twenty tanks killed in the canyon, two of them might just be mobility kills, the rest are trashed. Three mobility kills outside of the canyon, seven retreating toward the remains of the CP. Request permission to engage retreating tanks with TSAMs."

"Estimate on enemy infantry killed in the canyon?" Spears asked wearily over the battlenet.

"Impossible to estimate. They're in pieces or worse. Based on what I observed prior to mission strike, possibly twenty."

"Engage with TSAMs, no risk. Coordinate with Bane Actual."

"Copy that, engaging now."

"Nice job Raynes, don't wait for us to get to you, bug out now."

"WILCO, way ahead of you sir. Out."

With a lurch, the stability braces extending into the moon retracted back into the mobile artillery platform as the missile racks rotated back into their nested position. Raynes nudged his driver and felt the wheels hastily engage as he maneuvered into the path leading out of the canyon. Raynes picked up a small piece of chalk with his gloved hand and turned to the metal side of his compartment. With a half smile he slowly began to mark off each killed tank on the wall. It was getting crowded for this early in a war.

CHAPTER 12

Captain Julio Menendez finished his brief and turned expectantly toward the small crowd in the secure conference room. Arrayed before him were the base commander, his staff and the CEO of the KaliSun Corporation. Behind them were several of the key players in the recent battle, some still wearing their armor and barely qualifying as participants due to exhaustion.

"Thank you Captain. I've got some general questions to ask, I'd like you to keep your answers brief as these are mostly intended for you to answer next week in the more detailed after-action report, I don't expect you to know all the answers in the flash report," Commander Forsythe said.

Menendez took a breath and waited at the podium, a globe view of the moon slowly rotating on the screen behind him showing the battle and the recon results in an orgy of colors across the gray surface.

"We were able to capture significant data from the command module. I want you to take what you know from that data and bounce it against the data from the first raid. I need a status on cracking their operational codes, beyond just snatching volumes of data. Lean on the captured Chinese to provide you the data you need. But I need to know if we have any hope of cyber attacks or if this is going to be a straight slugfest."

"Yes sir. Preliminary data indicates that at the least the command modules and the food modules use different encryption. However there were some firmware chips in the command module that seem to be intended to insert into the computer and emulate the different types of encryption. Right now we're trying to work that angle. To reiterate my previous point, we found more firmware than known encryption, implying there are other encryption protocols out there."

Forsythe nodded and continued. "My next question is more of a clarification question. The recon flight found dozens of small outposts seemingly abandoned or minimally staffed on the dark side of the moon. They also found one deep underground facility that seems more factory than base. Can you give me your opinion of those facilities? I know you don't have facts, but what does your gut say?"

"My gut says . . . Sir, in my opinion, they did essentially the same thing we did. Built their army out of sight and surged it forward to the closest point to us. They hid their work on the moon, we went to Saturn. Their logistics footprint is tiny compared to ours, supply lines are significantly shorter." Menendez paused before continuing carefully. "In my opinion, they significantly outnumber us. Some of the new equipment we saw in this latest conflict, in addition to their ability to rapidly bring in reinforcements, brings into question whether our two-hundred man offensive force is sufficient to continue offensive actions." He finished with a rush.

Forsythe tapped his pen on the table pensively and looked over at Stokes. "Do you have any questions, Chairman?"

"Those tanks they brought in at the end. Ever seen anything like that in your intel assessments?"

"No, sir."

"Please go through the imagery the Angels brought back. They had to have tested them somewhere. I want to know where they tested them and where they're making them. That might be our highest priority target."

"It's possible they did it underground," Menendez volunteered.

"Possible. I think it's unlikely however. Find what you can, we need information before we can figure out a suitable counter to that tech," Stokes said firmly, before looking over at Forsythe with a nod.

"LTC Davies, Chief Robbins, and Chief Morris please stay. The rest of you are dismissed. Get some rack time but stay ready for further combat."

The tired men and women of the KaliSun Corporation filed out, leaving just a small knot of senior leadership clustered around the conference table.

Chief Morris sat in his SARine armor with his helmet on the table, smiling happily while Stokes and Forsythe compared notes. Finally Robbins looked over at him questioningly and asked what he was so happy about.

"Much to be pleased about. I brought all my SARines back more or less intact. Accomplished the mission, extracted that Angel crew nearly flawlessly. It was a team effort today, but my part of the team exceeded my expectations." He paused smiling broadly and winked at Robbins. "I love it when they do that."

"Me too," Forsythe said with a smirk. "Alright, I just want to talk about a few things quickly. For starters, based on the initial recon data, we may have a major problem. The recon flight detected dozens of those command modules parked at the Chinese base. We struggled to defeat that single one, with the majority of our offensive units. The longer we let them rest, the more likely we're going to have to deal with those things entrenched all over the moon."

"I'd consider nuking them," Davies said deliberately.

As Robbins started to object, Forsythe held his hand up. "It's not off the table, but it's not our first option."

"We could also drop big rocks from high orbit on them," Chief Morris said with a smile in Robbins' direction.

"Also an option, but since we have no big rocks ready to go, give me options now."

"We need to keep them off balance, but we don't really need to beat them right away," said Stokes. "I don't want to get hungry and go for the killshot only to wipe out our forces on a heavily defended target. In my opinion we hit them with dozens of quick strikes along their perimeter. It will keep them on alert endlessly, diminishing their readiness levels. We can probe their strength and it might disrupt their next attack."

"It also gives the men more trigger time. Each one of their outposts gets limited experience while our dedicated units build on unit cohesion and pile up practical low gravity combat experience," LTC Davies said, writing notes as he spoke.

"I'd recommend including smaller units from the rest of the companies on these raids, so they can get combat experience too and don't get barracks rot," added Chief Morris.

Forsythe nodded, writing on his tablet. "I'd take it a step further. I want a list of deep targets, behind their lines, that we can hit. Low value targets that we can smash and take our time to exploit. If we make them defend their rear, that larger footprint they occupy on the moon starts to look more and more of a disadvantage rather than an advantage. Turn a potential major strength into a weakness, even if it's not a huge one." He paused, reading before continuing. "I do not want any more offensive attacks that are even fights. We should have force superiority or abort. The only time I want a fair fight is if we're on defense and have our fortifications as an added bonus."

"So we keep them on their heels, watch closely for indicators of a pending attack and try to disrupt it without exposing ourselves too much," Stokes finished with a satisfied nod.

"How does that fix our problem long term? We have a freighter coming in very soon with additional troops from Saturn as well as the remains of that Congressional Delegation. How am I supposed to manage that with the enemy hitting us in the face the entire time?" Chief Robbins asked with a worried tone.

"I think we're going to have to attack them the day we begin ops, try to hold them in place while we get the freighter through. If we try to defend it at the point, somebody will get through. It only takes a missile in the back of a tug and the whole thing comes apart," Forsythe said grimly.

"I'm certain they'll expect that!" Robbins said, agitation creeping into his voice.

"I think I have an idea," Chief Morris spoke up.

Everyone turned to look at him expectantly, and he coughed and continued. "If we can get into their sensor and communication networks with a cyber attack, we might be able to spoof them into thinking a much wider attack is going on. Say a perimeter-wide probe from the south. They would be forced to take it seriously. Then we sneak a strike force in range of the main base and pop it with something hard and nasty. Small pinch nuke maybe. They'll be rushing to deal with the aftermath of that mess while we unload the freighter."

"We really shouldn't be using nukes . . . " Robbins began before stopping at Forsythe's hand signal.

"Work out a mechanism to do it, we'll consider how to actually attack as we get closer. I'll have Menendez set up a war room for you in the secure area. I know you need some down time Chief, go get some rest. We have a few more things to talk about."

Chief Morris nodded, picked up his helmet and left with Davies. Robbins rose to follow him but froze in place before sitting back down when he saw Forsythe's face.

"James, you need to understand that we're not going to win this conventionally unless something drastic changes. Captain Menendez was correct in his assessment—we are significantly outmatched. That armor alone is enough to negate our ground force advantage in technology. Those tanks will instantly kill any infantry they hit. No armor will help. I need to be brutally honest; if they had brought gunships to that fight with the armor, Spears' company would probably have been wiped out. I have no idea why they didn't, but I'm grateful for it."

"You can't say that for certain, the artillery strike could have still made it through," Robbins said stubbornly, arguing on principal more than belief.

"It's unlikely. Their point defenses would destroy that kind of artillery strike easily, that's why we only sent two artillery units in the first place. But it's kind of a moot point, since they wouldn't have survived during the SAR mission on the Angel..." Forsythe paused as he realized they probably wouldn't have had any air cover if the gunships had been present and continued. "We can play the what-if drill all day. But in all seriousness, we're in danger of losing this war. Losing means death, they aren't going to give us a lift home. Losing means Saturn Base is cut off and may die. We simply cannot afford to lose. So we're going to consider all options, even nuclear ones."

Robbins looked over at Stokes who was observing silently, and seeing no help he relented. "Fine. I still have a freighter coming in. It's got damage from that radiation storm and it's full of incoming trained Marines. Assuming we can offload it under fire, do you want me to send it back to Hatfield? We were planning on sending him parts for his auto-factories, specialty equipment they can't make and food, in addition to another two hundred Marine applicants that are crowding up the transit area. Are you sure you want to risk all of that? Why not keep the Marines here, it's not like he needs them out there and I'm sure they can get a ton of training on the fly in the coming months."

"I think we should send at least half of the Marine recruits and the pilots. He still has the best training facility and well, there is that other problem," Stokes said.

"What other problem?" Robbins asked, confused.

Forsythe shot a raised eyebrow at Stokes before answering. "It appears Saturn base has been attacked by aliens. They were able to fend them off. We're waiting on details."

Robbins sat motionless, his mouth hanging open before he shut it with a click. He blinked rapidly and stuttered. "Hos-hostile aliens?"

"Apparently. Like I said, we're still waiting for details."

"Did they cause the radiation ball thing?" Robbins asked with alarm.

"We don't know, although that would be one hell of a battlefield preparation technique," Forsythe said.

"Have you told Earth yet?"

"We were waiting on the recon flight data to come back," Stokes interrupted Forsythe as he was about to speak. "I thought it might be best to give them all of the bad news at once."

"Oh … oh."

"James, why don't you get with Captain Wilks when he comes off his downtime and see if you can come up with a mechanism to better defend the freighter. Ed and I will clean up in here."

His face ashen, Robbins left the room deep in thought. Forsythe turned to Stokes and raised an eyebrow. "Why did you let slip the alien thing to him?"

"He seems reluctant to go the whole nine yards against his fellow man. Perhaps fear of being eaten by some big scary alien will get him to focus. I know you guys are close, but you've been letting his dovish mentality persist for too long," he said sternly.

Forsythe took the admonishment and mulled it over in his mind before responding. "Maybe so, but it was done on purpose. He's a bit naïve, especially for this corporation. But that mindset is the type of thing I'd prefer to keep around, unsullied, in case one day I need his judgment to prevent me doing something I may regret. A moral compass if you will. Besides, he amuses me sometimes. Remind me later to tell you about what happened when he tried to grow shitake mushrooms on a condensate line and the spores ended up in the air ducts. We had mushrooms popping up everywhere."

Stokes sighed and threw his pen at the table softly. "I know, I didn't mean to snap." He rubbed his chin, running his fingers through the stubble that was starting to form. "So the recon team made it two full orbits, undetected the entire time. The Chinese seem like they pulled some punches on our ground team, skipping the gunships and bringing the tanks in hours after they should have. There are a lot more Chinese than we expected. I don't get it, you'd think they would be all over us now."

"Captain Menendez has a theory about that. What little intel we have on their command structure seems to indicate that whoever triggered the original attack has been sacked or killed. Right now, they're competing to see who gets to be in charge. The Chinese high command on Earth is still in disarray from the radiation event, trying to find a way to feed a lot of starving people and possibly having their own command disruptions. So it seems while they've merged all those small bases together, they don't quite agree on who gets to tell who what to do. I wish we could find a way to exploit it, but I'll be damned if I know how."

"There's no way to know, but if we can keep the pressure on, maybe they'll implode on their own. Nothing like a civil war to give us some breathing space."

"I'd hate to count on it. If there's one thing we've learned, it's that their leadership structure is resilient. They may be disagreeing now, but in two months they could be right back in step with each other."

"Yeah. So which one of us wants to be the one to tell Hatfield he might be on his own?" Stokes said lightly.

"Play you Russian roulette for it . . . winner gets to tell him," Forsythe said with a chuckle.

CHAPTER 13

Hatfield rapped his gloved knuckles on the table sharply and raised his voice. "Enough! This arguing is pointless. The next two freighters might be the last—both were damaged in the radiation storm, we're not even certain they can survive the return trip, so debating an evacuation is a moot point. Even if we wanted to, we couldn't fit everyone on the ships. The life support systems would collapse halfway home."

Molly started to interrupt him, waving her head in the vague direction of the stars as she did so. "Look, you can't force us to st . . . "

"Ms. Caan! Stop. We cannot evacuate all of the people. We cannot take enough food and water to make the trip. This isn't a viable option," barked Hatfield, his face beginning to redden in anger.

"Then let those of us who don't want to stay risk the flight home," Molly said, exasperated.

"I think, perhaps, you are forgetting something very important Molly," Brenner interrupted them.

"Oh yeah? What's that? That you basically kidnapped me? Or maybe that you're using the scientists as a cover for your little bullshit science project?"

"No, that we have discovered aliens. They have spaceships. It seems unlikely that they have only one," Brenner said, pausing to let his statement sink in.

"Furthermore, look at the weapons they had on that ship. Almost all highly effective defensive weapons on a ship designed to hide, designed to reflect energy weapons. In other words, their entire ship looks like it was built to defend itself against a foe that has better technology than ours. Ergo, they are not likely the only enemy out there. Either they have other factions within their race attacking them or they're fighting other species. In both cases those other factions represent a threat to us. Fleeing across the vacuum to try to reach an Earth that evidently is in the middle of fighting a civil war is foolish. The entire reason these might be the final freighters coming out here is because it is unclear that we will have a presence on the moon when they get back."

"No presence on the moon means no tugs to slow us down. We would just wing past Earth into deep space," Sloan said softly. "We can't even promise we could protect the freighters on the way back to Earth, it's probably a suicide run."

Molly bit her lip and glared around the room, tears forming at the corners of her eyes as she looked for any allies. Hatfield was practically boiling with anger, Brenner looked frustrated, Sloan looked sympathetic, while the Wing Commander and Marine Commander stared at her stone faced. She let out a sigh of defeat and looked back at Hatfield, speaking in a final act of defiance.

"You realize this is your fault I hope," Molly said. Hatfield remained silent as she stared at him, so she dared to continue. "Your ego drove you to build that ship without testing it properly and you brought the aliens here. Then, without even waiting to see if they were hostile, you attacked them, starting a war with an alien race that you don't even know how to talk to, never mind where they're from or how strong their Navy is. You agitated the Chinese into starting a war with us again when we're barely recovered from the last one, stealing trillions from your own country in the process . . . you're a monster."

Brenner shot a glance over at Hatfield to see his reaction. Remarkably, his mood calmed and he seemed to resettle himself before he responded to Molly in even, cold tones.

"The war with the Chinese was inevitable. If it had not been, there would have been no push within Congress to pay us to build weapons. If anything, the United States Government caused this war. You must realize the Chinese figured out we were building weapons for you, in direct violation of the Armistice treaty and every space treaty ever created on Earth. They know, as well as you do, that the high ground wins wars. The moment you signed the first funding line for space weapons, you set the ball rolling for this war ... "

"I didn't do anything, I was just the Chief of Staff to Senator Hernandez!" Molly exclaimed in anger.

"Right, the Chief of Staff who manages all the staffers. The people who actually write and implement the bills while the Senators posture on the cable news networks. No, you are buried hip deep in this mess, just as much as we are. I don't need space weapons, I'm clear out by Saturn, almost unreachable by any conceivable foe ... " He paused, eyes squinting before amending his statement. "Earthbound foe."

"Oh bullshit! You are dependent on the moon base and Earth, you couldn't possibly have thought you could just ignore the Chinese, sooner or later you would've needed protection from them, we just gave you the money so you could protect yourself ... " She faltered as she saw Hatfield's smile flash across his face before he settled into a neutral expression. "No ... no, the CEO would never have let you get away with it ... " The truth finally dawned on her.

Hatfield looked at Sloan and Brenner steadily as he replied, watching their reactions too. "It's irrelevant what he would try to do. The plan, my plan, from the start has always been the same. Build this base up to be self-sufficient, and if we determined that belonging to KaliSun was no longer beneficial, we could just leave. It's imperfect, but if the ship had worked out, we'd be the only people with access to other stars. We could trade that access for whatever we needed," Hatfield said, watching to see if Brenner or Sloan looked uneasy.

"You people are crazy, all of you," Molly said with horror. "First you betrayed our trust and stole from us; I don't care how you justify it, it was stealing. Then you refuse to hand over the military we paid for. Now you would have me be-

lieve you'd betray your own leadership, your own corporation, just so you can be the King of Saturn."

"Emperor. Emperor sounds better," Sloan said with a
laugh.

"How can you condone this! This is not the kind of person
you are Sloan. I know you care for people, I know you have
honor! Why..."

"Molly, I like you. But you are a bit naïve sometimes. You
act like we should have remorse from stealing from Congress or seceding from the Corporation. Honestly, it's hard
to care. I love my country, but it's being run by some real
douchebags and has been for sometime. If anything, we're
stealing from them. Most of the money we took they printed
out of thin air anyway, so it's not like we stole something of
real value. The only value it had was as a reserve currency
backed by the force of our military, and the idiots in charge
managed to starve the military and lose that dominance. We
stole electronic money; look what we built with it," Sloan
said patiently.

"Great! You stole money and used it to build a ship that
nearly ended life as we know it on Earth!"

"Don't be melodramatic. Look at what we actually *did* with
it," Sloan said, exasperation creeping into her voice as she
began counting successes on her fingers. "We built a solar
system transport system equivalent to the great railroad ex-
pansion of the 1800s, we built two major installations on
celestial bodies other than Earth, we built the first self-con-
tained food system in history, and those are just the things I
was involved in. We've developed cancer treatments, kidney
failure medication, advanced materials, and learned more
about our solar system than we've learned in the previous
eighty years of space exploration. All of that and we built a
faster than light travel system to explore our galaxy."

Sloan looked at Hatfield, who met her with a smile before
she continued. "But maybe we should ask what you would

have done with it? What if that money never got redirected to us? Would you have recovered from the Sino-Pacific war as quickly? No, our products were all produced in America—we got the industry rolling again, we got people good jobs after cheap Chinese junk products were pulled out. If not for us, you'd be wallowing in more inflation than you could possibly shovel out of. What would you have spent it on Molly? WHAT?"

"We could have fed the poor..."

"Who had a job because of us, made money because of us and could therefore buy their own food."

"We could have cleaned up the environment, fought global warming and repaired the cities damaged in the war!" Molly said, getting angry at Sloan's aggressive prodding.

Sloan laughed. "Well I think we just fixed global warming for you. That nice little plasma comet knocked out half the world's power requirements in one shot. You can send us a thank you card at your own petty convenience!"

Molly sputtered at her, outrage stripping her speech as she struggled to respond. Lips trembling, she finally calmed down enough to grit out an answer. "You've killed us all. You may be able to grow food in that cave, but eventually equipment will break down and you won't be able to repair it. We're just going to die slowly, like being stranded in the desert."

"Sloan, please explain to Molly about the cold storage facility," Hatfield said, with a trace of a smile.

"We've been padding our orders of equipment since the Director got here. We've got six cold storage areas buried deep under the base. Spares are stored in vacuum there. Every critical piece of equipment for the base has spares there. We can last a long time, a very, very long time," Sloan said proudly.

"I've been planning this since before I came here," Hatfield said with a triumphant grin. "Don't believe for one second that I didn't approach this from the perspective of long term isolation."

Brenner finally reacted, slapping the table with his armored hand and laughing. "I really wish you'd told me. I've had Ed looking everywhere for the equipment we seemed to always misplace when it came in on the freighters."

"Well, you ordered Ed to look for it. But he wasn't wasting time doing so. He's been aware of this activity from the beginning."

Brenner threw back his head and laughed before turning his chair to face Molly. "Look, I know you're mad. But let's be honest with each other. You can't do anything about your situation, so railing about it won't change anything."

"I have a *family* on Earth! I don't even know if they survived the radiation event. Don't you have a family back home Brenner? Somebody who you actually care about?" she asked him sharply.

Brenner's smile died and his eyes closed briefly. He stood up, gave Hatfield a small wave and walked out through the hatch, spinning the lock behind him.

"What the hell?" she demanded towards the hatch Brenner had closed.

"Ms. Caan, you should avoid making assumptions," Hatfield said as he stood. "Sloan, I've got to deal with our other little problem. Please brief Ms. Caan." With that he walked out another door, the military officers following after him and closing the hatch.

Molly turned on Sloan. "Yes, please brief me on what the hell just happened," she said bitterly.

"Which part? We're stuck here. Stokes isn't sure they can continue the freighters and it looks like the Chinese had a surge of their own on the Moon and now we're on the defensive and may not survive." Sloan spoke distractedly, watching Brenner's exit with concern.

"Not that, what's the deal with Brenner?"

"I probably shouldn't say anything."

"Sloan... you are the closest thing to a friend I have here, even if you do look down on me. I need to understand what that was about."

"I wouldn't say that, you and Erik seem to get along great."

Molly made a dismissive gesture, causing Sloan to raise an eyebrow in surprise as she spoke. "Stop changing the subject. What is wrong with Brenner?"

Sloan pulled her command suit glove off and began grinding a splintered nail against the edge of the table as she considered her words. "It took me a lot of effort to get the story and I'm still not entirely certain it's the full truth."

"Accepted; now spill it."

Sloan's face contorted as she considered her conflicted emotions. "From what I was able to find out, after the strike on the Three Gorges Dam there was a concerted effort to protect those involved, including their families. They split the design team for the weapon system up and sequestered them where they would be relatively safe. Think of it like a witness protection program, but for people that the Chinese considered war criminals. It was a huge disruption for their families; they didn't just take the immediate families, it was everyone in their extended families that there was any evidence of close contact with.

"Nobody is certain how the Chinese found the team members—the going theory is they hacked into the government databases and stole the information that some fool left in there. Others think one of those big classified data leakers who came out after the war started might have released the information. In any event, the Chinese sent hit squads out after them—the designers and their families. Brenner was on loan to the carrier program building the last of our allowed carriers. It was a secret assignment, fake name, job history the entire deal." Sloan paused, swallowing hard, before continuing.

"They used micro-drones to nerve gas the compound Brenner's family was in. Killed them all. Considering he used a drone to destroy Three Gorges, they may have done it out of a sense of irony. They gave him the full treatment after that. Obituary in the paper, new identity, the works. That's when I learned his name wasn't really Brenner."

Molly sat in shocked silence, absorbing Sloan's words as the pieces gradually fit into place.

"I did some research, apparently he took the last name of the Dutch Governor who bought Manhattan for a bunch of useless trinkets. I don't know why he chose Brenner. I don't really have the guts to ask him, to confront the truth. But if you want to know why Brenner feels no desire to go home, it's because all that remains for him there is a death squad and the memories of a family that died because of him."

"I remember the story," Molly said quietly. "The massacres happened right as I became an intern in the Senate. It was one of my first classified meetings; they were blaming each other for whoever was responsible for the leak that led the Chinese to them. Nobody knew who caused it."

"Or admitted to knowing. Interns in classified meetings…" Sloan shook her head sadly. "That's probably how the leak happened in the first place," she said bitterly. "He effectively ended the war, brought the world back to peace before a full nuclear exchange happened. In return, he lost his entire family, his name, his history, his friends and all they gave him was a million dollars and an NDA prohibiting him from discussing it, ever. And yet, you wonder why he has no problem taking the Government out behind the wood shed for a thrashing."

Molly swallowed, looking away from Sloan's eyes and blinking back tears. "I … I don't know what to say."

"Our Government, for years, has acted with impunity. Enriching themselves, their friends, doing whatever they pleased with no concern for the consequences. You want to know what to say? You can start with "I'm sorry." If you really want to make amends, you can stop spreading fear in our employees and work with the cards you've been dealt. It's a shit hand, but you're only here because you've been swimming in shit your whole career." Sloan paused, before awkwardly reaching out to grasp Molly's hand. "I know that sounds harsh. I really do sympathize with you and I realize that we've treated you in much the same way many of us were treated. I know that's not... fair," Sloan said, tripping over the final word awkwardly.

Molly sniffed hard, rubbing the tears out of her eyes and trying to put a brave face on before she looked Sloan in the eyes. "I know. I think, I know you've been through a lot. The war hurt us all in different ways, sometimes it's hard for me to understand the true impact because I never really was directly impacted. I mean... I... we went out partying when the Armistice was signed. It was just an excuse to go party, but nobody from my hometown died in the war. We didn't suffer food shortages or any of the missile attacks from China. I know building this base was very challenging. And... I know you've been nothing but kind to me since I got here, even when the Senator was badgering you, you still treated me well. I just..." Her voice trailed off, searching for an answer, tears springing anew from her eyes.

"It's just you've never lost your freedom. Never been a refugee." Sloan's eyes took on a distant look as she thought back to the war. "I remember the evacuation from Portland, after the nukes hit. We got lucky and headed south into the forest down OR 224. Many people headed east, down I-84, into the path of the fallout. I remember the complete lack of government support in the evacuation. The armed forces were all deploying, or preparing to, the police were trying to evacuate their own families. It was chaos. Looting, rape, no food, the roads were clogged with stalled vehicles. People were dropping and lying on the side of the road exhausted from the radiation exposure. Nobody had told us how to care for radiation exposure, it was a total breakdown of society, of government.

"You'd see people with horrific burns or concussive injuries from the actual nukes themselves mixed in with the people who were injured in the rush to escape. People were packing out the most senseless things ... I ... I lost my nephew in the crowd there. He thought he saw his mom and just took off into the middle of a huge crush of refugees. We never found him, I just hope somebody saw a small child and helped him escape." Sloan stopped talking, staring blankly at the wall.

After a few moments she looked back at Molly, speaking firmly. "You are a refugee now. The best thing you can do is survive, until the situation changes. The first rule of surviving out here, of surviving Hatfield, is to make yourself useful. Right now, he has a task for you."

"A task?" Molly asked numbly.

"Yes. Tomorrow morning, you and I are going to take Erik to the Eden Cave. The Director thinks he needs a break. He's one of the smartest people out here, but he's suffered a series of pretty serious setbacks. We had a failed weapons test, the ship he was responsible for testing returned only to sling a ball of energy through the solar system irradiating everything in its path, and now this latest weapon fiasco that nearly killed two thirds of our pilots. He blames himself. I've known him for years; he was always cheerful and fun to be around. But lately he just locks himself in his room. So we're going to test out the Director's theory that the Eden Cave can be used to help stabilize people teetering on the brink of a mental breakdown."

"What am I supposed to do?"

"You are going to go there and keep him company, to cheer him up and distract him. Sasha has already prepared rooms for the two of you."

"I am not going to be some plaything for your weapons designer to hump so he feels better!" Molly said, anger creeping back into her voice.

"*Stop!* You need to knock that off. You always assume the worst," Sloan said angrily. "You are not being sent there to be a sex toy—if Hatfield thought that would work, he would just send one of the girls from Phoebe's, who incidentally are probably a whole lot better at it than you. You are being sent there because during the alien attack, he responded to you when you talked to him. You are also being sent with him because frankly, you can be a royal pain the in ass when we include you in meetings. I think he's testing to see if you'll come back with a better perspective on our situation."

Molly recoiled from Sloan's anger, holding her hands up in surrender. "I'm sorry, I just . . . I've come to expect the worst from him."

Sloan sighed and rolled her eyes at Molly. "Oh really? Let's have a little reality check. You arrived out here in the company of a spy, when the spy got caught and all hell broke loose he *rescued* you from your demented boss. When he was confronted with the choice of feeding, clothing and housing you or throwing you out the airlock, he chose to let you live. He's included you in discussions about the plan forward, despite your clearly negative attitude toward his leadership style, and let's not forget that you aren't sitting in a cell next to your boss all day long. I'd say the worst he's done to you so far is bruise your ego and slap you with reality. This is the big leagues, time to understand that."

"He still prevented me from going home."

"No, Senator Hernandez holding a knife to your throat prevented that. Your own boss is the precise reason you are stuck here," Sloan said sternly.

Molly pursed her lips together tightly before taking a deep breath and letting it out slowly. "What do I need to bring with me to the Eden Cave?"

Sloan relaxed, leaning back and sliding her glove back on her hand. "Well I'd start with a happy attitude. Some clothes to relax in and that swimsuit Erik bought you wouldn't hurt. We do have a beach after all."

Molly let out an inadvertent laugh that caught in the back of her throat making her cough. "A beach, right." She stopped for a moment, thinking. "Actually a beach sounds very nice right now."

CHAPTER 14

Hatfield stood next to the SARine interrogator known simply as Joe in the company directory, and contemplated the scene on the other side of the observation window. He'd known Joe for years, a competent, if sometimes brutal, jack-of-all-trades who had been fundamental to maintaining his control of Saturn Base from the very beginning. It was that legacy of trust between the two men that checked his anger at the current situation.

"Have we made any progress at all in figuring out who's supporting Von Tremel?" Hatfield asked.

"We swept up the ones we knew about from cracking his files." He reached over and tapped on the thick glass one-way window next to him. "And a few of them like this clown occasionally pop up when we least expect it. It's going to be like whack-a-mole for a while unless one of them cracks I'm afraid."

Hatfield scowled, looking down the hall at the series of cells holding the prisoners of Saturn Base. On the right side were single occupant cells with pressed Phoebe rock furniture, a simple cot of nearly untearable fabric, and a basic bathroom. On the left side was a large single room cell with observation windows down its length.

In the first cell, he had one disgraced United States Senator, officially under medical treatment for a mental breakdown, unofficially in seclusion for attempting to murder her Chief of Staff during an abortive rebellion in the Research Center.

In the next cell he had brilliant materials scientist Dr. Augustus Von Tremel, who had been working for an unknown intelligence agency. Von Tremel had mentally cracked, then conspired with Senator Hernandez to try to destroy the Research Center. He'd also been designing weapons intended to penetrate the heavy command armor the senior leadership of the KaliSun Corporation wore, in an apparent bid to assassinate Hatfield. He was completely batshit crazy and only getting worse in solitary confinement, drawing obscene pictures on the wall using blood and feces while mumbling through his jaw, which was still wired shut from being broken during the rebellion.

The next cell held a new addition to his prison, Dr. Meckler, who upon interrogation had admitted to being aware of Von Tremel's plan before it kicked off. Meckler was now sitting miserably in the corner of his cell, crying into his hands. The final four cells held members of an intelligence operation that had been inserted into the Saturn Base employee rolls by an unknown party. Each had apparently been unaware of the other, only working through their handler. That same man had been handling Von Tremel, but had escaped on the last freighter out, at least temporarily. The last batch of trained SARines being sent to the MBTC had searched the ship and found him trying to blend in with the rest of the returning crew; he was still being interrogated as the ship transited back to Earth.

"A regular rat's nest," Hatfield said disgustedly. "How soon until you have it unraveled?"

"Fully? Maybe never. I think we've caught all the people who weren't supposed to be here. Now we have to figure out if there are more like Dr. Meckler; supposed to be here, but working for somebody else. That could take some time. Especially given the recent turn of events."

Hatfield grunted an acknowledgement as he turned and looked through a window on the other side of the hallway. Crouched in the corner was their other prisoner. With its small legs tucked in tight to its carapace, its big claws locked into a guard position over its face, and its damaged overclaw tucked tightly down its back, it looked almost like a rock, blending seamlessly into the color scheme of the walls behind it.

"That doesn't seem to be the color I remember from the initial pictures you sent me."

"It's not. Over time it has adapted to the wall color, both in the UV and visible light spectrum actually. Nearly perfect natural camouflage," Joe said with admiration.

"Have we made any progress communicating with it?"

"None. It doesn't seem to talk. Autopsies on the corpses don't indicate vocal cords as we would know them. But to a larger point, even if it could communicate in a way we understand, would it?"

"Look, we don't know how long these things have been in the system. We assumed they came here after the KaliSun's flight. But in reality that's because we could only see them when they were practically on top of us. They could have been here for years, decades even. Listening, watching. If you spent the last 100 years watching our species, would you want to talk to us?"

"A valid point I suppose," Hatfield said wearily. "What else do we know?"

"It's virtually invisible in IR, although when you get them fully stirred up in combat they do exude some IR, especially when they vent gas to push themselves in vacuum. Dr. Kapple's team has studied data from the attack. It looks like their internal body temperature is about twenty degrees warmer than ours, and they can regulate it via either a chemical reaction internally or through some kind of, uh, well they seem to be able to modify their carapace in such a way as to absorb radiation and convert it to energy. Here let me just show you the results."

Joe pulled his flexible display out of the shoulder of his command suit and stuck it to the wall. He backed away so that Hatfield could read while he pointed.

"First things first. We have found at least two variants of the . . . crabs. First variant is what we captured. It has those little T-Rex manipulator claws, a pair of gripping and or cutting claws, and an overclaw that seems to have a hinge enabling it to strike pretty much in any direction except underneath it. The three big claws are all armored to a degree, they absorb coherent light and are almost immune to any kinetic damage we can do with small arms. For that matter, the actual carapace is pretty heavily armored as well.

"Explosively formed projectiles and Von Tremel's zip gun could penetrate almost all of their armor. Shotguns at close range can damage the joints. SMGs and rifles just ricochet off, especially if the round strikes orthogonally to the surface; it's like shooting a steel plate.

"We had trouble discerning how their eyes work, they seem to have a nictating membrane like you would see in a underwater creature, but it's durable enough to act as a pressure seal in vacuum. There were other odd things about the eyes. During the autopsy we noticed that of the ten eyes, there seem to be four types. They're arranged in clusters of three with a bigger eye in the center. The bigger eye is utterly different than the others, we can't really tell what its purpose is; my personal opinion is it's a signal light of some sort, but I can't prove it. The three clusters of three remaining eyes give it a two hundred and seventy degree field of view. Each cluster seems to have an eye for different types of light, although we haven't determined exactly which types they can see. When they die, the membrane relaxes, so all of the dead ones suffered damage to their eyes. We can't communicate or even approach the prisoner, so that may be an unknown for some time."

"That matches most of what I learned from Brenner's report. Though he mentioned something about the blood being a meteor patch too, which didn't make much sense."

"Yes, we've gotten a couple of the biologists from the research group to look at it. Apparently if you make their blood expand rapidly, via heating or a pressure change, it hardens up." Joe chuckled. "It's almost perfect. Say you shoot them with a laser and actually get through their shell, their own blood forms a new barrier which you then have to cut through as well. You blow a hole in their shell with a gun and the rapid release of pressure causes the blood spilling through the hole to form a scab in an instant, containing the wound.

"I've never seen anything like this, but it makes them tough bastards in virtually any environment. It's like they evolved somewhere where even the slightest damage to the carapace could end them. We can't attack their armor with strong acids or bases; the bonds are so strong the acid can't oxidize the material. Dr. Kapple said he thought their shells appear to be a type of silicon based crystal structure." Joe flipped to a new chart. "He started to lose me when he talked about silicon encapsulation as a form of protection from oxidation, but from what I gathered, the structure of these molecules is basically a sea of organic material protected by a shifting silicon crystal lattice . . . it's inert body armor. Something far more advanced than we have, but heavier at the same time. Incidentally, we found this same molecule under that shiny reflective layer on the alien ship as well."

"Is it something they added to themselves? Something they extrude?" Hatfield asked as he flipped through the briefing material.

"We can't tell, but we know it's not the same for the second variant of crab we found. The two crabs we found orbiting Phoebe and attacking the MIC from the other side of the moon are different. Not so much in terms of internal structure, although that assessment has been hampered by the fact both corpses were mangled, but their externals were substantially different."

Joe shifted views to a whitened corpse, its innards blown clean away and shell shattered. He split the view to show gun camera footage from the Mongoose attacking it. "If you compare these two images you start to get an idea of the differences. The first, obvious difference is the small belly claws. On the first variant there are many of them and they seem to be almost secondary manipulation claws. On this variant there are fewer of them, they appear focused more on locomotion and are more substantial. The two front claws are also beefier, but also have bio-mechanical attachments; where that energy weapon was attached for instance. The claw is basically a claw and energy weapon in one compact package. They have more eyes, between three and five more clusters, giving them nearly universal coverage. Then there's the overclaw. It's capable of firing a dart of sorts, it's organic, weighs about two kilos and when we inspected one of them we detected a veritable shopping list of neurotoxin and other toxin components in it."

Joe looked uncomfortable and shifted to a new view, showing a scanning electron microscope's view of human blood under a microscope. "This is a sample of human blood." The view shifted to a video of the blood sample. "Here you see the introduction of a small portion of the stuff we found in the dart."

Hatfield leaned in and watched the display on the wall intently. A small tendril of dark purple liquid entered the plasma and started to spread out. At first nothing of interest happened, then the first red blood cell encountered it. The screen paused and indicated that the video had been slowed down. When the video restarted, the cell's membrane instantly dissolved, exposing the lipids and proteins beneath to the purple liquid, which violently expanded to wrap around the molecules, ripping them apart and spilling the hemoglobin into the plasma. The purple fluid ingested the hemoglobin greedily before the video abruptly stopped.

Hatfield stood stunned, staring at the screen. Before he could say anything, Joe played a second clip, this one from a more expanded view of the blood sample. As they watched, the toxin shredded blood cells, dissolved platelets and used their components to replicate itself, rapidly expanding to fill the entire slide with swirling purple fluid.

"We exposed it to plant material as well, pretty much the same result. Basically it's a chemical soup of organic compounds that can attack virtually any organic material they put in front of it. They destroy it, ingest it and then use the material from inside to replicate themselves. It works stunningly fast. We have no chemical, biological or mechanical system that can do this. If you get this on you or in you, you're going to die a horrible death."

"Even a surface contact?"

"Dr. Kapple seems to think so. He said it would take longer, but basically it attacks all organic molecules. We did expose it to a piece of carapace—it didn't do anything. 'Functionally uninterested' as Dr. Kapple said. When we exposed it to a piece of the crab's uh, meat, it attacked and destroyed it. We're not sure if the dart is used full time as a projectile or how they'd get another one. We can tell the toxins are produced in a gland located at the base of the overclaw that does not exist in the other variant. He's working on genetic sequencing of the two variants now to determine if they're actually different, if one is a female and the other is a male or . . . whatever else is going on," Joe finished awkwardly as he flipped through the last images.

Hatfield stared through the glass at the creature thoughtfully. "Did Kapple say when he would have a more complete workup on their biology?"

"He said he'll have a flash report in a few hours. Then they'll cross review that with the databases to determine if it's likely it originated from Earth."

Hatfield turned slowly toward him. "What?"

"Kapple said, and I quote, "We have deep oceans.""

"Bullshit. If we saw anything like this on Earth it would be the ultimate apex predator, we wouldn't even have finished swinging from tree to tree before this thing dominated us."

Joe smiled and gave an exaggerated shrug. "Hey, it wasn't my theory."

Hatfield sighed and glared at him. "So, what's your theory? And your opinion of them militarily while you are at it."

Joe paused, looking thoughtfully at the creature through the glass. "I don't think they're from Earth. I'd buy from an ocean planet or maybe even a gas giant. I dunno, maybe they can make themselves neutral in a gas atmosphere like they do in space. Kapple's assistant said, and I agree really, that these things look like they started off in some volcanic vent on the bottom of an ocean. He said very acidic ocean, but I can't speak to that. Then evolution took them up on land and eventually they made it to the stars. They are generations ahead of us in terms of technology and it's tough to see the line between their natural state and whatever genetic tampering they may have done. I think we shot a radhaz near them when we flew the *KaliSun* out there, they saw it or maybe got nailed by it, and tracked the ship back to find out what was going on." He stopped, letting seconds tick by before continuing. "They found us, we shot them up."

Hatfield looked at him sharply. "You sound like you think we shouldn't have fired."

Joe took a deep breath and smirked. "I'm just Monday morning quarterbacking. I think this was a scout craft, something that belongs to something bigger. The crew is too small, weapons too insignificant, and it spent considerable effort hiding. All of their technology seems to indicate they are used to fighting something at least on par with their tech level, yet they only brought ten or so crew to investigate a hostile system. It screams recon unit to me. Just those two variant Bs were enough to prang up one of the Mongoose, then you have the others we encountered. No weapons, no real tactics, they just tried to get in range to use their claws."

"Well we did hit them rather suddenly, maybe they didn't have time to get to their weapons."

"Would you approach an unknown base without being at battlestations? Especially if you were used to fighting dangerous foes?"

"No, not at all. We'd be buttoned up tight in full kit." Hatfield went silent, thinking, while Joe looked at him patiently, waiting for instructions. "Joe, work me up a contact plan to deal with this thing. I want to see a structured approach, with many safety features. This prison is already separated from the main facility, but just in case, strip all of the spare suits and other EVA equipment out so nobody here can escape. I want contact with this thing extremely limited until we understand its capabilities."

"Yes sir. One more thing, we have no idea what to feed it, have the other teams found anything like food on the ship yet?"

"They found some weird canisters that seemed to be sealed and need one of their claws to open. Some small shells, like you'd expect at, well, a crab cookout and not much else." Hatfield turned to head back to the airlock, before he got there he spoke over his shoulder. "Worst case, we can always feed him Meckler."

"I'm not sure subjecting it to that idiot is a good first step in diplomacy," Joe said with a laugh.

CHAPTER 15

Dance music thumped the series of small stages in Phoebe's burlesque section with a rhythmic pounding as Jacobs leaned back in a plush armchair and enjoyed the scene. In front of him was one of the small side stages, a ten-square-meter glass aquarium almost a meter tall with three poles sticking up out of it.

The glass walls were triple-paned, heavy-gauge scratch resistant glass, intended to protect the salt-water fish that swam through the coral reef from the loud music and repeated strikes of the dancer's heels. Lights embedded in the cutouts for the poles illuminated the vibrant colors of some of the most fantastic corals from Earth. Fish darted among the coral, and brilliantly colored mantis shrimp and snails roamed the sandy bottom.

The wall behind his chair was also an aquarium that ran from floor to ceiling, and was nearly seven meters across. Inside, schools of small fish and a couple of baby sea turtles cruised about, looking for food. A stream of bubbles in the center of the aquarium prevented people on the other side from seeing in to Jacobs' booth, which was just fine as far as he was concerned.

Unlike most strip clubs back home, this club also doubled as a brothel, so the normal rules about not touching the dancers didn't apply; so long as they were agreeable that is. For that reason, he liked the cozy, secluded, burlesque section over the main stages. Sure it cost a bit more, but it was definitely worth it, especially now.

He admired the dancer working the poles before him; Amy. It was amazing to watch her work. She'd been some sort of near-Olympic gymnast back on Earth before an injury made it impossible for her to compete. After a few stints trying to run yoga studios and step exercise classes, she'd run into a

KaliSun recruiter for the MIC. She'd been here ever since, one of the family.

The stage had small compensators near the ceiling, making the gravity higher toward the ceiling than the floor, allowing her to perform some truly amazing stunts as she shifted from pole to pole. Holding herself horizontal between two poles, just her toes on one and her hand on the other, she walked herself up and down the metal, swinging about inverted, twirling and spinning. It was something to look forward to. He watched as she climbed to the top of the pole and twisted a wheel on the ceiling. In the aquarium below, chaos erupted as a spurt of fish food blasted into the water.

The fish darted around in a feeding frenzy. As the food drifted to the bottom and the fish followed, the mantis shrimp struck, beginning a frenzy of their own. Soon the bottom of the fish tank was a mix of swirling sand, fish food, fish parts and gorging marine life. Jacobs smiled broadly. This never got old. Normally he could only afford to spend the day in Phoebe's casinos, dance halls and brothels once or twice a month, but these were hardly normal times.

The music died down as the song ended. Amy finished her routine by turning upside down on the pole, legs straight out with her hair dangling below her, and slowly twirling down to the glass floor to let her hair splay out above the fish. Jacobs gave a smile and clapped a few times as she untangled herself from the pole and hopped off the stage. She paused, throwing her hair back and putting it in a pony tail before landing bonelessly in one of the fake leather chairs next to him with an exaggerated sigh.

"So what did you think?"

"Looks like a new routine. I approve!" Jacobs said, taking a sip of honey liquor from his mug before handing it to her.

"Awesome!" she said, taking a sizable gulp before handing it back to him. "We've been short booze for weeks, I'd love to know where you rounded some up." She fought the seams of her costume and mopped sweat from her face and chest. "And yep, new routine. Brenner ordered us some new music and got some discs of the last couple of years of pole dancing championships sent down here to help us out. There are a lot of good ideas in there, but I do like to improvise a bit."

"I knew I liked that guy. First he brings booze to the moon and now he takes a moment out of his day to support single mothers!" Jacobs raised his hand in mock horror as Amy slapped his arm with exaggerated outrage.

"Come on now, I don't have any kids that I know of … "

"Wish I could say that same! But nope, I've got a real winner running around Kansas right now. Heard he was trying to breed his own football team. Too bad I got stuck with his student debt eh."

"Apple doesn't fall far from the tree," Amy said sweetly as she leaned over and planted a lipstick kiss on his cheek.

Before he could respond he saw her eyes shift over his shoulder, and he turned his head in time to see Sloan walk into the stage area with two of the Mongoose pilots behind her. She paused at the entrance of the alcove and admired the two tubes of backlit jellyfish that framed the door, the jellyfish floating serenely under the light as the music thumped in the background. She had two bottles of booze from her personal stash in hand and a fist full of martini glasses. Amy leapt out of her chair, jumped on the stage and ran over to Sloan to give her a hug and a kiss on the cheek, before grabbing her hand and pulling her over towards Jacobs, the Mongoose pilots following along behind them bemused.

"When Brenner told me that Hatfield gave you a five day all expenses paid MIC pass, I figured I'd find you in here," Sloan said with a smile as she slid open the bottle chiller in the table and placed the two bottles inside carefully.

Jacobs reached out and corralled Amy into his lap, doing his best covetous hoarder impression up at Sloan. "She's mine! Allllll mine." He sent a suspicious glare at the pilots and dropped his voice several octaves and grated out. "Miiiine."

Sloan laughed at him and dropped into Amy's chair, pointing at two others for the pilots. "So noted and don't worry, I know you earned a bit of a break." She pointed at the other pilots and smirked. "They did too, I'm not sure if you've met Kimmie Sinclair and Henry Terns?"

"Met sure. Know, eh. You know how it is," Jacobs said with a smile as he snaked a hand out from behind Amy's back and reached over to shake hands with the two pilots. "Though I seem to recall their names from the after action report."

"Yeah, what a shit show. I mean we won, but I'd rather not do it that way again," Henry said as he held a hand out for Sloan to pour him some booze. She winked at him and stole Jacobs's bottle off the table.

"Hey, that's my reward you're giving away."

"Yep, but Henry there, he earned it. His bird got pranged up and he ended up floating around in space for like seven hours waiting for a pickup. He's got the arm-chair equivalent of PTSD!"

Jacobs made a short sharp noise that almost sounded like a laugh before giving Sloan his best 'I'm too drunk to care' look. "I'll just have to drink it out of your bottle. Besides, sitting around in your titty tub waiting for a SAR bird is nothing compared to what my crew goes through every freighter run."

"Oh really," Kimmie said with a slight frown. Sloan rolled her eyes and leaned back in her chair, waiting for what she knew was coming.

"Sure, did you ever hear the story about Bill Stoogins? Probably not, it was before your time." He took a drink, starting again before anyone could really respond. "So Bill was my lead line jockey for the freighter runs, basically in charge of taking our small EVA pods out and connecting the cables between the two ships. Back then the controls were pretty primitive. Much of the tow package itself was actually Earth COTS products they had bought prior to deploying us, so none of the fancy stuff you might have seen on the way out here was in use yet. No IR painted cables, no beacons, no holo-HUD to fly by, real touch and feel flying. Probably not that different from when you came out of flight school in the Navy. Anyway, one trip we're trying to reel in this freighter that was loaded wrong. Somebody had made a last minute change to the cargo package and it unbalanced the center of mass."

Jacobs shifted his weight and Amy switched her seat from one of his thighs to the other. He rubbed her back as he continued with the story.

"So anyway, ol' Bill is zooming around checking the cables out. Never found out exactly what happened, but somehow either the cable he was carrying snapped or he hit something and it snapped the cable. Since it was under tension, he got slung away from the towing group at high speed. As he was going, he hit another cable and damaged most of his thrusters. So here I am on the bridge, watching him on radar and we keep trying to talk to him. Over and over again, with no luck. It happened so fast, none of the other EVA pods could get a line to him or grapple him. In less than half a minute, he was too far away to rescue. Destined to float through space until he died."

Jacobs paused, sniffing a bit and taking a drink. He looked up from the drink and stared directly at Kimmie before continuing. "So here he is, adrift. No fancy RTB button to help get him home, no SAR squad racing to his rescue. I've got this little pee shooter on the top of the *Atlas*, for fending off rocks and stuff, so when we finally get him on the radio I ask, "Hey man, do you want me to make it quick?" Now he's all breathing heavy, sounds like he's suffering a great deal. But he's not actually responding. So I activate the gunnery console and lock on, I'm saying a bit of a prayer for him before I hit the trigger and he comes back on the line. "Will you stop fuckin' praying Jacobs! I'm trying to jerk off here! I can't focus with you mumbling about God and his Angels in my ear!" So we're all just like, wait what was that? We're looking at his diagnostic and it shows he's leaking oxygen, no working thrusters left and he's in there spankin' it like he's sixteen again. Come to find out, Bill had decided that if he's going out, he's getting off first." Jacobs raised his glass and clinked it with Sloan. "I guess it was a form of auto-erotic asphyxiation, just kept going until the O2 cut off. Should be an interesting conversation with God when he gets there, eh? Anyway, the point is, seven hours waiting on a SAR bird is like getting stuck at the airport. He's going to be floating out there for an eternity, dick in hand."

Kimmie looked over at Sloan to confirm if it was a true story or if Jacobs was pulling her leg. Sloan smiled broadly and gave a shrug before commenting. "Funny thing is, they were close enough to Saturn that after a couple of years, Saturn managed to pull the pod into orbit and twice a year it's close enough for us to go recover. But nobody wants to go out there and look inside and see poor Bill's face as he finally crossed the GO/NOGO for launch threshold."

"He's one of the first pictures we put on the wall upstairs in the Employee lounge," Amy said soberly, stealing a sip from Jacobs' glass.

"Oh, wait. The red haired guy?" Henry asked, searching his memory for what the man looked like.

"Yep. Scrawny little dude. Damn fine pilot though, we found him up in Alaska working for an oil company."

Sloan started to say something when the music abruptly cut off and an announcement came over the speakers instead. *"Chief Goldsmith, please contact the watch officer immediately."* The voice repeated three times before the music kicked back on. She reached over and pulled a discrete phone off the back of the table and called the CIC.

After a few minutes of conversation she hung up, glumly handing her glass over to Amy and getting up. "I need to get back on the clock. Enjoy the booze, don't do anything too dumb." As she walked away the pilots put their glasses down and got up to follow her. She turned and stopped them. "No, you guys can stay. You're officially on required R and R, so enjoy yourself and Hatfield's vouchers," she said with forced cheer.

"What happened?" Jacobs asked her.

Sloan froze, her face an inscrutable mask. "Leblanc is dead, cause unknown, but not natural."

"The Marine Drill Instructor?" Kimmie asked with surprise. "But he's in great shape . . . "

"Yeah, I don't think . . . hmm, we'll talk when I know more for certain. In the meantime, have a good time, and don't forget Hatfield authorized an account for you at the casino, if you don't use it and lose it, it was a wasted reward!"

With that she flashed a smile and walked away, leaving Jacobs to stare at her retreating back, his hand no longer rubbing Amy's shoulders. Amy turned, looked down at him and gave him a wet kiss on the forehead.

"Hey guys, I have another new routine to show you. You'll love this one, I call it *'Love in Motion'*." She climbed off Jacobs' lap and did several provocative stretches in front of him before climbing back on the stage, her shadow causing the fish to dart around in a swift rainbow of iridescence.

Hatfield and Brenner stood next to Leblanc's bed and looked at what was left of him. His dark features were contorted in pain, jaw locked by rigor mortis in a silent scream. A red smear had spread through the sheets down near his stomach, and a technician was carefully lifting them away to expose a discolored prick mark on his side and a fist-sized hole leading into his stomach. The rest of his chest cavity and stomach area were shrunken, the skin tarped over his bones and nothing else—all the organs and muscle had been removed.

Hatfield tried to rub his forehead as he stood looking down, but ran into the helmet of his command suit instead. Moving his hand away in irritation he looked around the room. Nothing seemed out of place, Leblanc had been a very organized man. Originally from Ottawa, he'd spent much of his time in joint deployments with the United States Special Forces before teaching as a foreign instructor at Ranger School.

The history of his life was in this room. Framed pictures hung on the wall, a battle damaged Canadian flag was framed over his desk next to a professionally mounted display containing all of his rank insignia and medals from his time in service. The only thing out of place was his lifeless corpse on the bed.

Hatfield turned slightly to Brenner, activating his private channel. "Do we know who killed him?"

"No. There's no evidence in the log of anyone but him entering the room. They swept for evidence and found nothing particularly enlightening. Actually, they didn't find much of anything, he must have recently deep-cleaned this place."

"This better not be another of Von Tremel's bastards running around," Hatfield muttered as watched the tech work.

"I don't think it is. Von Tremel's guys were all into theatrics, you know, shutting off life support or blowing the seals on an airlock. Whoever did this removed his organs through a pretty small hole. If this is one of his guys, we've got a serious problem. This isn't murder, this is almost... I don't know, human sacrifice or something. I don't think we've seen organs removed this effectively since the Pharaohs ruled Egypt."

The tech looked back at Hatfield, his face tight with concern through his faceplate. "Sir, you better look at this."

Hatfield pulled up the image from the tech's probe, watching it pass through Leblanc's chest cavity. "What am I looking for?"

"Nothing. There is nothing left. No connective tissue, no veins, no blood. It's all gone. Some of those organs couldn't have fit out through that hole; the heart, liver or lungs, they're just too big. It's like they vanished. Also, if you look, there seems to be a hole to the left of his spine that's bigger than the entry hole."

"Maybe that's how the killer extracted them," Brenner said, stating the obvious in a patient voice.

"No sir, that's just it, if that was the case, the area under the back would be bloody too. No, whatever emptied him out, did it from that smaller hole, then punched a hole in his back after the cavity was more or less *dry*."

Brenner and Hatfield shared an alarmed look as the tech used his remote to move the probe through the hole in Leblanc's back and into a hole that seemed to penetrate into the bed. "Can you brighten it up, it's dark in there," Brenner asked.

The tech flicked a light on and instantly the medical probe was ripped out of his hands, pulling him off balance to land on Leblanc's corpse with a screech of pure panic. The corpse shook violently several times before the video feed went from shaky movement to a blank screen, the sensors crushed one by one.

Hatfield backed away quickly, almost tripping over the tech's evidence box and called out on the broadcast channel. "MARINES, INSIDE NOW."

Two large Marines, who had been standing guard outside the room since they'd found Leblanc, burst in through the hatch, swinging their close quarters weapons from person to person looking for the threat. A SARine stepped out of Leblanc's closet, swinging his weapon to bear, first on the two Marines then on the quivering corpse on the bed.

"Techs! Drop it and clear the room. Don't take anything with you," Brenner ordered as he reached up and grabbed Hatfield's shoulder. "You too sir. Now." Hatfield paused before heading out into the hallway. Two more Marines ran up and took protective positions around him.

Brenner looked at the SARine and made a hand motion. All four of them jumped into the same communications channel. "The corpse just started moving, we think we saw a hole under the body that goes down into the bed. Something is in there and it just took out the tech's probe."

The SARine nodded, looked around the room and spoke to Brenner in even tones. "Sir. I need you to get out and close the hatch behind you. Don't open it again unless you hear one of us give the all clear."

Brenner nodded and ducked outside, spinning the hatch shut and tripping the electronic locking mechanism. He pulled up the SARine's point of view camera on one side of his HUD and one of the Marine's gun cameras on the other and waited.

They watched as the Marines maneuvered through the room, keeping each other out of potential shooting lanes. When they were ready, the SARine reached down and grasped Leblanc's leg. He paused, giving it a soft squeeze of goodbye and then yanked his body off the bed. The two Marines leaned down their sights into the hole, waiting for something to happen.

They didn't have to wait long. Three miniature versions of the crabs they'd fought earlier shot out of the hole, charging after them on their little legs, their two main claws in an upraised position like crabs on Earth. A fourth crab hovered down inside the cavity in the bed, its big claws and a budding overclaw protruding, watching to see how the attack went.

The SARine raised an armored boot and brought it down with a sickening crunch on the smallest of the three attacking crabs, smashing its soft exoskeleton into the rug under Leblanc's bed and then kicking it off the floor like a soccer ball to smash into the wall. The other two were dispatched by quick bursts of shotgun fire at close range. Their carapaces not yet fully hardened, they exploded like melons, spraying blue blood all over the room and the Marines themselves.

The fourth crab sunk down into the hole and covered up, changing the color of its shell to match the surrounding bed material and the shadows. Seeing the non-aggressive behavior, the SARine pulled a small wire net used to transport materials in zero gravity out of his suit storage unit and opened it up. The Marines each took an end, then he stuck his gun barrel at the crab. It instantly seized the barrel and tried to pincer it in half, fracturing the anti-rust coating and spraying it around the room. Once he was sure the crab had it, he gave a tug, tearing it free from its hole and slinging it off the end of his gun barrel into the net. The Marines quickly secured the net's opening and stepped back. The self-closing safety mechanism activated, tightening the net down to a smaller and smaller size until the struggling package could no longer move.

As the Marines secured the crab, the SARine poked his weapon back into the hole and scanned for any more hostiles. There was nothing alive, just empty shells that had been discarded. He hooked one of the shells and pulled it out of the hole, letting his POV camera get a good look.

Brenner looked at it and swore. "John, I think these might be baby big crabs. That looks like it molted its skin to grow a new one."

"I know."

"We could have an infestation," Brenner said insistently.

"Yes, I know. I want you to go back through the tape from the fight in Broadway. Find out how these things got from vacuum to Leblanc's bedroom. Check everything, sensors, air quality handlers, the works. Hurry." Hatfield started to turn away before stopping. "And Brenner, I want you to close off the food tubes and Eden Cave. We can't afford these getting into a large body of water."

The thought of the crabs loose in the Eden Cave sent a chill down his spine as he ordered a lock down of the mil side. He started jogging back toward the CIC just as the SARine poked his head out. Seeing Brenner's retreating back he turned to Hatfield.

"That was the top of my 'shit I don't need to see' list, sir. The very top."

CHAPTER 16

Erik sat quietly under a tent that was flapping in a stiff breeze coming off the water. It smelled like the ocean, felt like the ocean, but he knew it wasn't a real ocean, not even a respectable sea. It was little more than a lake with artificial currents and wicked, unpredictable tides. But as he sat there, digging his toes in the sand, he had to admit it was still better than the best the MIC could offer. He scanned the horizon. A kilometer of sand stretching in either direction along the beach, a deceptively calm water surface, only broken by feeding fish and the occasional whitecap. Behind him stretched fields of short grasses, orchards and crops. Some of the land was clearly of lesser quality, with nothing but scrub to prevent erosion. There was a strange lack of the sort of insects you'd expect on a beach, and the grains of sand were rough, unweathered. There was no driftwood or shells, just pure, ground-up crystalline material and silicon, unblemished by the debris of mankind. He ran his fingers through it, feeling the sharp purplish crystals slide through the finely ground brown sand. It just didn't quite feel right.

He lazily stretched and took a drink of water from a jug nearby, his movements waking up Molly as she lay sunbathing a short distance away. She rolled up on her side, looking at him as she adjusted the two piece bathing suit he'd bought her during the flight test. He smiled at her noncommittally; she was fun to be around when she dropped the obsession for politics and just tried to act like a normal person.

"You want something to drink?" he asked her as he held out the jug. She shrugged and rolled over on her stomach, reaching out for the jug.

"So what do you think of the Eden Cave Erik?"

"I'm torn between being pissed I didn't know about it and amazed they managed to build it in secret. Now that I think back, I remember Sloan being gone a lot more than usual and a lot of hints. But somehow I missed the entire thing. It's not quite like a beach on Earth, but still, it's pretty amazing. Sasha says she's going to start releasing sea birds next week, maybe that will be the thing that makes it feel more right. That and a bonfire on the beach with some beer and fresh steak wouldn't hurt."

"I have to admit, when they brought me here I was stunned. Congress had no idea that he was building this, and frankly we'd have been pretty angry if we had known."

"Still burns me a bit that they showed you first," Erik said, looking over at her with a weak grin. "No offense."

She shrugged. "Sloan said Hatfield didn't want you distracted from the ship."

"Yeah, that ship," Erik said morosely, thinking back. They'd tested the engines on it with subscale tests, never going fully critical, never running it very long. When the ship had launched on its test run, they'd paid the price for that mistake.

"Hey, you're here to relax, not fixate on that thing," Molly said kindly.

"I know, but it's hard not to remember that you're at least partially responsible for sending half the human race back to the Stone Age, and maybe started a war with an alien species."

"I'd blame Hatfield, you were just doing what he told you to. Let it go."

"I seem to recall that's how the Nazis at Nuremburg defended their actions. 'I was just following orders . . . '"

Molly looked at him, her eyes inscrutable behind her sunglasses, but she didn't rise to the bait. "I don't like Hatfield, but I don't think he's quite that evil. I think he just spent more time trying to keep it secret than worrying about how badly it could go wrong. But that's not the point, you're supposed to be here relaxing. So relax."

A faint smile crossed his lips before he looked back out over the water. Without looking back at her, he spoke again.

"Speaking of relaxing, this is probably the most abandoned beach in the solar system, it's not like you can't avoid tan lines."

Molly's cheeks flushed and she flicked some sand in his direction. "Who says I care about tan lines?"

"Sure, sure, wouldn't want to blemish that uptight, proper, image of yours," he teased.

She scowled at him. "I'm sure you have no ulterior motive to getting my top off either."

He looked at her, a lopsided grin plastered on his face. "Who said anything about just your top?"

Her face turning lobster red, Molly did her best to glare at him, but the fake innocence of his look in her direction was too much and she couldn't help but laugh. "Such high hopes you have…" Her voice trailed off as she heard a rattling noise approach them along the path leading to the beach. They looked back toward the landward side of the cave in time to see Sasha Reynolds bouncing down the trail in her work cart.

Erik let out a sigh. "To be continued, I think."

"What, the great lady's boy gets nervous when somebody watches him work his game on a different girl?"

"Don't use the term lady boy please." Erik shuddered as a chill went up his spine. "I worked three months in Thailand once; the things I saw…"

Sasha left the trail and drove across the sand toward them, the six wheels of her cart throwing up small rooster tails of sand as she sped along. She slid to a stop not far behind them and hopped out, reaching back to pick a wet brown ball of fur out of the container of water strapped to the middle seats and striding through the sand to them.

She lifted the flap of the tent and plopped down on the sand, putting the little furball on the towel in front of her. She pulled out a jar of worms from her cargo pants and un-screwed the top. "Are you guys having fun out here?"

Erik looked at little ball of fur with distrust in his eyes.

"What is that?"

"This is Tipper," Sasha said, as she held a worm in front of its face. Eagerly the creature ran its bill down her arm into her hand and took the worm, immediately looking for another.

"That's its name, what the hell is it?"

"Seriously? It's a platypus. You've never seen one before?" Sasha asked.

"Uh maybe once in a book. Why is it here?" Erik said with distaste as he watched the small creature gorge itself on worms.

"Sloan smuggled them out here," Molly said helpfully. "They're her pets."

Sasha flicked a look at Molly before answering. "Sloan likes them, so she smuggled some out on one of the last freighters. They live in the river systems and will be the predator to keep the prey animal populations in check. This little girl got abandoned by her mom though, so I've been raising her since she was the size of an apricot."

"Looks like badly designed prank," Erik muttered under his breath as the platypus rambled around the towel, poking at his clothes, sunglasses and knocking over his box of crackers. "Gah, the thing is a menace." He reached a hand down to fend off the little bundle of fur's aggressive curiosity.

"Oh relax. She's harmless. They're just hungry all the time. Fortunately since we've been trying to compost all the plant waste we can, the population of worms has really taken off. So there is no shortage of food." Sasha leaned over to pluck the platypus off the towel and plop it down again between her legs. Immediately it started snuffling her hands and trying to get under her knees to explore.

Erik sighed, but a smile tugged at the corners of his mouth as he saw the creature try to crawl into the cargo pouch that had held the container of worms and get stuck. Its bizarre tail was poking out and its head was trapped in the pocket, its legs trying to find enough purchase to back out of the hole. He looked over at Molly and noticed she was captivated with the creature, half crawling toward it across the sand.

"So anything going on today Sasha? Do you need any help?"

"I'm under orders that you aren't to help me unless it's an emergency," Sasha said with a smile. "However, I did have one bit of news for you. For some reason they've temporarily sealed the tunnel back to the main base and we have ten Marines setting up shop at the entrance. Here's the note that Brenner sent me." She handed her tablet over to Erik and he peered down at the screen.

"Some kind of quarantine, evidently they are searching the entire mil side for something. Hopefully we don't have more saboteurs running loose," he said dismissively. He looked up at her suddenly. "What did the Marines say when they saw the Eden Cave?"

Sasha brushed some stray platypus hair off her pants and shrugged. "It's hard to say, they had their faceplates opaque. But I did catch two of them standing on the overlook staring at the ocean. I don't think they were expecting to see the ocean."

"It's not really an ocean," Erik said with an eye roll.

"It is to me. Since I am the master of this cave now, that means it is to you too," Sasha said pertly. "Now let's head back up to the house, I've made you guys some lunch. Don't worry about the tent, I don't think anyone is going to steal it."

She got up off the sand, cradling the platypus in her arms as she walked over to the rover. Molly and Erik followed her to the cart, brushing the sand off as they went. Sasha put Tipper in her water tub, where she proceeded to dive down and quickly scan the bottom, checking for any surprise tidbits to eat.

"There is one more thing you can do for me, if you really want to help," Sasha said as she turned toward Erik.

"What's that?"

"Brenner gave me fishing gear, but it's all still in the original packaging. I've never fished a day in my life, if you can figure out how to put it all together and maybe see if you can catch a fish or two for dinner, that would be great!"

Erik slung himself up in the seat and looked over at her. "Sure, how many rods are there?"

"Couple hundred, I think he intends to eventually let people sportfish on the Atlantic salmon we planted. So he got extras."

"A couple hundred ... Sure, I'll get right on that." He nudged Molly sharply in the ribs, catching her off guard. "Maybe he got a few kid-sized rods, you know something you can handle ... "

"I can handle an adult's rod!" Molly shot back.

"Oh, is that so? You'll have to show me sometime," Erik said with a laugh, tossing a wink in Sasha's direction.

"Wait ... damn it Erik," Molly said with exasperation, punching him in the arm.

Sasha spun the cart back toward the trail to the main house. Up ahead, the glimmer of Sloan's diamond monument glittered like a beacon, beckoning them home.

CHAPTER 17

Christie Elliot followed Kyle Winters as they were escorted from the tram station around the damaged Broadway section of the military side to a conference room. Along the way they saw numerous checkpoints manned by armed Marines, crews searching the air ducts and electrical panels also escorted by Marines, and the base's three bomb disposal dogs being led around to sniff the corridors. As they entered the room, Christie did a quick scan of the table to see who else had been invited. Seated along one side of the table she saw Major Stringer, Sergeant Major Marin, Major Sirano and Chief Graves. Along the other side of the table was the Deputy Director, Chief Sloan Goldsmith, Dr. Walter Kapple and a couple of people she didn't recognize.

She opened a private channel to Dr. Winters and muttered into her helmet mic. "I see a few people missing . . . "

"Yeah, I'm not getting a good vibe off this. We're the only two members of the research team here."

They took their seats and Christie looked around. She'd never been here before and the room was impressive. Lining the walls were banners for military units, scale models of different space ships sat in glassed-in recesses underneath them and there were video displays everywhere. Scenes of the various moons played out on the perimeter monitors like vibrant screensavers, live feeds from the observation satellites studying the Saturn system. The monitors hanging over the conference room table itself presented updated views of all spacecraft traffic in the region, with a clock ticking down in the corner until the next freighter arrived.

She had just taken her helmet off and was hooking it on the back of the chair when Dr. Rogers, the base's lead planetary scientist, entered the room with Hatfield, the Director's aide Jim Dover immediately behind them. They took their seats at the end of the table as the SARine guarding the hatch slammed it shut and locked it tight. Her wrist interface beeped several times indicating that the system communication gear had been disabled. Christie raised an eyebrow at Kyle as his lips set in a firm line, but she said nothing.

Hatfield spent several moments conferring with Brenner and preparing his presentation. Christie was shocked by his appearance. While he was still alert and focused, his body language betrayed a weariness and fatigue she had never seen before. There was a tightness about his eyes and lips that suggested somebody under a great deal of stress. He looked up and rapped the table hard with his gloved hand, causing the quiet buzz of conversation die.

"I've been sent a rather pointed request for information from CEO Stokes to update him on our current status. All of you have been called here so that we can get our house in order. I want to send information once. I want the story we send to be complete. The more times we transmit this data, the higher the chance they'll crack our encryption. This is one time the enemy reading our mail can have severe consequences, so I ask that any notes taken during the meeting be secured prior to leaving the room," Hatfield said in clean, stern tones.

"Which enemy are you worried about?" Dr. Winters asked delicately.

"Any enemy. Right now that means anyone outside the leadership of the Corporation." He paused, giving Brenner a nod.

The Deputy Director hit a button on his console, changing the screens above the table to show a mix of pictures of the alien ship, the alien itself and the damage to Broadway.

"First thing. We have encountered an alien species. It is a spacefaring race and has better technology than we do." He stopped, letting it sink in for those who hadn't already known. "They approached the base in a stealth ship, we were able to detect them intermittently, enough to launch a strike."

"So we initiated the hostilities?" Dr. Rogers asked.

"Yes, we weren't even sure it was a ship when we engaged it. The ship's stealth capacity was . . . is very impressive. But yes, we fired the first shots," Hatfield said.

"Are we sure they were hostile?" Christie asked cautiously.

"No, we are not. Although it seems reasonable to conclude they are now. All of you should be aware by now that we've been training military forces at this base. Pilots, Marines and SARines," he said with a gesture at the armored figure standing near the hatch. "Most of those forces were sent back to Earth prior to a recent experiment we conducted, in case there was blowback."

"That radiation event, we caused that?" Christie said with sudden realization, interrupting the Director and causing Dr. Winters to shoot her a quelling look.

Hatfield grimaced as he answered. "That is one possible theory. Another theory is that the aliens sent it in system toward Earth as they arrived to knock us off balance, then proceeded to this base to investigate us." As he finished Brenner gave him a quizzical look, but remained silent. "At present, we have their ship, heavily damaged, and one of their crew in our possession. As of right now, all other scientific activities are suspended. All assets will be redirected to examining the ship and trying to understand the species. For reference, this tiger team will be denoted 'Gravel Patch', Dr. Kapple will lead the biology assessment with Dr. Winters in support. Dr. Rogers is leading the origin investigation, Dr. Surjit Malhotra is going to lead the assessment of the ship's construction. He has already been dispatched to the ship in fact. Dr. Samuels will be working on trying to get a handle on the ship's equipment, he and Dr. Malhotra will likely need assistance from the other team leads from time to time." Hatfield turned his gaze toward Christie. "And you Dr. Elliot, are to begin full time operation making more Type 37 particle pairs. Brenner and Chief Graves will coordinate a storage process for you as well."

Christie gulped and nodded. At least now she knew where Sam had mysteriously vanished off to in the middle of the night.

"I want a five day intense review of the data, at the end of that, we send what we have. Brenner and Sloan are going to red team this presentation and try to hit you with every question they expect Stokes to ask. Let me be clear, if you don't know, say so. Don't make wild-assed statements. Treat it like an intel write up, I'll have the SARine Commander give you a sanitized example, but to summarize, every single assessment must be preceded with a classification identifier and concluded with the name of the person who made the statement and a confidence interval; low, medium, high and fact. Any questions?"

"Are we going to co-opt any of the contract researchers?"

"No," Brenner said coldly. "If you have a specific person you need from a different KaliSun team vet them with Joe," he said, gesturing at the SARine by the door. "There is to be no interaction on this topic with the contractors. We have reason to believe there are security risks still in that population, we can't take any chances."

"Is that why we have the security sweeps and checkpoints in the hallways over here but not on the civilian side?" Dr. Rogers asked.

"No, sadly that's a different matter, which we should address now. Drill Instructor Leblanc, a long-term member of the team, was killed in bed eighty hours ago. Brenner, please take them through the timeline."

Brenner stood up, moving over to a large wall that turned into a projection display. "What we have here is a timeline from detection to today," he said, pointing at a fairly complex timeline that looked like a skeletal fish, with on ramps and off ramps as various events converged on the main story arc. "We engaged the ship with spacefighters, eventually disabling it. Upon disabling it, we boarded with a mixed force of SARines and Marines. During the course of that insertion, we encountered the first alien, which is the charming creature on screen four. It inflicted a number of casualties on the Marines before retreating into a room where it has remained ever since, we can't get in and we can't get it to come out. As they were dealing with that creature, the alien ship fired a weapon of some sort that did extreme damage to the section of the base referred to as Broadway. Immediately afterward, they sent a landing party toward the large hole in the side of the base."

Brenner brought up a picture of the gaping hole in the moon rock, causing both Dr. Rogers and Dr. Winters to make startled sounds and lean in to look at it. Brenner held off while they inspected it.

"Energy weapon I presume?" Dr. Rogers asked.

"We think so, the Marines blew the power coils for it while it was firing. If they hadn't, it probably would have made it to the main base reactor. Adios muchachos," he said with a shrug. "We engaged the landing party near the end of the damaged portion, encountering four surviving mature creatures. Three were killed during the exchange; a fourth was captured. We've made attempts to communicate with it, so far unsuccessfully."

"Mature creatures? Have we found immature ones?" Kyle interrupted to ask.

Brenner shot him a look and continued without answering. He expanded the view of the timeline, bringing several things into focus simultaneously on the screens. "As we proceeded with cleanup and recovery, the tug *Atlas* managed to secure the alien ship, which had been continuing toward the base. He had to use an ad-hoc towing system to try to kill its inertia—it was a close call. The ship was eventually moved to an area away from the base for further study. We don't understand how it's powered, so we're trying to keep it far enough away that if the reactor or whatever goes, we're not sitting on a bomb in the middle of the base. Also, since there's still one alien on board, we want it sequestered for now."

"Jacobs managed to grab that thing on the fly? I hope you slipped him a bonus check," Rogers said with a chuckle.

"He's being well taken care of in the MIC as we speak," Hatfield said, with the first trace of a smile he'd displayed in the meeting.

Brenner smirked and continued, serious once more. "While we were securing Broadway, one of our senior design engineers, Dr. Erik Bilks, located an injured Marine who had been reported missing. He'd been in a room just off Broadway when the strike occurred and was unconscious with his suit leaking atmosphere. My interdiction team, having secured the bodies of the three dead crabs and the live one, moved to assist him. It was at this time, when we didn't have tight observation on the corpses, that this happened."

He played a short surveillance video taken from a mobile SARines recon eyebot that had been recording the corpses. One of the corpses heaved under its restraints, cracking open near the rear. As they watched, a series of small shapes left the crack and headed, single file, into the debris field, scooting through the vacuum as if propelled by something. The video stopped and several enhanced images of individual frames replaced it. The string of objects resolved into a line of crab-shaped creatures, very similar to the alien adult next to them, but with one glaring exception. Instead of the overclaw, each one had a large golden colored liquid bubble attached to their rear.

"Evidently, while we were distracted, these things left the mature crab and entered the debris field. Based on evidence we recovered at the scene and pieced together afterward, we believe these creatures, whether they are young crabs or parasites, are what killed Leblanc." He pulled up a picture of a chest piece from a set of command armor. "If you look closely, you can see in the abrasion layer some claw marks or small cuts. This is Leblanc's armor; he came to inspect the battle scene after the fight. We believe as many as four of those creature attached themselves to his armor, changed their coloration to match the armor and were able to ride like ticks back to his room. Once there he took his armor off and took a shower. He climbed into bed, where at least one of them stung him; whatever was in it, caused him to be immobilized. Then the crabs cut a hole in his side and crawled in, where they devoured his organs and muscle tissue."

Brenner brought a picture of Leblanc's emaciated body up on the display, followed closely by an internal view of what had been his thorax. Christie felt her stomach heave as she saw the shrunken features and plundered insides. She closed her eyes, fighting the urge to vomit. Brenner saw her reaction and hastily changed the image.

"Sorry Christie, I just wanted you to know what we were dealing with." He took a deep breath and continued. "After they were done . . . feeding, they cut a hole in his back and burrowed down into the bed, which is where we found them a day later. During the time they were digesting, they appear to have gone through several molting stages, getting bigger and shedding their carapace. One of them became quite a bit larger than the others and seemed to be telling them what to do when we discovered them. Three attacked our Marines and were dispatched, we captured the fourth one."

"I thought you said you only had one in captivity?" Dr. Rogers asked as he took notes.

"We currently only have one in captivity, the little one died. We'll get to that momentarily with Dr. Kapple. After the incident in Leblanc's room, we locked the base down and set up the checkpoints. Currently we've accounted for eighteen of the estimated twenty little ones that escaped into the debris. The four in Leblanc's room, plus we think fourteen more in one of the primary air ducts."

Brenner pulled up an image of the air duct, showing a menagerie of different sized crabs piled up in a corner. Their golden globules were gone and their carapaces trying to match the walls of the duct.

"I only see twelve in the picture," Christie said.

"Yes, we think those golden sacks attached to them are like egg yolks of a sort, a source of food. Once it runs out, they appear to cannibalize each other. We were able to determine fourteen possible individual bodies, there could actually have been more in there, but it's difficult to tell because they were badly mangled when discovered by the eyebot, one of them attacked it and it discharged its primary energy cell into them. Their equivalent to DNA appears very similar, like siblings."

"So the checkpoints and scanners are to find the last two?" Dr. Winters asked.

"Yes, we want to make sure they stay out of food tubes at all costs and would prefer they don't prey on any of our people too," Brenner said with a grim smile. "Dr. Kapple is going to brief you on what we think we know."

The German smiled at the assembled group. "Somewhat unusual task I've been given, I look forward to your help Dr. Winters. The cell biology is quite exotic. I've made some progress in sequencing their genome, which is structured very differently from ours. Basically all of the four main specimens have very similar gene patterns, siblings or maybe even clones. The other variant is a different genetic pattern . . . "

"Which other variant? The baby ones?" Dr. Winters asked.

"No, we encountered two others that appear to have been ejected during the space battle. They're different. I'm sorry, I skimmed past that," Brenner said.

"It's a small matter, the variances are tiny and seem to be focused on recessive genes," Dr. Kapple continued. "They have a very interesting biology. Their blood is actually somewhat similar to what you would see in a lobster, with Hemocyanin present and the oxygen transported via hemolymph instead of red blood cells. Because of the Hemocyanin, there is a surprising amount of copper in their system, which results in the blood looking blue when it has been oxygenated. This implies they evolved in a low oxygen environment, and they appear to be able to survive in a low oxygen condition for considerable amounts of time. There are, however, a number of unexpected proteins present, one of which likely increases the efficiency of the Hemocyanin as an oxygen transport mechanism, far beyond terrestrial crustaceans. One could theorize this directly impacts their brain development and could be the reason they ascended the food chain. The blood strongly absorbs the UV spectrum in the 420nm area, resulting in it appearing that vibrant color to us. The blood also contains a number of coagulants that are of significant interest. Essentially, when exposed to a decrease in pressure or change in temperature, the blood hardens. They don't use a typical cardiovascular system like we do, so hardened blood doesn't pose a risk."

"What do you mean?" Dr. Winters asked, puzzled.

"The blood seems to reach an equilibrium state with its surrounding plasma. So it doesn't really flow through the creature, but sits in reservoirs throughout the body with gasses equalizing the pressure throughout the system. As such, it lacks a heart."

"It would have to, to do that to Leblanc," Master Sergeant Marin said under his breath.

"We're not sure the little gobbers are intelligent yet Gene," Major Stringer muttered back.

"The Major is correct, it is likely the little ones act on instinct. Escape the dead parent, hide, find a host to feed off and grow. Judging by the carcasses that were more intact, we don't believe they get sentience until they approach the size of the one we captured in Leblanc's room," Kapple said kindly. "Moving on, typical earth peptide chains would be around 660 to 665 peptides long, these seem to have close to two thousand, but much of it is redundant. It appears this could make them virtually immune to diseases such as cancer. We found some evidence to suggest that genetic tampering may have occurred. I've already sent significant amounts of data down to my team on project Steakhouse to see if they can make any progress with them," Dr. Kapple said, with a nod toward Hatfield who made a note on his tablet.

"By all appearances, they molt to grow. We can't figure out how they communicate with each other. We found no written text anywhere. When we introduced the small crab in the enclosure with the adult one ... well it wasn't pleasant." Dr. Kapple played a video clip.

The small crab was dumped into the room through an airlock. It ran quickly away from the door and tried to hide against the wall. The big adult crab in the corner remained motionless until the smaller crab had changed his colors to match the wall. With a sudden burst of speed the large crab lunged forward, pinning the small crab down with a massive claw before driving its overclaw down into the small crab's carapace, crushing it to the floor. The adult crab positioned itself over the corpse and lowered itself down. The video fast forwarded ten minutes and showed the adult move back to his original location. There was no trace of the little crab, not even a blood smear.

"Poor little guy, never had a chance," Sloan said.

"We don't know how to explain that," Dr. Kapple said simply.

The room fell to silence as each of the assembled mulled over what they had been told. Finally Hatfield spoke up softly from the end of the table.

"I've got the SARines developing an analysis report on the tactics and techniques we used to win. I need this group to expand on Dr. Kapple's initial analysis. As of right now, the auto-factories are authorized for initiation. Major Stringer and Major Sirano, I want a full list of what you need immediately. We'll prioritize spares and replacements before we make entire new spacefighters. Chief Graves, make sure you get your list in too. If there are no questions, you are dismissed."

The group silently got up and filed out through the hatch, each trapped in their own thoughts. As Christie linked up with Dr. Winters to walk back to the tram she couldn't help but remember the image of Leblanc lying on his bed, a shadow of a man. She felt a shudder as she pulled her helmet back on and stepped into the scanning field, sweeping her spacesuit for any trace of alien babies tucked away, hiding.

CHAPTER 18

Forsythe leaned forward in his chair, resting his chin on the metal knuckles of his glove and watching the display in front of him intently. It had been nine days since Hatfield's report had arrived with little fanfare, another two days before they could decrypt it all. Since then the MBTC had been on full lockdown, communications to Earth were heavily restricted, flights were limited and the entire engineering core had been racing to implement Saturn Base's survival plan.

He looked over at the sensor operator and spoke quietly. "Is it performing within tolerance?"

"Yes sir, the radars are communicating well within the latency margins and we're getting clean beams on the search function." He swallowed significantly before continuing. "Either these things aren't here or maybe they don't even exist . . . "

Forsythe took a breath and leaned back as he answered. "They exist. One of them shot up Saturn Base, they captured it."

"But maybe it was the only one . . . I mean we've seen no evidence of them since," the sensor tech persisted.

"We keep looking," Forsythe said firmly.

The tech turned back to his work and Forsythe went back to studying the report. It certainly didn't lack detail—it was over two thousand pages. He should have known to press Hatfield to focus on the critical aspects of this thing. He really didn't care much for its cannibalistic traits, he wanted to know how to see it before it landed in the middle of the base.

He looked up as Captain Menendez walked in and sat next to him. The intelligence officer looked tired. His team had spent the last four days digging through every UFO report in the United States databases hoping to find some sign that these things had been seen before. They'd come up with nothing. Now they were trying to see if any more were hovering around the MBTC using Hatfield's new scanning technique, a technique that had yet to detect a ship, but in theory should work.

"You doing alright Julio?"

Julio stretched and tried to scratch his shoulder through the collar of his armor. "Just tired. We've been grinding pretty hard on this data and so far we've got almost nothing. I took a break from it and have been working the freighter problem with Robbins."

"I'm sure he appreciated that, he's been pulling what's left of his hair out trying to figure out how to get that thing in here safe. What did you guys decide?"

"We need to work it out with the Wing Commander, but we've got ten courier Angels now, so the plan is we do a high speed recovery of the critical personnel as early as we can. Maybe even before the tugs hook up. We tank halfway back and then try to scoot through too fast for them to interdict us. We're also discussing having them make moonfall to the east, it will burn a little more fuel, but it adds three hundred kilometers to the Chinese intercept efforts, so there's a chance we can make them choose between letting them through or sending their fighters on a one way trip."

"Ten Angels ... even if they use the most basic suits they can only bring about a hundred men back at once. There are almost four hundred people to ferry. You'd need to do multiple trips."

"Yes, after the first one, we expect the Chinese will probably catch on and move to intercept. Then there's the fact we don't know if any of those aliens are lurking around out there."

"We're working on that now, if we can detect them early enough, do you think we can deal with them? I'm not asking the Marine in you, I'm asking the intel analyst. The Marines already told me they'd have a crab bake by the end of the week."

The Captain shifted uncomfortably before reluctantly answering. "If it was just one ship, we might be ok, if we used nukes. But we don't have any of Hatfield's weapons around and we'll be so extended there it's likely they would tear us apart. Hell, some of the courier Angels don't even have guns."

"That's what Stokes thinks too. I think if we can isolate..."

"Holy shit!" the sensor tech yelled from his console. "Director! Look!"

Forsythe and Menendez looked up at the system map display and froze. Hovering in a shifting pattern around Earth and the Moon were four red icons. As they watched, a fifth icon appeared, then a sixth.

"How did you do that?" he demanded of the tech.

"Uh, I changed the Saturn Base parameters," the tech said tentatively.

"How though?" Forsythe persisted as he saw three more ships appear on the screen.

"Well, the Saturn team said they had optical camo that shifted when light hit it, so I was thinking that light and radar waves aren't really that different, they're both waves of a sort. So I made the sensors use a randomized pattern on the beam sweeps and composition. Then I overlaid different radar systems on the same area. You know an area with X-Band would also have an L-Band component hitting the same area, like a dual band radar but with two different systems. I figured if they were trying to hide from our sweeps by camouflaging themselves somehow, getting hit with multiple different types that are very different in wave form might be hard for them to deal with."

Forsythe blinked and looked at him intently. "That's pretty ingenious. I want a write up on it by tomorrow."

"Hey. Look at that," Captain Menendez said as he watched the screen intently.

Forsythe watched with him for several moments and grunted. "Interesting. What do you think of it?"

"I'd say they're aware they're being scanned repeatedly. Look how they turned to present their smallest profile to us and are backing away slowly."

"Yeah, maybe it's a gut reflex. Maybe it's more tactical than that. Either way, now that we can find them, I want you to keep the scans on them short and light. Linger long enough to detect them and keep a rough error bubble on them, but don't just pound them repeatedly."

"Yes sir," the tech responded as they began giving orders to the remote crews.

Forsythe leaned close to the intel officer and whispered, "Stay here and observe, make sure their behavior is recorded. I'm going to go tell the boss."

Forsythe got up and put his helmet back on as he stared up at the display. Twelve hostile icons winked back at him, hovering menacingly over their world. With a grimace he ducked out through the hatch, shutting it behind him. His two bodyguards stepped out of an alcove and fell in behind him as he strode down the hall, deep in thought.

The CEO of the KaliSun Corporation, a man with power beyond measure and the ability to shape the future of governments, economies and technology, was perplexed. He had created this Corporation, nurtured it, molded it and turned it into one of the most expansive entities in the modern world, but as he watched his employees work he realized that it had grown beyond his own knowledge. No longer was he the final voice to be heard in a decision—they had evolved and matured into an organization where he was more a guiding voice than an interactive leader.

He realized he was being minimized during the planning phase of the freighter recovery. He was watching Operations Chief Robbins take his team through the recovery operation step by step and discovered he had significantly misjudged him. Back when he'd first met him in Forsythe's office, he'd struggled to understand why Forsythe gave him such power and included him in his decision cycle so regularly. He'd seemed limited by his moral code and paralyzed by his internal ethical dilemmas. But watching him manage his team blew that assessment out of the water.

Robbins exuded confidence in his staff and the planned operation. He was firm and decisive as they red-teamed the plan, sharing criticism and praise with the staff in a way that kept them engaged, interested and focused on the mission. This man who he'd assumed to be a nervous, misguided albatross that had somehow snuck through the HR screening, was actually the rock the freighter operations team was anchored to.

If he could misjudge a man so completely, how trustworthy were the rest of his assessments? The freighter operation itself had come a long way since those early operational development briefings. They were taking steps to mitigate problems they hadn't even thought of fifteen years ago when he had last had an active voice. The Wing Commander and his squadron leaders paid rapt attention to Robbins as he spoke and interacted with the tug crews like equals, no hint of the cultural conflict they had been so concerned with when the Saturn Base had first been conceived.

A smile tugged at his lips. For all the gnashing of teeth that had happened during the planning phase, the sheer number of things they had been wrong about was astounding. Their successes were more a testimonial to the men and women who had pushed themselves to execute the mission then some omniscient leadership cadre.

The door swung open and Forsythe swept in. The room hushed to silence as dozens of faces turned to look at him.

"We've found the aliens. They are practically among us." With that, he kicked on the repeater display, punching in a special code to allow the display to show the classified data feeds from the CIC.

"Twelve. Twelve of those things," Wing Commander Prieter whispered.

"At least two of those are in the corridor the freighter has to transit," Robbins said thoughtfully.

"Yes, more likely three of them. If you notice that grey one has a huge error margin on the probable location. The good news is that when we start to detect them, they tend to shy away. So it's possible if we keep them painted as the freighter comes in and have a strong escort, they might consider staying away."

"I'm not sure what a strong escort will do for us sir. We've reviewed the data from Saturn Base and our local units were not effective against those things. More than one would almost certainly be impossible without blowing a nuke," Captain Wilks said.

"I know, we're going to have to try to bluff them. I'm thinking feints in their direction and hope they back away from the freighter. They may not know the freighters are mostly unarmed. We have to assume they saw the Saturn Base defense and are aware we can kill them. The trick is to bluff them long enough to get the freighter unloaded."

"Yes, we have some thoughts on that matter," Prieter began. "We'll use the standard two tug configuration with their drones to retro the freighter's velocity as it approaches, doing our best to keep them inside the normal approach vector. We'll also send two additional tugs out there with spare fuel cylinders. They won't be intended to help with the freighter but can if one of the other tugs gets damaged. Mostly they'll be used as refueling stations for a squadron of Mongoose and support Angels. Then we maintain an aggressive patrol around the freighter until we get the moon between us and the Chinese. Once we've got the moon blocking for us, we'll modify the freighter's trajectory so when it comes out from behind the moon, it's not where the Chinese expect. Hopefully, they'll be far enough out of position that we can get it on its way before they can catch it."

"That leaves the MBTC pretty lightly defended. Not to mention those pilots are going to be deployed in their suits for a long time," Forsythe said as he squinted at the display showing the projected path.

"We'll have to depend on the ground forces to provide local security. We have enough surface-to-space weapons that we should be able to make a pretty good defense," Captain Jill Belle, commander of the 1st company of Marines said.

"This will limit our ability to keep the Chinese busy," Forsythe said, looking over to Stokes for his reaction.

"Chief Morris assures me that they can perform a limited probe to one of four installations they've picked out that should trigger some Chinese response," Stokes said, gesturing over at the MBTC's senior SARine.

"Did you make progress on a cyber attack protocol to use on them chief?" Forsythe asked the large SARine.

"No, we've had limited success translating the language we get when we decrypt their systems. I think, at this stage, it's a waste of time. What the CEO is referring to is strictly a smash and grab."

"I, for one, am not convinced that the Chinese will bite on your diversion," Robbins said quietly. "I think we'll just be needlessly spreading ourselves even thinner than we already are. They can see the freighter approach, they've watched us recover them in the past. I think any small-scale attack on them is bound to be seen as the diversion it is. If we're going to hit them, we need to hit them somewhere they're protective of."

Forsythe looked to Morris, who shrugged and nodded in agreement. He rubbed the stubble on his chin and walked over to one of the nearby chairs to sit down. "Alright, let's do this systematically. What do we expect to happen? I know Captain Menendez was down here giving you some input, where are we at with it?"

Robbins and the Wing Commander exchanged glances, with the Wing Commander deferring to Robbins. "Well, I can't speak to the aliens. We came up with the previous plan on the assumption we might run into one, not twelve. As for the Chinese, we expect them to take a crack at the freighter. They have to know that more Marines and pilots are coming back with that ship, with the extra benefit of taking down a sitting United States Congressman. For most of the flight profile, the freighter will not just be out of range for them, but significantly out of range. They can't even burn all their fuel and coast at it, the probability that it could zip past is too high. That leaves us a relatively small window to protect against them, and a large window to protect against this new alien threat."

Robbins pulled up a series of charts. "We've pondered what to do if they throw rocks in the path of the freighter as well. We're basically going to randomize, to an extent anyway, the thrust profile of the tugs. There won't be the usual smooth deceleration, instead we'll cycle the engines to max like normal then occasionally let off on them. Those periods of coasting will make the recovery of the freighter containers difficult, however since they're mostly empty it won't be as big of a deal. Once the slingshot is complete around the moon and we need to put the next containers on, well that's a different issue. We're still waiting on you to determine what gets sent back to Hatfield."

Forsythe smiled as he looked up from his chair at his Operations Chief. "My action eh? I'll get you an answer by tomorrow morning. I think Ed and I need a strategy session on that first."

"We could also see another ground strike against us from the Chinese," Davies said. "We know they have tanks and presumably a large amount of infantry. If they can get close to us with that, we'll have a hell of a time fighting them and the space forces we expect them to send."

"We've given a lot of thought to that. Based on geography to our west and north, we're relatively certain they won't insert tanks into those areas. Too many craters, too many choke points. The south remains a problem. I was thinking of having you employ a blocking force to the north and west, utilizing mines in the choke points to slow down any fast moving armor and then employ the majority of your forces to the south or close to the base. Obviously the farther we keep those tanks away from our surface structures the better," Forsythe said to Davies.

Davies looked down at the map as his five company commanders huddled close to him. "We could have Spears keep his 3rd Company in mobile reserve with the scout units, then we'll keep 2nd Company for internal security on the base and push a task force under Captain Belle south." He gestured to the map while she looked on. "We'll give you command over the 4th and 5th and some artillery. Use 1st Company to secure this high ground here and hedgehog the position with your armadillos and ground artillery. We can push elements of the 4th out to your southeast a bit as protection for your flank down to that crater. You can use 5th Company to push to the north from your firebase until they get to this impassable terrain," he finished, tapping the map with his pen.

"Doesn't leave you many people to cover those northerly and westerly approaches," Stokes said apprehensively.

"Yeah, we'll use a virtual defense system in conjunction with mines. Observation cameras, radar and SIGINT systems tied back to the main C2 backbone. We scatter a few squads from the reserve into observation posts along the front with some artillery backup. If they see anything, they call down the artillery on that position and try to delay them long enough for Spears or the Combat Space Patrol to deal with them. The terrain is rough enough that if we get totally surprised we should be able to redeploy some of Task Force Belle to help," Davies said.

"Things are going to get really messy if those gunships show up again," Spears said. "The fighter squadrons are already at half strength to protect against the aliens. If the Chinese try to pincer us again, we could be in for a nasty fight. No air cover, strung out in the open with gunships pounding us, and tanks trying to flank us. I'd be prepared for casualties."

Forsythe studied the map intently, tapping his gloved fingers on the table as the thought. He could see the Captain's point; if the gunships showed up in any kind of force, and were able to engage the dispersed ground units away from the base's defenses, there was every possibility of this turning into a slaughter. He grimaced before finally standing up straight.

"Pull up the intel from the recon flight," he asked a nearby tech from Robbins' team. The globe materialized in the air before them, showing the moon with an updated imagery intelligence display. The moon was banded with different shades, depicting different sources of data and how long ago it was collected. He reached out into the hologram and made the map rotate until he was looking at the rearguard areas for the Chinese.

"I think I agree with Chief Robbins. We need to hit somewhere important when we send the Strike Force in. But we also need to hit somewhere that will make them respond with space assets. If I'm not mistaken, we saw several different facilities in their rear areas during the recon mission. One of those areas, specifically, strikes me as a valuable target that might get their rapid reaction force out of bed." He manipulated the virtual globe with his hands and pointed. "These large algae dome farms are still more or less active. The intel assessment indicated that they were using a type of algae that consumed food and emitted a diesel like fuel, which they refined into what is essentially jet fuel. Then they use oxygen from the lunar soil as an oxidizer and that fuels all of their ships and rovers."

He looked up to see a chorus of nods from the SARines and Marine Commanders. He started to trace a flight path on the globe as Stokes spoke up.

"So if we wreck it or damage it, they should come running. Losing that facility would constrain them a bit operationally for the time being," Stokes said with a smile. "I like it. Now tell me why that wasn't the original plan," he said calmly.

Wilks shifted uncomfortably and spoke. "The Angels can make that flight. But it's far out of range of any of the fighters, it would be about two refuel stops, each way, for the Mongoose. Even the Angels would probably want to refuel prior to contact so they don't run dry bugging out."

Forsythe nodded as he spun the globe around and expanded it into a flat map. "I think if we run two Angels out on this flight path, we can make it with just the one refuel along the way. No escort, limited munitions. Keep the radar profile as small as you can, slip in and out the right before the freighter gets in range. With any luck, they'll be letting most of their pilots sleep in anticipation of the attack the following day. Might buy us some time, but the short of it is, we're going to need to be quick and destructive."

"Ten Marines and three SARines to take down a whole facility?" Morris said softly. "They certainly won't expect that small a force to be a threat."

"Well, I'd focus on blowing the oxidizer tanks and fuel tanks at the same time, see if you can make some fireworks. Any structure you puncture would be a plus," Forsythe said.

"I wouldn't expect a straight puncture to work. Based on Menendez's analysis, these are modular structures shipped nearly whole from Earth. If you blow a hole in them, they seal shut autonomously. I think I'd rather try to start a fire inside them, instead of just venting them into space. The fire will cause more permanent damage."

"I like it. Can you prep this mission in time?" Stokes asked.

"Wait. Before you get too far, this mission is going to take two Angels out of the inventory for us to use. Two fewer

Angels is going to throw a wrench into our timelines," Robbins said.

"No, it won't. You won't lose any Angels," Forsythe looked to Stokes as he spoke. "We have some special Angels in the hangar we've been saving in case we had to sneak around. They're made to operate in pairs, each with their own unique abilities."

"More toys?" Stokes said with a degree of forced casualness. The creases of his eyes tightened in suppressed anger. Forsythe smiled weakly. "I was going to surprise you with them. Surprise!"

CEO Stokes just gave a non-committal grunt and looked down to the map. "So Chief, the question still stands."

"We'll be ready sir," Morris said confidently.

"Good, make sure your pilots practice before you leave. Special projects sometimes need special care," Stokes said with a meaningful look at Forsythe, before motioning him to follow as he headed for the door.

"Finish the planning, I want to review the coordinated plan in twelve hours. The window for recovery starts in five days and I want plenty of time to make sure we're squared away." He nodded at them and followed Stokes into the passageway leading back toward the main command deck. Their escort fell into place behind them as they trudged along in silence.

"Sorry," Forsythe began diplomatically.

"Don't be sorry," Stokes said over his shoulder as they walked. "Just find the time to brief me on all your little projects. Soon."

They approached a T intersection as Forsythe responded. "I will do so immediately, it's overdue and I understand your concerns..." He trailed off as he saw a slight, pregnant woman round the corner and walk toward them.

Before either of them could react, one of their SARine bodyguards pushed them out of the way and gave the woman a bear hug, driving her into the passageway she had just walked from. The other SARine scooped them into a corner and laid on them, placing his armored hands over their heads as a final layer of protection. Forsythe had just gotten his helmet in front of his face when the woman exploded, knocking the SARine off her and banging him into the opposite wall. The blast continued on, tearing his helmet from his grasp and bouncing it off his face.

As he lay under the SARine looking up toward the ceiling all he could see was the flashing of strobes, his head throbbing in pain. His ears rang and he looked around as much as he could. Ed's body stirred under the SARine slightly, the mechanical assist allowing him to maneuver the man's bulky arm off his face, but he couldn't get the leverage to get his body off. Forsythe tilted his head back and looked up the corridor as Marines and SARines poured down the hallway. He reached out and lifted the head of the SARine who was laying on him. Blood was smeared on the helmet and for a moment, he thought the man was dead. Then he saw his eyes, looking through the faceplate intently at Forsythe, and he realized the blood on the helmet was from his own smashed nose.

The SARine carefully levered himself off them and drew his weapon, covering the hallway behind them. Chief Morris charged down the hallway from the meeting room and began carefully removing the downed SARine's helmet, while a Marine used a special tool to disengage the armor plates allowing them access. A pilot ran by, Wilks, stopping just long enough to hand Forsythe his helmet back before running over to help the downed SARine.

Of the pregnant woman, all he saw was a stain on the wall.

For the first time in a day, he could hear sounds clearly again. It wasn't much, just the steady beeping of the life support monitor and a weird clicking sound, like a stone rebounding down a rock face. He reached his hand up and rubbed his face, careful not to touch the large bandage on his nose or any of the stitches on his forehead. He opened his eyes and gave a start.

Hovering directly over him was Captain Spears, a curiously detached look on his face. He coughed lightly, causing Spears to back away. "Seriously Mike. You are not what I want to see when I open my eyes in bed," he said thickly, his unused voice rasping in his throat.

"At least you still have eyes. Good thing Alex covered your face with his hand. They took a three-inch chunk of shrapnel out of his glove armor. Would have carved up that face of yours pretty good."

"Are Alex and Steve ok?" Forsythe mumbled out.

"Alex is fine, his armor is pranged up, but Steve took most of the blast. He's going to pull through, it was kind of touch and go for a moment. That bitch was packing."

"Suicide bomber?"

"Yeah, we've searched her room already. She sanitized it before she went on mission. So now we're down to scanning surveillance footage to see who she associated with. She worked in the kitchens. So that list is really long."

"How did Steve know?"

"Oh that's easy. He said you slowed down approaching her, so I figured you had the same idea. But there shouldn't be any pregnant women in this base. So he assumed body bomb or worse. They recovered a small bit of the trigger mechanism, it appeared to have been rigged to her heartbeat. If he hadn't bear hugged her and just chose to shoot her, you'd be in a body bag now."

"Did Ed survive?"

"He's unharmed. Most of the damage you took was from your own fool self, putting the helmet in front of your head instead of on it. It got blown out of your hands and off your face. The boss was protected by Alex almost completely, just some minor hair loss from the flash and ringing in his ears. He's already been released. They were keeping you here to make sure your brain didn't swell up with blood. Don't worry, I told the Doc there was no risk of that," Spears said with a grin.

"How bad is Steve now?"

Spears rubbed his hands together and frowned. "Well, he's not going to win a beauty contest, his faceplate cracked and put shards through the left cheek and ear area. Then he has blast injuries around his chest. Fortunately most of the material she packed the bombs with was low density; the armor soaked it up."

"I guess we weren't the only ones thinking of a pre-emptive strike to try to disrupt the freighter handover. Was it the Chinese?"

"We don't know. Like I said, she sanitized her room. You're repeating yourself a lot. I'm going to leave now, get some sleep. You only have a few days until things get really interesting here." Spears got up to leave. "Oh and one more thing. Remember how you had the hangar guys take those two spare hangar grav generators we were going to use in the new building and turn them into a system to defend against the Chinese throwing rocks at us? Well, they turned one into a gun. We can throw rocks now!"

With a quick turn he was out the door, winking at the nurse as he left and leaving Forsythe to his thoughts.

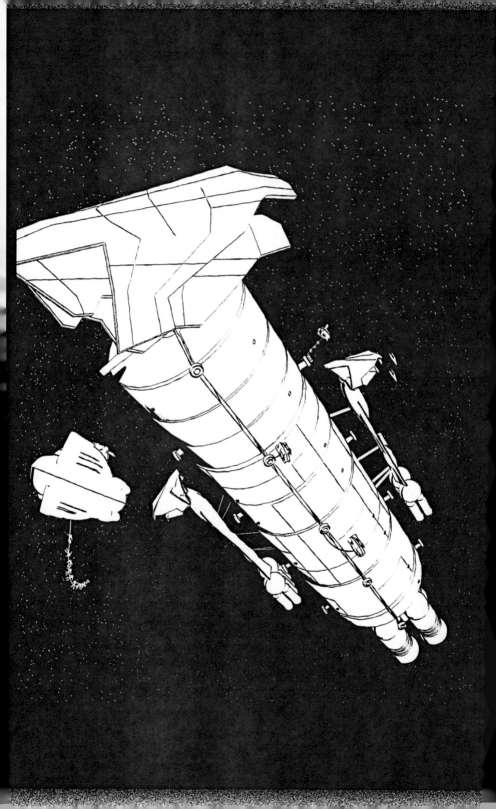

CHAPTER 19

S tand by for maneuver," the Angel pilot said calmly over the local battlenet.

Throughout the crew compartment of the Angel, Chief Morris's best SARine triplet checked their straps and gear one more time to make sure nothing was loose. A clock ticked down from ten on their HUDs and then the pilot did a gradual roll. As they flew inverted a bare fifty meters above the lunar surface, the pilot connected a tight laser link with the other Angel pilot.

Gingerly they drifted closer to each other until they were flying in tight formation, belly to belly. A vibration ran through the floor as refueling probes extended out from the underside of each ship and inserted into the socket for their sister ship. Angels weren't designed to pull fuel from their own in-flight refueling system, so they had to refuel each other.

"You're in good with the base commander aren't you Chief?" the youngest SARine asked his triplet leader.

He grunted in response, watching the external video feeds of the moon race past on his HUD.

"You go ahead and tell him, this refueling method sucks," the young SARine cracked as he clutched his restraints.

"It's still better than walking the whole way," the older man replied as he felt the system vibrate again, the probes retracting. He watched the external feeds for slight puffs from the maneuvering jets to indicate they were separating. Finally he saw a few bursts of white gas and breathed a sigh of relief.

He looked to the mission countdown clock and sighed. It had only taken a few minutes, but every time they went through this process, he expected to end up smeared all over the moon. The countdown clock ticked over—eighty minutes to the LZ.

"Eighty minutes. Try to get some shuteye," he said over the battlenet before leaning back in his chair. Before he closed his eyes he noticed that the pilots had dropped their altitude another twenty meters, right down to the rock.

Matt Kline, Chief of Staff to the senior Representative of the State of Massachusetts, lined up behind his boss in the passageway of the freighter. Six months they'd been in transit from Saturn Base, a trip that included riding out the radiation storm, flying through a huge field of micrometeorites, and was ending in barely controlled chaos, passengers hustled around the freighter at the last minute.

First they'd been told they were not going to be allowed any baggage on the trip down to the MBTC. Then they were told this was an active combat zone and to expect significant maneuvering during the return. Now this—standing in a single file line wearing thin spacesuits, one hand clutching a tether ending in a D ring as they waited for the big SARine at the end of the hall to motion them forward. He felt the hatch behind them grind shut, and the floor shuddered as the air was sucked out of the hallway. He reached forward and gripped Representative Sanders' arm, partly to comfort the older man and partly to assuage his own fears.

The airlock at the end of the passageway cycled open, exposing them to the vacuum of space. He felt an icy chill run down his back. The SARine was motioning the line of passengers forward, ten at a time. The first ten were a mix of pilots and Marines, and they reached up to a rope attached to the inside of the airlock and clipped their D rings into loops. As soon as they were all clicked in, the SARine went through the group quickly making sure they were properly connected and then gave an arm signal. Suddenly the first man was jerked off his feet and pulled into the void with the others following immediately afterward.

The SARine stood in the open portal, calmly watching to make sure they were clear before motioning the next ten people forward.

As they got closer, another SARine started walking the line, checking their harnesses one more time and making sure everyone was doing ok. When he got to Kline and Sanders, he stepped into the line ahead of them, turning around as he made his faceplate transparent, smiling encouragingly at them.

Matt reached up and tapped on the SARine's shoulder, looking into the young man's faceplate with concern.

"Have you done this before?"

"No, but it's in the book," the SARine said with a friendly pat on Matt's shoulder.

"What book?"

"Stokes' 'oh shit manual'," the SARine laughed at him, before stepping into the airlock.

They crowded into the airlock and hooked into the line. The two SARines bumped armored gloves and then the line released, pulling them free from the ship and rapidly into space. They soared through the formation of ships as the line was reeled in toward a waiting Angel.

At first terrified, Matt finally looked around at what was before him. In the distance below his feet lay the Earth, a bright blue marble against a dark starfield. Nearby was the moon, seemingly larger and lifeless. As he twisted around the line, he noticed the Angel was boosting away from the freighter slightly as it reeled, keeping the line under tension and moving into formation with the other Angels. He looked off to his right and saw an extra tug hovering in the distance, several more Angels and fighters circling it like bees around a hive. Looking behind him he got his first external view of the freighter they had ridden in on. The front and top deck were riddled with impact marks and temporary patches, evidence of the damage the ship had taken from the asteroid field that had been pushed into their path by that strange ball of radiation.

As the line got shorter he began spinning around it violently causing the starfield to change into a smear of light. Finally, he felt a strong grip steady him and pull him into the Angel. A few senior Marines were already strapping in, as well as their SARine escort. One of the Marines roamed down the length of the Angel, making sure everything was tied down and secured. He paused at their seats as he checked straps and cleared them from the rope, which was secured on an overhead reel that tucked into the ceiling.

Having satisfied himself with their condition, he hit some buttons on the bulkhead, closing the external door. Carefully he weaved his way into the top turret and secured himself. Seconds later, the ship slightly pressurized and the pilot came over their headsets.

"Brace yourselves. This is going to be pretty rough for about fifty seconds. The Chinese are making a play for you, so we're going to head for the moon at full speed. Stay strapped in and try not to get slapped around too much."

A countdown clock suddenly appeared in the center of his suit HUD, counting down from ten. At zero, Matt felt a sudden slap as the ship accelerated far harder than the compensators could handle. His breath knocked out of him, his eyes crept up toward the acceleration meter on the wall, its blocky red lettering climbing from 1.5 to 1.8 g and then higher still, eventually stopping at 2.87 g and holding there for several moments until the compensators could catch up. Gradually, the pressure eased off his chest and he was able to breath normally. With alarm he looked over at Representative Sanders, seeing his pale complexion through his faceplate he instinctively started to unbuckle his belt. The SARine to his left grabbed his hands and shook his head.

"Here we go!" the pilot yelled over the intercom, before throwing the Angel in a twisting, turning descent toward the moon. The top turret gunner swiveled rapidly, but only fired short bursts if he shot at all. The hull of the ship rang as a series of heavy impacts slammed into the belly, and the pilot heaved the sticks in a different direction. The top gunner continued to hammer away before suddenly cursing over the intercom.

"What?"

"Roadrunner Four is hit, I see smoke and debris. Son of a bitch rammed him."

"Is he on fire?"

"No, he's still coming down with us. Wings are jacked, I think he may have just lost cabin pressure . . . seems that was condensation and ice crystals, not smoke."

"Ok . . . ok I just flashed the SAR birds. They said the base is expecting incoming, we are to come in on a vector that's going to put us down near the graveyard. He said we need to land hot, so if you have a prayer, now would be a good time."

The ship rocked under multiple impacts as a new threat pounded them. The pilot spun away, the gunner blasting furiously before giving a cheer as he finally found his target. Once more the pilot kicked in his extra thrusters, slamming them all back in their seats as he pulled out of his dive, leveling out a bare twenty meters over the surface.

Matt Kline prayed.

"Sir, the first batch of passengers is down and safe. We lost Roadrunner Four to a mid-flight collision with a Chinese fighter. They were able to land, but they are no longer functional. SARines are working to extract the crew, there were casualties among the passengers," the communications tech reported to Will Forsythe.

"Understood. Thank you." To come all this way and get killed before they could even get down. He shook his head and checked his battle display. Still twenty minutes until the diversion force got to their site. He glared at the map. Leaving sooner than usual was supposed to let this first batch sneak past any possible Chinese response. It appeared they'd been ready for it, sending fighters with drop tanks out almost immediately upon their move to pull the crew off. The freighter modules had been damaged enough to slow everything down so that the Chinese were able to catch the tail end of their convoy. His eyes narrowed in thought.

"Comm, tell me the Congressman wasn't on that bird that's down."

"No sir, he and the company commanders were on Roadrunner Eight. They are down safe."

"When possible, get me patched to the company commanders."

"Yes, sir."

Forsythe looked over at Stokes, rubbing his head where the stitches itched. "I guess we dodged a bullet on that one."

"So it would seem. Are you sure it was wise to hold off trying to interdict those fighters as they made the intercept?"

"They only had a couple of minutes to engage on that pass. After that, the Angels were through and clear. The next convoy is going to be subjected to almost fifteen minutes of combat. I want to make them dump their external fuel tanks early. I think this plan only works once or twice." He paused taking a drink of water. "If at all."

An alarm rang through the room as the regional map flashed three times and dropped red indicators in four places. "Sir, we have troops in contact, multiple sectors. We have possible contact to the northwest and heavy contact being reported in vicinity of the seam between 1st Company and 5th."

"What about space assets?" Forsythe asked.

"Nothing yet, sir."

Colonel Davies walked over from his station and kneeled down, his armor scraping noisily on the floor. "Sir, I would guess they had their space assets on alert five, when they saw you kick off early they scrambled to intercept, but the ground forces were not in position yet. I'd like to move Spears into position to reinforce that seam. If they push through there we could be encircled and forced to perform a breakout under adverse conditions."

"Colonel, this is your show. But I have to ask, that's not really a seam, more like a gap in the line there. Is he going to be able to cover it? Do I need to get you out there to assist them?"

"Captain Spears is very capable. I know we've predominately had him hitting fortified structures and space bases, but he was a maneuver warfare expert during the Earth wars. For all his joking around, he's actually an avid student of history and he has learned from it. Talk to him and you're just as likely to get a dissertation on General Balck's use of the 11th Panzer division in Russia as you are to hear about his latest conquest in the rest and recreation area. I'd rather give him operational control, with loose, general guidelines, then try to direct him remotely from back here."

Forsythe pondered for a moment and nodded. "Ok, like I said, this is your show. Just make sure he and Captain Belle are talking. I don't want to see any fratricide out there when the artillery starts falling."

"Yes sir."

"So we've got our own Hannibal of the Steppe eh?" Stokes said in a bemused voice.

Forsythe looked at him with surprise. "You caught that reference?"

"Come on. The best leaders understand the past."

"Still, that was a long time ago and generations of technology have been created between then and now."

"I've always felt we lost more tactical genius as we got more technological assistance with our war-fighting." Stokes looked down at his armor with a sad smile on his face. "There isn't much glory in pushing a button from far away."

Forsythe made a sound that was half grunt and half laugh. "Well, when Balck was rampaging through the Russian lines, I imagine they didn't feel there was much glory in getting rolled repeatedly either." He shifted his eyes to the sensor stations and barked at them. "How about an update on those quick alerts, it's been seven minutes!"

"Sorry sir, we haven't got much. Whatever was to the north isn't moving right now and we can't figure out where they are. The recon units sent some drones to check it out. The enemy forces to the southwest are massing, we're working up numbers on them now."

"Give me a ballpark figure."

"Maybe two thousand, with at least five or six tanks," the sensor tech replied nervously.

Stokes let out a low whistle. "Ok. This is going to get pretty sporty."

"Looks like they're going for a killshot, that gives them close to seven to one numbers superiority overall. Probably a lot closer to eleven to one at the point of attack... What about space assets?" Forsythe yelled over to the sensors officer.

"Still nothing up yet."

"I'm not sure if I'm happy or sad about that," Stokes said.

"Yeah, I'd almost like to know how bad it's going to get," he turned back to the sensors tech. "What about the aliens?"

"They're still maintaining distance and appear to be observing. If we scan them for too long, they back away."

"Maybe if we put on a good enough show, they'll get scared and go home," Forsythe mumbled to Stokes as they watched the battle map update, the mobile response force heading to the weak point in the line.

"Let's try for a clean dispersal," the senior SARine announced over the battlenet as two Angels dropped down into a space between several of the buildings in the Chinese base.

They hadn't detected much activity on approach, but as they landed they saw several technicians round the corner in a rover. The rover stopped suddenly, hopping forward in the low gravity as the crew turned to stare at the Angels crouched on the regolith disgorging heavily armored troops into the center of the base. Like deer in headlights they stared at the Marines as they broke up into three squads and headed out.

"Take them Dagger 1-2," he said casually as they bounded over to the nearest airlock, charges in hand. One of his Marines crouched and carefully squeezed off three short bursts. The driver's head exploded into vacuum as he took the brunt of two of the bursts and the third burst splintered the thin plastic shell protecting the motor. The Marine bounded over to the destroyed rover as the two remaining occupants struggled to get free.

He knocked them both down and studied their outfits at a glance. Making a decision, he reached down and savagely cut open the space suit of one of the men with a combat knife, pushing the thrashing man away to die silently on the ground nearby, and then subdued the other man. One of the SARines bounded over and trussed the man up before putting him in a special bag for prisoners. With two hops he was back at the wing of the Angel the SARines had come in on, attaching the prisoner to a special hardpoint on the wing.

Meanwhile, the other three teams had breached airlocks leading into different buildings, standing back as debris and atmosphere jetted out violently. Once inside they sealed the hole with two layers of flexible plastic and proceeded deeper into the installations. After the initial airlocks, most of the doors were weak and intended to survive the bare minimum pressure differential. As they opened each one, the outer areas that had been exposed to vacuum gradually re-pressurized. The fire teams exploited whatever visible intelligence was available, stealing documents and hard drives as they planted thermite throughout the facility.

Only the second team ran into significant numbers of Chinese. The building they'd broken into was the operations building for most of the rest of the base. As they searched the dead bodies of the caretaker crew it became evident that much of the facility was automated and that the crew were only here to push the reset button when things failed.

The senior SARine checked his HUD and watched the mission time elapse. After fifteen minutes he gave the recall order and they raced back out to the Angels, carrying what they had collected. After spending an agonizing ten minutes attaching bags of captured data to the hardpoints normally used for missiles, they reboarded and took off.

As they wheeled away, one of the structures superheated and ruptured into space, thermite ravaging the building in a 2500 degree inferno.

"Sir, Captain Belle is reporting a breakthrough in the seam. Large numbers of mechanized infantry, spearheaded by tanks," Captain Spears' APC commander reported.

Spears studied the blue-force tracker intently. Right now he'd arranged his company down under the lip of a crater that was smack in the middle of the seam, between 1st and 5th Companies. They were close to the lip, with their heaviest guns facing toward the edge. He watched as his recon units swept out from the edges of the ridge leading to Captain Belle's position, engaging the enemy column from range and darting away.

"Any sign of enemy space assets?" he asked the commander as he searched his map for enemy position updates.

"Captain Belle reports she is taking fire from several gunships supported by single-seat fighters. No enemy air transports visible. Command has sent two sections of Mongos to help drive them off."

"Well, it looks like they learned to be a lot more cautious about exposing those big troop movers to our forces anyway," Spears said. A few new icons popped up on the display. Frowning, he cycled through them—heavy mechanized rovers, open topped rovers and anti-space point defense rovers mixed together in a column trundling along behind the armor, which was arrayed in a flying wedge formation.

He looked up into the right corner of his HUD and blinked the communications app open. The menu took up the central part of his HUD and he used his eyes to scan through the list, finally opening a private line to Captain Belle.

Her voice booming and echoing with static as the encryption software mangled the data transmission, she answered. "You've got incoming Mike."

"I see them. I need a fire mission call out. Give me an artillery barrage in grid 2232 and walk it to Hill 18. Then I want a few rounds at grid 2248 and walk it back toward you."

"Uh Mike, that's off target. You're going to bracket them. Recommend you reset to grid 2238 and 2239 and walk north to south along column route."

"Negative Jill, if we disrupt them before the crater, they'll disperse. I need to take that armor on the spearhead out or else the rest of the day is going to be very difficult. They have point defense rovers in the mix, any artillery you drop on the column itself will likely get shot down. I need you to drive them toward us if possible."

There was a pause as Captain Belle digested what he was saying. "Ok, I see what you're up to. Artillery barrage in three, good hunting."

"Wait, not done yet. I need a pre-registered area denial barrage. Danger close, grid 2240. Sustained barrage fifteen rounds per minute. Once we bloody their nose, I'm going to use it for cover."

"Don't delay bailing Mike, that's practically right on top of you."

"Yep, I know. Hoping we can mobility-kill the tanks and then cause enough panic in the column that your rounds finish them off. Either way, they don't leave the crater rim. Make sure your people upload the exclusion zones to the BFT, those scouts are very mobile."

"Solid copy. Be advised we just picked up some probes on our front flank and what looks like enemy rovers massing by the seam between 1st Company and 4th Company. Belle out."

As he watched, a large red hashed marking began to appear on the battle map. His scout units continued to duck in and out of the danger zone as they shaped the path of the enemy column. A flashing alert in the corner of the map drew his eye. He blinked twice bringing it up.

"Recon complete. Previous estimates accurate. We engaged the enemy lightly along the length of the column. Heavy volume of fire picks up around three, zero, zero meters. We took no losses, inflicted minimal losses. Planting mines in their tracks in case they back-track or a second column comes through."

Captain Spears shifted his map over to look at the cut that the enemy column had pushed through. There was a blind corner, with a small hill on one side and a five-meter-deep crater on the other side. As he watched, small blue icons lit up the map display where they were stringing anti-vehicle mines. With any luck, they could plug that spot with wreckage and force any reinforcements to go around or stay stationary.

"Enemy armor is two, zero, zero meters out and closing quickly sir," the APC commander reported.

"Going to step outside, keep the engines hot," Spears said to the commander as he reached over to the weapons rack and pulled two rocket propelled grenade launchers off the wall. He stepped out the open door of the APC with a puff of lunar dust. Carefully strapping one of the launchers to his armor, he walked over to his headquarters group that was crouched between the APCs with their own rockets. He settled down on one knee with the launcher at the ready and waited, his command armor automatically shifting colors to match the surrounding regolith and shadows, his faceplate opaque with the laser shield down.

He could feel them coming, the vibration of their tanks and rovers rattling the lunar surface in a counter symphony to the APC's engines. He looked down the line at his men, watching the dismounted Marines prepare themselves for close contact in the shadows of their APCs. Two thousand enemy troops in mechanized transports supported by armor approaching his scant one hundred men; if they'd tried to set up a static defense, like Captain Belle had done, out in the open, they would surely have been massacred. He had something different in mind.

The vibrations increased, small cascades of lunar rock rolling down the crater lip in slow motion. Dust shimmered out of the soil, building up a static charge and adhering to their armor and vehicles like chalk. His HUD displayed the enemy column, the armor surging slightly ahead as it approached the crater lip.

He licked his lips and lifted the rocket launcher to his shoulder. The rocket was semi-guided, but had a smart targeting system that enabled him to aim it without having to look precisely down the sights. With startling speed, the first tank appeared over the rim of the crater, pausing as it surveyed the situation, its belly armor exposed to the KaliSun Marines below. For an instant they stared at each other as the other tanks aligned with the lead tank along the rim.

"FIRE!" Spears screamed over the battlenet. Along his line, rockets ripped out and slammed into the soft underbelly armor. Nobody had been sure what it would take to destroy a Chinese tank with one of the man portable systems. But one thing was certain, what they used was excessive. The wave of rockets blew the tanks up and backward, flipping them away from the crater rim as they exploded, throwing shrapnel in all directions. Secondary explosions rocked the wreckage as they tumbled away from the vicious attack.

"Displace FORWARD," he yelled as he stood and dashed up the shallow crater rim, using his command suit's maneuvering jets to hop up the slope while he swapped the empty rocket launcher for the second launcher he was carrying. Getting to the top, he stopped and steadied himself long enough to align his shot on the lead rover. "Free Fire and retreat!"

With a silent flash of light, the rocket left the tube and zipped into the tightly packed enemy column, detonating on the front of a lightly armored, open-topped troop carrier. The rocket penetrated the driver's bubble and exploded, tossing enemy soldiers high above the regolith and spraying them with shrapnel. Without pausing, he jumped back down the crater rim and ran to his APC, heart pounding as he saw return fire from the enemy column kick up dust all along their line.

The enemy troops had dismounted and were charging after them, some of the heavy rovers inching along to support them. The KaliSun Marines sprinted back to their APCs and loaded up. As the last Marine entered his APC, the commander began backing away, keeping their guns on the crater rim. Spears lurched through the interior cabin to his battle map display, double checking to make sure nobody was left behind. They were retreating at speed toward their rear area as the enemy reached the rim and took up firing positions. Gouts of lunar soil erupted as the heavy rovers fired large caliber weapons at their retreating forces. The constant pinging of lunar rock and rifle rounds slamming into the APCs armor accompanied the bouncing path the driver took.

Spears locked his suit into his chair as the APC took a ponderous turn and sped away at max speed. He studied the rearview camera feed. He had just gotten the camera focused as the first of Captain Belle's artillery rained down on the crater rim. With the point defense rovers hanging back to avoid the ambush, there was no protection from the steel raining from the sky. He grunted in sympathy as the artillery turned the crater rim into a red stained ruin of twisted metal and exposed human bodies.

"Take us to Waypoint Bravo two-three," he instructed the driver before switching over to the command battlenet. "CIC, Spears. Enemy armor has been defanged. Troop concentrations have pushed two klicks into the seam. They are not contained. Spears out."

An observation drone high above the battlefield to the south relayed a continuous stream of visuals back to the CIC. Using only passive sensors and limited maneuvering thrusters, the drone was nearly invisible to the Chinese fighting on the moon's surface below. Its sensor pods used multifaceted bug-eye cameras to study the battlefield, allowing the operator to keep a full battle picture while following multiple specific targets at once.

The artillery strike on the lead elements of the Chinese attack force was just dying down as the drone observed the dune buggies of the recon force race in from the south. They followed directly along the path that the column had originally taken, plowing through the lunar dust that hung over the surface as they charged the enemy's rear. The Chinese were still stumbling away from the crater rim, trying to get back to their rovers and disperse before another artillery strike landed. Their commander had been in the lead tank and they were disorganized.

The scouts raced along the length of the column, targeting the point defense rovers that protected it from direct artillery attacks and KaliSun spacecraft. They pounded them with weapons fire, aiming for the wheels and sensor domes.

The drivers swerved back and forth, running over Chinese infantry with their buggies as they struggled through the dust cloud, throwing them high above the surface. As they reached the edge of the artillery impact zone they spun around and headed back down the column, spraying fire at the wheels of the rovers, again focusing mostly on the point defense vehicles as they pushed through. As they pulled away back toward the south, Captain Belle dropped another artillery strike on the convoy, this time aiming for the most concentrated cluster of vehicles.

While the scouts had managed to disable almost two-dozen rovers, hitting the sensor domes had proved to be too difficult while bouncing through the dust. The Chinese column's networked sensors allowed them to destroy almost the entirety of the incoming artillery, with just a few sub-munitions deploying prior to intercept. The column weathered the storm and continued to reassemble as they prepared to move away from Captain Belle's area.

Colonel Davies drummed his armored fingers on the table. "Well, Spears had the right idea. Let's just hope they damaged their point defenses enough we can get some Mongoose in for gunnery runs."

"How many casualties did we take?" Forsythe asked as he multitasked between the space and ground battles.

"Two injured Marines, neither serious. One sprained knee from jumping off the crater rim and one gunshot wound to the back of the thigh, which his suit and a penetration repair kit was able to stabilize. Marine armor isn't really designed to protect you when you're running away," Davies said, reading the report. "The recon units have pulled back to Captain Belle's firebase and are rearming, they report no major damage to their units."

"That's not bad at all," Stokes said, surprised.

"The battle is still in its early stages. They still seem disorganized. Most of their space assets seem content dealing with the freighter and trying to keep Captain Belle pinned down. I've gotten the impression they weren't expecting to see Spears out in the open like that."

"How many casualties have we inflicted so far?" asked Forsythe.

"Task Force Belle has downed two gunships and one single-seat fighter. The first skirmish to the north resulted in the Chinese probe being wiped out, recorded twenty EKIA in that conflict. Then we've got Spears, who appears to have killed six tanks, fifteen heavy rovers and whatever infantry got caught out in the open during the artillery strikes. We can't get a firm handle on that until the dust dies down. It's progress, but he's still outnumbered and they'll be out of range of Belle's guns soon if they keep pushing ahead."

"Out of range of her guns, but eventually in range of ours," Forsythe said. "The only problem is, once they get closer to us, the terrain starts to really favor their approach over our artillery. We could be duking it out with that column in the middle of the base. It'll be worse than the first time—now they have heavy weapons instead of just infantry."

"That may not be our only problem," Colonel Davies said, reading a report that flashed on his screen. "Captain Wilks just reported that they've located a second pincer moving on the seam between the 1st and 4th company that's stronger than the one that Spears just hit. It looks like they're trying to encircle Belle, while pushing into the base from the south. That will leave the 4th cut off from their line of retreat back to the base, the 1st encircled, and the 5th Company's left flank flapping in the breeze, with Spears wandering the no-man's land in between."

"Do we have a drone over 4th company?" Forsythe asked the sensor tech.

A new view appeared on one of the monitors, the drone's view with a superimposed blue-force tracker. The enemy armor column was pushing along the bottom of a crater rim as they maneuvered to hit the seam between the two companies, spearheaded by twenty tanks and a heavy contingent of anti-space point defenses. The computer counted up the rovers and displayed a number on the screen. As he saw the number, Forsythe took a deep breath, careful not to let the rest of the control room see his dismay.

"Looks like another fifteen hundred plus infantry, a bunch of tanks, and heavy rovers. The path they're taking is going to threaten the 4th Company's flank," Colonel Davies said.

"My God they have a lot of infantry. Each of those pincers outnumbers our total force independently," Stokes said quietly.

"They do have inferior space suits and weapons. Or did anyway. But yeah, this is going to get pretty hairy," Davies said.

"What is that Angel doing hovering off to the south of the enemy column? He has to practically be on the ground at that altitude," Forsythe said as he pointed at the blue-force tracker display.

Davies turned to investigate from his console. As he typed, the enemy column seemed to hesitate, before it ground to a halt in the shadow of the crater rim. Somebody climbed out of the lead tank and bounded back toward one of the lead heavy rovers. The drone circling overhead zoomed in, so close that they could almost make out the lettering on commander's helmet. He was holding a big plastic sheet and pointing angrily to their left. Several soldiers dismounted and climbed the edge of the crater rim, setting up a temporary observation outpost looking in the direction of the dug-in KaliSun Marines to their north.

"Are they fucking lost?" Stokes said in quiet wonder.

"Better. I just got off the net with Wilks. He has his support Angel sitting out there on the edge of visual range, just below a rocky hump, jamming them. They can't talk to each other, their navigation systems are probably down and their sensors are blind. I think you're going to want to see this," Colonel Davies said with a smile as he modified the view on the display.

Streaking in low and fast from the southwest, twelve icons appeared on the blue-force tracker. Arranged in four groups of three fighters, they were coming in at a slight angle down the long axis of the armored column at high speed, dangerously hugging the terrain below them. Further back, a second Angel hung above the moon's surface, a small tag next to it indicating it was target painting with its lasers.

The drone image flickered as the lasers began reflecting off the armor elements of the enemy column. Seconds passed and the squadron of Mongoose raced closer. The tank driver and a soldier from the heavy rover were standing helmet to helmet, angrily gesturing in the general direction of the seam. As the squadron got closer, each fighter began individually painting a target. Near the north edge of the screen, several fast moving icons left Captain Belle's position as she fired an artillery barrage at the stalled enemy column. Seconds after the first grouping of artillery shells showed on the screen, another appeared.

At a range of five hundred meters, the Chinese became aware of the threat, dumbfire missiles ripping from the racks of the approaching Mongoose fighters, flaring intense light out around them. Some of the troops scrambled to dismount and take cover, others tried to swing weapons to bear on the incoming missiles, and several of the drivers tried to swing out of the column and race away causing a tangled traffic jam.

Badger Squadron fired again as they approached, picking different targets as the first salvo tore into the flank of the armored column. Light armored rovers were slammed sideways, exploding into clouds of shrapnel that ripped through the dismounted infantry with devastating effect. Several tanks were blown clear off the surface of the moon as their heavier armor absorbed the full force of the explosion. For brief moments they hung above the surface, rotating and smoking before gravity took hold and dragged them down. The second wave of missiles hit just as the squadron began an intense gunnery run down the length of the column, stitching high explosive and fragmentation rounds up the length of the stalled rovers.

Fifteen seconds after the Mongoose squadron had cleared the battlefield, the first artillery rounds rained down. Some came in as solid pieces of explosive that carved up the lunar surface, while others broke apart to drop bomblets over a football field sized area. The crater rim protected the column from some of the incoming rounds, kicking up great clouds of dust as they landed short. But waves of artillery continued to rain down. Vehicles that were hit by the solid artillery rounds simply vanished. Tanks and heavy rovers hit with bomblets had their external sensors and communication gear vaporized, creating a haze of shrapnel that shredded the infantry taking shelter next to their bulk.

Captain Belle hit them again and again. Six total salvos of artillery fell on the column before her guns ceased firing. As the final explosions died down and the dust hung heavy in the air, Wilks' squadron did another slow pass over the area, firing rockets where the tanks had been and engaging concentrations of troops with cannon fire. Weak return fire greeted them, signaling the location of surviving troops. Whenever a rocket or stream of tracers lifted from the moon in the direction of one of the Mongoose sections, the entire section would return fire. By the second pass, most of the survivors just hunkered down.

"Colonel. Captain Belle requesting an urgent resupply of artillery ammunition. She's down to seven rounds per gun," the communication officer shouted to Colonel Davies over the cheering from her fellow techs. "Captain Wilks indicating he is RTB for fuel and ammo as well."

"Detail five Angels to get them some ammo ASAP," Davies said with a smile before turning to Forsythe and Stokes. "That was textbook. Stall them and pound them. Captain Wilks continues to impress me with each engagement."

As the dust cleared from the strike location, several tanks came into view on the drone feed, followed by a half dozen heavy rovers and a mixed bag of troop-carrying rovers and point defense vehicles. Almost all of the vehicles had extra soldiers hanging onto them as they surged out of the dust cloud.

Stokes gestured up at the screen. "Unfortunately, it wasn't the knockout blow we'd hoped for I'm afraid." The room grew quiet as the crew realized they hadn't wiped the Chinese out after all.

The enemy column raced along the crater rim before the lead tank fired its main gun into the rim itself, collapsing it in a cloud of dust. Without pausing, the tank plowed up the slope of the crater and out into the open space beyond, the column following behind.

"Well, I guess it's going to be one of those kind of days," Forsythe said tightly as he watched the enemy column pick up speed and head for the light screening force connecting the 4th Company to Belle's far left flank.

"The Badger Angel is still jamming them. I guess whoever's in charge . . . well he's certainly more decisive than the last commander," Colonel Davies said morosely. "We'd better warn 4th Company not to try to tangle with those tanks, just delay them and try to inflict mobility kills."

Colonel Davies shifted back over to his console, and Forsythe looked over to Stokes and sighed. He was about to speak when the sensors officer interrupted him. "Sir, we just detected a large scale force of Chinese fighters, with some gunship support, heading to intercept the freighter. There is also a large ship in the center of the formation that the fighters seem to be refueling from."

"So much for only having to deal with them for fifteen minutes," Forsythe said with a sideways glance at the system traffic monitor. "Give me an intercept plot and warn the Wing Commander that he has big trouble heading his way."

Spears stared at his options on the battle map. He had successfully broken the first attack column into two pieces. The first group was stalled at the point of contact where they'd taken out the tanks, struggling to repair their vehicles and get mobile again. They'd left a reasonable ground force there to protect the repair crews and had circled the point defense systems to make it hard to approach them. He'd called for an artillery barrage and it had been destroyed easily, with only a few bomblets passing through.

The second group consisted of a few heavy rovers and most

of the light rovers. It was pushing hard toward the base but without defensive rovers to protect it against starfighters or artillery. The column had already escaped the range of Captain Belle's guns and was working its way through the helium-3 mining pits toward the southern extent of the base.

He had ordered 5th Company to send their reserve to chase them, in the hope that they could keep them disorganized before they reached 2nd Company who were defending the base. It might result in the destruction of the enemy force, though it was still numerically superior despite the pounding it had taken.

But that plan had gone right into the trash before it could even start as the Chinese launched probing attacks along the entire 4th and 5th Company lines, a second pincer was in the process of punching through the Marine screening force between the 4th and 1st companies, and a large fighter force was lining up to attack the next wave of Angels transiting to the base.

He sighed in frustration, realizing there was no good option. Chase after the first force and leave his rear exposed to the armor breaking through to the southeast. Attack the armor breaking through and risk 2nd Company being overwhelmed at the base and not having a home to go back to.

"Or I can sit here confused and lose by default," he mumbled to himself. His senior SARine, sitting across the table, leaned forward and tapped the front of his faceplate. With a scowl, Spears killed his suit mic, hoping that had only gone out over the command net.

He kicked on a private channel to his XO and the senior SARine. "I think if we chase after the rest of the first force, we might wipe them, but we'll lose in the end. We need to keep the heavy armor away from all this open space between Belle and the base. So we're going to head to the second seam, we'll approach from the back side of Captain Belle's defensive hedgehog push right into their flank. If we leave now and the screening force holds we can get there just as they punch through. Focus fire on the heavy armor and grind into them. We'll lose a significant amount of our effective force if we only use APCs, so once we've closed the gap, we're going to need to dismount. It could get ugly."

The XO grunted his agreement but the SARine hesitated for a moment. Spears looked over at him. "Go ahead."

"I'd split off some of the recon units and have them harass that column going north. They're fast enough to keep up and have a decent amount of firepower. It will let us maintain contact with the hostiles and make sure they don't split up. Maybe we'll get lucky and the scouts can find a place to drop some mines in front of them and weed out another couple of their fire support rovers."

Spears pulled up the recon force on his map, studying their status. He split the force into two smaller units and pulled the commander into their battlenet. "Alder, need you to take the units I've designated and go chase down that first column, keep them honest. Get moving now, I'll give you a more detailed plan in a few minutes."

The scout leader acknowledged, and Spears ordered his company to fall in as they skirted the edge of the immobilized Chinese force and headed for Belle's position at high speed. The Chinese fired into the dust cloud the APCs kicked up in a futile effort to inflict some damage.

"What is 3rd Company up to? He's split his force." Ed Stokes stared in confusion at the map display.

"I don't know, we'll work on that in a moment. Right now we have bigger fish to fry," Forsythe said, staring at the intercept plot.

"Weapon is ready, standing by for firing solution," the weapon tech said from her station. A few moments passed and she turned slightly, speaking into her helmet microphone. "Solution received, countdown at five... four... three... two... one... weapon away... weapon away.... weapon away... weapon away. All weapons heading downrange sir."

Across the base, in a hangar that hadn't been used since the first attack on the base, several large bundles shot into space at nearly fifteen gs. The hangar door slowly closed as the last bundle left, once again the façade of a heavily damaged abandoned building.

"Now the waiting," Forsythe muttered, rubbing his thumb against the console as though he was trying to wear a groove into it.

"Sir, Expeditionary Force Marines arriving now along the northwest perimeter. We're short transport, so they're filtering forward to the recon outposts on foot. We expect it will take another two hours before they are fully deployed," the communications tech reported.

"Make sure we get some additional O-two generators out there, send a mix of the small outpost sized ones and a few of the big units so that they can fully pressurize the casualty collection tents if things get ugly."

"Yes sir."

"Fresh off the boat and straight into battle. I shudder to think how much atrophy they suffered on a six month cruise after getting a radiation bath," Stokes commented to Forsythe under his breath.

"We're short bodies right now. I can't tell what the hell the Chinese are doing up north. They might be trying to recon a path through for an assault force we can't see, or maybe just infiltrate the base. Either way, I can't afford to send 2nd Company up there to deal with them while we have that column approaching us from the south," Forsythe snapped.

"I know. I was just thinking it's a rough transition," Stokes said with a smile as he nudged Forsythe's shoulder. "Lighten up a bit. We're doing better than we expected and we knew this was going to be a bit of a shit show."

"I'm just waiting for the other shoe to drop," Forsythe said tensely.

"Intercept in ten seconds," the sensor tech reported.

High above the moon the bundles from the hangar blossomed into dull starbursts, several metric tons of rock debris exploding outward to form a dense cloud approaching the oncoming Chinese formation. A flight of Angels flying ahead of the newly formed meteor patch amped up their jamming to max, focusing specifically on the known sensor wavelengths and long-range comms the Chinese used. The gunships in the formation began taking extreme-range potshots at the Angels, trying to get them to peel off. The pilots randomly juked their Angels around, praying that no computer had figured out how to predict their next move and blow them out of the sky.

As the Angels closed distance with the formation, the enemy fighters stopped refueling and began to spread out, randomly changing direction in the hope of preventing a hidden missile strike. But with just a few Angels approaching them, they made no major course corrections, continuing on their intercept course with the freighter as it offloaded the next batch of incoming pilots and Marines.

The two tugs serving as starfighter tenders started to inch away as the Mongoose pilots and their support Angels began to push a perimeter out toward the Chinese fighters. The Mongoose pilots broke formation into sections, but didn't move to engage the mass of Chinese fighters pushing toward them.

Just outside gunnery range from the enemy, the screening group of Angels peeled away from the debris, continuing to jam the Chinese as best they could as they banked toward the freighter. The dark moon rock continued on at high speed, directly in the path of the surging fighters, gunships and fuel ship. With their sensors blinded by the Angels, and no thermal threat detected from the rock, the Chinese never saw it coming.

One moment the lead elements were preparing to drop their fuel tanks and accelerate toward the freighter, the next the stars were filled with the bright flashes of fighters exploding as they were riddled with rock traveling ten kilometers per second. The gunships reacted instantly, firing in all directions in a preprogrammed flak pattern that lit up the darkness. The fuel ship shuddered from multiple hits, fuel and oxidizer leaking into space briefly before igniting in a huge fireball that sent a wall of debris and burning gas outward into the formation.

The gunships shot down some of the larger incoming rock, but the explosion of the fuel ship and rock fragments were too much for their defenses. With sequential flashes they exploded, venting gas and bodies into space. Massive secondary explosions lit the stars as their ammunition detonated.

As the last of the clouds of rock passed through the formation, the remaining forty Chinese fighters dropped their fuel tanks and accelerated toward the freighter, angry killer bees that just had their hive kicked.

"I think Joe has his work cut out for him," Stokes said, as the Wing Commander's Mongoose squadrons broke their holding pattern in the freighter formation and blazed toward the oncoming Chinese.

"We still have a couple of surprises left. I just hope it doesn't come to that," Forsythe said, watching the two opposing fighter formations approach for a head to head pass.

"Bad news Captain. Task Force Belle reporting that the screening force was unable to retreat prior to contact with the enemy armor. They were trapped and pounded, 4th Company is reporting they lost both screening squads and half a platoon sent to help extract them," the 3rd Company senior SARine reported to Captain Spears as they bounced along the moon in the back of the APC.

Spears winced at the report. To lose nearly twenty-five percent of 4th Company in one engagement was painful. He looked down at the map; they were still five minutes out. He'd just been too slow. He reviewed the orders he'd sent out. After hearing how deadly those tanks were against infantry at close range, he was second guessing himself. The display before him continued to update as the time to contact ticked away on his HUD.

The SARine nudged him hard. "Don't change your plan sir. We're a too close to make a new one and not have it go sideways on you. We'll just need to execute."

Spears nodded back at him and checked his rifle and the rocket launcher he'd strapped to his back. Only two rounds for the rocket launcher and a couple of breaching charges—they were going to have to kill the tanks quick.

"THIRTY SECONDS!" the driver yelled over the local net.

The company raced around the last ridgeline that separated them from the Chinese, who were reorganizing their convoy after wiping out the 4th Company squads. As the lead APCs came into line of sight they spread out in a wide line, advancing across the relatively flat lunar plain, leaving roostertails of dust to hang above the surface as they accelerated. The Chinese didn't react immediately, many of their external sensors destroyed during the earlier artillery barrage.

The 3rd Company's ten APCs raced toward the tanks with the scout units trailing behind them, using their bulk as cover. One hundred meters from the Chinese, the main guns opened up, focused on the treads of the enemy tanks exclusively. The anti-infantry turrets sprayed down the line of light rovers, trying to pick off Chinese infantry before they could dismount and find cover.

The six remaining Chinese tanks immediately accelerated, trying to turn their heavier frontal armor toward the oncoming assault. In seconds the APCs were among them, ramming them and trying to prevent them from swiveling their guns to fire on the KaliSun Marines. As soon as contact was made, the rear doors of the APCs opened and Spears' company poured out. The rest of the Chinese column closed distance and began racing through the fight, dumping troops off as they tried to run down the Marines.

Spears leapt free and charged toward the tank that was trying to claw its way out from under the front of the APC. He used his suit to boost himself in a long bound to the back of the tank, landing on top. Kneeling, he slapped his breaching charges on the tank, one on the hatch leading to the turret and two on the engine compartment. He checked his work before jumping off the tank and leaping to cover in a nearby crater. He pulled the rocket launcher from its smartmount and clutched the detonator.

His driver put the APC in reverse and popped off the tank, skidding to a stop just as Spears detonated the charges. With a bright flash, the armor across the top of the engine compartment peeled away to expose the engine, while the turret bucked hard from the explosion against its thick top armor.

Seeing that the tank was still moving, one of the Marines from Spear's APC ran toward it, leaping up on the rear. He grabbed on to the sharp edge of the damaged engine armor and tossed in two high explosive grenades before jumping off. As he ran away, the tank lurched toward him, swiveling its turret around to bear.

The grenades exploded, destroying the engine and sending molten metal into the back of the crew compartment. The metal superheated the light atmosphere inside and eviscerated the commander, igniting the stored ammunition inside. For a brief instant a spout of fire and gas erupted straight up out of the turret before a lack of oxygen killed the flames, leaving nothing but thick smoke to billow out in an expanding haze.

The driver opened his hatch and tried to escape the tank, his spacesuit melted onto his body and smoking heavily. As soon as he tumbled clear, the top turret gunner of Spears' APC cut through him with the heavy cannon.

Spears turned away, looking for targets. A dozen meters away, one of the APCs lay on its side, a huge hole blown through it from tank fire. Two SARines were working to open the driver's compartment as the Chinese infantry continued to fire on them, their rounds repeatedly striking the heavy SARine armor with hammer blows, knocking them to their knees as they tried to work.

Spears slung his rocket launcher and brought his rifle bear just as one of the recon dune buggies jumped a rocky hump in the lunar dirt and plowed into the crouched enemy infantry, scattering them like bowling pins as it accelerated up the column, guns spitting fire. Spears ducked down by the side of the smoldering tank, alternatively scanning the battlefield for his next target and watching the updates flow across the mini-map in his HUD.

The initial surprise against the tanks was over so he ordered the APCs to disengage and attack the infantry and light rovers. The battlenet screamed with chatter as the 3rd Company Marines ran from cover to cover, trying to engage the infantry and avoid the remaining three tanks that were maneuvering through the area at speed, chasing the APCs and shooting at anything that moved. Enemy heavy rovers began to break away from the column so they could target the Marines taking cover behind depressions in the lunar soil.

Spears crouched behind the destroyed tank letting it's heat hide his thermal signature and assessed the situation. His men were engaging the Chinese by squads, focusing on pockets of resistance and eliminating them one by one. A Chinese heavy rover drove past, heading for a small elevation to get a better firing angle on the Marines. As it settled into position, Spears darted out from his cover to a spot forty meters away. He knelt down and brought the rocket launcher up, aiming carefully for the joint between the forward wheels and the main body. Taking a deep breath, he squeezed the trigger. The rocket shot silently through the brilliant sunlight, trailing a yellow-white plume of smoke, and detonated on the side of the rover, driving a shaped charge deep into the hull.

Without waiting to see the damage caused, Spears ran toward the rover's stern, reloading as he went. As he approached there was a large internal explosion, completely destroying the rover and spraying the area with shrapnel. He just had time to cover his face with his arm before the debris slammed into him, knocking him flying through the light lunar gravity to land in a puff of dust. He lay there, wheezing from the impact, as his suit informed him that he had several tears, was losing atmosphere and bleeding in several places.

The passive medical system kicked in, an anti-coagulant paste congealing around the injuries and applying direct pressure. Wincing, he took out his penetration repair kit and began applying it to the areas that the suit indicated were suffering from a loss of pressure. Six patches later, the atmosphere loss alarm ceased its frantic wailing, and his suit showed he had regained integrity. He groaned as he looked at his status and how much air he had left.

Struggling to his feet, he searched around for the rocket launcher, realizing it was nowhere near him. He unslung his rifle and unsteadily panned it around the battlefield, performing more on memory than conscious thought. Remembering that his suit had a blue-force tracker, he sat back down on the regolith, breathing hard as he blinked the tracker onto his HUD. Surprised, he saw there was a blue icon almost on top of him. He looked up to see an Angel hovering overhead with its door open. A large SARine dropped from the door to land with a flare of his retros nearby. He ran over to Spears with a cable in hand, hooked it to the back of his shoulders and then grabbed on while the Angel towed them up off the moon.

As he was nearly halfway to the Angel, he noticed there were still two tanks roaming around shooting. Before he could process the scene in front of him, two missiles streaked away from the Angel, twisting and turning before slamming into the engine compartments of both tanks. A minute later, two more missiles left the racks and hammered a cluster of enemy infantry and a heavy rover. He reached the cabin and the SA-Rine helped him lay flat on the floor as the Angel peeled away, headed to Captain Belle's position at high speed.

The SARine flipped up Spears' laser protection visor and peered into his eyes. He pulled out a tool from his thigh pouch and started removing parts of the command suit. "Well, you got lucky Mike, we were about to nail that rover when we saw you shoot it. That explosion must have thrown you half a klick."

Spears coughed mightily inside his helmet, struggling to see who had rescued him. When he finally got his eyes to focus on the SARine's nameplate he let out a laugh. "Glad to see you Morris." With that he coughed once more and laid on the floor to let the SARine tend to his injuries.

CHAPTER 20

Sir, the tug *Jotun* is reporting major damage. Multiplemissile strikes and at least one Chinese fighter rammed them in the engines! They are evacuating...Scratch that sir. *Jotun* just suffered a major explosion, they are no longer in controlled flight," the sensors tech reported soberly.

Forsythe closed his eyes for a moment, clenching his fists. "Roger. If possible send a SAR unit to extract any survivors."

"Sir, we also have reports that Captain Spears is down and is in transit to the field hospital at Captain Belle's position."

Colonel Davies and Forsythe exchanged a grim look before Forsythe asked, "Was Spears able to stop that enemy column?"

"The armor and heavy rovers are all destroyed. They have disabled all the remaining enemy rovers and are currently trying to deal with the infantry. They're still outnumbered two to one easily and the APCs are low on ammunition," Colonel Davies reported.

"Casualties? Beyond Spears," Forsythe asked.

Colonel Davies sighed. "4th Company reports twenty-nine KIA, 3rd Company reports three dead APCs, maybe sixteen KIA, but that number is suspect since the discipline on the battlenet is breaking down."

Forsythe swore under his breath. "All of the enemy rovers are disabled?"

"Yes sir, they were targeted heavily by the APCs and rocket teams," the intel officer reported.

"I want a fighting retreat. Have them extract any dead or injured they can and pull back, use the remaining APCs as shields. Once out of range, I want a designated fire team to remain behind and shoot anyone that tries to access our dead or the damaged APCs. The remainder of the force is to pull back and rearm with Captain Belle. Get me a no kidding count on how many effectives they have left."

"You want us to take the pressure off of them?" Colonel Davies asked curiously.

"I want to avoid further losses right now and get our mobile QRF back to being mobile. You said their rovers are dead. They won't last long out there with no rovers and limited oxygen. There is no reason to waste resources killing them the hard way," Forsythe said patiently. "I know you don't like to back away from a fight, but realistically they are no threat; just like the other stranded group Spears left behind before."

Stokes, who had largely ignored the interchange once it was clear that Spears wasn't in critical condition, had been studying the base map. For the past twenty minutes, they had been observing 2nd Company shooting it out with the remains of the first Chinese column. Progress was being made, with the Chinese gradually pulling back and 2nd Company following them in hot pursuit, with the other half of Spears' recon unit harassing the Chinese from the rear. Now, as he watched, several perimeter sensors along the northwest corner of the base were flashing red; nonfunctional.

"Colonel, what's going on to our northwest?" Stokes asked, interrupting the two men.

Colonel Davies squinted at the map with concentration before pinging the observation post up on their battlenet. He frowned, then tried a second outpost. After he tried a third, he began to look worried. He called up the combat space patrol battlenet. "CSM, this is CIC. I need immediate eyes on the base's northwest quad, sector four-seven."

"Acknowledged CIC, Angel two on task now."

The CIC was quiet as everyone watched the feeds from the Angel's observation orbit over that part of the base. The pilot brought up a thermal scan of the area and several hotspots immediately appeared in the shadows of the building. As he banked to come around, his gunner swung his weapon down to look at one of the hotspots. Immediately ground fire swept up at them from a dozen locations among the buildings. The

Angel shook violently as it took repeated hits and engaged its afterburners to escape.

"Heavy contact, maybe fifty foot mobiles inside the perimeter!" the pilot reported as he swept away.

"That southern attack is trying to drag 2nd Company out of position!" Forsythe hissed at Davies, as the latter began recalling units from the 2nd Company.

The blue-force tracker updated, showing 2nd Company units pulling back, probable locations of enemy units, and the CSM patrols rapidly shifting to ground attack mode. As the 2nd Company tried to break contact with the Chinese they surged forward, breaking up the maneuver and forcing the Marines to take cover.

"CSM Angels, I need you to break formation and proceed to Marine Expeditionary locations we are sending you. Pick up as many Marines as you can and combat drop them to the roofs of the buildings," Forsythe said as calmly as he could.

"How many Marines do we have in the base right now?" Stokes said nervously.

"Less than a hundred scattered throughout the base. No real concentrations anywhere, just enough to provide security against saboteurs. Most of them are on light duty due to injuries sustained in recent battles," Colonel Davies said tightly.

"Well get them into one battlenet and pull in anyone else who manages to get back to the base. We need them to . . . "

"Building 17 has been breached!" the communications officer yelled from his station.

Stokes pulled up a diagram of the base and winced. Building 17 was where most of the civilians were supposed to be sheltered. He looked at the tracker and saw that there were actually fifteen Marines in the building, but sensors were indicating nearly forty enemy soldiers had penetrated the area.

"I wish we knew how many there were," Stokes said nervously.

"Building 17 Marines are responding, they have set up a

defense at the entrance to the shelter-in-place area and are holding their ground there," Colonel Davies reported. "About forty-five minutes until the Expeditionary Marines can get back. I'm not sure how much it will help, they don't know their way around the base at all."

"God damn eternity," Forsythe muttered. "Sensors, can you give me any idea how many there are and where?"

"They seem to have split into two groups, one group hit building 17 and we can't find the other group."

"Can't find or are not sure they exist?" Forsythe asked pointedly.

"We assume they exist because we detected more troops than those that entered 17, we aren't sure where they are."

Forsythe grunted and turned to Davies. "Assemble what Marines we have in non-critical buildings into a rapid response unit. I want you to track down these assholes quickly, before they find something important to wreck."

"Already working on it," Davies said as he turned back to his station.

"Found them! They broke into an access tunnel from the secondary landing pad and are heading this way. Security footage shows at least two KaliSun employees are with them," the intel officer yelled to them.

"As captives or guides?" Stokes asked icily.

"They are not restrained and appear to be leading them."

"Leading them here?"

The intel officer swallowed nervously. "Yes sir, that tunnel leads to a mainline maintenance tunnel that can either goes here or to the recreation center."

Stokes' bodyguard left his post and walked into the hallway as they talked about what to do. When he re-entered he was carrying an assault shotgun and a shoulder bag full of ammunition. He dropped the bag at Stokes' feet and handed him the shotgun. "Are you familiar with this model sir?"

"Yes. It's been a while however." Stokes took the shotgun and peered into the chamber. Satisfied, he slid a box magazine in the receiver and let the bolt close, checking the safety before laying it on his lap.

"Just remember, it's an automatic shotgun, aim low and walk the rounds up their chest. I've given you armor piercing flechettes, just don't shoot one of us," the SARine said as he checked his own weapon and headed into the hallway.

The intel officer turned and looked at them. "They'll be here in moments, those two assholes are leading them straight to us."

Davies and Forsythe exchanged a look and then put their helmets on. They locked them down and checked each other's seals before pulling their close quarter weapons off the back plates of their armor.

"I guess this is better than having to track them down," Forsythe said with a resigned sigh.

"Yeah. Good luck Will," Davies said as he shook the MBTC Director's hand. He turned to the nervous faces of the crew in the CIC. "Stay at your posts, keep your helmets on in case the pressure falls. The freighter crew is counting on you to get them home. Good luck."

The crew watched the Director and the Marine Brigade Commander leave the CEO of the Company sitting in his chair facing the door, shotgun in hand. Several of them nervously checked the seals on their suits before returning to work. The hatch made an ominous clang as it slammed shut behind them.

Wilks was doing a slow loop over Captain Belle's position after his strafing run on the stranded Chinese troops near 4th Company's position when the message came in across the radio.

"All space assets be advised, the hangars are currently in lockdown. Enemy troops have entered the base, proceed to backup landing zone." As the communications officer finished speaking, Wilks could hear the distinctive sound of automatic shotguns in the background.

Savagely he slammed the throttle forward, turning north toward the base. "Badger Squadron, reform on my wing."

Screaming past the ruined hulks of the first Chinese column, he scrolled through the weapons status of his squadron. Extensive strafing runs on the enemy rovers and engagements with the few fighters that had dropped down from the furious dogfight around the freighter, had significantly depleted their inventory. The Badgers gradually caught up to him and formed into a standard three-ship strike package as they dropped in altitude down toward the deck.

Brilliant flashes of light off to his left drew his attention as he yawed the Mongoose's tines around in a wide circle to give him a clean visual of the area. They were muzzle flashes from the Chinese rovers as they tried to press in on the scattered 2nd Company. 2nd Company was designed to act as a localized security force for the base—they weren't equipped with rovers, APCs or heavy weapons, yet they had tried to engage the Chinese in the open field. As he approached he got an urgent message on the base battlenet.

"Approaching Mongos, Captain Williams, 2nd Company, I need immediate support in my area. Enemy rovers are putting intense localized pressure to my center, we're about to break."

"Badger Squadron copies, rolling in now," Wilks said, forcing the excitement out of his voice.

"Angels, give me a paint on those rovers."

The support Angels acknowledged him and his HUD lit up with indicators on the leading rovers. Seconds later, an additional icon appeared over three of the rovers as the Angels designated them as targets. Wilks smiled and bore down on the enemy with the sun at his back. The rovers were pushing forward, the infantry creeping along behind using them as shields against everything the 2nd Company could throw at them. At one hundred meters, they ripple-fired dumbfires into the advancing Chinese formation.

The missiles streaked in, obliterating the leading element of the Chinese column, and scattering the rest in confusion. As the squadron pulled away, Wilks flipped his fighter over so he could watch without changing his vector. Out of the corner of his eye he saw a flash of light as two of the recon buggies came flying out of a small crater and charged into the scattered infantry, guns blazing. Several squads of Marines, seeing the enemy in disarray, charged in, engaging them at point blank range.

With the forces mixed, all Wilks could do was orbit above them slowly and watch, the struggle devolving into a hand-to-hand fight between the larger force of Chinese and the desperate KaliSun Marines.

The Marines with their heavier armor, heavier guns and better suit design were able to bound around through the firefight, engaging enemy soldiers quickly before jumping away into the hanging clouds of dust that had been kicked up by the airstrike. The Chinese lacked blue-force tracking to deal with the low visibility and were unable to effectively use high explosives against the sturdy Marine armor, and they were gradually being worn down.

The rest of the 2nd Marine Company collapsed down on the center, flanking the Chinese as they did so. Wilks watched as the Marines increasingly ran out of ammunition and resorted to beating the enemy with their rifles and combat knives. Eventually, the dust became so dense that he could no longer make out more than the occasional flash of a grenade or body flung high by an explosion.

"CIC this is Badger Actual. 2nd Company has engaged the Chinese southern thrust at point blank range; we have no visual, but believe they could use backup," he said over the battlenet. Getting no response after a minute he tentatively asked, "CIC, are you there?"

He was greeted by static.

Forsythe flipped another trashcan on top of the temporary barricade they'd erected in the hallway, quickly ducking down as the Chinese sprayed bullets in his direction. He felt something slam into his shoulder armor, driving him back slightly, the camouflage rippling in response. Next to him, Colonel Davies levered himself up off the floor and fired a quick burst down the hallway before ducking back down with a smile on his face.

"Two more that time, double headshot!" he said with a grin as the SARine bodyguards next to them alternated firing down the hallway.

"Try not to enjoy this too much," Forsythe snapped at him as he accessed his wrist interface. "I'm going to adjust the gravity between them and us. I'll increase it near the ceiling and see if we can mess up their aim. It'll only work in the center of the corridor, so just compensate for it."

"Not sure it's worth trying sir. At this range, the shift in direction will be minimal," one of the bodyguards said as he took two rounds that penetrated the flimsy barricade and ricocheted off his chest plate.

"You're probably right." Forsythe shifted his position and peered through the gap in the barricade. Fifteen meters away, at the T-intersection, the remaining twenty Chinese special forces troops were taking turns firing around the corner. At their feet were eleven corpses, killed during the exchange of gunfire, including the two men who had been wearing KaliSun Corporation spacesuits. Forsythe made sure they got dropped in the initial ambush.

"Sir, battlenets are down. Looks like they blew a repeater. The CIC is cut off from external communications and our localized nets are being disrupted by the structure," the SARine to his right reported. "We're on our own."

"Ammo check!" Colonel Davies ordered. As one SARine kept the enemy pinned down, the three of them took stock.

"I have two ten-round mags for my shotgun and that's it," Forsythe said softly.

"I have about twenty left in my SMG, four in my sidearm," Colonel Davies said as he examined his weapons.

"I've got eighty rounds left on the SMG and two spare shotgun mags," the SARine to their left reported. "Have an SMG mag." He handed the Colonel a magazine and looked at Forsythe expectantly, making his faceplate transparent. "Do you need more ammo Director?"

"Keep it," Forsythe said with a grimace. "I'm not hitting much so far anyway."

"Out of practice eh?" Davies said with a grin, ducking suddenly as a burst of gunfire smashed into the barricade. "How are you doing for ammo Chief?" he asked the other SARine.

"Twenty rounds of SMG, thirty of shotgun and a sonic grenade, which is pretty much useless right now. Sidearm is winchester."

"Well, I guess we could just charge them," Forsythe said thoughtfully. "Push forward hard, while we still have ammo, count on our armor to protect us."

Another burst of weapons fire hit the barricade followed by a grenade explosion that nearly destroyed a third of their cover, scattering metal off the walls and ceiling.

"Might be our best bet. Just keep your faceplate covered and let the two SARines go first. We'll toss the grenade out, see if we can get them to back away from the hallway and then rush them. It's only a few meters, if we get in close we can light 'em up. We wait here playing whack-a-mole and we lose." Davies shrugged debris off his shoulders.

The SARines nodded in agreement and waited for Forsythe to give the go ahead, crouching with their bodies angled toward the enemy, faceplates turned away for protection against lasers and direct hits. Forsythe gazed at them, considering one last time before giving the order. What had been pristine armor twenty minutes ago was now crisscrossed with impact and burn marks from the grenade exchanges. He felt tired.

"Ok, we go when he tosses the grenade." He struggled to his feet, checking the action on his shotgun to make sure it had a round in it.

The SARine raised his stance slightly as his partner fired a few shots down the hallway. As soon as the rounds hit, he threw the grenade. It flew on a flat trajectory down the hallway, bouncing around the corner, and they took off at a dead run. They had only made it a few steps when the grenade went off, bathing the hallway in high-pitched sonic screeches. Several steps later a loud explosion and a rattle of gunfire sounded from the hallway ahead. As they approached the T-intersection, a roar of gunfire from the left spewed fire and metal as it cut down the Chinese, blowing some of them into the intersection. The gunfire continued for several seconds longer as their bodyguards slid to a halt and then pushed them back toward the barricade quickly.

"Any callsign this net. Respond," the SARine Senior Chief said over the battlenet. "Any callsign this net, respond immediately." There was no response. The four of them raised their weapons, holding the laser designators at head level against the corner of the wall before the next hallway.

"Shit. Do you see them?" Forsythe whispered into his helmet microphone.

"No, but everyone should be on this battlenet," Davies whispered back.

As they stared at the smoky corridor a single laser light slowly tracked around the floor, pausing on each body briefly. Davies heaved a sigh of relieve, the laser showed up clear as day on their helmet HUD displays, but was invisible to the unaided eye. Only KaliSun Marines and SARines used that particular frequency of laser. Just the same, he was worried they couldn't hear them on the battlenet.

As they stood there, a Marine poked his head and shot-gun around the corner in their direction, scanning the hallway. They stood motionless, their armor camouflaging itself seamlessly into the haze. The Marine peered into the smoke, hesitantly advancing several steps before he froze and crouched. As they watched he seemed to stare directly at them, before they saw his helmet tilt to the side slightly.

Abruptly a SARine stepped from around the corner and strode toward them, stopping a few meters away with his gun pointed toward the ground.

His external speaker scratched to life. "Strike force reporting in, sir. We ran into Captain Wilks on the way back and he told us to investigate."

Forsythe and Davies looked at each other with relief. They had intentionally not loaded the strike force with the defense force's crypto for the day in case they were captured. They lowered their weapons and Davies took a step forward to smack the SARine on the shoulder.

"Damn good timing Chief."

"No problem sir. We had a pretty low risk raid. Looks like you guys caught it rough here," the Chief said as he looked around the nearly destroyed hallway, electrical panels arcing through the smoke.

"We still have another group of hostiles over by the civilian side," Forsythe said as he moved to unlock the hatch leading into the CIC. "We'll need you to leave some ammo here and take a force over there to break the siege."

"Already taken care of sir. We fast roped into building eleven to get down. On the way, we saw what they were up to. I sent second squad over to ass-jam them. Last report indicated they had taken down the main force and are mopping up the rest now. 2nd Company seems to be finishing off the rest of that Chinese force to the south. I think the base is secure except for any remaining solos."

"We're going to need to scrub the base top to bottom for

sabotage. The group coming to the CIC had two KaliSun suits with them helping them navigate and opening doors. We need to assume they left other surprises. Check the critical areas first, but realistically we need everything checked. We'll have to make sure they didn't hack the life support systems too, and get communications back up here," Colonel Davies said rapidly as he sketched out his response plan.

Forsythe saw that they had it under control and opened the door into the CIC, only to stare straight into the muzzle of a shotgun. Stokes smiled through his faceplate at him, not the least bit fearful with the rest of the crew strategically placed around the hatch holding improvised weapons.

"I was hoping that was you coming through," he said as he lowered the muzzle.

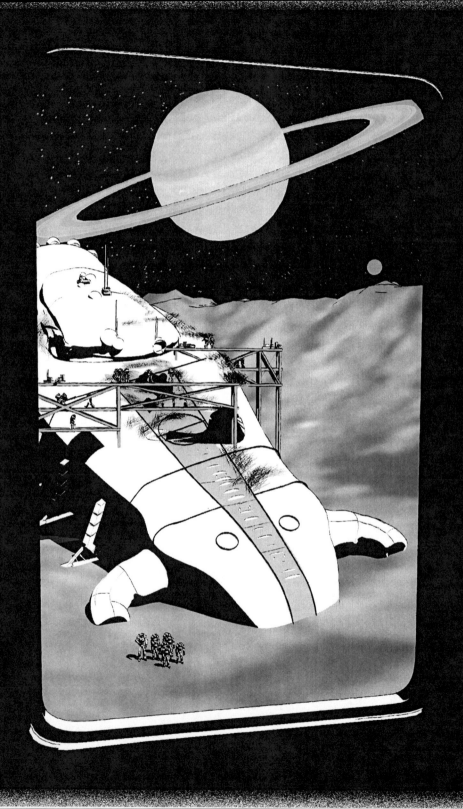

CHAPTER 21

The hallway was dimly lit as the four of them stood silently at the observation window in in their bulky command suits. The chill of crossing the crater floor still clung to them as the warm air of the Saturn Base temporary prison left a sheen of condensation on their armor plates.

"It looks sickly to me. The shell is starting to turn grey, almost like the others did when they died," Sloan said skeptically.

"It hasn't moved in two weeks. It just sits in the corner ignoring any stimulus we try on it," Joe said softly into the private battlenet.

"Well, Dr. Kapple has been trying to figure out what to feed it since we captured it. It never responds. It just stares at what we put in the room," said Brenner.

"Maybe we're too chemically different from them for it to recognize what we're giving it is food," Sloan said. "Have you tried giving it more basic chemicals or synthetic protein or algae?"

Joe shared a file with her through her HUD. "So far, we've tried soy products, raw grains, frozen meat, cooked meat, fruit, nuts and rice. It never shows any interest."

"Still no way to communicate with it either?" Hatfield asked hopefully.

"Nothing. Hardly any symbology present in the ship. No pictographs or hieroglyphs. We've put our entire computer science team against the ship and gotten exactly nowhere with penetrating their computing systems. Best guess at this point is they use some form of body language driven communication. But this one never moves, so we can't even study that possibility," Joe said.

"Have you tried talking to it?" Brenner asked.

"We tried flashing lights that step up through numbers,

short wave and long wave radio...even a laser. All it did was cover its eyes," Joe said dejectedly.

"But it did respond. Interesting," Hatfield said, considering his options. "Alright, get Dr. Meckler."

Joe looked at him quizzically before shrugging and walking to Meckler's cell. Brenner looked at the Director curiously.

"You aren't going to ask his opinion on what to do are you?

"No. I'm going to see if he can get this thing to respond."

Brenner gave a short laugh as Joe hauled a disheveled Dr. Meckler over to stand in front of them. His face was pale and a nervous tic was constantly working one of his eyebrows. He stood before them barefoot, in a plain jumpsuit that barely contained his pudgy stomach.

"Director Hatfield...the way you are treating me is unconscionable! Solitary confinement has been known to cause serious mental health issues, I must protest this in the strongest possible way..." His voice faded as he saw that none of them took him seriously.

Hatfield pointed at the door leading into the crab's enclosure and stepped back. Joe half lifted the scientist off the ground and slung him through the door to land in a heap. Sloan closed the door behind him with an ominous clang.

Meckler stood slowly as he clutched his butt cheek in pain. "From one small room to another," he said bitterly as he looked around, his eyes adjusting to the dim light. He wandered toward one end of the room, looking miserably at the floor. "I don't even get a bed or a toilet in here?"

Hatfield nodded to Joe, who projected an image of himself on a screen by the door. Meckler strode over and looked at it expectantly. Joe very casually, but very clearly pointed off to his right, the side of the room Meckler hadn't inspected yet. He looked over at the corner and was about to make a sarcastic comment when he finally saw it.

With the low light of the room and the crab carapace's ability to blend in with his surroundings, it almost looked like the walls of the corner. But as he stared in horror he realized it was some kind of horrific creature crouching in the darkness. He sprinted to the door, tugging on the handles and banging on it, begging to be let out.

On the other side of the door, the four armored figures stood motionless in the dim light of the hallway, watching the crab for any signs of life. The creature did not stir, change color or emit any sound. After watching for several minutes, Meckler pleading through the door in giant racking sobs to be saved from the creature, Hatfield gave a resigned sigh.

He blinked the communication channel for the door up on his HUD and spoke over the intercom with Meckler. "Go talk to it. This is the creature you let attack the base with your little stunt. Ask it why it attacked us."

"I didn't have any idea, you can't blame me for this!" Meckler pleaded with Hatfield.

"Try to talk to it," Hatfield said, abruptly cutting the transmission.

Still sobbing softly, he walked to the middle of the room and stood quivering as he looked at it. He seemed to try to pump himself up to talk, but instead stood mute before them.

"Say something," Hatfield said with agitation over the intercom.

Meckler started at hearing Hatfield's voice again, a small pool of urine forming on the cold metal floor at his feet. He began to shake harder, shivering in fear as he stammered out a few timid sentences toward the crab.

Sloan shook her head. "This is never going to work. I can barely understand what he's saying and I speak English."

"It hasn't eaten him yet," Brenner said thoughtfully. "Another datapoint."

"Come on, if you were a predator, would you eat a pudgy prey animal that just pissed all over itself?" Sloan said mockingly.

"It could be an ambush predator. Maybe it only attacks things from hiding," Joe said. "That would explain the tentative approach to the base. Maybe."

"It's a spacefaring race. While it might prefer to ambush prey to obtain the element of surprise, no creature ever ambushed its way to the top of the food chain. No, there is just something it doesn't like. Maybe it thinks this is a trap," Hatfield said.

"Can't blame it given how we killed its friends," Brenner said. "But I agree with Sloan, this isn't doing anything but coating the floor with piss right now."

"We have one more thing to try," Joe said as he walked over to a stack of cases and opened one. Inside was a strange metal tube with unique end caps. "We found a room on board the ship stacked with these things. We cracked one open, its full of a paste like material, just a bit more solid than, say, gelatin and denser. They've been running analysis on it for three weeks, and we still have no idea what it's for. The going theory is that it's an MRE of some sort. But we can't be certain it's not a weapon, I mean the poison venom had to come from somewhere."

Hatfield looked at it and gave a sharp nod. "Put it in there, let's see what happens."

Joe shrugged and opened the door, sliding the tube along the floor toward Meckler. Meckler stopped mid sentence and started to run for the door. Joe slammed it shut quickly. He looked down at the tube as it rolled slowly back and forth through the puddle of piss and started to say something.

Abruptly the crab unfolded itself from its corner and charged Meckler. He panicked and tried to kick the tube to the crab before running to the door. The crab was too fast however, and it closed the distance and whipped its overclaw down in a sharp arc, connecting solidly with his shoulder in a brutal impact that sent Meckler flying into the observation window.

Using its small T-rex claws, it reached down and plucked the canister off the floor and backed slowly into its corner again. It cradled the canister in its claws as it settled down to the floor. The smaller claws made rapid movements along the canister, cleaning off all the urine and small smudges of dirt like a high-speed buffing wheel. Restlessly, the overclaw hovered over the top of the crab, its two pincers open in a defensive posture as it slowly re-matched its shell color to the surrounding walls and floor.

"Wow," Sloan said.

"Joe, I want you to tell Dr. Kapple we need those canisters analyzed immediately. Whatever that stuff is, this thing finally showed some life. I want to make sure we didn't just give it a bomb or something," Hatfield spoke in the silence that followed.

"I'd say judging by how he treated it, that it's neither a weapon or food. Maybe that's a baby one," Brenner said.

"We've seen the baby ones I think, they don't seem to come out of test tubes." Hatfield said, remembering Leblanc's desiccated body.

Brenner shrugged helplessly. "I have no idea really."

"Joe, get Meckler. Make sure he's not dead and toss him back into his cell," Hatfield said.

Sloan unlocked the hatch and opened it while Joe leaned in, grabbing Meckler by his left calf and dragging him around the corner, up over the lip of the hatch and onto the deck outside. Sloan slammed the door and locked it. She looked down in time to see several of Meckler's teeth fall out of his mouth.

Joe started performing very rough first aid as he tried to wake Meckler up. After a few minutes he came around and groggily tried to stand up. Joe helped him get off the ground, stuffing some gauze in his mouth, and half carried, half dragged him to his cell.

Hatfield turned without further word walking to the airlock deep in thought.

CHAPTER 22

Brenner slowed the rover to a stop a short distance away from the creek that ran through one quadrant of the Eden Cave. This was one of the areas Sloan had gotten more or less complete in the run up to the flight test, and as such it was farther along in development than most of the rest of the cave. The banks of the creek were steep, with water undercutting them and cascading vegetation falling into the water, rocks scattered throughout the creek bed. The water that flowed past was crisp and clear as it shot toward the sea.

He set his helmet on the seat next to him, enjoying the breeze that swept down the cavern walls and through the young trees nearby. He could smell evergreen and moss with a hint of wildflower. As the air passed over the creek it noticeably cooled, occasionally causing wisps of fog to roil off the surface where the water crashed over the rocks. He let his gaze drift down the river until he saw Erik perched on a rock overlooking a deep hole, with a fishing pole in his hand.

Brenner looked down at his command suit, its armor plates scratched and dented, the paint chipped and worn. Even the emblem of a female warrior holding a sword on his shoulder looked faded. He flipped his wrist interface into view, saw the time and briefly closed his eyes. Taking one last look at the serene young forest around him, he heaved himself out of the rover and started down the path to the river.

As he went down the trail he happened upon Molly laying out on a blanket, shielded from view by some trees, as she soaked up the artificial sun's rays. He smirked—she was clearly asleep, her swimsuit top lying on the towel next to her. As he clomped by, she opened her eyes and squinted at him through the sun's glare. Realizing who it was, she hastily scrambled to cover up as he went past. Brenner didn't say anything, walking on toward Erik in silence.

As he rounded the final bend he saw Erik standing in the shallows with his net in hand, a struggling fish splashing at his feet. After several tries, he finally netted the fish, standing up triumphantly and turning toward the shoreline. When he saw Brenner he flashed a smile and held up the fish, shouting over the sound of the tumbling water.

"You should see the colors on these fish. I don't know if it's because the water is so clean or if the artificial sun does something to them, but man. The spots on these cutthroats really stand out!" he said with admiration.

Brenner smiled at him encouragingly and closed the distance. "I'm glad somebody is getting to enjoy the fishing poles I added to the list," he said as he looked around at the muddy bank. Insects covered the surface of the water, and cutthroat trout were rising to the surface to inhale them. The entire area was alive with life, with the sounds of frogs croaking, insects buzzing and the splash of fish.

"Whatcha looking for Brenner?"

"Platypuses," he said with a laugh.

"Ah Sasha and Sloan released them on the other side of the spine."

Brenner arched an eyebrow at him questioningly. "The spine?"

"Oh yeah, sorry, I forgot you've been busy. You know that ridgeline that Sloan insisted on halfway down the coast. The one she said would help create storms by forcing the air to move vertically instead of just horizontally? Well it resembles a spine on the maps of the cave because some of it eroded away during the first big storm before the ground cover had a chance to take. So it's a big ridge with ravines in it that runs from the cavern wall down to that bluff overlooking the sea.

"She put the platypus on the other side with the excess wetland wildlife so they wouldn't destroy this side's ecology if they got to breeding uncontrollably. I guess she figured they wouldn't go up and over the ridgeline so it acted as a natural divide. I'm not sure it mattered to be honest. The other side is doing just fine, although some of the trees may be stunted for a while until we can get more soil and fertilizer over there."

"We?" Brenner said with a smile. "Are you going farmer on me now Erik?"

Erik laughed. "Clearly not. Sasha went off to spread nightsoil from the reclamation tanks on the other side of the ridgeline and I went fishing. I help where it seems . . . beneficial to both parties. It's not like I'm leaving Sasha on shit detail alone, she's got all those drones doing the actual spreading and planting," he finished defensively while the fish wriggled in his hands.

Brenner motioned him up away from the water and sat down on a rock nearby. Erik wandered over and kneeled next to him, taking out a small knife and cleaning the fish.

"Yeah, we've been pretty busy lately," Brenner began tentatively, trying to figure out how to broach the next topic. "Let's see you've been on R and R for what, six or eight weeks. Something like that?"

Erik grunted an acknowledgement as he tugged on the fish's gills and pulled all its guts out through the slit he'd cut.

"In that time we've managed to repair the Promenade. The MIC is fully functional again but Broadway is going to take a long time to repair. There was a pretty big fight at the MBTC when the last freighter arrived and we've learned a few things about the aliens we found."

Erik stepped back to the river, rinsing the fish off and tossing the guts out into the water before he walked back and put it in a nearby cooler, wiping his hands on a rag. "How bad did we get hit at the MBTC?"

Brenner shifted on his rock, his armored plates causing the pieces to crumble away. "Pretty serious. From what Forsythe said they hit them mid transfer, nailed one of the tugs in the process, and managed to penetrate all the way into the CIC before they were stopped. Captain Spears was among the casualties although it looks like he will recover fully."

Erik let out a whistle and shook his head. "Did they complete the freighter handoff with just one tug then?"

"From the sound of it, the tug that was damaged wasn't on tug duty, it was acting like some kind of mobile refueling station for the Mongos running defensive screen. They didn't provide a ton of detail on that aspect of the fight."

"Did we take many losses?" Erik asked anxiously.

"Apparently the Mongos got off pretty light. The Chinese went straight for the throat and avoided dogfighting. As a result, they didn't do too much damage to the fighter screen. We lost a few Angels, including one to ground fire. It sounds like the Marines took it on the chin though. They obscured the numbers in the report they sent us for security reasons, but the inference was that some units suffered twenty percent casualties."

Erik looked up in alarm. "Twenty percent? Do we even have an effective force now?"

"For defense we'll be spread thin, but should be able to manage. Offensive operations could be pretty dicey until the latest batch of Marines gets settled in and acclimated. The Chinese suffered terrible losses. Almost none of their ground forces returned and a significant portion of their fighters fought until the bitter end." Brenner closed his eyes, fighting memories of the previous war on Earth before continuing. "I don't know how they can continue doing this. They've lost so many men at this point. At some point they have to run out of trained people. They have to..."

Erik kicked a small stone away as he thought. "Remember that first battle they had? Captain Wilks led that assault on their forward base and smashed up a couple of rice factories and water reservoirs. I've been thinking, maybe they're so reckless with their men because they can't support them all logistically. Maybe it's a use or lose situation. I think they knew that freighter was loaded up with more Marines and pilots. If that's the case, and they're having problems with logistics due to the supply line back to Earth being shit, maybe this was an attempted knockout punch. Maybe they knew that if we landed more troops they couldn't win or build up the forces they needed to win, so they threw a big punch and hoped it landed."

"That's a lot of maybes," Brenner said dubiously. "In any event, word is they only managed to load half of the expected trainees on the freighter as it made its pass. That means we're not getting the reinforcements we were hoping for when it eventually gets here in six months. Which brings us back to our current problem."

"Aliens," Erik said with a snort as he threw the rag in the cooler and shut the lid.

"Yes, aliens. Forsythe's guys were able to take the data we collected during our fight and your notes and develop a radar search algorithm that seems to be fairly effective at detecting the ships through their camouflage. We've been able to implement it here. The catch is, when you see them they know you can see them and they move away. So you can't keep a sensor lock on them without them moving around," Brenner said as he watched Erik's reaction to his notes being used for good.

"I take it to mean that since you implemented it here and believe it was successful that means you found more aliens?"

"Yes, at least two. They're parked about as far away from us as they can be and still be orbiting Saturn."

"How many did they find around Earth?"

Brenner paused, licking his lips. "At least twelve."

Erik leaned back looking at Brenner intently, then he started to laugh, a slow, disjointed, laugh that shook his whole body. "There are fourteen of them? Of the thing we fought and nearly lost to?"

"Fifteen if you count the one we've captured, which by the way still appears to have at least one of them onboard."

"We barely beat one," Erik said with a laugh, his eyes shifting past Brenner as he caught sight of Molly walking down the path toward them, her towel wrapped around her tightly.

"Yes, we're in a tight spot. That's why I need you to come back. We can't make any sense out of half of the alien systems, we haven't gotten the prisoner to talk and I think we're starting to run out of time. I need you Erik and it wouldn't hurt Sloan's feelings if you sent her a message, I think she misses you."

Molly walked passed Brenner, giving him an undecipherable stare as she bent down to look in the cooler. "Oh good, you caught something finally."

Brenner saw Erik wince at her dig and smirked. He should have asked him how long he'd been trying to catch a fish when he first got there.

"It was an epic battle. I had to convince him to hit my bait over all the other bugs in the water. It must be some kind of hatch," Erik said, flicking a small larva off his ankle in disgust.

"Are you ready Erik?" Brenner asked patiently.

"Sure Brenner, I've been on light duty long enough," Erik said as he looked down at the creek sadly.

"You can come back here as often as you need," Brenner said, gesturing at the cave. "Soon we're going to start allowing people the doc says are stressed out to come here regularly. John's just timing the release of that information so it does the most good. He needs Sasha to give him the ready to go and he wants to spread out the good news. First thing was the Promenade being repaired. I think he'll start giving tours back here in another month. KaliSun employees first, then we'll consider the contractors."

"Still some spies running around loose I take it?"

"We think so. During the assault on the MBTC, two employees assisted the Chinese in penetrating the base. It allowed them to bypass a lot of security measures and head directly to the CIC. As I understand it, the whole thing ended with Forsythe, Davies, and Stokes' bodyguards in a shootout in the hallway outside the CIC against twenty to thirty Chinese."

"Last stand at the Alamo," Erik said, shaking his head in disbelief.

"Wait, what happened?" Molly asked.

"Long story, I'll explain later."

Brenner narrowed his eyes as he looked at the two of them, his lips pursed. He'd have to remind Erik about sharing confidential information with Molly later. He stood up and dusted his butt off.

"So, you ready to head back or do you want to stop off back at the house and cook that thing?" Brenner said, gesturing to the cooler.

"Let's cook it, I need to get my stuff anyway. You look like you could use some downtime."

"I'm afraid there isn't much time for that these days. But I can probably kill another hour."

"Good, I've built something I want to show you at the house," Erik said with a grin.

Brenner looked at him and waited, motioning with his hand to get Erik to spill. Erik leered over at Molly, who blushed as she glared back at him. "I made a hot tub. It takes a little work to get it heated up, electric coils aren't the most efficient. But it really takes the stress out when you can sit in there and look out over the sea."

Brenner smiled at Erik and started walking back toward his rover. "We'll see."

He heard Molly cough loudly. "Excuse me," she said as he turned back around. "Do I get to go back to the base with you?"

"Sure."

CHAPTER 23

The command staff filed into the conference room for an 8am standup meeting that had ominously been called 'tactical regrouping' on their schedules. They arrayed themselves around the table with the military leadership on one side and a select few research staffers on the other with the KaliSun employees and Molly. Brenner and Hatfield occupied the end of the table in silence.

As they all got settled, Hatfield motioned to Joe, who sealed the hatch and turned on his electronic counter surveillance suite. A soft hum spread throughout the room briefly before dropping to a near inaudible level.

Hatfield leaned in and started the meeting off. "I'm sure you are all aware of the general facts of our current situation. Today is primarily information sharing so that we can all brainstorm on how to proceed."

The researchers shifted in their seats, aware that it was uncharacteristic for Hatfield to share his vision for the future. Major Stringer and Chief Marin sat in stoic silence, while Captain Martin stared at the researchers intently, studying their reactions.

Hatfield let the silence hang for a few moments longer. "The basics are simple. We performed a secret flight test from Saturn Base to Gliese 581, a red dwarf star about twenty-three light years away. The trip took about three days. When the ship returned it was followed by two things. The first, an energy emission of a size and scope we are still struggling to quantify, that disrupted communications, power grids and basically civilization as we know it throughout the solar system. This object rapidly slungshot around the sun and impacted a sizable asteroid. The radiation has since dissipated, leaving behind a large number of irradiated asteroids that have been knocked out of orbit.

We are trying to determine their orbits now and determine how safe the freighter racetrack back to Earth is.

"The second challenge that returned with the KaliSun has not left us. Shortly after the plasma ball hit the asteroid belt we were approached by a single ship of alien origin. This ship approached the base here on Phoebe in stealth mode, but was detected before it could close to weapons range. The ship was engaged and defeated. The base was damaged during the confrontation and several of the ship's crew succeeded in penetrating into the military side of the base. That's the damage you see being repaired on Broadway.

"The local security forces were able to defeat the enemy landing party and capture one of their soldiers. At this point, it is not clear if the enemy discharged the plasma ball or if it was the result of our ship. We have been unable to communicate with our prisoner, despite our best efforts. Any questions or comments so far?"

Molly started to raise her hand, but Dr. Rogers spoke first. "You mentioned a single alien ship, have we detected any others since the confrontation?"

The slightest hint of a smile twitched at the corner of Hatfield's lips as Dr. Rogers spoke up on cue. "Yes, after the military confrontations that we've had with the Chinese on Earth, the MBTC commander, Will Forsythe, using data collected during the alien attack here, was able to develop a method to more effectively detect their ships. To date we have found fourteen. Two here and twelve around Earth."

The scientists around the one side of the table were stunned briefly by that admission, before breaking into discussions among themselves. Hatfield let it play out, shooting a look to Rogers who nodded his head back and acted surprised when Dr. Winters asked him if he'd heard about this before. Finally, as the discussion started to get out of hand, Dr. Winters held his hand up and calmed the other scientists.

"Director, I was under the impression that the fight with the last alien ship didn't go well, that we came very close to losing in fact. Now you tell us that there are two more of those ships out there and more around Earth. Perhaps it's time to discuss evacuating the base ... "

Brenner held up his hand forestalling the uproar that was about to start. "We can't evacuate. The next two freighters coming in were both in transit when that plasma comet shot through the system, both freighters took significant damage from the event. We're not certain of their full condition as of yet. We did lose several people due to radiation exposure and one hull breach. It's possible those two freighters won't be capable of a return trip." He held up both hands again as the room erupted with questions, calming them briefly. "The freighter that just did a stop at the MBTC was also damaged during the storm and the Chinese attempt to down her in transit. We're not sure how much of that ship can be repaired, they're assessing her on the outbound flight. The MBTC lost a tug in that battle. If they continue to lose tugs, we may not be able to continue the freighter runs at all. No tugs means no way to slow ourselves, you'd just shoot off into space."

"Then there's the whole armada of alien ships waiting around Earth that can shoot you down as well," Major Stringer quipped.

"Why doesn't your Navy deal with them? I mean what did we pay you for anyway?" Molly added sarcastically, finally able to get a word in.

"I don't have a Navy," Hatfield said bitterly. "I have a couple of trainee fighter squadrons, with no capital ship support and no independent ability to detect the alien ships. The MBTC isn't much better off."

"I thought you said we could detect them now?" Sam Malhotra said, alarmed.

"The sensors required to see them are too large and energy intensive to fit on a small ship," Captain Jasper Wilcox drawled from his side of the table. "We need to be in sensor range of the ground radars or else we're blind as a bat." He glanced at Major

Stringer, giving an apologetic nod for talking out of turn. The Major shrugged indifferently in return.

"All the more reason to take our chances evacuating as many people while we can!" Molly said.

"I suppose you put yourself near the top of that list?" Dr. Kapple shot back at her.

"I am not a combatant, you started this fight. I just want to go home!" she snapped, tears welling up in her eyes.

"Ms. Caan, enough. We've discussed this before, you know the reasons we cannot evacuate," Hatfield said sternly.

Dr. Winters started violently and looked at Hatfield. "You've discussed this with her already, but not with us?"

"Yes," Hatfield said, a frustrated sigh escaping as his teeth clamped shut.

"Don't be offended. The conversation at the time was not intended to exclude you, it was a spontaneous discussion," Brenner said apologetically to Dr. Winters.

He started to say something in return, but a glance from Dr. Rogers quelled him as Hatfield continued.

"For the rest of you, the reasons we cannot evacuate the entire base are quite simple. For starters, we cannot protect the freighters on the way home. We don't have the ships, radars or weapons to spare to modify them to be defensible. It's possible there will be no tugs left to slow you down when you get there and there are too many people to get on one freighter. It would take three freighters at least, assuming we abandon all of our gear, weapons and armor with each successive freighter making the base less defendable."

"Additionally, right now, humanity is in three places—Saturn, the moon and Earth. The aliens may hesitate to attack so long as they cannot easily wipe us out in one shot. If we head back to Earth, we're putting all of our eggs in two baskets, painfully close to each other," Dr. Rogers said thoughtfully.

"Yes there is that," Hatfield conceded.

"So, if we're not evacuating, and the freighters may not

keep coming, how long can we last before supplies run out?" Christie asked quietly.

"Nearly indefinitely," Sloan replied forcefully, drawing looks from around the table.

"How is that possible?"

Sloan glanced over at the Director who nodded his approval. She smiled at Brenner, who leaned back in his chair to watch the faces of the research staff as she unveiled her masterpiece.

"For some time now I have been tasked with making the base here self sufficient. Many of you know about the food tubes and efforts to grow more diverse crops. As a function of that task, we have created a new food tube, substantially larger than previous ones." Sloan paused dramatically before hitting a key on the table, flooding the screens with images. "I give you the Eden Cave."

There was a startled silence around the table as the civilians looked up in awe at the vast vistas on the screens. Dr. Winters looked sideways down the length of the table with an accusatory glare at Hatfield.

"Why weren't we told about this?"

"For security reasons primarily. We've had a distressing number of attempted sabotage events on this base, which led us toward a policy of caution around who knew," Hatfield said. "If it makes you feel better, we also didn't tell the MBTC or Corporate Headquarters exactly what we were doing. Aside from the caretaker, the people in this room represent the majority of those who know it exists."

"As you can see, we don't need to evacuate," Brenner said softly.

"I see a beach," Major Sirano said happily. "When do we get to go?"

"Very soon G-LOC, very soon. It's my intent to use this facility as a rest and recreation area as well as a source of food. That ocean has a maturing population of salmon, shrimp, crabs, lobster and a few other fast growing fish," Hatfield said with a smile.

"Mahi?" Major Stringer said hopefully.

"Yes, it's a salt water sea with freshwater rivers. Mahi and the various species of salmon are our apex predators. We've got a warmish side and colder side of the sea that we use to induce weather and wave patterns. As a result, we have warm water sea life and cold water sea life in the same, small body of water," Sloan said with pride.

Molly looked around the table with despair as she realized that for most of the people sitting here, the Eden Cave was a fascinating, shiny toy that had taken their minds off of their predicament. She knew she wasn't going to get any help, but decided to try one last time.

"Maybe you should allow people to take the risk going home. Let them know they can't be protected and they may die. But give them the option before the freighters stop coming."

"I take it you still want to go back then?" Dr. Rogers asked her kindly.

"Yes, absolutely," Molly said firmly

Hatfield and Brenner exchanged a brief glance, Hatfield writing a couple of notes. Sloan shook her head sadly and said nothing.

"We'll consider it. There will only be a limited number of seats," Hatfield said.

"Thank you," Molly said with surprise.

Major Stringer looked at her with irritation before speaking up. "Well, so we have food and water. We can spot the bastards before they get here and we know the MBTC has their hands full. What do we do next?"

"You saw the data from the fight at the MBTC, what do you think?" Brenner asked him.

Major Stringer pondered the question for a few moments before responding. "I think they have the MBTC in a bad bind. If the Chinese keep doing the human wave style fighter attacks on the tugs, eventually they're going to get them all. If that happens, it could be years before we can re-establish the supply lines. The Chinese seem very aware of this; they ignored the freighter itself and went right for the tugs and the Angels. In my mind, that's bad. Very bad."

"What about the actual combat?" Dr. Rogers asked

"Well, we still have a clear advantage with starfighters. There is no doubt our electronic warfare is miles above their ability to counter it. As a result, they're always behind when it comes to situational awareness and that gives us a huge edge. Plus, our ships are just plain tougher. They shoot at us with fifty caliber machine guns and we shoot back with twenty-millimeter cannon, it's not even a fair contest in most dogfights. The ground is a bit of a different story."

"You mean the tanks?" Brenner prodded.

"Yeah, the tanks. Most of our tactics and weapons depend on a certain fragility of the enemy armor or structure. Those tanks are going to be a serious problem, especially if they have a lot of them or we get caught out in the open with no Mongos overhead. To a certain degree, it's the same problem we have with the aliens. Our weapons are just not designed to deal with their armor. I've asked Dr. Bilks to help us develop new weapons, but he's been sequestered for a few weeks."

"Sequestered?" Sam asked.

"He's been on company mandated R and R," Hatfield said firmly, cutting off further discussion on the topic with a chop of his hand.

"Really, the only reason we keep winning is because Chinese weapons and technology are lagging behind ours. There's nothing really wrong with their tactics, it's fairly advanced deception in most cases, with a heavy reliance on spreading our defense out. With the casualties we've taken since the war kicked off, eventually they're going to wear us down," Major Springer said.

"Just a matter of time then?" Dr. Winters asked.

"Yes, unless they've shot their wad or something changes dramatically. Eventually we're going to run out of bullets and bodies to throw at them."

The room grew silent at the grim assessment. Hatfield waited until he saw that each of them had come to grips with the issue before he started talking again.

"So my plan is straightforward. First, we assemble the people at the base and explain the situation to them. Not detailed, just kind of where we are. The rumor mill is going crazy now and we need to get that under control. Second, we're going through the data from the flight test and combat data that we have on the crabs, sorry, the aliens. Once we get through that, we're going to make some adjustments. Thirdly, we have a freighter arriving in a few weeks, we need to assess the damage to it, repair what we can and offload the cargo successfully without getting roped into combat with the two ships watching us. Once we get that far, we'll let a select few people evacuate on the freighter and reassess our manpower requirements."

Hatfield saw that the crowd agreed with the plan and it looked like they were starting to settle down from the shock they'd taken early in the meeting. "If there are no further questions, I think its time to break this meeting up. Dr. Winters, I'd like to have this meeting weekly with you and Dr. Rogers from now on. That should keep you updated and we can avoid any more surprises."

Winters smiled and thanked the Director before leading his people out through the hatch, leaving just Sloan, Dr. Rogers, Brenner and Hatfield at the table.

"Still no data on that strange worm or snake thing we saw down in the clouds of Saturn?" Sloan asked Rogers hopefully.

"Nothing. I think we're going to have to assume the radiation storm drew it to the surface from down deep. I don't think its related to the crabs however."

"We'll keep an eye out. I need some time to write a speech, so I'm heading to my quarters," Hatfield said and stood up to leave. "Try not to get in any trouble for the next couple of days."

CHAPTER 24

Christie and Sam settled nervously into their chairs in the PRC. The chamber was normally used for presentations and group meetings, but today it was to serve as the assembly hall for Director Hatfield's 'State of the Base' speech.

Christie craned her neck around looking for any of the senior staff from the KaliSun Corporation to make an appearance, but they were nowhere to be found. Instead, she saw that the majority of the scientists were milling around aimlessly, nervously greeting their colleagues and debating what the meeting might mean. She couldn't blame them, in her entire tour on Saturn, Hatfield had only done one of these speeches before. That time it was to announce that the Promenade was complete and that a new era of occupation on Phoebe had begun. Recent events did not lend themselves to such positive news, and the academics were fully aware of it. As far as she could tell, most people were assuming the news would be bad, very bad.

Sam tugged at the elbow of her spacesuit and nodded to the top of the amphitheater. She followed his gaze and flinched slightly. Lining the top of the room were several SARines and a full squad of Marines in riot control gear. The lights at the top had been dimmed low and their suits' optical camouflage nearly perfectly blotted out their outline to the crowd before them. As she surveyed the room she noticed that several other Marines were interspersed throughout the crowd in casual attire, blending in as best they could.

"Are we expecting trouble?" Christie whispered to Sam. She was tempted to put her helmet on so she could talk to him in private, but didn't out of fear it would raise suspicions.

"I think the Director is just being prudent. Look at their gear, they aren't kitted out for a gunfight. Its more like they're expecting panic and the need for crowd control," Sam said in soft conversational tones.

Christie looked again and breathed a sigh of relief. Most of the Marines were stationed near groups who had been difficult to deal with in the past.

The massive projector at the bottom of the amphitheater came to light showing Director Hatfield's aide, Ed Styles, on the screen. He was a harmless looking man, with a calm face, but Christie knew that under that façade was a competent manager equivalent to any US President's Chief of Staff.

"Attention ladies and gentlemen of Saturn Base. The Director will begin speaking in three minutes, please make your way to your seats," Ed said pleasantly through the projection, which was being sent to assembly areas throughout Saturn Base.

Christie couldn't be sure, but she'd bet that the Director had segregated different populations of similar function throughout the base for this briefing, specifically in an effort to get a better feel for how each group reacted to the news he was about to share. A cold chill ran down her spine at the thought of those crab things getting lose in the base's civilian areas.

Sam looked over at her curiously but said nothing, instead reaching a hand over to grip her knee firmly as he smiled reassuringly at her. He put his hand back in his lap as he turned to look across the room, watching intently as the scientists found their seats. It was an interesting dynamic, with groups of scientists automatically clumping together based on their expertise rather than company affiliation.

The Director appeared suddenly on the screen. He was wearing his recently repainted command suit and was sitting behind the beautiful wooden desk that Christie had seen in his private office. He looked calm and in charge, the large armored suit and non-sterile surroundings combined to give the impression of somebody wholly comfortable with where he was, and with who he was.

"Residents of Saturn Base and KaliSun employees, I come to you today with an update on the status of our base. As many of you know, a series of events have occurred at this facility that have been the cause of concern and rumor. Today I will try to address those concerns and give you all an understanding of where we are going from here.

"A short time ago, a United States Congressional delegation arrived to inspect the science facility. During their time here, the senior member of that committee, Senator Hernandez, suffered an unfortunate mental breakdown. She remains in protective custody and is receiving the best medical care we have to offer. During the course of that breakdown however, several other members of the research staff were caught up in a rebellion led by Dr. Augustus Von Tremel. As some of you are aware, a number of junior researchers were killed during that incident."

Hatfield paused, looking contrite as headshots of those who had died were displayed on the screen. After an appropriate pause, he continued.

"As we investigated those murders, and they were murders, we were able to prevent several other acts of violence that had been bubbling under the surface. Through that investigation, we arrested a number of violent offenders who were plotting additional attacks."

A gasp ran through the audience as pictures of the criminals flashed across the screen and Dr. Meckler's image showed. Each image had a list of crimes next to it, starting with their worst and usually ending with conspiracy. The contract scientists in the room started shifting in their seats. Those who had been present when Meckler had been arrested looked over at Christie and Sam with wary eyes, unsure what to make of the situation.

"Parallel to these investigations, the solar system suffered a significant radiation event of unknown origin. The base suffered minor damage and has since been completely repaired, but the incoming freighters and Earth were damaged more significantly. While the bulk of Saturn protected us from the worst of the radiation, most of the rest of the system was not so lucky, which brings us to the most pressing problem I need to explain.

"At present, it is unlikely that we can allow anyone to transit home. The incoming freighter scheduled to arrive in a few weeks was damaged in transit by the radiation. They have been working tirelessly to repair the damage on the way here, and we stand ready to meet them with additional repair crews, however there is only so much we can do in a single pass."

Hatfield paused, fully aware that his statement would cause significant discomfort to his audience. He sat patiently at his desk, silent.

Sam leaned over and whispered in Christie's ear. "They must be monitoring the rooms in real time so he can tell when it's time to speak again. I wouldn't be surprised if there are extra Marines in the hallways outside the assembly areas."

"Yeah," Christie replied, as she listened in on the conversations nearest to them. People were scared, very scared.

A sharp tone sounded from the speakers and Hatfield continued. "An additional complication has manifested that is related, we think, to the radiation event. We have made contact with our first alien species. They are intelligent, warlike and technologically superior to us. One of their ships has attacked the base, we were successful in defending ourselves."

He paused again as the science assembly room broke into pandemonium. There had been rumors of a space battle fought above the base racing through the community for weeks. Everyone had assumed it was a Chinese attack based on the information that had been released about the fighting on the moon. Aliens were an entirely new problem that nobody was prepared for.

Christie looked up at the Marines, her face lined with worry, but they seemed calm and unperturbed by the confusion that had erupted below them. The plainclothes Marines started to calmly interject themselves into the more panicked conversations, bringing up the good things about the situation and trying to defuse the situation without the researchers realizing they were doing so. She frowned and leaned close to Sam.

"I don't remember this type of mob psychology training for our Marines before," she whispered.

"I think Brenner added it when he got here. He said he'd rather talk somebody down than gun them down. I heard he convinced Hatfield to add it as required training for the permanent Marines. Looks like they took to it well, no threatening body posture, non-aggressive language. I'm actually pretty impressed."

Finally, after almost fifteen minutes of relative free-for-all, the scientists had mostly calmed down and were back to talking about the impact it would have on their research. Some were even openly raising the possibility of academic papers on the new alien species. It was at that point that Hatfield grabbed their attention again.

"The presence of hostile aliens in proximity to our base is a further reason we are hesitant to allow people to try the transit back home. We did capture one of the aliens during the attack and are attempting to communicate with it now. If we succeed in that respect, it is our intent to open a dialogue with them that will hopefully defuse the situation. However, as of right now, we are effectively at war with an alien species and the MBTC is at war with the Chinese. These two things combined mean that travel home, for the moment, is restricted to those with a medical reason to leave or those who are willing to take what we believe will be an enormous risk."

The image of Hatfield held up his gloved hand as though to forestall another outburst and smiled. It was genuine smile, not gloating or superior that drew the eyes of the research staff toward his image.

"The news is not all bad. Over the course of the last three years, the KaliSun Corporation has been endeavoring to bring a new facility online within the base. This facility follows the path of the Morale Improvement Center and the Promenade in its purpose, a facility that provides an area of relaxation and peace. It also happens to allow us to expand the dinner menu in the restaurants and casinos in the MIC, something that has been a regular request during the guest surveys. So without further comment, I give you Eden."

The image on the projection screen of Hatfield's face gradually faded to be replaced by an incredible panoramic shot of the Eden Cave taken from the entrance. There was a stunned murmur from the scientists as they took in the lengthy purple-white sandy beaches, the crops spread out like a checkerboard across a landscape studded with rivers, creeks, waterfalls and parks. The image gradually faded away to show baby goats bouncing playfully in a pen while chickens ran free throughout the area. The next image showed a series of faux log cabins lining a cliff face studded with purple crystals that poked through rock, each with a porch, a small grassy area with a picnic table and a grill. The image faded again to show a man fishing in a river, catching a large brightly colored trout on a fly rod as the wind blew through the young pine trees around him. Another showed a smiling redheaded woman crouching next to a little red wagon piled high with green beans and cucumbers.

The slide show continued on and on. Christie was able to pick out members of the senior KaliSun staff in the images. Erik fishing in the river, Brenner turning a wrench on an autonomous tractor, Sloan using an army of robots to plant seeds, and several people she didn't recognize. All in deliberate poses of relaxation, none of them wearing their spacesuits, but showing signs of a healthy tan. As the image shifted to a picture of several buff Marines playing volleyball on the beach, a cheer came from the men lining the rear of the room, several of the Marines clapping and hooting at the men and women on screen.

The image gradually came back to Director Hatfield once more, still smiling as he spoke to the stunned crowd.

"As you can see, we've been very busy. Up until recently, the facility was not ready to receive visitors. However, at this point we feel it is safe to allow small groups to visit for recreation breaks. We're going to allow people who have been on station longest to go first and then we'll move down the line. At this point time, we're considering allowing people to volunteer their free time to work to improve the Eden Cave, volunteers will earn points which move them up the roster to vacation there sooner. It's the fairest way we could think to do it.

"I know it's been a stressful few months for many of you. Again I encourage you to visit the facility medical wing if you feel the need to talk to somebody. I speak for all of us at the KaliSun Corporation when I wish you the best of health as we fight through these troubling times. This is Director Hatfield, signing off."

He finished speaking, his image fading back to the montage of pictures from the Eden Cave. Christie felt drawn to it, mesmerized by the artificial beauty of the imagery. Next to her Sam chuckled softly.

"Clever, maybe too clever by half."

She looked over at him curiously. "What do you mean?"

"He gave them all the bad news. We're at war with a strange race of monsters, but never showed them a picture of one, leaving it an abstract. He told them the incoming freighters were damaged, but didn't detail how, allowing their minds to construct a worst case scenario that will make it so they don't want to board one; it plays upon their internalized fears. He told them there had been murders at the base then showed a montage of people he claimed were victims and a montage he claimed were villains, but I think we both know Meckler wasn't a murderer, just a moron. By sharing data that was previously restricted, he managed to convey a feeling of transparency. Then he let them blow off some steam, when he wasn't in the room, with his Marines infiltrated into the crowd to guide the discussion in the least harmful direction. Then when they had all gotten to a point where they were distracted and in need of some kind of reassurance or plan for the future, he shares the Eden Cave while simultaneously giving them a way to compete for access. That last bit is pretty brilliant; he's going to get free labor out of the deal while making them feel a part of something grand. But that's not the best part," Sam said with a smile.

Christie smiled lopsidedly at him as she prodded his leg. "Oh really, and what's the best part?"

"Whoever vigorously volunteers and strives to build points the fastest stands a high probability of being a possible spy or saboteur. Most of them will be innocent, but a spy will want access immediately so they can report back. This will help him narrow the field of suspects as he tries to clean out the rat's nest."

"Unless they're too smart to fall for it. Maybe they just interrogate whoever gets to go first?"

"Trust me, the list of who gets to go first has been rigged. Think about it. Who has been here the longest?" Sam looked at her expectantly before saying with a smirk. "KaliSun Employees. Yes, I think our Director is quite clever. Look at the way the scientists look. No fear, they've dismissed going home and he's given them a new thing to go after in the Eden Cave."

Christie looked across the room. It was true, the scientists were all excitedly talking or looking at the montage of pictures going by on the screen. As she watched, a number of the Marines in the group were guiding the discussion and pumping up the excitement level as they continued to work the crowds. She had to admit, being manipulated never felt so good.

CHAPTER 25

The bandage is a nice touch," Stokes said to Forsythe as they sat waiting for their guest. "If I didn't know better, I'd say you'd hung out with Hatfield too much."

Will Forsythe put his hand to his forehead, pushing the tape holding the bandage against his skin. "I did bump my head this morning, there was blood everywhere."

"Yes, on an open drawer. You know he's going to assume that enormous bandage is from the battle," Stokes said with a smirk.

"Maybe it'll make him more amenable to what we have to say."

Before Stokes could respond, Representative Sanders stormed into Forsythe's private office, boiling with anger. He approached the desk and raised his voice to berate them when he saw Forsythe sitting in his chair with a huge white bandage on his face. He stumbled slightly, caught off guard, and sputtered his opening barrage at them.

"It's been weeks since I returned and you're just now agreeing to see me!" he raged at them, stomping his boot on the deck for emphasis. "I demand to be given access to a radio so I can report in with my comrades in government."

Forsythe couldn't help but chuckle at the use of the word comrade, but held up a hand to politely calm him down. "I know and we do apologize for that. We've been a bit busy since you arrived."

"We needed to secure the base completely prior to broadcasting the details of our condition back to Earth," Stokes said calmly.

Sanders turned his glare on Stokes. "You tricked us into going out there, knowing that Hatfield is crazy. You knew what would happen."

"Actually, we specifically told Hatfield to make his best effort to make your stay enjoyable," Stokes said. "As I understand it, he didn't initiate any of the problems. If I'm not mistaken, there was at least one of your spies along for the ride as well, not to mention Senator Hernandez."

"You sent us out there to get us out of the way. You knew that by the time we got out there and were able to report back, you'd have the Marines and pilots back here at the base. You knew by the time we filed our report, it would be clear you had an army, but no intention to hand it over to us," Sanders said bitterly.

"True on all accounts. You were strategically out-maneuvered, that is fact. Think of it like Judo, we used your aggressive attack to bring you close and defeat you with your own energy," Stokes said without emotion.

"And you admit to it? Do you realize what's going to happen to you when the government figures out what you've done? Do you even fathom how severely we're going to punish you? And yet, here you sit, proud of what you did."

"In all honesty, fooling your government is not something to be proud of. You're bloated and difficult to manage, even in your own office. Half of your senior leadership can't even remember the names of all the agencies they're supposed to oversee. There are more difficult challenges dealing with program leads in our own company than there are dealing with your government. Something I suspect you discovered first hand with Hatfield," Stokes said.

"Speaking of which, what did happen out there? All we have is his version for the moment," Forsythe broke in.

Sanders stood there fuming at them. "You don't even know? How can you claim you don't know?"

"You've met Hatfield, you were there in person. I bet you don't know everything he's up to," Stokes said unperturbed.

"But he works for you!" Sanders sputtered.

Stokes shrugged noncommittally and smiled. "As for what

your government is going to do to us, right now, I'd guess almost nothing."

"Nothing? Nothing! I think you underestimate how angry this will make them."

"A lot has happened since you've been away, particularly since the radiation event. Please take a seat. I think there is some information sharing that should occur."

Sanders angrily muttered a curse under his breath and yanked a chair out from the table, sitting down on it hard, his space suit making the seat's support groan in protest. He made an expansive gesture with his hands, waiting for them to continue.

"For starters, I have much bigger problems than Hatfield killing some spy he caught messing with his life support and your Senator going crazy out there."

Sanders tried to interrupt him, but Stokes raised his hand, stopping him. "Right now my ground forces at the MBTC have lost nearly a full ten percent of their strength. Many of our ground vehicles are damaged or destroyed, our fighter strength is down twenty percent, I lost one of my tugs and I just had an enemy force blow holes in a dozen surface buildings in the base.

"The Chinese continue to hit us with a seemingly endless supply of troops and we're starting to run low on ammunition to deal with them. This is a war of attrition, until your freighter showed up, we were effectively decimated across the board. We have two more freighters of pilots and Marines on the way, after that, we may be out of reinforcements. Saturn Base has its own problems."

"Like what? When I left there, the biggest problem they had was figuring out how to subvert our investigation. I had the entire flight back to think about this, I am convinced Hatfield gave us the run around," Sanders said, slapping the table with his hand in frustration.

"I understand that. You experienced the radiation event we had to deal with ..." Stokes said patiently.

"Experienced? Experienced is hardly how I'd define it. That was terrifying, your doctors told my staff those freighters were shielded enough to handle anything, but one solar flare and half of the equipment stops working. I'll probably die of cancer because of that!"

"Well that wasn't a solar flare. It was a giant ball of radiation that came into the system at high speed. We don't know where it came from, though we think we have a theory, more on that in a moment, but it caused significant damage to Earth. That damage is why we are not terribly worried about how your government is going to respond. It's also why we haven't given you access to a radio just yet."

"What do you mean?" Sanders asked, fear in his voice.

"The President, Vice President, Secretary of State and many of the Joint Chiefs are dead. The government is currently being run by the Speaker of the House from, we believe, Cheyenne Mountain in Colorado Springs."

"The Speaker moved the government to a museum, I find that hard to believe," Sanders said slowly as he processed what they were telling him. "How did the President die?"

"A combination of controls failure and pilot error on Air Force One, during the radiation storm. We think. Nobody recovered the wreckage, so it's difficult to say what actually happened."

Sanders stared at them open mouthed as the significance of that statement sunk in. "What about everyone else?"

"The Speaker's control is weak at best. Several parts of the US have effectively devolved to local control. There have been no new countries announced, but people are definitely on their own. Speaking only of our compounds, our security has joined forces with local police units to provide protection. But we are small enclaves compared to the bigger territories like Montana or Texas."

"Protection from what?"

"Bandits mostly, or people trying to survive. The food situation in the United States isn't critical, but there has been a breakdown in its distribution. As a result, many of the urban areas are being abandoned as the people there spread out into the countryside to . . . obtain food. At our main compound, we have prevented this so far by supplying the nearby cities with food we are able to move in from the mid west, but fuel is limited. Right now we're trying to get the city people growing gardens and teaching them basic survival skills. It's a tough slog, most of them are incapable of surviving on their own," Stokes said. "Not all of our facilities survived equally unfortunately. It was mostly the sites where we had employee dependents housed that did the best. Some of our research sites were less fortunate."

"Are you saying the United States has slipped into some kind of apocalypse?" Sanders said in disbelief.

Stokes and Forsythe exchanged looks before Forsythe answered. "Well, they aren't as bad as the Middle East, Africa, Latin America and west Asia. Some of those areas have gone almost tribal at this point. Europe has the Germans and Austrians attempting to reinstitute some kind of feudal system and we can't tell what's going on in Russia or China. Knowing the Russians, I'd guess they are coping. China was sending up a steady stream of weapons and reinforcements, but that stopped not long ago."

"What about my district . . . "

Stokes just shook his head. "There are people there, but they lack the equipment to talk to us. One of our observation flights says they believe people are fortifying the area, which is either promising that they have the sense to put walls up, or worrying that they need them. But we haven't been able to reach out. As near as we can reconstruct, your family has been home for the last three months or so. So at least they weren't stranded in Washington D.C."

"Why, what happened to D.C., did the Chinese attack?"

"It's still smoldering," Forsythe said glumly. "It started as a riot or looting. Since then, we think just random arson. There appeared to be a sizable police force protecting the main Federal Enclave, but most of the north and south are rubble. It spread into Arlington too, mostly in the residential areas. I think the last imagery shows an area from Alexandria to Ballston to Rosslyn just burned to the ground."

"We have another problem. Perhaps a more significant one," Stokes began.

"More significant than our country being destroyed?" Sanders sputtered at them.

"I wouldn't say destroyed . . . " Forsythe said, but Stokes kicked his leg under the table.

"Yes, more significant than that. A hostile alien force has engaged us. We survived the first encounter, barely, at Saturn Base. We think they were responsible for the radiation event—think of it like preparing the battlefield by knocking our technology offline and causing a humanitarian crisis in the process. We captured one of their ships, we've seen at least twelve more."

"Aliens . . . " Sanders repeated dully. "We've been attacked by aliens?"

"It would seem so."

Sanders looked away from them, his breath speeding up as he slowly sank into panic.

"Aliens, and the fact the Chinese on the moon are shooting at anything flying toward Earth, makes us reluctant to try to take you home. You might not make it. At best, it would be a rougher ride than the one you experienced landing from the freighter."

Sanders shuddered at the memory of being bounced around in that Angel; he'd puked all over himself when they had finally landed. Then again when they had encountered Chinese soldiers near the shelter in place. He had no desire to do that again.

Stokes keyed something on his wrist and a large SARine entered the room, standing behind Sanders quietly.

"I know it's a lot to process, but we think it's safer if you stay here a while longer. We'll try to get in touch with your family and your government as soon as we can. Please follow the SARine, he will take you to a guest room we have arranged for you," Stokes said, gesturing to the SARine to help him get up.

As Sanders was led from the room and the door shut, Forsythe turned to Stokes. "Cute, blame the plasma comet on the aliens nobody can talk to."

"Right now he's quite receptive to new ideas. Shock has a tendency to do that, I'm hoping as he sits in his room thinking about this over and over again it will lock into his head as the truth and he can be our voice on the matter with Earth. He'll seem sincere and he won't be one of us. He's mad enough at Hatfield it should lend some credibility to the whole affair."

The console in front of them pinged a calendar reminder. Stokes looked at it sadly. "Never any time to relax."

"At least this next meeting should be a bit more exciting."

Captain Wilks walked along next to Captain Spears on their way to Forsythe's meeting. Spears had brand new command armor on, still with the basic camouflage scheme and lacking insignia and awards.

"So how does it feel to get out of the hospital Mike?"

"Great. I just love to have lots of things to worry about again," Spears said sarcastically

"Who are you kidding, you were worried about your unit when you were in the hospital," Wilks said with a laugh.

"True enough, I got one of the medics to give me the casualty figures. There are going to be a lot of new faces when I get back."

"Yeah, sorry to hear about your XO. Jamie wasn't it?"

"Jamie Novak," Spears said sadly. "Did you see the report?"

"Just skimmed the casualty list, what happened?"

"It was after we dismounted the APCs and charged the tanks. Everything was going more or less according to plan, but the tank managed to swivel its turret unexpectedly, hit him square in the head and drove him into the APC armor. Our armor's good, but that was too much, broke his neck on impact. When the SARines found him, they thought he'd passed out, almost no visible damage to the neck sleeve, but he was dead inside."

"Shitty way to go."

"I dunno, I imagine it was a lot better than the Chinese we left stranded out there. Report said we just stood off with Angels and watched them suffocate as they tried to walk across the surface to our base." Spears shuddered, wincing as he tweaked his ribs.

"Yeah, Forsythe gave the order to save ammunition, so we just watched them. You'd see a line of them charging ahead, then one would start to stumble, then fall down scratching at his faceplate or neck. Then it was over. The others would keep going, you'd see another go down and another. None of them made it to the base."

"Almost feel sorry for the bastards."

Wilks looked at his friend in surprise but said nothing. As they approached the entrance to the conference room they saw a space-suited figure being led by a SARine walk into the hallway. He passed them, eyes forward and unfocused, his face ashen.

"Well, doesn't he look like he just got donkey kicked in the groin?" Spears said as they pushed open the door and walked in.

Stokes watched the staff file in. Operational commanders, section chiefs, the Brigade Commander and Wing Commander all walked in and took their seats around the table.

Most of them were exhausted, and several still bore the scars of recent combat on their suits and in their eyes. He let them get seated then rapped his knuckles on the table.

"I want to keep this short and to the point," he said as he looked around the table, meeting each man and woman's eyes as he did so. "Over the last few weeks we have discovered that the Chinese have a significant advantage over us in forces, and possibly an edge on equipment. We've engaged them—beaten them. But the fact of the matter is, just based on the casualty statistics so far, that they outnumber us about thirteen to one in total manpower and about six to one in equipment. That means in every defensive fight, we're disadvantaged. Our offensive engagements have to be constrained by what kind of response they can throw at us. We are lacking my friends. We cannot afford to grind it out with them."

A number of the military members nodded their heads in agreement, but said nothing. The KaliSun civilian employees shifted nervously in their seats, afraid of what was coming next.

"We can't pick up and move to Saturn. We can't evacuate to Earth. Whatever we choose to do, we are here until the Chinese are defeated and the aliens are dealt with. We have some additional reinforcements coming from Saturn Base in the coming months—trained pilots and Marines. But at our current rate of attrition, these will only be enough to bring our units back to full strength then . . . then we will gradually lose. That is my opinion as CEO; my military commanders agree." Stokes gestured toward the seated senior military commanders, who nodded in unison as he spoke.

He pulled up a map of the moon on the main display and overlaid the Chinese positions on it.

"We currently have just this one facility on the moon proper. It's a large facility and very capable, but still very much an island being encroached upon by the Chinese. As you can see, they have gradually pushed out fire bases in recent weeks in a double pincer encirclement. When that closes, we will be surrounded."

"Since our initial attack on this big Chinese base here, they have heavily fortified that area. We cannot possibly hope to attack again with conventional forces, it would be a meat grinder that would cripple us for future operations. However, this is also where they've concentrated much of their total force. It's the central hub for a significant portion of their bases and we believe is their main food supply location. Based on those facts, this is where we'll strike," Stokes said firmly.

"But you just said we can't possibly win an attack on that base," Chief of Operations Robbins said carefully.

"A conventional attack yes. I intend to nuke them, multiple times," Stokes said, looking Robbins directly in the eyes.

Robbins worked his mouth several times, clearly upset about the possibility of nukes but not sure what to say. Spears saved him by interrupting.

"Excuse me sir, but having attacked that facility before, I know much of it is underground. We're not likely to take out much of the actual base."

"Do you remember the final targets Wilks' task force hit as you were leaving?" Forsythe asked Spears.

Spears looked at Wilks and furrowed his brow, thinking back. "Heat exchangers, some water tanks and rovers I think. Why?"

"All on the surface correct?" Forsythe said patiently.

Spears smiled lopsidedly. "Yes."

"So do you see why it would be effective now?" Forsythe said.

"I don't," Robbins interrupted. "All that rock is going to block even the radiation from hitting their crew areas."

"If you lost every single heat exchanger and major water reservoir in one attack, how long could you keep our base functioning?" Forsythe asked.

"Oh, I get it," Robbins said, downcast. "So we cook off all

their support equipment and let them struggle to survive afterward."

"Correct, it may not kill them. But what it will do is force them to distribute their forces again to places we can effectively attack. It will make them expand their logistical footprint and maybe, just maybe we'll do enough damage that they can't mount an attack again. At the very least, we'll destroy a lot of support equipment they can't replace from Earth," Colonel Davies said.

"Are you sure you want to open Pandora's Box?" Robbins asked sadly. "Especially with the aliens watching."

"We are going to lose otherwise," Stokes said.

"I'm not sure what your concern is Chief," Spears said slowly. "The only difference between an air strike, nuclear strike, and executing somebody in the street is scale. They can't defend themselves in any event. Failing to admit that the moral impurity of any given act of murder is equivalent is just hiding behind your momma's skirt to avoid feeling bad about your actions."

Robbins flushed as Spears finished speaking, but bit his lip rather than respond.

"This is a big step, we'll need a vote," Stokes said.

"We never voted before?" Wilks blurted out.

"This one time, with this group, we'll vote on this," Stokes said firmly. "All in favor, raise your hand."

Gradually hands went up in the air. Those aware of the purpose of the meeting ahead of time raised their hands quickly, the others more slowly. Eventually all hands were raised except for Robbins, who sat glumly in his seat. He looked around and raised his hand, barely making it above his head.

Stokes looked around the room again. "So be it. Senior military command staff, prep your plan. Small footprint, big payloads. Good luck everyone, and keep a tight lid on this."

CHAPTER 26

"Ok Dr. Rogers, we're all ready now," Hatfield's chief of staff said to Rogers and his team as they prepared to brief.

"Thank you Ed. We all know why we're having this briefing, but since it's being recorded, I'll summarize for posterity. On October 3rd, Earth standard date, we launched an experimental spacecraft in the direction of Gliese 581, a red dwarf about twenty-three light years away in the constellation Libra. This spacecraft is the first extra-solar craft we have created that was able to return back to the solar system, and the first craft to leave the solar system since Voyager did back in my youth," he said as the crowd chuckled.

"We chose Gliese 581 due to the fact that it was one of the first solar systems they discovered planets in that might be in the goldilocks zone, and because we have the most data on it. We were not expecting to find life there, although we brought equipment to look for it. The plan was to stop short of entering the system, drift by taking measurements, make sure we knew where we actually were, then turn around and return. Total trip time was about three days. There was no crew aboard the ship, just a menagerie of animal test subjects and sensors.

"We all know the results of the test flight, the ship successfully left the system and returned. We believe, upon its return, it discharged some kind of plasma ball into the system, which caused significant damage to human civilization. We also believe . . ."

"A moment Dr. Rogers," Hatfield interrupted him. "Please state for the record, we have no specific proof that the ship caused the plasma comet."

Rogers smiled and looked down briefly before looking into the camera. "We do not have proof that the ship caused the plasma comet. However, the ship and comet showed up at the same time. We believe aliens arrived at nearly the same time. It is possible, although unlikely, that the plasma comet resulted from alien action. It's my understanding that the alien ship we have captured did not have any equipment that could have produced the comet either."

"I would like to amend that statement," Erik Bilks spoke up. "We can't tell what most of the equipment on the alien ship does. We also did significant damage to it when we captured it. The weapon they used to assault the base could have potentially created the plasma comet."

"Let's not get ahead of ourselves," Hatfield cut the argument off. "Dr. Rogers, please continue."

"Sure. Our ship arrived at the proper destination, and proceeded to get oriented and perform scans of the local area." Dr. Rogers pulled up a series of displays on the overhead monitors showing a massive planet, larger than Earth and with several moons orbiting it. Another display showed the orbital tracks of all of the major planetary bodies in the system.

"As you can see, this is a very busy solar system. Aside from the numerous planets, there is also a huge comet belt that circles the sun, roughly ten to twelve times the size of our solar system's comet belt. As we arrived in system, there were twenty-seven comets orbiting inside the comet belt, one of them was almost forty times the size of Halley's comet."

"That's practically a small moon," Sloan said

"Actually, it's larger than a small moon," Dr. Rogers replied with a smile. "This comet is actually about three times the size of Phoebe."

A stunned murmur ran through the room, only silenced when Hatfield rapped his gloved knuckles on the desk. He made a note on his tablet and motioned Dr. Rogers to continue.

"The comets aren't the only big objects in system. Specifically we're here to talk about Gliese 581c, a large tidally

locked super earth that is the third planet in the system."
Dr. Rogers pointed up at the monitors and the system map
individually before speaking again. "It is about 5.4 times as
massive as Earth, with a number of unexpected moons orbiting it. The moons all orbit the planet very slowly and we
expect they suffer brutally cold winter periods when in the
shadow of the planet. The largest moon is just a little bit
larger than Mercury.

"We'll get to that moon in a moment. For now I want to
talk about the super planet. This is one crazy planetary system. It's tidally locked, but not completely, so it does slowly
rotate to an extent we think; we only observed three days
of data. But given its orbit and the intensity of the sun, its
climate is pretty rough and tumble.

"On the sun side, it is very hot, with full day sunlit exposure. There are vast deserts that approach a hundred degrees Celsius at the equator. No significant bodies of water,
volcanic activity is common and we believe regular earthquakes. One thing we did notice was that there are areas on
the day side that appear to have been carved by glaciers and
evidence of large lakes that once existed. On the dark side of
the planet, it's an ice and snow hell, perpetually cloaked in
darkness that sometimes approaches fifty below. The vast extent of the dark side of the planet appears to be frozen water
with occasional warm spots caused by volcanic activity."

"As we approach the day and night terminator line however, things change significantly. The temperature settles
into a very comfortable 15-28C range, the right levels of oxygen and carbon dioxide; very breezy."

"You mean we could survive there?" Sloan perked up
with interest.

"Well, no," Rogers said apologetically. "The gravity is still
quite outside our comfort zone, too heavy at about 1.85 Earth
standard and the pressure is a fairly uniform 400 KPA, about
four times what we prefer."

Sloan sat back in her seat again, making notes on her tablet and kicking Erik under the table. Erik shot her an annoyed look and turned his attention back to Dr. Rogers.

"The width of this terminator zone is actually very large, perhaps as wide as Canada, though that varies depending on the latitude, with the far north being quite a bit narrower and the far south being wider. The interface where the hot air from the day side meets the frigid air from the night side produced some incredible storm fronts during our observation period. Think thunderstorms and blizzards larger than Europe hammering the area for days on end.

"We witnessed one blizzard that is estimated to have dropped two to three meters of snow in the time we were in system. As we were leaving, the sun poked through in that area and was melting it, resulting in massive rivers of water flowing into the day side deserts. That ice water hitting the baked ground resulted in some amazing weather, with thick blankets of fog shooting out into the desert as the first water was turned to steam, only to be chilled by the rivers of water that followed."

"A pity you won't be able to release that data back on Earth," Brenner said softly. "It would make a great paper."

Rogers shrugged before continuing. "The planet as a whole is very active tectonically, but volcanoes also seem to appear in line with the path that the larger moons orbit. We believe that as the moons orbit, their gravitational pull causes significant tidal forces on the planet, causing massive tidal shifts where liquid water exists and volcanic eruptions. It's as though somebody took a knife and lightly dragged it across the surface of the planet as the moon passes, leaving a trail of volcanoes in its wake. This is particularly important on the dark side of the moon, where the volcanoes create locally warm areas, which in some cases would be habitable, at least temperature wise. The constant volcanic action also seems to be causing a reflective effect on the planet as a whole, keeping its average temperature at the terminator to something we could, possibly, tolerate."

"It doesn't sound very habitable," Hatfield said pensively. "What about the moons you mentioned?"

"Not habitable by humans," Rogers corrected him. "The three major moons orbit very slowly around the planet, and as such they experience very long hot and cold periods. The planet's gravity caused several visible earthquakes while we were observing it. The largest moon had frozen water on its surface, but no visible signs of vegetation. We did detect an electromagnetic signature from the pole area."

Several members of the command staff sat bolt upright at the mention of an EM source. Hatfield held his hand out to quiet everyone.

"What kind of signature?"

"Fairly organized, consistent with electrical equipment operating. We also detected some light radioactivity in the area."

"Did you detect any spacecraft or structures?" Brenner demanded with concern.

"No, although from what Erik has told me, the instruments on the ship wouldn't be able to unless you saw them decloak."

"Assuming they are the same aliens as the ones we are dealing with," Hatfield said thoughtfully.

"Erik, did you make any progress on the alien ship?"

"Not really. We can't figure out what most of the equipment does. The damaged areas seem to be slowly regenerating structure, but not components. There's a hidden room in the ship that resists all of our attempts to scan it, we assume that's where our final alien is hiding."

"Regenerating via what mechanism."

"Well, it looks, I dunno, it kind of scabs over then starts to heal. Not all areas are doing it."

"Is there a priority to what is being repaired?" Brenner asked.

"So far as we can tell, no. It looks like a passive repair system based on an organic platform."

"Dr. Rogers, do we have any evidence that the crabs came from this Gliese?"

"I'll speak to that," Dr. Kapple said from his side of the table. "I've reviewed Dr. Rogers data and compared it to our prisoner. Aside from the recent changes in our prisoner, I see nothing that would imply that they could not live there. However, given they have space travel, I also cannot say that it looks like their probable home world. Certainly the pressure and temperatures are within their range, it may be a matter of choice. The only thing we can say for certain is that that strange thing we saw swimming through the upper atmosphere of Saturn during the alien arrival is not biologically related to them."

"Wait, wait," Brenner said with frustration as he tried to slow him down. "What change in our prisoner?"

"I was going to save this for later, but there have been some distressing changes to the prisoner since he was given that cylinder," Dr. Kapple said.

"Explain," Hatfield said.

"It opened the container several days ago and has been ingesting the material within. This morning when we checked on it, we noticed that its overclaw, the claw on its back, had fallen off. It was eating the claw as it sat there. We have some footage of that, but it's still being analyzed." Dr. Kapple swallowed as he continued. "He or she has also gotten bigger and appears to have molted, shed some skin, which it also ate. We have analyzed that paste more extensively since we gave it to the creature, it appears to be a high density food source wrapped around their version of stem cells."

"Meaning what?" Brenner demanded.

"You remember the bee hives we have right? They feed royal jelly to certain baby bees and out pops a queen . . . "

"Shit," Sloan said as she rubbed her forehead.

"It might not be a queen or whatever that equivalent is. It could be that it is able to select or choose through biochemistry what it becomes," Dr. Kapple said.

"Yeah, wait until it chooses to become some giant face-ripping warrior crab," Erik said as he shook his head in annoyance. "Who fed it the damn thing before we knew what it was anyway?"

"I did," Hatfield said firmly. "We thought it was starving. Major Stringer, I want you to increase the guard on that facility. Also, let's consider the possibility it gets too big for its containment."

"What about the alien in the clouds of Saturn?" Major Stringer asked. "Do we need to prepare for that too?"

"That is better news," Dr. Kapple said. "We think that is a totally different species, something that we haven't detected before. We think it lives far down in the atmosphere of Saturn where we can't see well and that the radiation storm caused it to surface. Every indication we have is that it is non-sentient." He paused and leaned forward conspiratorially. "We have taken to calling it a cloud serpent around the lab."

"And it's gone now?" Erik asked pointedly.

"Yes, we think it went back down into its normal habitat."

"Are you sure?" Erik prodded him.

"No, of course not. But we haven't seen it since it went back down into the clouds."

Hatfield held his hand up. "One alien species at a time. If it's a non-threat, we'll ignore it for now. If we figure out a solution for our current problems, then you can write up a mission request to go serpent hunting. But for now, let's stay focused."

Erik looked over at Brenner, distaste on his face, but remained silent. Brenner returned his glance and shrugged before turning to Dr. Kapple.

"So is Dr. Winters going to have the analysis done for the plasma comet any time soon?"

"Yes, he's actually working on it now. He's still amazed at how intense the radiation spike was, he's going back over the sensors and cross correlating them to determine if there were any errors before turning the report in," Dr. Kapple replied.

Hatfield leaned back, his chair creaking in protest, and looked at the overhead screens. As he watched the planet's storm cells track across the day-night terminator he couldn't help but feel a sense of wonder. This is what they had risked so much for and it wasn't even habitable.

"Package your data up, give me two hard copies on portable drives. Bag up one of the crab bodies and a full sampling of the material we found on the alien ship. The freighter should meet the tugs in about seventy-two hours. We're going to have to do a pretty strange handover, so I want the science data onboard fast, try to shield the crab body from sensors…"

"Which kind of sensors?" Erik asked.

"Any you can think of, I know what you are leading up to, I don't know if they can detect their own kind remotely. But I do know I don't want them hitting the freighter," Hatfield said. "We'll have to take steps to slingshot them around Saturn away from those two ships watching us and maintain some level of security. Also, remember both the crew and the passengers on this freighter had a hell of a trip out here through the radiation storm, they're probably going to be slow to get settled in."

"What about those who decided they want to go back?" Dr. Kapple asked, sneaking a glance at Molly, who had been sitting silently in the back of the room the entire meeting.

"Once the science package is onboard and we have a full assessment of how bad the damage is, we'll send them out to catch the freighter as it makes its final alignment," Hatfield said.

Molly stared at Erik intently before looking down at the tablet in her lap without comment.

"Dr. Rogers and team, that was excellent work. Thank you all, let's have a good week."

Erik Bilks stomped down the gangway to the alien ship angrily, ignoring the Marines guarding the makeshift hatch they'd shoehorned into the side of the ship. He paused briefly at the entrance to collect his eyebot, Zealot. He downloaded the current duty roster to his HUD and walked toward the bow of the ship, ducking temporary lighting and data cables that had been strung by the exploitation crew.

He reached the room he wanted, a small alcove near where the starboard claw had been attached, and stopped, carefully unpacking Zealot. With a flicker of lights the little inspection drone came to life, calibrating itself to the local atmosphere and gravity conditions before silently rising from his gloved hands to hover in front of his face.

He cleared his throat and opened a channel to the little drone. "Zealot, access indicated air duct, explore. Search for open spaces or animals of any shape. IR, UV, hyper-spectral, visual, atmosphere. Execute."

The little drone spun on its axis to inspect the air duct, small puffs of gas escaping as it maneuvered close to the hole. It scanned the hole with a laser, making sure it could fit into it then transmitted an acknowledgement of the order back to Erik's HUD. Silently, the neon green bot entered the gap and proceeded down the tunnel, scanning and measuring as it went.

Erik unrolled a large, flexible display and stuck it on the wall. With a flick of his thumb he powered it on and watched to make sure it synced with Zealot. When it did, he gave a satisfied grunt and sat down on a folding chair somebody had left in the hallway, watching the display as the drone slowly explored the recently found portal.

He kicked the wall in frustration and thought back to the argument he'd had with Molly right after the Director's meeting.

She had grabbed him immediately outside the meeting and confronted him.

"I'm taking that flight back."

"Why? Aren't you happy here?"

"Happy? Happy? I don't belong here, I don't belong under that asshole's control!"

"Who? Hatfield? We're all under his control, he's the boss here."

"Right! Exactly! I just want to go home to my family, to get away from this place."

"So that's that. Just going to leave me, eh?"

"You could come with me Erik, he said it was open to all."

"Oh please, I'm not going back to Earth. From what I hear it's one big disaster area. I haven't been back there in close to a decade, there's nothing for me back home."

"But there IS something for me back there, my whole family, my job!"

"Your job? What's the biggest change you could cause while working for a Senator? Maybe you slip a line or two into some legislation? Out here, we're influencing all of human history. So you could go back to that tower of babble in Congress, one voice lost amongst hundreds, or you could stay here with me and participate in history ... "

"I don't want to be part of history, I just want to be happy," she said as a tear rolled down her cheek. Angrily she wiped it away, looked at the stubborn expression on his face, and stomped off.

A steady pinging in his ears broke his focus on the past. The little drone had somehow managed to get into a flat circular room which was about three meters tall by ten meters across. Small tubs lined the floor and flickered with motion. The drone panned around and froze when it saw pictographs on the walls. In the visible spectrum, they looked like crude cave paintings, but when Erik looked at the hyper-spectral view he stared in astonishment.

The images weren't just simple drawing, but complex fractals that contained huge amounts of data. He zoomed in and noticed that the wall section of the room the drone was inspecting contained a number of ships of varying sizes. After a few moments of inspection he saw that one of the smallest images was actually an image of the ship he was standing on. It had a second image next to it, one that seemed to depict fifteen of the ships hooked together to form a cylinder, eight of them facing one way and seven facing the other. As he watched, the image pulsed in the IR spectrum, showing the eight firing beams of light from their noses to a central point, which then glowed brightly. The ship formation seemed to move on the wall without really moving, and as he watched the rearward-facing group fired another combined beam in the opposite way. The image seemed to bend in on itself and disappear with a flash, only to reappear at the start of the sequence moments later.

Below the image additional ships were depicted, something that was as large as the entire scout formation and whose animation indicated that it was shooting other ships of a design not on the wall panel.

Erik squinted his eyes in thought as the strange alien video repeated again before mumbling to himself, "Like a cruiser, meant to engage the enemy . . . oh shit."

His eyes tracked down to the next image which showed a large cylinder, its animation showing it dispensing dozens of the 'claws' off its hull to land on a watery world below. The image below that depicted a massive ship that had numerous weapons emplacements and a strange hole in the bow that released dozens of small ships, while the big guns blasted down at the surface of a planet below.

Zealot finished its scan and moved to the next panel, which showed a similar series of ships. In this case, the animations identified the ships' function, but there were also secondary animations that showed the first panel's ships moving in and shooting at specific points. A third panel showed the same thing, again with the first panel ships attacking specific points. Erik was watching breathlessly as the drone moved to a fourth panel, this one barely occupied.

"Oh, shit. This is not good," he said as he looked at the fourth panel. At the top of the panel were representations of Angels, Mongoose and the various Chinese spacecraft. Below them were images of the tugs and freighters, each with animated depictions of the ship's vulnerabilities.

The drone slowly circled the room, inspecting the remaining panels. Each one was a combination of images that didn't make much sense to Erik. Finally it stopped on a panel which had a visual representation of a ship; the ship that he was on. The damaged areas glowed under the UV filter, with some areas pulsing as though they were being repaired. As he watched the ship image became animated, going through the ship deck by deck. Bright IR images flashed on the screen in various parts of the ship. Nervously, he pulled up his blue-force tracker and overlaid it on the map of the ship. He swallowed; the moving IR images were KaliSun employees.

The drone beeped at him repeatedly, its tempo increasing in alarm. Erik shifted his eyes back to the visual and froze. It was hovering over one of the tubs on the floor, tilted forward to look down into it. The tub contained a small version of the crab they had found under Leblanc's body, staring up at the drone with its overclaw extended in a defensive posture. He had the drone climb higher in the room and inspect the other tubs—each one held a miniature version of the crabs, peering up at the drone with their claws extended.

"Oh shit... shit... shit... shit. The ship is growing new crewmembers," Erik swore as he hurried to open a battlenet channel and dragged in all senior level KaliSun members.

"Urgent, I have figured out what the dead space was in the alien ship. We have major problems. Need additional Marines to the ship immediately..." he said breathlessly over the microphone, recording it and telling it to repeat before he was distracted by the target of the drone's attention.

It was hovering toward the rear of the room, looking at a pulsing, organic object. He'd seen the dissections of the

dead crabs from the hallway, and what he was looking at
were enlarged versions of the same organs. He had the drone
pan around the room again and he started to recognize other
organs. He realized then the floor and ceiling were actually
the same as the crab's flesh.

"Zealot . . . you're inside one of them . . . the whole ship is
one of them," he breathed into his helmet before he quickly
worked his wrist interface, sending the data he'd collected so
far to the base storage system, flagged for immediate review
by Kapple.

CHAPTER 27

Sloan held the probe next to one of the thicker trees on the Promenade, listening to the soft clicking as it detected residual radiation. She wanded a few rocks, bushes, a bench made from compressed stone and another tree before shrugging her shoulders in resignation and putting it away.

"Well, it's mostly repaired. I'm still detecting a fair bit of radiation on some of the stuff," she said to Brenner, who was sitting at a picnic table a short distance away reading his email.

He mumbled distractedly at her as he flipped through the messages that had been stacking up all morning. She looked over and saw he wasn't paying much attention, so she launched a handful of gravel at his helmet. He flinched as the rocks bounded off in all directions and looked up.

"You were saying?"

"The Promenade still has residual radiation present," she said with an irritated wave.

"Is it dangerous to occupy?"

"Well, not really. I wouldn't eat anything we end up growing in here though." She reached a gloved hand up to a low hanging branch from one of the trees, fingering the ink black leaves tenderly. "The genetically modded plants seem to have handled it the best. If I'm not mistaken, several of the varieties even went through major growth spurts."

"Hmm, make a note of that for Dr. Winters. I'm sure he'll want to know."

Sloan walked over to him and perched herself on top of the table's surface, leaning back and looking up at Saturn through the clear roof.

"You know, aside from the gravity, those mountain chains on Gliese are high enough the pressure wouldn't be too difficult to live with," she said thoughtfully as she upped her helmet's magnification to see the polar storms swirl in the distance.

Brenner stopped reading his messages and looked over at her with exasperation. "You mean the old volcanoes left over from when the moons orbited through that area? I don't really want to live on an active volcano ... and it will be active next time the moon passes over that spot."

"Maybe, maybe the plates have shifted enough there is no path for the magma to get back to the surface again."

"With just a few days of data, I don't think we can know. But volcano plus oppressive atmospheric pressure plus earthquakes plus heavy gravity plus crazy huge blizzards doesn't sound particularly enthralling. The moon we saw looked more tempting."

"Except it's in the dark for long periods of time."

"Just like living in Alaska, sometimes the sun never shines, sometimes it never sets," he said with a laugh.

"Eh, well I still think we should make a go of it. Modify some livestock to survive the conditions and let them go. Any time we need steak, it's just a short hop away. No more six month freighter waits."

"Might not be any more freighters soon enough, you're assuming we can even go back there. I don't really buy John's insistence that the aliens caused the plasma comet. If we did cause it, it's not like we can use that ship again. We'd have to build a way-station out there, build a bigger ship to handle livestock and do a survey of the area before we risked it. Not to mention, I think the research guys would go nuts on you if they found out you were going to contaminate the first world we found with some kind of genetically modified cow just so you could have steak with your seafood."

"Then I guess you better figure out how the alien ship works so we can use their method," she said sullenly.

Brenner looked over at her sharply before shifting tone. "We'll look into it, Dr. Rogers will want to do another mission out there anyway, to get a better feel for the history of that solar system. But for now, we're at a bit of a loss. No matter how you shape it, that ship we fought doesn't have the engines to get out of the solar system. Even if it did, we can't find anything that might control them, the computers are rudimentary at best."

"Maybe it has a mother ship, something that brought them all here and dropped them off to do recon," Sloan volunteered.

"Yeah, that's what worries me . . . " Brenner's voice trailed off as he blinked in confusion. The email he had been reading on his HUD had been replaced with an emergency action message that was repeating on his screen. He blinked the audio on and listened to Erik's voice as he requested extra Marines on the ship. When he realized that Erik had included almost the entire senior leadership he looked over at Sloan in alarm.

Sloan finished listening to it for the third time and gave as short laugh. "Maybe he found the computer."

"Normally you don't need Marines for a computer," Brenner said with concern as he stood up and headed for the tram station.

Hatfield turned away from the medical technician working in Meckler's cell in disgust. He glared over at Joe.

"How is it he was able to attempt suicide with your team observing his cell day and night?"

"Clearly we've had a breakdown. Just be glad he wasn't a boy scout, the knot might have held."

"I'm not really concerned whether he lives or dies, I'm more worried that we're losing our edge watching the prisoners. Remember, most of these people were actively trying to sabotage the base. We can't afford a prison break, especially not with that thing doing . . . whatever it's doing," he said with a gesture across the hallway toward the imprisoned crab.

"I've scheduled a team meeting for this afternoon. We'll correct it."

Hatfield closed his eyes briefly before striding across the hallway to the observation port for the crab room. He stared through the window at the crab thoughtfully.

"It's gotten significantly bigger."

"Yes sir. I never would have thought it could find enough calories in that goop to grow so much. It's molted three times and ate the shell remains each time."

"Its head and remaining claws don't seem that much bigger."

"Most of the growth appears to be in the back. It's gotten thicker and longer, so much so that it can barely maneuver."

"Can you tell how much of that goop it ate?"

"Not without going in there and trying take the tube away. Which, to be honest I am not looking forward to."

The SARine who had been working on Dr. Meckler walked into the hallway, shutting the cell door and walking over to the two of them.

"He's stable. We've taken his clothes away and turned up the room temperature, he shouldn't be able to hang himself again." The SARine shook his head and held up one gloved hand, showing them the edge of the palm. "You know he's crazy right? I was trying to treat his neck and he bit my hand, bit the armor so hard it cracked one of his teeth off. We had to remove the tooth, but I'm not sure he really even noticed. You might need to sedate him, for his own protection."

Hatfield nodded at the SARine and dismissed him, turning back to the crab in silence. After several moments he turned back to Joe.

"Is there anything else you think can be gleaned from Dr. Meckler?"

"No."

"Let's start end of life planning for him. We can send his cremated remains back on the freighter," Hatfield said.

"Yes si . . . " Joe replied, pausing as he was interrupted by a critical message from Erik. The Director listened in as well before banging his fist against the wall in frustration.

"Why do I think this is more bad news . . . "

"Dr. Bilks does seem to have a talent for it."

"Alright Erik, we've got half a company of Marines roaming around the surface of Phoebe right now looking for escaped crabs from the ship and the entire command staff here. What's going on?" Brenner asked patiently as he entered the cargo module that had been moved near the alien ship as a makeshift HQ.

"I found something in the bow of the ship. The dead zone we couldn't figure out how to scan, I managed to get Zealot into it. You won't believe what I found." He pulled up the little drone's data feeds on the displays.

The assembled leadership core of the KaliSun Corporation's Saturn operations watched in silence as the drone bumped and bounced its way down a tight tunnel before entering a large chamber. As the drone replayed its footage, Erik looked at them expectantly, watching for a reaction. As the final clip showed zoomed-in detail of the cluster of organs, Dr. Kapple spoke up.

"You guys are going to hate me for saying this. But I think Zealot is inside one of the . . . "

"Crabs!" Erik finished for him exuberantly. "The whole space is inside one of the crabs, a really big one. I think this is like a nursery, I've been recording for about two hours, the same imagery and animations have played over and over again. Like a learning program; all those baby crabs sitting there observing the panels . . . it's like school!"

"I agree. This looks like a training room for crab young. The organs match the organs from the ones we killed, though much larger," Dr. Kapple said quietly. "Given one of the ones we killed in the hallway leaked a bunch of baby crabs into Broadway from its rear, I'd guess this is the inside the rear of one of the crabs."

Hatfield exchanged a meaningful glance with Joe. "So, taking what you know about the prisoner and what we think we've found, do you think it's possible the cylinder we fed to the prisoner is triggering it to grow a nursery inside?"

"Well it's speculation . . . " Kapple began slowly as Erik shook his head in exaggerated agreement. "But I'd say that it triggered the parenthood stage of their life. Which means the prisoner could soon start producing little crabs." He looked at Hatfield with a slight grin. "Congrats, you may soon be a father."

"Not just that, but it's training them. Training them how to fight! Look at the panels, there are three for ships we haven't seen and one for ours! That means there could be a total of three other species out there!" Erik said with excitement.

"That's speculation, but it does seem probable." Hatfield zoomed in on one of the ship panels. "I hope it's wrong, but if I'm reading this right, they have an entire fleet structure, including something like our wet navy carriers. I think if they exist and they find us, we're finished."

"This might explain why we can't figure out the ship computers as well," Brenner said.

"What do you mean?" Sloan asked as she flipped through the hyper-spectral images of the room.

"Well, if the ship is basically built around one of the big crabs, the computer would logically be the crab's brain, probably hard wired into the external ship components. That would explain why the ship heals, why there are no computers we can find, and why there was no real bridge area. Those panels on the wall may explain why they haven't attacked us yet either. They've been analyzing our attack methods and observing us. This is not good. Next time they hit us, I think we're going to be in for a beat down."

"Why do you say that?" Major Stringer asked.

"We won't catch them off guard again. If they have any common sense they will whittle away our external assets like the tugs and freighters until we're constrained to a small area, then send in an endless number of ground assets to hit us," Brenner said thoughtfully.

"The babies that ate Leblanc were aggressive, almost mindless. The ones in the tub are aware they can't hurt the drone. Maybe the baby ones come out with primitive brains and have to be educated in the nursery to prevent them from being a threat to each other. I mean, half the ones we found were eaten by their siblings," Dr. Kapple said.

"So the big crab, we'll call her a queen, controls the ship and grows the type of small crabs she needs for crew. We saw on the panel that there are bigger ships, do you suppose that means bigger crabs, or more medium-sized crabs running one big ship?" Brenner asked.

"No way to tell until we see a big ship," Dr. Kapple said. "However, I would assume they would be loyal to their queen. So every genetic line producing babies probably answers only to their specific genetic line. Perhaps the three different panels are not three different species, but rather three different genetic lines, using pheromones and social cues to identify themselves to each other."

"Giant load of speculation Walt. Three species or three genetic lines, doesn't really matter. If we run into any of those fleets, we probably die quickly. If they land a ship on Earth and get into the oceans, the people on Earth die quickly. Same with the Eden Cave. We need to warn Stokes immediately. Brenner come to my office, we'll try to figure out how to tell him," Hatfield said.

"And Erik. Excellent work. Have Zealot install a camera pod inside the chamber. I want to know the moment the crabs move or the images change. We need to know how fast they learn and what they're being taught. Maybe we'll catch a break and it'll teach them interstellar space technology or something."

CHAPTER 28

President of the United States. For years he had dreamed of this job. For years he had carefully plotted a course and waited his turn for a nomination. Yet now, it seemed like a hollow victory. As the former Speaker of the House, now President, listened dully to his aides recount the status of what was left of the country, he considered the Pyrrhic nature of his ascension.

He had been on a tour of a military base slated for closure in his district when it happened. Deep in a drab office building listening to the base commanders try to convince the local populace that the base closure wouldn't destroy their economy, he hadn't even noticed when the first wave of radiation hit Earth. The lights had dimmed occasionally and his cellphone stopped receiving emails, but he was practically asleep during the speech anyway.

Then a messenger had run in and spoken to the base commander. The President, Vice President and a host of others were dead he said. They'd all turned to him, the new President by line of succession. The whirlwind of events that followed still overwhelmed him, and led to where he was now, sitting deep in the bowels of a mountain in Colorado, listening to a depressing litany of status reports from across the nation. Things were improving, but slowly. The briefers changed and he snapped back into focus as the woman in charge of the northeastern part of the United States, the area he represented, took the podium.

"Mr. President, we have good news from Maine. They have successfully restarted one of the power plants in Canada, electricity is starting to flow back into the country. We've reestablished a line of contact with the National Guard units in the region and they report that there was limited rioting and looting. Most of the residents just hunkered down and waited. As we go further to the south, things are not going as well.

"Previous reports that substantial portions of the northern end of New York City were burned during the event have been confirmed, there were significant casualties with some areas apparently abandoned. The fires appear to have started as the event was unfolding, likely the result of overloaded power lines or people using candles.

"We have sketchy reports from Philadelphia and Boston indicating that they are still struggling to get their ports open. With the help of the Kalisun base at Keokuk we have been able to get major shipment of grain from the Midwest into the area, so there is food. There has been some difficulty processing it locally. The rail links between Pittsburgh and . . . " She paused as a messenger burst into the room breathlessly.

"Mr. President, you are needed in the situation room immediately!"

Grateful for the interruption, he snatched his notebook and strode quickly out of the room, his aides trailing behind him. A short walk down the passageway, they cut through the cafeteria and into the hallway beyond.

He entered the room and blinked in surprise. Nearly half of the remaining Joint Chiefs of Staff were clustered around the central table in the room, each reading a hard copy printout to themselves. Feeling a bit like he'd just interrupted study hall in school, he walked over to the table and picked up a hardcopy.

An Admiral looked up from his papers and snapped to attention. The President waved them down. "Ok, what's happening?"

"We intercepted a message sent from Saturn Base to the KaliSun CEO about three hours ago. This is the first time they've sent a message like this without double encryption, security padding or the usual cryptic code words, so we were able to decrypt it for once."

"Ok, so what does it say?" the President asked impatiently.

"It's confusing, but one thing is clear. They repeatedly refer to "aliens", "Crabs" and "Alien Fleets"," the Admiral said uncertainly.

"They also provided a significant amount of other data about the ships, most of it seems to be general observations. But one thing that seems important to them is this," the Air Force four star General held up a diagram.

The President stared down at the image of fifteen ships in a cluster with red notations drawn around it. In big block print along the bottom a statement read '**Beware of dangerous energy emissions**'. The President studied the diagram longer, pretending to understand what he was looking at before finally looking up at the Air Force General, Connors.

"What's your take on this Connors?"

"It appears that cluster of ships emitted some kind of energy weapon at them."

"You mean like the event that wrecked the country?" the President said sharply.

"It's hard to imagine that happened, but it is possible, if unlikely."

"So aliens showed up and fired their weapon off and now they're mopping up the rest of the KaliSun Corporation's assets before moving on to us," the President said firmly.

The Joint Chiefs looked over at him cautiously as the General Connors spoke again. "That's a possibility sir, but not confirmed."

"Then confirm it," the President said with irritation. "I'm going to start working on a speech, we have to let the world know that this was not some act of God, but aliens. They have to know that we must all come together... it will be a good speech, a historic speech," he finished as he flashed them his best smile.

The President swept out of the room, leaving the Joint Chiefs to stare at his back, worry on their faces.

CHAPTER 29

Captain Wilks drifted away from the refueling Angel and rotated his Mongo out of the inverted maneuver. He goosed the throttles and settled back into the lead position in the formation. After a quick check to make sure the refueling Angels had cleared out, he flashed his running lights several times and the formation accelerated to cruise speed again.

He looked down at the map attached to his thigh armor and compared what he saw with the terrain flying past as they headed to the next waypoint, a scant hundred meters off the moon's surface. With all their networked communications shut off and radios silent it felt eerily like his first combat on the moon.

Back then they couldn't use their navigation systems or radios due to all of the ambient radiation. They'd stumbled into an oncoming Chinese assault force, bounced away and stumbled onto the Chinese base from the wrong attack direction. So many things had gone wrong during that attack and yet they'd still come out on top. He popped the thrusters to push the Mongoose up over a hill jutting out from the moon. This mission had the same air of desperation about it.

He scanned back over the formation, making sure everyone had avoided the hill. His squadron of Mongoose, the Badgers, flew in neat four-ship clusters, two clusters to a support Angel. Staggered throughout the formation were the assault Angels, two loaded with two nuclear weapons each, two SA-Rine Angels to provide recovery and fire support with their conventional weapon payloads. His strike force this time was less than a fifth of what he'd had during the first attack. The target was more heavily defended and fully aware of the threat the KaliSun Corporation posed to them now.

The best they could hope for was to surprise them with the attack direction and pray they got the nukes off before the defensive batteries made a metal fog above the base.

"Director, *Atlas* reports freighter capture almost complete, they will have the ship ready to offload cargo shortly," Higgins reported from her sensor station.

"Thanks," Hatfield said as he slumped in his chair and watched the proceedings.

The CIC had been lightly occupied while they waited for *Atlas* to complete the maneuver, but as news of the status went out, additional crew began to flow in and take their stations. Light chatter rose up out of the crew area to wash over Hatfield as he stared at the two red icons on his system map.

The two alien ships had been slowly moving back toward Saturn for the past day as the freighter approached. They weren't overtly moving to intercept, but there were clear opportunities for them to do so if they kept it up. He'd pre-positioned a squadron of Mongoose and their support Angels on the *Heritage*, but it was still two ships. Even with the special dumbfires, the situation could quickly get out of control.

Erik entered from the rear of the room and took a seat next to Hatfield, plugging in his suit for a quick power charge as he brought up the console in front of him. He looked over at Hatfield's posture and raised an eyebrow.

"You alright boss?"

Hatfield gave a half smile before responding. "Given the situation, yes. Worried your boss might be a little stressed out are we?"

"Well you look a little down is all," Erik said with a smile. "Maybe some time in the Eden Cave or a swing through Phoebe's will cheer you up."

Hatfield gestured at the main screen, which showed the alien ships and possible intercept routes between them and the incoming freighter. "Take a good look. For more than half the freighter's path, we can't provide an escort from the *Heritage*. If they attack, they'll have plenty of time to destroy the ship and we won't be able to do anything to stop them."

Erik studied the screen intently for several moments. "I guess we could attack them first, take the initiative."

"If we attack, they just drift away from us. They are more maneuverable and have longer range than we do, like a boxer staying at jabbing range. Or they decide to engage with one ship and flank us with the other ship, hitting the base. I think we just have to defend for the parts we can, keep an eye on them and minimize what's on the ship during the slingshot, hope they leave it alone or something happens to change the equation."

"I don't like relying on hope. What did Stokes say when you sent that report back? Also, Brenner told me we sent it back barely encrypted, why the hell would we do that?" Erik asked with surprise.

"I'm hoping the Earth governments can decrypt it. If we just told them that aliens had arrived in system and were making a general mess of things, or we blamed the aliens for the damage the plasma comet caused, they would never believe us. If they think they stole the information, they're more inclined to take it seriously. We sent a bunch of other transmissions with bad encryption at the same time, with the excuse being we'd taken some damage recently that hindered our encryption efforts. Ideally they will take it seriously."

Erik looked skeptical. "I guess that could work. But anyone with a brain in their head won't buy that a ship-based weapon caused the plasma comet."

Hatfield arched an eyebrow over at him and smiled. "Our two leading theories are that aliens caused it or we caused it; in both cases using a ship."

Erik grunted a noncommittal response and sat back in his chair, looking at the display thoughtfully.

"*Atlas* reports cargo container pull has begun on the freighter," Higgins called out from her console.

"At least it looks like we'll get the cargo unloaded before they can bother us," Erik said.

"Don't assume anything at this point," Hatfield cautioned before raising his voice to yell down to the sensors operator. "Let me know the moment you see any reaction from the aliens."

Higgins was bent over her console, staring intently at her screen, and didn't respond. Hatfield gave a sigh and leaned forward to repeat what he said when his console and two of the screens on the main wall began flashing.

"Sir, we've confirmed movement among the alien ships. They have split apart slightly and are coming toward the freighter. Projected intercepts on the main screen right about...now."

A room full of eyes looked up at the main screen as the projected intercept was displayed. A soft curse drifted up from below.

"Higgins, signal *Heritage* to get the crews to their fighters."

"Right away sir."

Hatfield looked over to Erik and shrugged his shoulders. "Now we see how this plays out." He leaned forward and hit a button on his console, sending a message to Brenner he'd crafted hours earlier.

"Shit," Erik said under his breath, watching the projections adjust to show the two enemy ships eventually bracketing the freighter formation.

"Badger Actual this is Strike Angel Two, recommend you hold behind this next ridge, I have a developing situation here."

"Negative Two, we're within their sensor envelope, we need to go now before they see us," Wilks responded calmly.

"Actual, I think the base is already under attack…"

"What?" Wilks said in surprise. "All sections, hold on me at the next ridge."

The strike group flared their thrusters and settled into a hover as Wilks struggled to get a handle on what was going on. He directed his support Angel to push up from the formation and take some observations.

Seconds ticked by as the Angel probed the distant base with its advanced radar and optical scopes. Nervously, he scanned the horizon expecting a missile strike or advancing ground forces maneuvering to engage them, but nothing was happening. Finally the support Angel began piping the battle picture down to his HUD—he stared in amazement.

Hovering over the Chinese base were three of the alien ships, firing at close range down onto the structures with their point defense systems. Further above them were several other alien ships, clustered together in a ball. As he watched the optical feed he shook his head. The Chinese were rushing out to engage the alien ships and being met with a blaze of energy weapons fire. Rovers melted under the barrage, tanks raced around the perimeter of the base trying to escape the withering attack raining down on their heads.

Buildings were venting atmosphere as infantry poured outside to shoot up at the ships. As the Angel began its descent, two squadrons of Chinese fighters raced in from the west to attempt strafing runs on the ships. The final sequence showed one of the squadrons getting too close to the formation of ships hovering over the attack force. With a brilliant spurt of energy, half the squadron disappeared into a cloud of melted slag, drifting back down toward the moon.

"Your orders sir?" prompted his XO over the private battlenet.

"A minute, I need to think," he said as he shared the data with the rest of the squadron.

"We can't keep sitting here…" one of the pilots mumbled. Wilks ignored him and tried to figure out what to do.

"Our orders don't include a contingency in the event aliens are here," he said with exasperation to his XO on their private channel.

"No, the orders say to nuke the Chinese base, I think the aliens being there is just their own bad luck. The longer we sit here the more likely we are to get a lot of unwelcome attention," the XO replied.

"Look, when I talked to Stokes he made it sound like they weren't sure the initial fight at Saturn Base wasn't just a case of miscommunication, that given their actions since then, they might not be as hostile as we think. If I nuke them, I can promise you they will be hostile after..."

"Sir, respectfully, they have a fleet structure we cannot match and they are attacking the Chinese. I hate the Chinese as much as the next guy, but they are still attacking other *humans* right now, and by the look of it, doing a stand up job of it. If we can take them out now, we need to. We won't be able to use nukes on them if they do this to our base...this is not 'the enemy of my enemy is my friend', this is 'the enemy of humanity is my enemy'. Pull the trigger, sir."

Wilks gritted his teeth and considered. They were burning precious fuel keeping behind the ridge and risking discovery at any moment. He laughed into his faceplate—what was it that G-LOC used to rant about? Analysis paralysis—don't overthink yourself out of a course of action, in a time of crisis do something, even if it's not the perfect choice.

"Strike Team, this is Badger Actual, we will proceed with our attack, with some modifications. Stand by for update in two minutes."

He quickly pulled a flexible display out of the cubby to his left, putting the Mongo into an automatic station-keeping mode. The data from the support Angel flowed onto his screen and he began mission planning the nuclear strike. The original plan had been four surface detonations, one in each quadrant of the base. With the aliens present, he was going to have to make some tweaks.

People's Republic of China Space Forces Colonel Cheng Vong surveyed the chaos unfolding in the base from an auxiliary airlock that led from one of the perimeter bunkers surrounding the base. They were twenty minutes into this vicious attack and already the main command center had been destroyed, the majority of the senior staff present. Thirty percent of the atmosphere in the base had been vented and they had taken untold casualties.

He stared up at the large space ships hovering over the base. They seemed so peaceful and serene until he brought his infrared filters down and could see the blaze of energy weapons fire emanating from them. How the KaliSun Corporation had managed to hide these weapons was beyond him. How they could sneak up on the base so effortlessly infuriated him. He'd warned the command repeatedly that they were expanding too quickly toward the enemy base, which left huge gaps in their sensor net. But the logistics situation demanded a quick victory, so they had pressed on. Now they would all pay for this error in judgment.

Taking a few deep breaths to calm himself, he sprinted from the airlock to one of the nearby structures that had been destroyed in the opening barrage. The walls were blown out and gaping holes had been punched down through the roof so he'd ordered one of the mobile command and control rovers to hide inside. He bounded through the low gravity as fast as he could, finally pushing through a hole in wall of the structure into the relative safety of the ruin.

He walked through the wreckage carefully, avoiding anything that could puncture his suit, passing the charred remains of the building's occupants. Even in the vacuum of space, burnt equipment out-gassed smoke and heat to hover inside the structure. He hoped the accumulated heat bloom would last through the battle, providing camouflage to the concealed rover, otherwise the building would be his tomb.

As he approached the rover, he saw that the crew was already driving stakes down into the remains of the building and erecting antennas near the gaping holes in the wall. He reached the rear airlock and banged on it several times before it unlocked and let him in.

He climbed in, cycling it shut and making his way through the cramped interior to the control area. A junior officer leapt out of the main chair and stood at attention. He returned the salute and climbed into the chair, taking his helmet off and looking at the displays.

"Report."

"Sir, we are taking very heavy casualties. As the soldiers leave the barracks they are being hit immediately with fire from those ships overhead. Our fighters are attacking the ships, but having no effect on target!" the junior officer reported. He was sweating heavily and looked terrified.

"Are we secure in this building now?"

"Ye-yes sir. We have covered the rover with IR camouflage and the destruction of the building is hiding us, but if they decide to strike again . . . I . . . I don't think the building will protect us."

Vong waved his hand dismissively at the officer, who turned and busied himself at the communications console. Leaning forward, he pulled up the command and control display and looked at the health and status of the base.

There was a deep gash in the lunar soil over the main reactors. It looked as though the ships above knew where the reactor chambers were and were trying to blow a hole through the surface of the moon to get to them. He realized the only reason they hadn't succeeded was that each successive strike was stirring up dust which had to be vaporized by the follow-on energy discharges before it could dig any deeper.

His infantry was scattered all over the base, returning fire on the ships ineffectually and without any cohesive action.

About half of the tanks had taken up position on a ridge to the west and were firing on the ships from there, the other half driving through the base madly trying to avoid being hit.

"Fools," he muttered under his breath. There was no way they could fire back at the ships overhead by driving directly under them; all they could do was die.

The space forces were trying to drive away the ships to no avail, and were taking heavy losses in the process. He frowned. It was strange, there was none of the pervasive jamming that normally accompanied the KaliSun Corporation's attacks. No jamming, no fighters and none of those cursed Angels. His eyes narrowed and he glared at the image of the space ships; something was amiss.

"Space Fighter Control, this is Colonel Vong, I am taking control of the defense of the base. The main command center has been hit and has lost communications." Vong winced at the understatement he had just made. They had been more or less vaporized. "Pull your fighters back to the western marker and get organized. Bring in the units from Base Viper and get me a defensive formation. I want the gunships to form a box and hold for my orders."

"Space Fighter control acknowledges, Colonel!" came the relieved response.

"5th Armor, STOP driving through the base like that. You are running over my infantry! I want you to find a shooting position and fire on what's left of the rover maintenance building number twenty-one, immediately."

"Sir, that's a friendly target!"

"Obey your orders 5th or I will have you shot," Vong spat back. The junior officer who had been running the C2 rover prior to his arrival looked at Vong nervously.

"6th Armor, I want you to target the water reservoir and cooling tanks two hundred meters to the east of rover maintenance building twenty-one, immediate execute."

"Sir . . . are you . . . yes sir."

Vong watched as the fighters pulled back and the armor began firing in sequence. Almost immediately the water reservoirs used to cool part of the base reactor system exploded in steam and ice crystals as the tank rounds crashed into them. A minute later, 5th Armor shot at the rover building, blowing debris and liquefied metal into the surrounding area. The dense fog of ice crystals covered the hole the enemy ships were drilling, followed closely by the liquefied metal and debris from the rover shed.

Alien fire plowed through the new debris field, each blast of energy absorbed and dissipating into energy and gasses. Metal turned to liquid, then gas, each phase soaking up more energy from the overhead ships. Vong smiled wolfishly at the monitor; there were weaknesses to energy weapons.

After another minute of futilely firing into the rapidly expanding cloud of dust, gas and debris, the rate of fire slowed. As he watched the IR screen, he saw them shift target to the tanks, sending energy beams down toward them. Several tanks in 5th Armor were hit almost immediately, the rest restarted their frantic race through the base. As he watched, two soldiers sprinting between buildings caught the full force of a passing tank. One was ground under the tank, life support system crushed and suit ripped to shreds, while the other was bounced upwards, ricocheting hard off one of the buildings before drifting back toward the moon, broken and lifeless.

"5th Armor pull back from the base structures, you are hitting your own support infantry!"

"Sir . . . Commander Sung is dead, they just . . . just blew him up!" a panicked tanker responded.

"Either hide your tanks in the damaged buildings or pull back and join 6th armor on the ridge, immediately," Vong ordered impatiently. Several of the tanks continued to careen through the base, but slowly others followed orders, slipping between narrow gaps or hiding in destroyed structures.

"Sir, the ships higher up, they're dropping some kind of large pods or landing shuttles on us!"

Now what? Vong thought as he swung his eyes to the monitor. Sure enough, fourteen pods were dropping down from the ships hovering above. They didn't seem to be accelerating very hard...

"Space Fighter Control, are you ready yet?"

"Yes sir! Awaiting orders!"

"Bring your formation over the base and engage these things, immediately. Destroy them, whatever they are."

"Yes sir!

Vong settled back to watch the scene develop. Small clusters of soldiers were still firing uselessly up at the ships above, their missiles intercepted by pulses of energy, their smaller weapons bouncing off the ships harmlessly. He shook his head. How had the KaliSun Corporation got this far ahead in technology? It couldn't be possible, unless it wasn't them at all, but somebody else.

"But who?" he muttered to himself. He watched the tanks on the ridge evade the long-range pot shots of the ships hovering overhead. His display showed the fighter wing approaching from the west, a half dozen gunships surrounded by forty fighters, effectively the last of the qualified pilots. After this, it was just the partially trained reserve force at the western base and whatever they could get from the Gobi Desert training facility, if they ever got anything from them again.

It couldn't be the Europeans, they'd been broke for a long time. It wouldn't be the South American Trade Union, they were effectively allies of the Chinese prior to the big radiation storm. The Russians could pull it off, they certainly had places in Russia they could hide the development of these weapons. The United States ... he narrowed his eyes. They had thought the US was paying KaliSun to build weapons, but what if they had their own program instead. It wouldn't be the first time the Intelligence Directorate was woefully wrong. He thought back to the final images they had received from their first attack on the KaliSun base, the Mongoose fighters chasing after the survivors. Fighters they hadn't even known existed until they'd fought them.

The onrushing gunships met the falling pods just before they reached the lower attack ships. The first pass was a blaze of speed and gunfire as they unloaded on the pods with everything they had. Mini-guns buzzed away, missiles tracked in on the pods, and the attack ships fired back up at the formation.

Several of the pods shuddered under repeated hits and were pushed around by the impacts of so many weapons, but only one was destroyed. The last pod in the formation took the brunt of the top turret fire from the gunships as they passed, peeling open like an onion to spill its contents into space. There was a flash of light and a spray of liquid and then the pod was gone.

Vong bit his lip and rewound the scene on his display, zooming in to the best of his ability. He stared at the scene several times, watching as the pod split open along its longitudinal access, spilling several shapes out into space where they were immediately hit by fire from the gunships. He froze the frame and stared at the screen in confusion.

"What is that?" he said aloud. On his screen was a strange ovoid looking shape, with what looked like claws...

"Sir, the fighters are swinging back around and taking another pass at the pods. One of the gunships is reporting non-functional, they took multiple hits to their primary computer core and they're struggling to control their craft."

"Tell them to return to base," Vong said distractedly as he stared at the shape. It didn't look like any of the imagery they had of KaliSun space armor, not at all.

The fighter formation struck the pods again, this time destroying two more, but taking more significant damage from the attack ships hovering over the base. The pods continued down toward the moon, firing off retros before landing in a cloud of dust.

The sides of the pods opened up like flowers and several shapes tumbled out, forming into tight bunches and then gliding along the surface of the moon in the direction of the reactor. His breath caught in his throat as he saw them more clearly. A nightmare of heavy claws covered the front and top of the body, a strange tail with spikes and an even more massive claw dominating the top.

"Sir, wha . . . what are those . . . things?" the officer behind him asked, terror creeping into his voice.

"The enemy," he said grimly as he keyed the radio. "All infantry and armor units, hostile forces have landed in the vicinity of the southern aquaculture complex, engage immediately. Destroy them."

Around the base, infantry began streaming in the direction of the hostile landing force. Having been unable to damage the ships above, the possibility of getting a crack at ground forces motivated them to rush through the base. The tanks spewed dust out behind them as they burst out and up and over the ridge, firing in the direction of the enemy formations.

As Vong watched, a tank that had been hiding near the landing zone bounced around the corner of a building, firing its main gun at nearly point blank range into a cluster of enemy creatures. The round passed through one of the creatures entirely before exploding in the middle of the pack, spraying pieces of carapace and blue liquid in all directions. He heard a cheer come over the net as the tank fired into another formation with similar effect, before it tried to run down a third formation.

When it hit this group, it didn't run over them. Instead, the creatures let the tank push into their formation, loosening it up until they could reform on the tank. As he tried to drive away, the group of creatures began using their huge overclaws to grip and pincer the tank's armor, peeling it away and plucking the crew out one by one to be cut in half and thrown aside. When the last of the crew were gone, they clambered off and resumed their path toward the reactor, leaving the dismantled tank in their wake.

The creatures changed formation into a diamond shape, four blockers using their claws to deflect infantry weapon fire while a fifth hovered in the middle, firing back with energy weapons attached to all three of its main claws.

Vong frowned as the casualties climbed. A single hit from the energy weapon would vaporize a Chinese soldier and could burn through much of the armor on a tank. Meanwhile, the small arms fire they fired back at the creatures had almost no effect beyond pushing them around in the low gravity.

Things were looking very bad until the 6th armor arrived from their perch up on the ridgeline. They raced down through the base in groups of three, concentrating their fire on the clusters of enemy with devastating effect. Clouds of blue liquid erupted into space as the tanks mowed them down, eventually wiping them out entirely.

As the fight on the surface was playing out, the fighters and gunships were making repeated passes at the hovering enemy ships, trying to distract them and provide cover for their men on the surface. The ships were dishing out incredible amounts of damage, and had already managed to shoot down over twenty of the Chinese ships before one of them was significantly damaged, a fighter crashing directly into the engine area at full speed. The explosion rocked the ship from stern to bow, causing secondary explosions within. As the ship limped away from the surface of the moon, the remaining Chinese fighters hounded it, repeatedly striking with gunfire and missiles.

With satisfaction, Vong compressed and archived the battle data before sending it to one of their new orbiting communication satellites. The Party officials on Earth would learn of his victory against impossible odds soon; a reward was inevitable. Maybe they would make him the new base commander, or perhaps a promotion to Command of all Moon forces. He clenched his fist and smiled at the thought.

After failing to destroy the reactor, the aliens began to pull back. The damaged ship struggled to gain altitude as its partner ships closed ranks to protect it from the swarming Chinese fighters. The ball of alien ships that had launched the pods started to spread out, pulling back as they took long-range potshots at the undamaged structures.

Vong heard a cheer over the communications link as the Chinese forces realized they had driven off the attackers and suppressed a smile. Whoever had just attacked them had been forced to flee, just as the original KaliSun attack had been. They had taken damage and losses, losses that would take a long time to recover from. But they had still survived, and with the other training facilities and bases they had secretly built on the moon, they would be able to fight again soon enough.

"Sir, look..." the officer behind him said.

Concerned by the tone in his voice, he looked over at one of the perimeter sensors, his heart skipping a beat when he realized what he was looking at. Almost twenty KaliSun fighters and Angels were fleeing at high speed away from the base. He stared in puzzlement before the realization hit him. He ordered the sensors that were left to perform an immediate scan of the surrounding area, his stomach souring as he suspected what he would find.

There, almost at the base, he saw them; four missiles racing toward them. Just four. He sighed, knowing what was to come next. They had fought so hard only to be blindsided. He closed his eyes as the first missile darted down the hole the original attackers had left, and the other three diverted up toward the retreating enemy ships. Seconds later the light and heat from the explosions washed over the structure as the ground violently tossed beneath them.

"All callsigns, get low and fast. GET CLEAR! GET CLEAR!" Wilks shouted into the mic as he hauled his Mongoose around and slammed the throttles forward. Behind them the exhausts of the four nuclear-tipped missiles glowed cheerfully as the weapons raced into the Chinese base.

He put a map showing the missile track and countdown clock in the lower right hand part of his HUD and pushed his Mongo to its max speed. They flashed over a ridge and dropped into the shallow crater beyond it. The entire formation flipped over, cutting their throttles, and using maneuvering thrusters to turn their ships before powering up to kill their velocity. The Mongoose settled down in the crater as low as they could, huddling up against the crater wall.

He watched the four missiles finish their path, one diving down the hole that the crabs had bored for them, timed to detonate above the reactors, the other three arcing upward toward the retreating crab ships. The alien ships had moved since they had fired, so what was supposed to have been two detonations in the middle of the formation and one above it ended up being two below and one right at the top. The Chinese fighter formation was focused on destroying the damaged crab ship, and the crab ships were focused on trying to defend their damaged ship. None of them saw the warheads.

With a brilliant flash the three weapons detonated simultaneously, sending radiation out in all directions. A second later, the underground detonation reached the surface, sending a wave of energy and dust out through the hole and causing the entire base to quake.

The energy wave passed by overhead, blocked from hitting them by the regolith of the crater. When the quake reached them it caused the ground to buck and the crater walls to crumble, dropping waves of gravel and dust onto the hovering ships. Several minutes passed before another large lunar quake shook the area. Then all was silent.

"Badger Angel One, take a look."

"Yes sir."

Minutes passed as the Angel poked up above the crater wall and scanned the base. Wilks put the time to good use, going over their new line of retreat, giving the location of the remaining crab ships a wide berth. Data began to trickle in from the support Angel.

The base was virtually unrecognizable. Large swaths of the crater had collapsed further into the ground, and many of the buildings were shattered or simply gone. Of the Chinese space defense forces there was no sign. No sign of any surface activity from their infantry either.

Gracefully falling from above, trapped by the moon's gravity, were two of the crab ships, no life showing aboard them, their structure mangled and blistered. He saw no sign of the third crab ship. As he watched the feed continue to play out, he noticed that the crab ships above had survived and were pulling away from the moon swiftly. None of them seemed to have the crab claw shapes on their bows any longer, and he made a note of that for the intel guys.

"All callsigns, let's go home," Wilks said with relief as he looked at their diminishing fuel margin.

The formation used their maneuvering thrusters to push away from the wall and gradually rose up out of the crater. As they headed back toward home at a relatively sedate pace they were engaged by an unexpected firebase that had been defending the perimeter.

Long lines of tracer fire raced past them, kicking up dust from the nearby ridgeline as the Chinese struggled to get a lock on them, the radiation from the nuclear blasts fouling their sensors. Corkscrewing missile tracks erupted from several launchers as they fired missiles in the hope they could find them. The missiles headed in all directions, some heading for the sun, others back toward the hot spot left from recent battles.

"Angels, jamming to max, all units stay on me, shift course

thirty degrees north, immediate execute!" Wilks felt the gas leak through the compensator as he wrenched the control sticks to his left.

"This is going to be a dangerous run home..." he said in the silence that followed, the lines of tracers flying past his tines in front of him.

CHAPTER 30

G-LOC has the *Heritage* squadron ready to go. They can launch on your command John," Brenner said as he looked back at Hatfield from the communications pit.

"Understood, hold the launch for now. Let's not show our hand just yet. Higgins, what is the expected time before those two crab ships enter the outer engagement envelope for the *Heritage* attack group?"

"About twenty-two minutes sir, assuming they continue on the same vector."

Hatfield leaned back and looked over at Erik. "You upgraded the warhead design on the bigger missiles. How confident are you about the explosion radius?"

"It's a WAG."

"What's a WAG?" Molly asked as she walked in with Sloan.

"Wild-assed guess," Erik said over his shoulder.

"I know what it means, what are you referring to?" she asked with annoyance.

"Oh." Erik looked over at Hatfield questioningly, and when he saw him shrug indifferently he responded. "How big a boom will go off if we use the new warheads. We've never tested them, the yield is uh, theoretical." A memory flashed across his face causing him to wince.

Hatfield caught the look and turned to speak directly to him. "If they are deployed it will be by my order, I will bear full responsibility."

Erik nodded, but said nothing.

"How big a blast Erik?" Hatfield prodded.

"Two or three times the size of the last one we used. But we have no test data and our understanding of how it works is limited," Erik said sadly.

"Brenner, I think we'll let them get about thirty minutes into the envelope before we launch the fighters. That gives G-LOC time to get to them and engage before they run away."

"And what if they don't run away?" Molly asked nervously.

"That gets them that much closer to the base, which means we can possibly use the remaining fighters at the base and their Angels to fight them too. I don't know why they chose to attack now, if they had waited another half day, the freighter would be out of our protection range. But I'm not going to be sad about it."

"You are assuming you can win, even if you use everything you have."

"No, I'm assuming I have a better chance of winning if it's not one squadron of trainees against two of those ships," Hatfield said. "Any improvement of the odds we face at this point is welcome."

Molly sat back in her seat, rubbing her face with both hands and breathing heavily through them. She looked over at Sloan and whispered. "Do you think they will win?"

"It's *we*, you're here too," Sloan shot back as she watched the displays update. "And to answer your question, I don't know. I'm not much into fighting, so I don't know how this will end. Probably not well, if I had to guess."

"Director! The alien ships are changing course! They're both curving out away from the freighter, heading away from Saturn too," Higgins shouted up from the sensor station.

"Wow, look at them go . . . " Erik said in awe. "If you were wondering if we'd seen their full capabilities yet, I'd say that's a no."

"Yes, they're looking more and more like a stealthy advance scout, the kind you'd use for a fleet. Sneaky, lightly armed but with the ability to flee quickly if they need to," Hatfield said quietly.

"Any idea what caused them to split?" Sloan called down to Higgins.

"Nothing we did, everything was goi . . . holy shit."

Hatfield stood up and looked down at Higgins, who was staring at her screen with her hand to her mouth.

"Higgins, what's happening?" Hatfield demanded.

She started and looked back at him. "NUDET detected on the moon. Maybe more than one."

Hatfield sat down, his face a mask in concern. The rest of the CIC started talking quietly, coming to grips with that news.

Erik leaned in close to Hatfield. "You realize the implications of this right?"

"We may have just lost the MBTC, which makes the freighter somewhat academic. If the aliens stay away, maybe we'll just capture the freighter and use it like the *Heritage*," Hatfield said quietly.

Erik grimaced and shook his head rapidly. "No, no. The alien ships responded to the NUDET before the *light* from the explosion reached us. They have faster than light communications!"

Hatfield's eyes narrowed in thought. "Brenner, get up here now."

Brenner looked back at him confused, saw the expression on Erik's face and bounded up the stairs.

They huddled together, Sloan and Brenner taking a knee while Erik and Hatfield leaned in. Molly was left sitting off to the side, straining to hear.

"Erik pointed out the aliens knew about the NUDETs before the light of the explosion reached us," Hatfield said softly.

Brenner snorted in surprise. "Uh, how is that possible? Oh . . . oh. Well, that makes things awkward. They could have already phoned home."

"Right, but that's not all," Erik began. "Think about it, a nuclear bomb went off and the aliens ran away. If they set it off as part of a plan they had, they wouldn't be running away. We need to know who detonated that bomb. Soon."

"Do we have any nukes on the moon?" Sloan asked curiously.

Brenner and Hatfield exchanged a quick glance before answering. "Yes."

"How many?" Erik prodded.

"Maybe a dozen weaponized missiles, with material to make more," Hatfield whispered.

Erik blinked in surprise. "Where did we get that much weapons-grade material?"

Hatfield chuckled. "We have an RTG factory in the United States that produces plutonium 238 isotopes for use in long range communication systems. We used the site to make a few more… useful isotopes as well. They inspected the place constantly, but since it was clear we really were using the RTGs on communication systems and they were borrowing bandwidth on those same systems, they didn't look very hard."

"So we know the isotope our missiles have right?" Erik asked.

"Yes, but I seriously doubt we'll be able to tell from here whose nuke it was. The Chinese have access to that same isotope, you'd have to be at ground zero to be able to tell which reactor it came from," Brenner answered.

"So wha…" Sloan was interrupted by Higgins yelling up from her station.

"Communication from MBTC, it's just two words. 'Crab Rangoon'," Higgins said with a lift of her eyebrows.

Hatfield leaned back and smiled. "We're good. Rangoon was the code word for "We nuked the Chinese." I can only presume based on the reaction of the crabs here and the lack of any other code words that we nuked the Chinese and the crabs, either at the same time or separately. Either way, I think that explains why they burned out of here so fast. It also means that the MBTC has not been destroyed."

"Higgins, where are the two alien ships going?" Brenner called down to the sensor pits.

"They're making tracks in the general direction of Uranus. They're not bothering to stealth, just running."

Erik nudged Sloan suggestively. "We have crabs heading for Uranus . . . "

She rolled her eyes at him and pinched his tricep through his suit causing him to wince in pain.

Hatfield shot a bemused look at the two of them and stood up. "Brenner, continue freighter capture. I'll be in my room, composing a message to Stokes."

CHAPTER 31

Forsythe pushed the plate of cheese and crackers over to Wilks as he sat down. "Care for a snack Captain?"

Wilks stared at the plate in silence for a moment. "I thought we were out of cheese?"

"The last courier we snuck through the Chinese blockade picked up a few wheels from the transit station. Evidently Marcus opened up a trade route from the Missouri base south of Keokuk into Wisconsin. They've been trading fuel for beef and dairy since about ten weeks after the Chinese attack on the base," Stokes said as he piled a slice of cheese on a cracker and stuffed the entire thing in his mouth.

"I'd heard that the Midwest wasn't looking too good these days, I'm surprised he was able to ship anything up there," Wilks said with surprise.

"Marcus did a lot of work for us obtaining restricted materials back during the build up to Saturn. He's got a solid mind for trade and knows how to work around the margins. From what I understand, he's been running barges up the river under cover of darkness, hiding during the day."

"They have to use smaller ships, but for now, it's enough to keep the farmers in Wisconsin working and keep the base supplied with protein to supplement the agri-towers. That's not to say there haven't been incidents. The route runs a bit too close to several cities for his taste," Stokes said, wiping off his hands and bringing up the report from the nuclear strike.

Colonel Davies walked into the room, waving at the three of them before taking a seat and reaching over to grab food off the plate. "Sorry I'm tardy, the readiness review of what's left of the 4th Company took a while."

"No problem, we're just getting started."

Davies squinted at the screen briefly before he started in on the topic. "Ok, so this is the most recent imagery from the Chinese base we hit earlier this week. We're seeing signs of life at the facility. As of now, we've seen a very large number of utility rovers and a scattering of combat rovers, tanks and other vehicles parked outside the main base perimeter. They're sitting just beyond a ridge which appears to be shielding them from the majority of the leftover local radiation."

Wilks leaned forward, looking intently at the screen. After a minute of study he frowned over at Davies. "What are they doing?"

"Leaving, if I had to guess. We've seen several gunships approach from the west, pick up individuals on the ground and then leave, and a lot of foot traffic hauling gear out to the rovers."

"Pulling back to the other bases then. I can't tell, how many vehicles are on the other side of that ridge?"

"The ridge itself partially obscured the observation Angel, but based on how many we can see and assuming they have them more or less evenly spaced, I'd say around eight hundred vehicles," Forsythe said.

Wilks looked up in shock. "How the hell did they make that many, or store them?"

"I'd they must have a factory or two we don't know about yet. Even so, just the material needed to construct them is enormous. If you look at the false color imagery of the tenth quadrant of the parking lot, it seems like many of them are not actually made of metal. Maybe a plastic or a net of some sort over some metal parts, I think a lot of them are just frames intended to get around inside the base. But, I'd say they're planning on using them in the near future," Forsythe said.

"Also of some concern is this scene," Stokes said as he pulled up another image. "It looks like they're disassembling parts off the two fallen crab ships and transporting them to the rovers and gunships. At this point, they've already gotten away with some of it, but we need to prevent any more from being extracted from the wreckage."

"So the plan, Captain Wilks, is for you to lead a forward deployed strike force to this area here," Davies said as he pointed at the map. "In an effort to both limit their ability to extract alien artifacts and decrement their remaining assets to the best of your ability. I'm looking at sending elements of 1st Company to assist you for ground security, with Badger and what's functioning of Talon Squadron as your strike element. The area south of their base labeled 'LZ Crop duster' is where you will set up a temporary ground base. From that position you are to proceed north and interdict as many of the rovers as you can, while sending Talon to break up the efforts to salvage the crab ships. Your first strike should be the Chinese spacefighter base due west of the facility. Try to damage their hangars and any grounded craft to obtain space superiority," Colonel Davies finished before grabbing several more crackers off the plate.

"Our forward base is a ground base sir? Our Mongos aren't really designed to take off from the surface of the moon."

"We're going to dispatch three rock haulers from the eastern mining camp to serve as your base platform. Support Angels will ground on the moon, Mongos will have to carefully land on top of the haulers. We've created some temporary living quarters inside the cargo haulers, but it's going to be tight quarters and be advised there is still a lot of pretty nasty dust on the inside, so I'd recommend wearing your helmets as much as possible."

"Sounds lovely sir."

"Hopefully this will be a short duration mission. 1st Company will provide ground security and use their man-portable systems to defend against the odd Chinese fighter that tries to get in. You'll have several support Angels that will provide sensor perimeter for the base, and four quick reaction Angels with SARine support in case you locate any alien debris that's worth recovering."

Wilks cycled through the imagery of the LZ, rovers and Chinese spaceport quickly, his eyes scanning the details, looking for anything that seemed out of place. The three senior leaders of the base were silent, letting him assess his task.

"I think I have it sir. I take it we need to get going soon."

"I hope you got caught up on your sleep Captain, the cargo ships should be ready to leave in five hours, 1st Company is doing equipment check and will be ready about the same time. Sorry for the short notice," Forsythe said apologetically.

Wilks smiled as he stood up, snapped a quick salute and turned to leave.

"Captain," Stokes said as Wilks turned to leave. "If you want, you can take the plate of cheese."

With a grin stretching from ear to ear, Wilks scooped up the tray and started to leave before pausing and pulling a bag out of his thigh pouch and covering the cheese from view before striding out the door, pulling it shut behind him.

Forsythe watched him go and gave a soft grunt. "He never argues, just takes it on the chin and keeps on going."

"There's a reason I promoted him to Squadron Commander and gave him command of the first strike on the Chinese," Davies said.

"A far cry from the current American President," Forsythe countered with a laugh. "Did you see his speech about the aliens? Never in the course of history has one man said so much wrong, to such a small audience, that created such a lack of caring. I think I missed half of the speech because I couldn't stop laughing."

"Yes, waving a few sheets of paper around and claiming you have evidence that all of the problems the people of Earth are suffering through are the result of aliens was probably not the best way to start the speech," Stokes said. "Although I seriously doubt, given the power problems and general state most communities are in, that many people had time to sit through forty minutes of that drivel."

"True enough. On that note, you mentioned Marcus earlier. Are we having problems with our facilities? I never got to see the Missouri base," Forsythe said.

Stokes brought a diagram of the facility up on the main screen. Situated on an island in the Mississippi river, south of a small town called Keokuk and near the Wisconsin, Illinois and Missouri borders, the base had two distinct parts.

The main facility was on the island, which had been increased in size and raised higher above flood stage by dredging the nearby river and putting the dirt on the island. The other half of the base contained the main residence and entertainment facilities, the two pieces connected by a covered causeway.

Two agri-towers dominated the south end of the facility, towering ten stories over the surrounding area. Inside each tower were tightly packed hydroponic growing facilities that grew specialty foods that were packaged as rations to be sent to the space facilities surrounding Earth, and the main cargo terminal supporting the MBTC. The plants inside were genetically modified to provide concentrated doses of critical nutrients needed to make a packaged meal as small as possible. Because they were genetically modified, they couldn't be grown in the open air, where they might contaminate normal crops through cross-pollination. The tops of each building bristled with solar panels and contained several integrated security stations that looked out over the river to the south.

To the north of the twin towers, two small manufacturing plants churned out specialty parts for the Angels. A railroad crossing and pedestrian causeway connected the island to the shore. The railway spur cut through the base before merging in with an original rail line that paralleled the river. Several warehouses and support structures dotted the northern edge of the island with security buildings and green spaces. The edge of the island was an elevated barrier that prevented boats from mooring or landing on the island without using the designated docking area.

On the Missouri shoreline a series of tall levies had been erected around a residential area, with several shopping malls and food stores. The levies had been created to defend against a one hundred year flood, but it didn't take a tactical genius to realize they made a highly effective defensive position, especially with nothing but fields of soy in front of them until the rail line.

Colonel Davies whistled through his teeth. "If that's not a fortress, I've never seen one."

"The western channel can be cut off as well. By dredging out the river the way we did, it actually redirects much of the current away from the island, so even if they blow a dam upstream from the base, the majority of the flow will push against the opposite shoreline. This also makes it hard for smaller boats to fight the current and reach the base. The northern storage area and agri-towers to the south give us a huge field of view around the base. The only real issue we have is a lack of elevated firing positions in the residential area, which based on the last report we got from Marcus, he seems to be rectifying," Stokes said with pride. "As for how they are faring, I'd guess the best way to address that is to let you read Marcus' last report."

> "Ed,
>
> I'm going to keep this short, we've got a lot to do with winter approaching. We've opened up an additional trade route to Eau Claire. They don't have much to trade us, but I do have a very warm beaver hat for you when you visit next time. I know we are sending fuel supplies we can scarcely afford to spare for limited gain, but I view it as stabilizing the area around our more productive trade partners. It's my feeling if we can get them through the winter, most of the criminals who are roaming the woods will either die of the cold or head south. That should provide them a chance to get settled for the coming summer.
>
> We continue to see a steady stream of refugees and bandit groups heading south as winter approaches. We're in a very rural part of the river and we keep the lights down at night, but even so, we've been regularly petitioned for shelter. I've had to make the

unfortunate decision to only accept a limited number of people based on skills. The rest we've given some food and sent on their way. There have been a depressing number of children among them, but there is nothing we can do.

Following behind the refugees there have been packs of bandits and individual criminals preying on the stragglers. I've pushed patrols out as far north as Keokuk and about ten miles out on either side of the river. They're on orders not to interact with any of the refugees, but to interdict criminal elements whenever possible.

Just last week one of our scout patrols encountered a group consisting of about twenty individuals who had captured two families and were tormenting them. The patrol was a SARine triplet and engaged the bandits as darkness fell. Between the use of thermal optics and silencers they were able to eliminate the threat, unfortunately several of the civilians were murdered prior to engagement; in that case we took in the survivors.

I did push a long-range patrol in strength up the Illinois River to scout out how bad Chicago is. It was bad before the fall, it's worse now. We located several refugees heading south along the river and interrogated them. As near as we can tell, Chicago went Lord of Flies within 48 hours of the power dropping and the local government has zero control over their city. The patrol pushed on to within visual range of the city and reported that there were several structure fires burning day and night, uncontrollably. The row houses to the southeast portion of the city have been decimated by fire. They reported there was no indication of a Chinese strike on the city, the residents did all the damage. In my opinion, Chicago is a total loss at this point.

We also located the recon Angel that was downed right after the electromagnetic storms started. Amazingly, the crew survived reentry and impact. They put down in Peoria, in the middle of a junior high football field. Based on their interactions with the locals I am going to push an observation unit to that area to keep in touch with the residents, who have done surprisingly well given the conditions. We sent a medical flight over to supplement their medics prior to winter start, as well as several combat engineers to help them fortify their enclave.

We are fortunate to be far enough north that the Chicago refugees that do head for the river are getting to the Mississippi well south of us and continuing downstream from there. We did manage to secure one fuel barge in Louisiana and bring it up to the base, but river refugees nearly destroyed it in the process. There were repeated attempts to board the vessel and we frequently took fire from the shoreline. At this point, we only navigate the river in darkness, with outrider zodiacs providing protection. The river is very dangerous, not just to us but to many of the people trying to float down it. The fuel barge reported seeing close to three hundred dead in the water on its way north.

The reactors are good for another forty years, so the fuel issue isn't critical except for some of the patrol craft and generators along the levy fortifications. To alleviate that further we've been scavenging heavy cable from the abandoned town of Alexandria just to the north. It's my plan to have power lines strung out to the defensive outposts along the levy by first snow. Even with the extra men that arrived right before the event, we're still woefully short of staff to man the defenses in the event we get attacked by a large force. A few of the refugees were former service members or police, we've accepted those and given them limited duties until we can fully trust them. There's a lot of concern among my senior staff that if we let them man the wall and a friend of theirs comes along, they may let them slip through. But we'll deal with it.

Pass on my regards to the men at your base and let them know that the families they left groundside are safe as long as I draw breath.

Sincerely,

Marcus Green, Commander Keokuk base."

"Well, that's depressing," Forsythe said as he finished reading the report.

"He's had a lot of challenges, more so than the other sites.

It's a combination of things; proximity to the river, well publicized food production system during the run up to the flight test, and being on the path of people heading north to south. Most of those who have been dependent on the government have been unable to adjust to the new situation, and there has been a stampede to warmer climates.

"Our other sites were more remote, but due to the number of family members of space-based employees that are living there, we upgraded his security forces in the run up to the flight test. We consolidated several smaller sites from the surrounding area and gave them a ground contingent of Marines and SARines disguised as security employees. Even so, he's going to have a rough winter."

"Yeah, I think everyone is going to have a bad winter," Davies said bleakly.

CHAPTER 32

It's not pretty, but it should do for the short term," Erik said dubiously as he looked at what the base engineers had cobbled together in the three days they'd had while the freighter rounded Saturn.

"It doesn't have to be pretty, it just has to look deadly," Brenner said firmly.

"I guess, still, they better hope the crabs don't come after them. It would be a short fight."

Hatfield rotated the image of the improvised defense system they had attached to the freighter. The base engineers had taken a single cargo container and attached a half dozen missile launchers and some tubes that looked like artillery pieces to the exterior, and structurally reinforced the interior. If the crabs approached the freighter, they were to fire the missiles with the specialty warheads and hope the explosions were far enough away not to destroy the freighter in the process. The plan was to appear deadly and hope the crabs just stayed away.

He sat back in his chair. "You're right Erik, we can't know for certain they won't attack. If they do attack, I seriously doubt we'll win the fight. The freighter is going to be mostly empty going home. I've decided not to allow any of the workers to transit home on this flight, not until we know what the crabs are up to."

Erik looked at him sharply before catching Sloan's eye. She shrugged back at him. "You know there will be a number of people on the civilian side who are going to be very upset they're not allowed to leave. Most of them are all packed and waiting for permission to board."

"Yes, Molly included I'm sure," Hatfield said softly. "The official story is that we have determined the freighter was damaged en route to the base, to the point that it's unsafe to use. We intend to send a repair crew with it only, and they will attempt to repair the ship while it's in transit home. Only critical medical cases will be on the manifest." He paused, tapping his pen on the table. "Erik, I'm leaving it to you to make sure that Molly doesn't contradict that story at all. It's critical for the morale of the base that no special cases are made."

Erik made a face but nodded that he understood, before sitting back in his chair thoughtfully.

Hatfield watched him for a second before turning back to Brenner. "What's the status of the aliens now?"

"They're still going all out for Uranus. Tight formation fly-ing, no effort at stealth at all. Uranus is quite a ways off, but in three days they've almost made it halfway there."

"If I had to guess, they aren't stealthing because at that speed their passive defensive system can't handle the gas, gravel or whatever else is out there," Erik said without looking up. "Or they can't stealth at that speed due to how it works, or they've decided that stealth doesn't work on us. I'm sure by now they know what our max speeds are just based on watching the freighter fly, and our fighters. Maybe they've decided that stealth doesn't work but speed will."

"So in other words, you don't know," Hatfield said with a smile.

"Do I look like a crab? No, I don't know."

"Crabby for sure," Sloan said with a smirk.

Hatfield held up a hand to forestall Erik's retort. "The point is, they're flying not just away from us, but also away from their comrade ships that headed to Venus. I want to know why."

The room was silent as they all considered it, images of the aliens, their ships and a live feed inside the captured ship's training atrium scrolling past on the monitors over the table.

"Let's talk about what we know of their two apparent desti-nations. The main body seems to have gone to Venus, these two outlier ships are heading to Uranus. The two planets don't seem to have much in common with each other," Brenner said.

"Well, Uranus is gassy and cold. Really cold. We haven't done much of a planetary survey on it yet. Dr. Rogers has the full details of what we did get from the few probes we sent there. There are some twenty-five to thirty moons that range from ice to rock. Some of the moons are tiny, we detected a lot of nickel if I remember when the last probe was there. Gas on Uranus is mostly hydrogen, we had plans to put a science mission out there early on, but there was no funding for it and getting there is a huge pain in the ass," Erik sighed as he finished.

"And Venus?" Sloan prodded him

"Acid rain, I mean like real acid rain, all the time. Greenhouse gas effect really makes for an unpleasant day, I think the temps get up around a thousand degrees and pressure is like being at the bottom of the ocean. Metal dissolves very quickly due to the acid in the air. Basically hell. If they can survive in both of those temperature extremes, in those conditions, we might as well give up. We won't even be able to fight them on all the places they could colonize. If we tried to land an Angel on Venus, it would dissolve."

"Great. Didn't you say the crabs were resistant to acid when you helped Walt on their analysis?" Brenner asked.

Erik shrugged indifferently and remained silent.

"So I come back to my original question. Why are they there? It sounded from Stokes that they thought the aliens were landing on Venus," Hatfield said.

"I have a theory," Brenner said, his eyes downcast as he doodled on the tablet in front of him. "We know they can regenerate soldiers from the room we found in the captured ship. We know they lost a fair number of soldiers attacking the Chinese, and by my count they've lost three or four ships now. We suspect that they have faster than light communications, though we don't know how or how much faster.

They clearly have faster than light travel, but based on the diagrams we saw in the training atrium it looked to me like the small ships had to work together as a unit to do it. Does that track to your understanding Erik?"

"It's as good an interpretation as any at this point."

"So if we've wrecked four ships and they need the full contingent of ships to leave, they may be trying to replace the ships. They could be going to the planets to get the needed resources to build them up, while they grow a new ship crab. Taking it a step further, we know they can grow crabs that are specialized for a given task, maybe they can make crabs that can handle extreme heat or cold, pressure and acid. If that's the case, we could be watching them get ready to leave."

"Or they could be building a bigger communications dish to phone home," Erik said sullenly. "If that's the case, and the training atrium is saying what we think it's saying, we could be in for a beat down."

Hatfield rubbed his temples in thought for several minutes as the team each pondered what Brenner had said. Eventually he broke the silence. "Well, we can't do anything about it. Given the speed they're using to get to Uranus I think they can just run away and avoid us at will. Even if we could catch them, I'm not sure we could win. So let's consider the only option I see left to us."

Everyone in the room looked over at him expectantly as anticipation built.

"Brenner used to build command and control systems and participated in building a wet navy aircraft carrier. Sloan has built up environmental systems in the past for spaceships, we have other experts in space-based manufacture and we have the auto-factories." Hatfield took a slow breath and continued.

"I want to convert one of the cold storage tugs into a carrier craft. The first space carrier. We have limited resources to work with and no idea when we will need it. So the plan, in broad strokes, is to crank up the auto-factories and get them producing Mongoose and Angels as fast as they can, modify the tug to be a carrier, slap missile launchers and point defenses on it and keep it as automated as possible. We're going to be short crew for it, short pilots and short building materials, so it's time to get creative."

Hatfield looked around the room, making eye contact with each of them in turn. "I want Christie to crank up production on our specialty particles. The particle smasher should be running full time. I want you to get Dr. Malhotra to start working on using his metallurgical advances to make the new parts of the ship using the smallest amount of metal possible, while retaining strength. Brenner, I need you to work with Dr. Rogers to make sure we can get hydrocarbons off Titan, we'll use them to make the insulation and composite panels for the ship. We have the current group of trainees that came in on this last freighter and the next freighter for sure, after that, new personnel could be very hard to come by.

"The reports we've got from the next incoming freighter indicate it was damaged extensively in the storm, but not irreparably. I want to capture that freighter and bring it into a stable orbit near the *Heritage*. Once we finish the current ship, we'll use that ship as a structure for another ship. After that, we should have two carriers, fourteen squadrons of Mongoose and support Angels. I don't ever want to be in a position where we can't defend the immediate planetary system again. I want the flexibility to be able to try to maneuver the crabs instead of just chase them. This is going to be difficult."

"Will we really have almost two hundred Mongoose pilots?" Sloan asked curiously.

"Not quite two hundred, but in general yes. The last freighter and the next freighter were loaded up with new pilot and Marine trainees originally intended to be surge trained and sent back to the MBTC as they dealt with the response to our refusal to turn over the troops to the Government. There were almost no civilians on these two freighters."

"How fortunate," Erik said sourly.

"Peace is just the time you use to plan for war," Brenner said quietly.

"Indeed. One final note, I want Sam to dedicate several of his people to look into making new rounds for the artillery and spacefighters that can survive being hit by the crab point defenses. We can't afford to keep burning ammo up on their defenses if they attack us with anything more significant." Hatfield paused, thinking. "I know this is going to be rough on people, I want to make sure that everyone gets enough downtime. We can't afford to burn our people out, so team leaders will need to work to spot trouble before it becomes trouble. The Corporation will give unrestricted passes to the MIC to those who need it, and access to the Eden Cave. Let's try to get a skeleton of a project schedule done by the end of the week. Everyone keep their heads up. Dismissed."

CHAPTER 33

Chief Graves leaned against the bar in the VIP section of Phoebe's and caught the glass sliding down length of the stone surface. "Thanks Amy," he said as he turned to Chief Stokes standing nearby and raised the glass in mock salute.

Stokes cracked a half grin and returned the gesture while he turned up the volume on the monitor. "We haven't had a solar system wide All Hands in ages. What do you suppose they'll talk about?"

"It's your cousin giving the speech, you telling me you don't have the inside scoop?" Master Sergeant Marin cracked from his spot at the bar as he nursed his drink.

"Not a clue, Ed's been hard to get a hold of on email since before that big gamma burst event; I'm in the dark, same as you."

"There's some solace in that at least," Ava Sirano said.

"How come you guys didn't want to watch this from the military side?" Amy asked from behind the bar curiously.

"Anytime leadership feels the need to talk to the entire Corporation at once, it's best to have a ready supply of alcohol available," Sloan said cheerfully.

"Ok quiet down, he just came on the screen," Marin interrupted, using his command voice.

The room quieted down as a handful of pilots, Marines and KaliSun engineers left the booths and wandered over to join the rest of them at the bar, watching the screen. Ed Stokes, the CEO, walked slowly to a large table, flanked by a large man with thinning gray hair and a senior Marine Officer.

"Who are the two guys on either side of him?" Amy asked Sloan quietly.

"The guy on the left is Will Forsythe, Commander of the MBTC. Not sure who the Marine is."

"Lieutenant Colonel Davies," one of the Marines said from behind them. "It might be Colonel now, it looks like they promoted him," he trailed off as the speech started.

"Good morning, afternoon and evening employees of the KaliSun Corporation! As I am sure you are aware, it's been quite some time since our last All Hands. Much has happened in the meantime, many of you have legitimate concerns about family and friends back on Earth, the new war with the Chinese and the appearance of an intelligent alien race. In light of these concerns, we called this All Hands. We rarely do a solar system wide announcement and there are some technical difficulties with doing so, primarily time lag for our communications. As a result, we will not be doing a live question and answer section at the end of this briefing, however, we have set up a special site on the portal where you can ask your questions and they will be answered and posted where everyone can see.

First and most importantly, I want everyone to understand that our facilities on Earth, with few exceptions, are secure. With the exception of a small number of employees manning two R and D facilities, all groundside employees are safe. Also of significant importance, the residential facilities that support our dependents on Earth are doing fine. We have consolidated several smaller facilities into larger residential compounds and have expanded the security envelope to encompass those residential and educational areas. Your families are safe, your children are safe and they are continuing to be provided with the best education and healthcare. Solid contingency planning and execution by those on the ground led us to be in this situation, much of Earth has not been as fortunate.

There are still grave risks on the ground. The areas around our compounds are not doing as well. Banditry and crime have skyrocketed, especially in the more developed areas. Even in the United States, there is much hardship. The KaliSun Corporation is taking steps to assist our friends in the American and Canadian governments. We are delivering aid to stricken communities and reinforcing police and National Guard forces as they combat the rising tide of crime. We remain committed as an organization to provide what aid and medical assistance we can to our fellow countrymen in their time of need.

As a function of the disruption on the ground, travel from the MBTC to Earth is being restricted. We do have launch facilities that survived both the radiation storm and the subsequent upheaval, however, for most of them winter is fast approaching. Adding additional employees to those sites, even for temporary visits to see family and friends, strains their resources.

Additionally, the Chinese are attempting to blockade the planet. These factors, combined with our current resource limitations and the active state of war that exists, means that only essential travel between Earth and the MBTC will be allowed. Travel back from Saturn Base to the MBTC is also restricted due to the threat of attack by hostile alien and Chinese forces. I know this is a hardship for many of you and goes against the spirit of your work agreements with the KaliSun Corporation. But these restrictions are in the best interests of your family, coworkers, and you.

During the radiation storms a number of nuclear events occurred on Earth. There were several bombs detonated in the Middle East and in southeast Asia, specifically India and Pakistan. The losses inflicted by these detonations are unknown. The immediate damage to those areas is also largely unknown, we have high altitude observational data, but no human intelligence data related to the current conditions of the populations in those areas. The fallout from those detonations has not crossed over the equator due to the prevailing winds. While fallout has landed on some of our south Pacific facilities, we have determined through direct testing and observation that it is not significantly worse than what was seen during the surge in nuclear weapons testing in the 1960s.

While any nuclear strike is non-desired behavior, the fact our facilities have survived is a good thing for you, the employees. It means that our primary launch sites near the equator are intact, and once the global situation improves, we will once again be able to launch fresh food and supplies from those locations. In the short term, you may have to deal with less food choices than we typically would prefer, but these shortages will be rectified, we hope, by next summer.

Now, the bad news. Once again we are at war with the Chinese. We will be posting battle summaries to the portal page shortly after this meeting, but rest assured your armed forces have been fighting fiercely. They have taken casualties, but at least for the moment, we are victorious. Despite the fact the Chinese hit us with a surprise attack, we were able to survive and counter attack. Since that counter attack there have been weekly battles between our armed forces culminating in a series of knockout blows that we have delivered over the last two weeks.

To summarize, the Chinese are in retreat. They are running as far and as fast as they can to put space between us. They have inflicted losses on our forces, but we have beaten them back, destroying each of their attacks in turn and launching our own punishing strikes in retaliation.

As for the aliens, that's a more perplexing issue. They arrived in close proximity to the radiation event that did so much damage to Earth. We don't know that they caused it, however the timing is very suspicious. They initially attacked the base on Phoebe and were defeated by our brave pilots and Marines. From there, another group of them approached Earth and took a high orbit around the moon, above the MBTC. We believe they were observing our capabilities and planning their attack. Shortly after the last Chinese attack on the MBTC, they struck a Chinese base.

Our forces were launching a surprise retaliatory attack on the Chinese and encountered the Chinese and aliens fighting over the base. After letting them fight for a while, we delivered a devastating strike that resulted in significant damage to the Chinese base and the destruction of three alien ships. Since that last attack, we have observed the alien ships retreat from the space around our facilities. For the time being, it appears we have driven them off.

They have not left the solar system, they are still a threat. We observed them fighting the Chinese and they have demonstrated the capacity to be a significant threat. We must remain vigilant the face of this and prepare for their return.

I know that many of you have had a very stressful summer and fall. But I want you all to know the good work your coworkers have been doing. *So, we have prepared a short video to close out the meeting. I want to thank you all for your efforts in these trying times and I want you all to know that the sacrifices you have been asked to make have been worth it. Without further comment, let's show the video."*

Graves turned the sound up as a stirring instrumental piece began to play, starting out softly and rising in tempo. On the screen an image of the Corporation logo appeared, with individual unit and base banners fading into focus over the image. The music increased in volume and showed a montage of employees smiling while working in the research facilities, space-suited figures performing tasks across the stark landscapes of the moons Enceladus, Titan, Phoebe, and Earth's own moon. The video sped up to show the intricate dance of a freighter capture and the construction of the Promenade on Phoebe.

The music shifted as the images changed to scenes on Earth as KaliSun employees participated in charity ten-milers, community outreach and mentoring young children at school. As the video played, there were more current views of employees handing out food to refugees, constructing temporary structures and performing medical screening on children who were smiling big for the cameras. The video faded out with an image of armored KaliSun security officers patrolling a snow swept landscape, a combat dog jogging alongside them.

The monitor faded to an image of the company logo, the portal link scrolling along the bottom with instructions on how to ask questions.

Sloan leaned back, gave three slow claps and laughed. "Well that was fun, eh?"

Sirano shrugged her shoulders back. "Not much different than the truth I guess. Hey we're doing ok, your families are safe. Oh and we're kinda fucked at the moment."

The crowd began to disperse, heading back to their tables as Amy served up a few drinks at the other end of the bar. Graves leaned over to Sirano and spoke in an even tone. "I think it's more interesting what they didn't say.

She looked at him and waited patiently for him get it off his chest. Marin slid down the bar, stood next to him and waited as well.

"It's obvious isn't it? No mention about how we defeated the crabs, nothing about us nuking the Chinese when the crabs were fighting them. Half that footage was stock footage from a couple of years ago when we did the last lunar survey around Saturn, the logo spam at the beginning had generic versions of a single Angel squadron and a single Mongo squadron, nowhere near the total we actually have. Stokes said that we were helping the American government, but if you look at the footage you see from Earth, I didn't see a single US uniform on any of those people. The patrols they showed are all KaliSun employees, not joint patrols. I'd say the situation on Earth isn't good at all."

"I've spoken to the Director recently about Earth. He said the same thing about our bases, the families are safe and transport is disrupted. They may have polished the turd a bit, but I think the underlying truth is there," Sloan said quietly.

"Do you think he told you the truth?" Sergeant Marin asked her pointedly.

"Yes, none of my family lives near any of our bases and I haven't been back in years. Lying wouldn't impact me one way or the other. I think . . . I think I've come to grips with the fact that anyone not near our bases could be lost. Stokes didn't say anything about them, if they're lying about anything I'd expect it would be about that. I don't think it's reasonable to expect they were able to track down all the extended families, just the immediate families who were living in Corporation housing."

Graves looked intently at Sloan for a few minutes before he grunted and finished off his drink. "Either way, it looks like this war is going to go on for a long time. Chinese . . . aliens, just another thing to kill," he said as he walked away from the bar, stopping at a table with a couple of the off duty girls from the brothel downstairs, chatting them up briefly before the three of them left, heading down the stairs.

Sloan looked over at Ava expectantly, meeting her eyes and raising an eyebrow.

Ava shrugged. "We're not exclusive, besides, it'll probably do him some good to blow off some steam."

Sloan laughed. "Yeah, maybe he has the right idea. I think the next couple of months are going to be really busy."

Hatfield stared balefully through the glass of the observation window at the alien inside. In the past weeks it had grown to nearly four times its previous size, so large now that it was wedged firmly into one end of the room, immobile. The previously dark shell had morphed to take on the coloration of the walls around it, turning subtle shades of grey where the overhead lighting created shadows. Its little eyes now seemed impossibly out of proportion to the rest of its carapace as the shell had expanded around them.

"It still doesn't eat?" he asked the SARine beside him.

"Nothing we've given it anyway. I'm not even sure it can eat now wedged in there like that," Joe said.

"You didn't give it any more of the canisters from the ship did you?"

"No."

"Then where does it get the energy to keep growing like that? It's like watching a starving bodybuilder get bigger; it just doesn't make sense."

"Kapple has a theory," Joe said hesitantly.

Hatfield shot a sideways glance at him curiously before nodding his head.

"He says that based on the autopsies from the ones they killed during the assault, it's clear that there is an interior bladder of sorts that contains the same basic contents as what was in the canisters. Some of the more exotic compounds may be missing, which he said may be a control mechanism to prevent them from growing like this one did. But it was his belief that the bladder acts as a food reserve of highly concentrated energy that behaves like our fat. They can draw on it to sustain themselves, and if properly triggered, to grow into something else. He also thinks it ate the claws more to ingest the claw material itself and reuse it for its expanding shell, than for energy production. He said it appears that since the creature has ingested the canister goo, its shell can convert light, possibly in the infrared spectrum, into energy as well. Like a plant."

"Are we providing light in that spectrum to it?"

"In limited quantities, yes. It's a byproduct of our normal lighting."

"Well, at least we aren't starving our prisoner. Any signs of little ones?" Hatfield asked cautiously.

"Not externally, we think we can see some via x-ray inspection, but we can only get one to two x-ray images off before it does something with its shell to block the imaging."

Hatfield sighed, tapping the window with his belt knife pensively as he considered his options. "No effort to communicate?"

"Not that we can detect."

"Alright. I want roving patrols around the building at random intervals. Sweep the dust in the crater smooth and install more security cameras watching the exterior of the building. Increase the patrols internally too, I don't want it to sneak out a couple of the little ones and have them either find a way into the base or back to their ship."

"You know they can scoot above the surface, sweeping the dust won't help."

"We also know that when we saw some of them early on, they were still towing their food sack. It might drag, we need to be cautious and vigilant. If one of these things gets into the base, we may have to tear the place apart to get them out."

Joe was silent for a long moment as he consulted his helmet

HUD and issued orders. "I've notified Marin of the need for increased security around the facility. We'll install a couple of guard shacks out here as well, to give them a place to shelter in place if need be."

Hatfield turned to leave, his head down in thought when Joe stopped him with a hand on his shoulder.

"Sir, what about the other prisoners? You'd asked us to arrange for Meckler to pass, but we are still awaiting the official word."

Hatfield stood motionless for a long moment before responding. "Hold off for now, I may need him in the future."

Without waiting for Joe's response, Hatfield entered the airlock leading outside and sealed it up. As the pressure equalized he looked at the displays on his faceplate. Updates flew past—Sloan sending him material updates, Christie sending him updates on the preventative maintenance cycle for the accelerator, and Major Stringer giving him a flash report on the new arrivals. His lip twitched as he opened the folders for Erik and Brenner; nothing for hours. His eyes narrowed in thought as he sat down next to Ed Styles and composed a brief message to Sasha in the Eden Cave while Ed drove toward the tram terminal. He read it twice, pausing before finally sending it, stamped important.

He looked over at Styles, the image of Saturn reflected off his faceplate like a skewed art deco piece as he carefully guided the rover over the crater terrain.

"You doing ok Ed?"

Styles looked over at him briefly with a grin visible behind his faceplate. "Sure sir, as well as can be expected. I was just watching Stokes brief the Corporation while you were inside, things are just peachy sir."

Hatfield considered this in silence as they approached the tram station. He stepped into the tram car and took a seat. As the tram smoothly accelerated, he opened up his personal account and moved a full day VIP pass for Phoebe's into Ed's account, with a note ordering him to take a day off soon. With a satisfied nod to himself, he leaned back and put Sloan's messages into full screen on his HUD as the tram raced toward the CIC.

───

An hour after the end of Stokes' speech, Sloan was still down at the bar sitting in the corner with her command suit half off, drink in one hand and a tablet across her lap. Her heavy booted feet were propped up on a chair next to the table as she went through her team's proficiency reports. It was the assessment time of the year again, and human resources were hounding her to finish up scoring her team. The whole world was in a shambles, yet they were still sitting comfortably in their office over in the MIC sending out nasty-grams like nothing had happened.

The bar had emptied out to a large extent as many of the previous occupants shuffled down to the casino below or over to the brothel to get the most out of their leave. Amy was wiping the tables down as Sloan got to the end of her list.

She bit her lip in annoyance, Henderson, Larry Henderson. He'd been a real pain in her ass for most of the year, but productive. He was just one freighter away from heading home on rotation to work at the MBTC when the radiation storm had hit the base.

She stopped, her mouth tight with annoyance before she typed in several terse sentences commending his service and indicating he earned high marks. She stared down at the tablet, reading over what she had written and making a few small corrections. With a heavy sigh, she stood up and took the tablet over to the far wall, near the back of the VIP area. After a moment of looking she found his picture on the wall and held the tablet up to take a snapshot. She made sure the dates weren't too fuzzy and went back to her spot at the table, typing one final line into her report.

"*See attached photo, employee deceased at eleventh month of calendar year due to radiation poisoning suffered several weeks earlier. Recommend full benefits for employee's next of kin."*

She hit the send key and put the tablet down, refreshing her drink and staring at it in the dim light. Hesitantly, she typed in a command to bring up his personal file and looked through the information. There it was, near the bottom. Emergency contact: wife. Her fingers hovered over the tablet's surface before she opened the file.

A pleasant looking blonde woman with two kids beside her popped up on screen. She was smiling for the photo and hugging her kids. A notation from HR along the bottom indicated that the photo was from four years ago and that the kids were entering middle school soon. Sloan's cheek twitched as she read the caption, but she forced herself to close the tablet and lean back in her chair, taking a swig out of her glass as she did so.

She'd been sitting there for a few minutes, staring silently up at the painting on ceiling of ancient Roman gladiators when a commotion drew her attention. Erik and Molly had entered, arguing at full volume as they went to the bar. Even from twenty meters away Sloan could tell it had been going on for some time, Molly being the vocal half of the conversation. Erik ordered two drinks from Amy and set them both in front of Molly, ordering one for himself and sitting on the bar stool unhappily as she continued to rant.

Sensing he could use some help, Sloan tucked her tablet under her chest armor on the table and sauntered over toward them. The bulky lower half of her command suit juxtaposed against her muscular torso created a strange dichotomy to the eye. She walked up next to Molly and took one of the drinks from in front of her.

"Aw you got me a drink!" she said with a smile at Molly, who was in the middle of tearing into Erik again.

Molly turned toward Sloan, surprised, her face red and her eyes red rimmed with tears. Sloan looked past Molly to Erik quickly, he mouthed "freighter" at her.

"Sorry to hear that your travel home has been delayed," Sloan said diplomatically. "I'm sure that Stokes and Hatfield will work hard to get people a ride back."

"Really? You really think that?" Molly spat back angrily. "What makes you think that *he* wants to make any effort to send me home?"

"Honestly, you aren't critical to our facility here and you eat and drink resources," Sloan said bluntly, causing Molly to blink in surprise as Sloan continued. "Additionally, the reason to prevent you from going home before has somewhat gone away. Earth is a mess, even if you told your story to the people back there, it's unlikely to have much of an impact. The President of the United States has publically blamed the radiation storm on the aliens and credited the KaliSun Corporation with saving Earth from being looted by them. I don't think you'll have much of an audience."

Erik shook his head sadly behind Molly and turned away, downing his entire drink in one shot and waving at Amy for another. Amy walked over and poured him his drink and handed Molly a cloth napkin to wipe her eyes.

Molly stared at Sloan. "Then why not just let me go?"

"Because there are big nasty aliens who might destroy the freighter before it gets home. Because the freighter is still pretty badly damaged from the storm and they need the entire trip home to try to repair it," Sloan said, reaching out and taking Molly's drink away from her. "Now I think you need to take a deep breath and realize a key truth here."

"What's that?" Molly sniffed back at her.

"Hatfield is pretty smart and he pays attention to detail, but he's not willing to modify his entire plan just to mess with you. He's doing what's best for the people and best for the Corporation; you are just a casualty of the situation. A situation that is beyond the control of any of us. Now take a deep breath and accept your immediate future for what it is."

"But I want to go home."

"I'm sure you do, but for now, why don't you stop drinking

and try to relax. Go back to the Eden Cave or go swimming in the ball, but you need to stop this relentless self-pity. Not just for your sake but for Erik's and mine too." She turned to Erik and glared at him. "Now Erik, you should know better than to take somebody who's emotionally distraught to a bar, even this one. *Especially*, this one. Go take her somewhere relaxing."

Erik flinched, but nodded his agreement and silently rubbed Molly's shoulder as he guided her out of the room.

Sloan looked over at Amy who slid another drink at her. "Kids these days eh? No sense at all."

"Erik's not used to dealing with people with real problems. Up until recently, he could always shrug it off with a laugh and a prank. His problem is that he cares about the girl. He's just lost," Amy said diffidently as she swept up the used glasses and put them in the sink.

"Well, well, I come into the bar and the first thing I find is our hard charging operations chief and a philosophical bartender. I feel like I just stepped into a bad movie!" Jacobs said as he rolled into the room from the stairwell leading up from the casino. As he got closer he threw a friendly wink in Amy's direction and took a seat at the bar. "So why did I just see Erik leading a teary eyed woman away from the bar?"

"She's upset about not being able to go home on the freighter," Sloan said neutrally.

"She wouldn't be if she'd gotten the view of it I did. Poor thing looks beat to shit."

"She hasn't adapted well to full time life out here yet," Sloan said.

"That's because she doesn't have goals. No goals, life here is meaningless. If you have goals, life here is the land of opportunity. Take me, I've got a few easy to judge goals. Get the freighters in and out with the best margin in the Corporation and get our friend Amy here to spend quality time with me without any monetary incentive." Jacobs smiled over at Amy with his best seductive trucker gaze.

Amy laughed at him and leaned over the bar to plant a kiss on his lips. "One step closer to goal completion!"

Jacobs spun his stool around in a circle with a 'whoop' before stopping it facing Sloan. "See, first I got that last freighter out the door with a record low fuel consumption, and now I've earned a gold star with our lovely bartender. Mission in progress!"

"I'm not sure I'd brag about that freighter sling, it shouldn't count against the record since it was almost completely empty."

"That just means we have no historical performance data for how the tugs handle it. But that's not the point, you need to give that woman something to do other than sit around and mope, or else she's never going to get better and she's just going to drag you all down. Erik's fun and all, but he's not a full time distraction given that he has to do actual work from time to time."

"Perhaps you have a point," Sloan said thoughtfully.

"Of course I do," Jacobs said. "Now let's have a drink and talk about that speech the boss gave. We'll make a drinking game out of it."

Sloan laughed. "I need to head back down the Eden Cave to check on something, how about you and Amy play. I'm sure you could use the time to work on your year end personal development goals." She smiled at the two of them, throwing Amy a wink before walking over to her command suit and shrugging it back on, sealing the helmet as she walked past the bar and down the stairs.

Behind her, Jacobs was messing with the monitor and flirting with Amy, who watched Sloan leave before seductively undoing the top button on her shirt as she leaned across the bar toward Jacobs.

CHAPTER 34

Brenner ran after the space-suited figure through a fog of flash-vaporized water as alarms sounded in his ears. After several minutes of struggling to close the distance between the two of them, the figure stopped suddenly and turned back towards him. He saw a ripple of flashes from the darkness to his right just as he reached her. As her faceplate turned toward him the glass exploded outward, spraying jagged lines of blood and gore across his visor . . .

Brenner took a surprised breath and opened his eyes as he floated in a pool of water near the top of the Eden Cave's spine. High above him, the muted artificial sun hung large, reflecting light off the purplish crystal of the ceiling. In the distance he could hear the surf crash against the beach. He took a deep breath and let it out in a gush, his body sinking lower in the water briefly.

He closed his eyes and tried to remember the woman from his dream again. Her features were elusive, covered in shadow, but it was still *her*. He lay silently in the water, reflecting on what had caused the nightmare. With a grit of his teeth he thought back to the footage from the recent combat on the moon. Captain Wilks had been on a tear recently, but even that combat paled to the slaughter that had unfolded during their latest battle.

His mind flashed back to the mixture of gunnery footage and high definition bomb damage assessment pictures that had been forwarded to them. Lines of rovers shattered on the surface of the moon with figures thrashing in the dust nearby, short-lived explosions as starfighter cannon rounds had torn through the utility rovers, spraying their passengers and cargo out to land in the dust along the length of the Chinese line of retreat. Wilks had caught the main column while they navigated a series of craters in the moon's surface. The walls of the craters were too steep for many of the rovers to traverse, so the main body was in a tightly confined column stretching several kilometers away from the base.

Wilks had relentlessly pounded them; flight after flight of Badgers had strafed and rocketed the convoy. Those caught in the barrage were shredded, those who escaped foundered in the thick dust at the bottom of the craters, their survival uncertain. He had made the mistake of looking for any similar air-to-ground slaughter in human history. Dunkirk was the first, but the Highway of Death in Kuwait was the most hauntingly similar.

He shook his head slightly and opened his eyes to study the area around him once more, taking his mind off the past. The rain systems had been unbalanced early in the process of bringing the Eden Cave online, resulting in occasional deluges that badly eroded the spine. Since there were no crops being planted in the area, Sloan and Sasha had ignored the problem. Eventually the dirt covering the pile of crystal and rock that formed the interior structure was exposed. When Sasha finally discovered how bad the problem had become, there wasn't much that could be done to fix it. She and Sloan had just dammed up the drainage off the slope and hoped for the best.

The result was this pool, elevated above the majority of the Eden Cave, with a stiff breeze blowing across it. Salt and minerals had built up, increasing the density of the water and making it inhospitable to algae and seaweed. A sheer cliff rising another thirty meters up formed one edge, and the dam's sharp drop off formed the other edge. Water flowed down the face of the crystal and stone dam like an infinity pool at a five star hotel. Being in direct sunlight for most of the Phoebe base day kept the temperature of the water artificially high.

Sloan had told Brenner about the pool weeks ago, suggesting that he could use some time alone. He'd been in the water almost an hour, floating serenely, the parts of him that were submerged pleasantly warm, the parts of him that were exposed to the wind chilled until he was forced to occasionally dip under water to warm up.

His eyes partially closed, he was startled when he noticed a shadow cross his face. It took him a moment to mentally wake up before he opened his eyes and tried to push away from the shadow as he blinked away the water.

Staring at him from the nearly shear crystal cliff face was a strange looking goat, with short stubby horns curving back toward its tail. As he treaded water he moved away from the cliff side of the pool, away from the strange goat. He was almost to the center when he heard Sasha speak from behind him.

"It's called an Alpine ibex," she said quietly from the shore.

He glanced over at her. She was wearing a pair of cargo pants and a long-sleeved sweater, with a set of binoculars around her neck. "How long have you been sitting there?"

"Well, I've been trying to find this guy for a couple of days now, I finally saw him from down there and followed him up here only to find him staring down at you," she said with a small smile.

Brenner glared back at the ibex. "Fine, how did that get here?"

"Turns out they are really good at climbing nearly impossible surfaces. My security camera footage shows this one figuring out the gravity transition near the wall. He literally walked up the cave wall and then jumped from the wall to the ground, just like he jumps from rock to rock up here."

"No Sasha, why do we have an exotic goat in the Eden Cave? Is this another one of Sloan's pets like the damn platypus?" Brenner asked exasperated.

"Oh we have no idea. She swears up and down she had nothing to do with it. We grew up twenty-five of the goat embryos to get the herd started and a few of them came out ibex instead of billy-goat. I'm a little uncertain what to do, when he gets full grown those horns of his are going to be almost a meter long and he'll outweigh the farm goats. I'm not sure we can really milk them either, certainly shouldn't mix it with the other goat milk."

"Goats are the reason classical demons have horns and hooves," Brenner said in disgust as he floated in the water. "How many are there?"

"Seven so far, we don't want to defrost the other embryos to check them, but at some point we're going to have to use them to get to the genetic diversity numbers."

When Sasha spoke, the ibex gave a snort and stepped from one tiny lump of crystal protruding from the cliff to another, smaller one. Somehow he tucked his body up against the shear face as he foraged for moss and grass that had begun to grow in the cracks. Brenner shook his head in admiration. At one point earlier in the day he had considered climbing the cliff face so he could jump into the pool, but had given up because of how slick the crystal was.

"Check with Sloan, but I'd think the best answer would be to just let these go. Get them out of the goat herd before they teach any of the goats any bad habits or start crossbreeding."

"You mean turn them loose entirely or put them in a new pen?"

"Turn them loose, any new ones that come out of the embryo store get turned loose as well. I'm not sure if this was done on purpose or by accident, but either way, they aren't domesticated." He gave a short laugh. "They'll just add to the wonder for our civilians visiting the Eden Cave."

He watched as the goat climbed the rest of the way up the face, pausing silhouetted against a large chunk of purple crystal, before it quietly walked away over the ridgeline. He spun around in the water to look at Sasha and realized she had shucked her pants and was sitting with her legs mid thigh in the water. But she made no effort to climb in any farther.

"I talked to the Director this morning," she began conversationally as she kicked at the water in front of her slowly.

"He said you had a new assignment coming, something to help protect us from the aliens."

"Yeah, looks like it," Brenner said cautiously, unsure of where this was going.

"He said you'd done this kind of work before, but that last time . . . " She paused searching for words. "But that it might bring up unhappy memories of the past. He said that last time you worked on a carrier, you were away from your family when they were killed by the Chinese. He said he's concerned, I guess is the word, that working on this new project might dredge up that past."

Brenner sank lower in the water, closing his eyes briefly as he remembered back to the incident. He remembered where he'd been told, down below decks during a meeting on an upcoming test, and the crushing despair that followed. He was silent for a long time, Sasha waiting politely for a response.

"I suppose that's a justifiable concern," he said.

"Is there anything I can do to help you?" Sasha asked with a neutral smile.

"What did you have in mind?"

"Somebody to talk to, vent at. I know you have other coworkers and friends you could talk to, but you see them day-to-day. Maybe you'd feel more comfortable confiding in me."

"You're still my subordinate, it would be inappropriate to burden you that way."

"Actually, as of this morning, I am not. The Director has informed me that he has officially promoted me. I am no longer in Sloan's org chart and I guess I no longer report to you. I am now the Program Manager of the Eden Cave, direct reporting to Director Hatfield."

"Congrats!" Brenner said warmly from his spot in the pool. "Not too shabby, from working girl to program manager in under two years. If Earth was in better shape you could make a killing with a tell all book."

Sasha flushed in embarrassment at the mention of her previous duties at the MIC but recovered before smiling out at him.

"Thank you, the Director said that moving through the org chart like this would give me many new opportunities to advance and find happiness."

Brenner was about to respond when he caught the odd inflection in her voice. He thought about it for a long moment, his mouth barely submerged as he realized what she meant.

"Yes, I imagine it will," he said back to her with a large grin, before dunking his head underwater.

He dove down several meters before slowly letting the water push him back to the surface speaking bubbles into the water. "John Hatfield, match maker." The thought felt odd, and deep in his subconscious he knew that it was just Hatfield planning contingencies for risks he saw ahead, but at the same time, he didn't care.

ΛBOUT THE ΛUTHOR

Originally from Michigan, Nick built his first 'big' rocket at age nineteen; about thirty minutes later he was staring in dismay at the pieces of it scattered across the field. Since that minor incident, he has designed, built or tested numerous smaller rockets, as well as satellites, space science payloads, command and control networks, radios, fire control units, and one killer tree fort. With fifteen years working in the space and defense industries, Nick still finds time to enjoy a lengthy list of hobbies, from fishing and hunting to writing. He currently lives in Huntsville, Alabama, but travels extensively around the country.